PICTURE OF DEATH . . .

A new image appeared on the computer screen. Two areas were circled in yellow. One was full of tiny blue spots. The other red ones.

"That's two villages," Kincaid said. "The blue dots are dead bodies. Recently dead and cold."

"My God," Lisa Duncan exclaimed, "there must be a hundred of them."

"I don't get it," Turcotte said. "Are they connected to the rocket that went down there?"

"I don't know," Kincaid admitted. "It just seems like too much of a coincidence. And what's even more bizarre is the other village, where all the people show up dark red. The shade indicates the average body temperature is over one hundred one degrees Fahrenheit."

"Everyone in the village is hot?" Turcotte asked.

"Looks like it," Kincaid said.

"What are we looking at?" Duncan asked.

"The end of the world. To be more specific, the death of every human being on the face of the planet who is not a puppet of the aliens. . . ."

ROBERT DOHERTY

AREA 51
THE MISSION

A DELL BOOK

ISBN-13: 978-0-440-22381-8
ISBN-10: 0-440-22381-4

Printed in the United States of America

Published simultaneously in Canada

February 1999

10

OPM

To my father,
George Mayer,
for helping make a dream come true

Prologue

A golden tendril was stretched out from the guardian computer under the surface of Mars and wrapped around the head of the Airlia who had awakened the first echelon and sent them off in their talon ships toward Earth.

The guardian informed her of the destruction of the fleet and the death of her comrades. The pupils in her red eyes narrowed as she processed this information.

She twitched as the guardian picked up a small anomaly near Mars. She had the surface sensors focus on it. Something was coming toward her location, less than thirty seconds out. There was no electromagnetic reading and she almost ignored it, but she paused. She was the only one left awake. She could afford to take no chances. She mentally gave the commands.

In the center of the solar field array a bolt of pure energy shot upward. It hit the incoming *Surveyor* probe dead-on.

The Airlia saw the nuclear explosion take place three miles above her location. It had been close but not close enough.

The Airlia began giving commands. She would wake the others. Then there was much to do.

The first battle had been lost, but the war was far from over.

Lisa Duncan adjusted the focus on the telescope. "There's the mothership. You can see it against the moon as it goes by."

Duncan was short, barely over five feet, and slender. Her dark hair was cut short, framing a thin face, etched with worry lines and stress. She had a glass of white wine in her hand, and gestured toward the scope, inviting the other person on the deck to take a look.

She wore khaki pants and shirt under a brown leather flight jacket that was worn and faded. The jacket was necessary, as a cool breeze was blowing down from the Rocky Mountains and the telescope was on a deck that wrapped around her house, precariously perched on the side of a steep mountain. The faint strains of jazz floated out of the open door onto the deck. A fire blazed in the large stone fireplace inside, the smoke curling out of the chimney above their heads.

The house, 7,000 feet up, overlooked the Great Plains to the east. The lights of the city of Boulder twinkled 2,000 feet below. The glow from Denver was farther away and to the right. The nearest neighbor was over two miles away up the packed dirt road that was the only way to get to the house.

The Rockies stretched north and south, the continental divide to the west. It had taken them over two hours to drive the rental car from Denver International to here, the last forty minutes from Boulder on a precarious narrow road that had degraded from paved to gravel to dirt the closer they got to the house.

Mike Turcotte put his chilled mug full of beer on the railing and took Duncan's place at the scope. He bent over, placing his eye on the rubber eyepiece. He was a solidly built man, of average height, about five-ten, with broad shoulders. His skin was dark, a legacy of his half-Canuck, half-Indian background. His black hair was peppered with gray and cut tight against his skull. He wore jeans and a black T-shirt with a gold Special Forces crest emblazoned on the left chest. He didn't seem to notice the cool breeze.

"That thing survived a nuclear blast," he marveled, seeing the mile-long alien ship through the scope as a sliver of black against the bright full moon.

"It was designed to cross interstellar distances using a drive system we don't have a clue about," Duncan said. "Remember, Majestic-12 couldn't cut through that skin for over fifty years when they had it at Area 51."

Turcotte straightened. "Is it in a stable orbit?"

Duncan laughed. "Worried it'll land on your head?"

"On somebody's head."

"It won't be coming down anytime soon. Larry Kincaid from the Jet Propulsion Lab says it's in a high orbit that doesn't seem to be decaying. The ship is tumbling very slowly. There is the gash the explosion put in the side, but considering the power that was expended, it's not much damage. Close-ups reveal the ship's skin is torn, but the framework seems intact. One of the talons is nearby, also tumbling."

He remembered that sixth alien spaceship chasing him, firing, just before the nukes went off. It had survived the blast intact, but the ship had gone dead—just in time before it blew his bouncer out of the sky.

"What about the other five talons?" Turcotte asked.

"No sign. Kincaid says they were probably caught inside the cargo hold in the explosion." Duncan leaned against the railing. "UNAOC wants to check it all out."

"Check it all out?" Turcotte repeated.

"Send astronauts up on shuttles and rendezvous with both the mothership and talon."

"Take Area 51 into space, in other words," Turcotte said.

Duncan frowned. "That's an odd way of putting it. This is the United Nations Alien Oversight Committee we're talking about, not Majestic-12."

Turcotte considered her in the dark. "Do you trust UNAOC?"

For a while the only sound was the wind through the pine trees on the hillside. Finally Duncan answered. "No, I don't. There's another problem."

"Problem?"

"With UNAOC," Duncan said. "The dig into the wreckage of Majestic's biolab at Dulce, New Mexico— to find what was on the lowest level and to try to find the guardian computer that was there—has been stopped."

Turcotte wasn't overly surprised at that piece of information. "Why?"

"I didn't get a reason, because I wasn't officially notified. I only found out through a source of mine in Washington. I would assume that the U.S. is pressuring UNAOC to stop. The disclosures at Area 51 were bad enough. I think whatever was going on in Dulce would be worse."

"From what I saw when I broke in there," Turcotte said, "they were doing illegal biological testing." "They took the Nazi scientists who worked the death camps and put them in Dulce and gave them the green light to continue their work. I'm not sure *I* want to know exactly what they were doing there." He shrugged. "Let's hope U.S. pressure is the reason."

Duncan pulled up the collar on her leather jacket. "What do you mean?"

"Dulce—and Area 51—were under the control of Majestic-12. Majestic—at the end—was under the control of the guardian computer from Temiltepec that was working for the Airlia group under Aspasia's control. If you follow the trail, maybe there's still that same faction that doesn't want what was being done in Dulce to be discovered."

"Majestic was broken up and the Temiltepec guardian buried when Dulce was destroyed," Duncan said. "Aspasia was destroyed by you."

"Majestic was only the American group that was under control of the guardian," Turcotte said. "I'll bet you my next paycheck there are other groups in other countries under the mind control of a guardian. Temiltepec wasn't the only guardian left behind by the aliens. We did find one in China, don't forget."

"Long buried," Duncan said. "And that one was Artad's guardian, not Aspasia's."

"True. But it would also be naive to assume there aren't more guardians out there we don't know about. Don't forget, the Easter Island one is still active. It would also be foolish to think that by stopping Aspasia's fleet we totally defeated the Airlia.

"And remember, it was a foo fighter that took out Dulce, which makes me think someone was trying to cover something up. And maybe whatever was supposed to be covered up is still going on somewhere else."

"You think the biotesting at Dulce was moved?"

"Either moved or being done elsewhere. It would make sense to have redundant facilities. The same is true with the guardians under Aspasia's control."

"Wheels within wheels," Duncan said.

"Hard to know what to believe and who to trust," Turcotte said.

"I trust you."

Turcotte rubbed the stubble of beard on his chin. Duncan came up next to him, standing close by his side. He regarded her for a moment, taking in her dark eyes. "Where's your son?" He felt bad for not having asked before, but it had been one heck of a trip just getting some time off and coming here. He'd noticed the picture of Lisa and her son on the mantelpiece inside.

"He's been staying with his father since school started. I knew this assignment was going to consume all my time, and it wouldn't have been fair to leave him here."

"It would be kind of lonely," Turcotte noted.

"It is, but we enjoy it when we're here together," Duncan said. "When I taught at the University we would drive to town together."

"You miss him." Turcotte said it as fact, not a question.

Duncan nodded. "They're away now on a camping trip. I'd hoped to be able to see him, but . . ." Her voice trailed off.

"I'm sorry," Turcotte said.

"Next time in town," Duncan promised, "I'll introduce the two of you. You'll like Jim."

"I'm sure I will."

"He got his license last year," Duncan said. "I was so scared, letting him drive these roads. I almost sold the house and moved into town. But then the presidential appointment came and, well, I didn't have time and Jim likes it here. He likes the quiet. I like it too.

"When we're done with all of this"—she pointed at the sky, and Turcotte knew she meant the mothership— "I want to come back here."

"I'm glad you didn't move," Turcotte said. "It's beautiful."

Duncan was the President's science adviser and primary point of contact for everything to do with the Airlia. This was the first chance the two of them had had in weeks to simply stop and be still for a little while. Turcotte knew it was a temporary respite, but one both of them terribly needed.

They lapsed into silence for a few moments, taking in the spectacular view. The moon was shining down on them. To the west it reflected off the white-covered peaks.

"There's Longs Peak." Duncan pointed to their left. "A fourteener," she added, referring to one of the many peaks in Colorado over 14,000 feet.

Turcotte nodded. "I climbed it when I was in Tenth Special Forces."

Duncan laughed. "I should have known." She gestured toward the south. "On a clear day you can see the top of Pikes Peak, over a hundred miles away."

"I always wanted to retire out here. I don't think you can beat the mountains," Turcotte said.

That brought another long silence. Turcotte looked up once more at the sky. Finally he spoke. "Anything from Kelly?"

Duncan sighed, realizing the real world was never far away. "Nothing. The only change has been that the shield surrounding Easter Island is now opaque. Overflights, satellite imagery, thermal, infrared, radio waves—nothing can get through. There's just a big black half-circle sitting on the ocean now. We don't have a clue what's going on inside of the shield."

"And Mars? The Airlia base?" Turcotte asked.

"Nothing. We hope the *Surveyor* nuke took out the guardian there."

Turcotte shook his head. "You've looked at the imagery from Hubble and the other data like I did. The bomb went off a couple of miles up. There's no surface damage."

"I was trying to be optimistic. Mars is a long way off." Duncan tried to put more confidence in her voice than she felt. The talon fleet had powered up after being left in storage for more than five thousand years and crossed that distance in less than two days.

They were lost in their own thoughts until Duncan broke the silence.

"Some people think we did the wrong thing."

Turcotte laughed. "That's understating it a bit. I have had a moment or two to watch the news."

"All right," Duncan said, "a lot of people think we did the wrong thing."

"We had to act," Turcotte said. "There wasn't time to sit around and have a debate."

"I'm not saying I agree with those people," Duncan said. "I think we did the right thing. What I'm concerned about is what happens next."

Turcotte took a sip of beer, then put his mug down. "Hell, Lisa, I'm not exactly sure what happened, never mind what is going to happen." He closed his eyes in thought. "First, we had the Easter Island guardian computer tell Nabinger what a great guy this alien Aspasia was. How he saved mankind from some other terrible alien force the Airlia were at war with by keeping the rebels among his own people from engaging the interstellar engine of the mothership and bringing those aliens here. So we stopped Majestic from flying the mothership. Then we get inside Qian-Ling and that guardian computer says no, Aspasia was the bad guy and this Artad fellow and his police, the Kortad, were the good guys. But that there was indeed an interstellar war between the Airlia and some other alien race and the mothership's interstellar engine shouldn't be engaged anyway. So at least both agreed on that, and stopping Majestic and keeping the mothership's interstellar drive off was a good thing.

"So then we get Aspasia coming in from Mars— where he'd been snoozing for a hell of a long time— with what looks like a fleet of warships ready to finish what he started ten thousand years ago. And his foo fighters destroy a navy sub and look none too friendly. So we stopped him."

"And the foo fighters," Duncan added.

"And the foo fighters," Turcotte acknowledged. "We stopped Aspasia based on what Nabinger told us and the actions of the foo fighters." He shrugged. "I don't know what the truth is, and I'm not sure Nabinger did either."

"He was trying to tell me something important when he got killed," Duncan said.

Turcotte nodded. "I think he figured out what was in the lower level of Qian-Ling we couldn't get into. Peter was a brave man."

"Quite a few brave people have died in this conflict," Duncan said.

"That's the nature of war," Turcotte said. It was a subject he was very familiar with, having been in the military ever since graduating from the University of Maine. He'd served in the elite of the U.S. Army, from infantry to Special Forces, to a counterterrorist unit in Germany until the assignment that had brought the two of them together when he'd been picked to join the top-secret security force guarding Area 51.

Now he was assigned to Lisa Duncan, to help her deal with the results of opening up Area 51 and the shocking fact that aliens—the Airlia—had arrived on Earth over ten thousand years ago and established an outpost. And that the Airlia had never left. They had had a civil war, during which the island humans knew in legend as Atlantis had been destroyed. It appeared now, at least from the evidence they had gathered so far, that an uneasy truce had existed between the two Airlia factions for millennia, maintained by computers—called guardians by the humans who found them.

Duncan interrupted his thoughts. "Did you know that ten percent of Americans don't believe we ever got to the moon? They think the whole Apollo program was done in a hangar out in the desert."

Turcotte raised an eyebrow.

Duncan continued. "CNN just did a survey and they found that over forty percent of Americans don't believe the Airlia are real. They think the whole thing was staged. That there was no fleet. No aliens. No base on Mars. None of it."

"How do they explain the bouncers secreted at Area 51? And the mothership hidden there?"

"Some say none of them exist. You have to remember that only a very small percentage of the population has actually seen a bouncer in person, even with the publicity tours we sent some on. With the special effects Hollywood can churn out now, many people think it's all fake. Or they think the bouncers are military prototypes and the government is trying to scam the public. That this whole alien thing is a ploy to misdirect attention."

Turcotte shook his head. "That helps explain some of the reaction, but it doesn't make me feel any better."

"This won't make you feel much better either," Duncan said. "The CIA has picked up quite a bit of Chinese Army activity in the Qian-Ling region. It's likely they might try to blast their way into the tomb."

"They won't have to blast," Turcotte noted. "The hole we got out of is still open."

"From the imagery it doesn't appear they've gone in yet, but it's only a matter of time."

"Once they go in they'll have contact with the Qian-Ling guardian," Turcotte said.

"The guardian might not communicate with them," Duncan said. The strange gold pyramids found at several Airlia sites were, as far as they could define it in human terms, computers. But the alien computers could do so much more—including directly interfacing with the minds of those who touched its surface—that no one was quite sure what they were. The alien computer uncovered under a dig at Temiltepec in South America had taken over the minds of several members of the covert Majestic-12 group—the event that had begun Turcotte's and Duncan's involvement in this.

"Even if they can't make contact with the guardian," Duncan continued, "they might be able to get access to the lower level and uncover whatever is down that central corridor."

"Nabinger knew what was down there," Turcotte said.

"There's no way we can get back into China to find out. God knows what will happen with the Chinese. They might simply blow the place up, as the Chinese government has more than enough to deal with right now with their own people rebelling."

"I don't think the Chinese, even if they go in, will be able to make it to the lower level," Turcotte said. "Nabinger was probably the only one who could figure out how to get in there."

"I hope so," Duncan said.

"And STAAR?" Turcotte asked. "Anything further?"

Duncan put a hand on his forearm. "Well, I was going to get to that."

"What do you want me to do now?"

"Lead a team to Antarctica. The engineers who have been drilling at the Scorpion Base site say they should break through very soon. I want you to be there when they go in."

"When do I leave?"

"Tomorrow afternoon."

"And where will you be going?"

"The Task Force off Easter Island. The navy wants to try an underwater recon by a probe. Try to get under the shield."

"You think that will work?" Turcotte asked.

"No, but we can't give up on Kelly."

"And if it doesn't work?"

"Then I go to Russia."

"Russia?" Turcotte thought about that. "Section Four?"

Duncan nodded. "There's more going on than we know. What Colonel Kostanov told you—it has me wondering. I sent a message to Section Four and finally managed to talk to someone named Yakov. He told me he would get back to me, but knowing Russian efficiency, I thought it best if I went myself."

"That's probably true," Turcotte agreed.

"They're going to come at us again," Duncan said.

"They?"

"The Airlia. The guardian computer at Easter Island. STAAR. Take your pick. We stopped them at Area 51.

We stopped the fleet. But they won't stop. And God knows what will happen next."

"I always used to tell my team in Special Forces that what you least expect is what will happen."

"That's why I'm afraid," Duncan said.

Turcotte stepped behind Lisa and wrapped both his arms around her, feeling the leather crinkle. "I know this isn't over. Is that why I'm here?"

"No," Duncan said. "You're here because I want you here."

There was just the sound of the breeze through the pine trees for several minutes.

"I'm cold." Duncan nodded toward the door and the beckoning fireplace. "Ready to go in?"

"In a second," Turcotte said. He watched her walk inside, then turned to the dark countryside. He sensed something, a feeling he'd had before while on combat missions—of being watched. His eyes scanned the nearby area, but he knew he wouldn't be able to see anyone, if there was someone out there. Finally he turned and went inside to join Duncan in front of the fireplace.

Fifteen hundred meters away, on a craggy hillside facing Duncan's home, a man sat cross-legged behind a night-vision telescope set on a tripod. He watched the two figures silhouetted by the fireplace. His flat expression didn't change, even as he watched the two begin kissing, his only interest professional. The watcher noted as the man in the house got up and pulled shut the curtain.

He had a small earpiece in his left ear, attached to a receiver he'd planted days earlier. It had picked up the conversation the two had had on the porch. The man was thinking about what had been said, condensing it for the report he would have to make shortly. A receiver he'd hidden inside the house now picked up the sound of the two making love, but that interested the man not in the least.

An MP-5 silenced submachine gun, round in the chamber, lay across his knees. Behind him, a backpack rested against a tree. A bulky plastic case was strapped on the side. The man laid the sub aside and reached for the pack. A large silver ring glittered in the moonlight on his left ring finger as he did that. He opened the plastic case and pulled out the two parts of a sniper rifle. His practiced hands quickly bolted the parts together. He pulled a different scope out of the pack and slid it into place on top of the rifle.

One never knew how those he worked for would react to his report, and he wanted to be prepared just in case. He looked through the scope and turned it on. The image came to life in an array of colors, from hot red through cold blue. He sighted in, the thermal sight letting him see through the curtain. There was one large red spot in front of the flickering deeper red of the fireplace—the man and woman sleeping arm in arm. Twisting the focus knob, he zeroed in on the man's head. He knew he'd have to take down the Green Beret first.

The rifle ready, he leaned it against the tripod. Then he pulled out a secure cellular phone. He punched in a number. He made his report in a few concise sentences. After a short pause, he received his orders. It was the same 99 percent of the time as it had been for generations of those before him.

Take no action—for now. Just watch.

2

A long black streak, over a hundred meters long amid a row of smashed and splintered trees, marked the crash site of the Blackhawk helicopter that Peter Nabinger had been on. It was on a hillside, in a remote area in the west of China, the terrain rough and difficult to reach by foot. It was thirty miles east of Qian-Ling, the mountain tomb that Nabinger had investigated, not too far from the ancient capital city of Xian.

The largest intact piece of the chopper was the armored cockpit and the area right behind it. All were dead, the two pilots still strapped in their seats, the control panel buckled against their chests. In the rear, Peter Nabinger's body lay on its back, both legs badly broken, his left side covered in blood. His sightless eyes looked up at the shattered rotor blades.

Clutched in his right hand was a leather notebook with his high rune translations and the drawings and photographs he had collected during his years of tracking down the source of the ancient language. In it also was the secret of the lower level of Qian-Ling, the ancient tomb of the Emperor Gao-zong and his empress. Given that a guardian computer had been found above that lower level, along with a large area containing numerous Airlia artifacts that no one had had a chance to investigate, that secret was critical.

Writing down what he remembered from his contact with the guardian and his interpretation of the high rune characters on the wall leading to the lowest level had been the last thing Nabinger had done. He had been desperately trying to radio out that secret when the foo fighters had caused the Blackhawk to crash. And now the secret lay here on the hillside with him, gripped by his dead fingers.

It was a terrible ending for a man who in the past month had made some most startling discoveries in the field of archaeology. He had penetrated the secret of the Great Pyramid, built as a space beacon during the war between the Airlia factions, and then the corresponding message built into the very shape of the Great Wall of China, beckoning to the sky for help. The entire previously accepted history of mankind had been thrown on its ear due to those discoveries and the world was still reeling, many not willing to accept these new facts.

The wind blew, ruffling the edges of the pages sticking out of the notebook. In the distance, the sound of helicopter blades approaching became audible.

Deep underneath Rano Kau, Kelly Reynolds had become one with the guardian. Her body, pressed up against the side of the twenty-foot-high golden pyramid that housed the alien computer, wasn't important to the machine. The golden glow that surrounded her body kept it in a stasis field where it hung in suspended animation. But a thick golden tendril that tapped into her mind was fastened directly to her head.

Kelly Reynolds had been drawn into the Area 51 mystery because of the investigation of her fellow reporter, Johnny Simmons. His death at the hands of the Majestic-12 committee that ran Area 51 and its sister bio-research facility at Dulce, New Mexico, had galvanized her. She had not believed that the Airlia were evil or bad, but that mankind's best hope lay in communicating with the aliens—and the best way to do that had been the guardian computer. But since coming down here just before Turcotte destroyed the Airlia fleet, she had not moved.

Easter Island was the most isolated spot on the face of the planet, part of Chile but over two thousand miles from that country on the west side of South America. That remoteness had obviously been the reason the Airlia had chosen it to hide the guardian computer.

The island was shaped roughly like a triangle, with a volcano at each corner. Landmass totaled only sixty-two square miles, but despite the small size it had once boasted a bustling civilization—one advanced enough to have built the Moai, giant stone monoliths for which the island was known. How the statues, some almost sixty feet high and weighing over ninety tons, had been moved from where they were carved to their positions dotting the coast had been a mystery, one that the presence of the Airlia computer might shed light on. There was no doubt now that the Moai were representative of the Airlia—the red stone caps like the red hair of the aliens, the long earlobes similar to what had been seen on the holograph of the Airlia under Qian-Ling. So another mystery of the ancient world had been partially solved.

The destruction of that early Easter Island civilization had always been accounted to the breakdown of the island's ecosystem. By the time the island was discovered by Europeans, on Easter Day in 1722—thus the English name—it was virtually unpopulated and stripped of almost all trees.

It was under Rano Kau that the guardian had been

secreted over five thousand years earlier. And on that strangely shaped computer a small panel, only four inches high by three wide, now opened. A microrobot, less than two inches in height, tottered on six mechanical legs, looking like a metal cockroach. It skittered across the floor to the base of the communications console. The pointy tips of the front two legs turned horizontal. They jabbed forward into the wooden leg of the table. The microrobot began climbing up the leg. It reached the top and headed for the machinery.

One of those devices was a computer with a direct sat-link into the Department of Defense Interlink system. The microrobot used its arms to pull a panel off the side of the computer. A thin wire came out of the top of the Airlia creation and poked into the innards of the computer. The screen on the computer flickered, then came to life.

High on the rim of Rano Kau's crater, a satellite dish aligned with the nearest FLTSATCOM satellite and made a connection. Built into the side of the crater itself, with technology that the UNAOC scientists had only been able to guess at, a communications array, an Airlia one, also came alive. It reached out into space, toward Mars. Making contact, it received a message from the Red Planet. A plan and the order to implement it.

The guardian reached out around the planet to other guardians.

Turcotte took thirty minutes to cautiously move down the last fifty meters. It had taken him an hour to walk around the mountain and climb over the top, but the last part was most critical. He quietly wove his way through the pine trees clinging to the mountainside until he saw what he was searching for—a small, level spot where a prow of rock thrust out from the steep hillside.

The watcher was long gone, but to Turcotte's trained eye there was no mistaking the imprint of a tripod and other signs in the ground. The grass and pine needles had been disturbed ever so slightly. Turcotte scanned the area for other clues. In his time in the Special Forces he'd spent time on hillsides just like this, doing nothing but watching and recording what he saw, so he knew what to look for.

Whoever had been there the previous night was good. That bothered Turcotte. There were a large number of alphabet-soup organizations—CIA, DIA, NSA, ISA, to name a few—from his own government that might want to keep an eye on him and Duncan. Then there were all the foreign agencies. But what truly disturbed Turcotte was that not only didn't he have a clue who had been there, but the person might have been from an organization Turcotte didn't know about. An unknown enemy was much more dangerous than a known.

Finally he spotted something. Against the bark of a pine tree there was the smallest of imprints, just under half an inch in diameter. As if someone had pressed the tip of a weapon against the tree. Turcotte looked at it closely. The imprint was circular. In view of the care the watcher had taken, this mark seemed strange. Turcotte pondered it for a few moments, but there was nothing more he could make of it.

He looked across the gorge at Lisa's house. He had left her sleeping comfortably, the thick blanket covering her naked body. The sun was coming up over the high plains to the east. Turcotte took the direct route back to her house.

·   ·   ·

The stone face of Kon-Tiki Viracocha frowned down on the traveler. Hewn out of a solid block of andesite and weighing many tons, the Gateway of the Sun was the entrance to the center pyramid of the city of Tiahuanaco. The sun god Viracocha's presence at the top of the archway told the traveler this was a most sacred site high in the Bolivian highlands.

"This way." The guide was anxious. The site was off-limits by decree of the government, and soldiers patrolled the area frequently.

The Russian who followed the guide through the gate was a huge man, almost seven feet tall and wide as a bear. Even his bulk, though, was dwarfed by the ruins he walked through. They approached the Pyramid of the Sun, a massive earth-and-stone mound over three hundred feet high. At the very top of the pyramid, a stone altar had been placed millennia before. On its flat surface thousands, if not hundreds of thousands, of people—prisoners, criminals, volunteers, the unlucky chosen ones—had had their still-beating hearts ripped out of their chests, the bodies thrown down the steeply stepped side.

The Russian was known by only one name—Yakov. Whether it was his first or last name didn't matter. Nor did it matter whether it was his given name. He had been operating in the gray covert world for all of his adult life, and that was all he knew.

Yakov cared little for the outside of the pyramid. His research had led him here and he knew what he wanted to see. The guide was clambering over a pile of broken rocks at the base of the pyramid, searching.

"Here!" The man pointed down.

Yakov joined him and looked. There was a black hole between two large rocks. It would be a tight fit. The guide held his hand out and Yakov tossed him a wad of local currency held together with a rubber band. The guide was gone.

Yakov paused before pushing himself into the dark hole. He took several deep breaths, his lungs laboring in the thin 13,000-foot atmosphere. He looked around, taking in the sight of Tiahuanaco as it caught the first light of morning. One of the two great ancient cities of the New World, Tiahuanaco was much less well known than the other, Teotihuacan, outside Mexico City. That could easily be explained by Tiahuanaco's remote location high in the Andes Mountains. Just getting there required an arduous journey from La Paz, the capital of Bolivia. But there was also a very negative policy enforced by the Bolivian government toward visitors desiring to see the ruins. Getting a travel permit to come to Tiahuanaco was almost impossible. Yakov had bypassed that requirement by ignoring it. He was well-versed in the techniques of entering countries illegally and moving about in the black world.

Both New World cities, because of their greatness, their pyramids, their sudden appearance at the time of the waning of the Egyptian Empire, had raised speculation that they were founded by remnants of that civilization. Now, with the awareness that there really had been an Atlantis, destroyed by the Airlia, the speculation had shifted that perhaps these Central and South American cities—along with the Egyptian, the Chinese, all the Old World civilizations—had been founded by those fleeing that disaster; this, the diffusionest theory of the rise of civilization, claimed that the various civilizations around the world had arisen at the same time because they were founded by people from an earlier, single civilization.

Yakov thought the diffusionest theory was likely, and he also felt there was much more to history than the books recorded. He was a member of Section IV, a branch of the Minister of Interior, sister to the KGB. More a bastard stepchild. Section IV had been formed by the Soviet Union to investigate UFOs and the paranormal. As the years had gone by, after various discoveries, the Soviets had little doubt that Earth had been visited by aliens at some time in the past, although the exact extent of alien involvement in human affairs had been unknown up until the cover being blown off of America's Area 51 just several weeks before and the information received from the guardian computer.

Yakov, while taking the new revelations in stride, was still on the path of something he had been tracking down for years. Today he hoped to find another piece in the puzzle. He turned toward the dark hole and lowered himself into the bowels of the Pyramid of the Sun. Turning a powerful flashlight on, he made his way through the stone hallways, hunching over to keep his head from hitting the roof.

At Area 51, Major Quinn was inside one of the surface buildings that had been turned into a makeshift morgue. In the middle of the Nevada desert, this location was also well off the beaten track. Part of Nellis Air Force Base, the location had gotten its designation from that post's map, being designated with that number training area. Quinn knew the entire history of the place, having been assigned as operations officer to the Cube, the command-and-control center for Area 51, five years before.

The location had been chosen because it was where the mothership had been found during World War II. The facility had grown over the years, especially when most of the bouncers—seven of the nine atmospheric craft of the Airlia—had been brought there after being recovered from their hiding place in Antarctica. Test flights of those craft had led to the rumors of UFOs for decades.

Two doctors from UNAOC—the United Nations Alien Oversight Committee—wearing their white lab coats, masks, and goggles, were preparing to do an autopsy on one of the two bodies of the STAAR representatives who had been killed trying to stop the mothership from taking off.

Zandra had been her code name, Quinn remembered as one of the doctors pulled back the sheet covering the first's body.

"Could have used some sun," the first doctor remarked. His name tag read "Captain Billings."

The body was milky white, the skin smooth. The other doctor set up a microphone on a boom in front of Billings. He clicked on a recorder. "All set."

Billings picked up a scalpel but simply stood over the body for a few seconds as he spoke. "Subject is female; age approximately forty, but it is difficult to determine. Height . . ." He waited as the other doctor stretched out a tape measure. "Seventy inches. Weight"—Billings looked at the scale reading on the side of the portable cart—"one hundred and fifty pounds."

Quinn stepped out of the way as Billings walked around the body. "Hair is blondish, almost white. Skin color is very pale white. Body is well muscled and developed. No obvious scars or tattoos. There are six bullet entry wounds on the chest. Four exit wounds on the back."

Billings leaned over and pulled up the left eyelid. "Eye color is brown . . ." He paused. "Looks like there's a contact." He put down the scalpel and picked up a small set of tweezers. He plucked out the contact lens and looked at it against the overhead light. "Hmm, the contact might have been cosmetic, as it is brown-colored." Billings looked down.

"Jesus!" Billings exclaimed. "What the hell is that?"

Quinn stepped forward as the doctor gasped and moved back. Quinn looked into the right eye. The pupil and iris were red, the pupil a scarlet shade darker than the rest of the eye and elongated vertically like a cat's.

Quinn pulled his cell phone off his belt and punched in to the Cube. "I am isolating this building as per National Security Directive regarding contact with alien life-forms. Request immediate bubble protection be put over us ASAP to prevent further contamination!"

In the Cube, the operations center for Area 51 buried deep underground, Larry Kincaid heard Major Quinn's call over the speaker. He'd worked at NASA for over thirty years, and STAAR personnel, with their sunglasses, pale skin, and strange-colored hair, had been around for every space launch. They had been there under the authority of a top-secret presidential directive and as such had had complete access to every NASA facility. It was the way of bureaucracy that the correct piece of paper could override every suspicion and every bit of common sense for decades. The warning that they weren't human was startling but not earth-shattering, given all that had happened in the past several weeks.

So as everyone else scrambled to comply with Quinn's request to quarantine the STAAR personnel autopsy area, Kincaid's attention was focused in an entirely different direction. He was tapped into the U.S. Space Command's Missile Warning Center.

The Center was located deep inside Cheyenne Mountain on the outskirts of Colorado Springs, alongside the headquarters for NORAD. The Space Com-

mand, part of the Air Force, was responsible for the
Defense Support Program (DSP) satellite system, which
Kincaid knew quite a bit about from his work for JPL,
the Jet Propulsion Laboratory, which had been responsible for coordinating the construction of the boosters
that had put those satellites into space.

He knew that DSP satellites in geosynchronous orbits
blanketed the entire surface of the Earth from an altitude of 20,000 miles. The system had originally been
developed to detect ICBM launches during the Cold
War. During the Gulf War, it had picked up every Scud
missile launch and proved so effective that the military
had further streamlined the system to give real-time
warnings to local commanders at the tactical level.

Every three seconds the DSP system downloaded an
infrared map of the Earth's surface and surrounding air-
space. Kincaid knew that most of the data was simply
stored on tape in the Warning Center, unless, of course,
the computer detected a missile launch, or something
happened to one of the objects already in space that
they were tracking. Right now, his computer screen
showed the current DSP projection and nothing out of
the ordinary was happening.

Kincaid looked like a burned-out New York City cop.
He was one of the few left at JPL and NASA from the
early, exciting days of the space program. He wasn't a
specialist, but a jack-of-all-trades. He had been mission
head for all Mars launches, a job that had thrust him
into the spotlight when the Airlia base on Mars had
been uncovered in the Cydonia region.

Kincaid checked his watch. He'd been staring at the
computer for the past three hours. He decided he'd give
it another half hour—then he froze as a small red dot
began flashing on the screen.

Kincaid used the mouse to put the point over the red dot and he clicked.

A code came up on the screen:

```
TL-SAT-9-3//MISSION-CIVIL//ARIANE/
/KOUROU
```

The code told Kincaid several things: First that it was a man-made object—a satellite. Second that it was a contracted, privately financed, civilian project. Third, that it had been launched by the European Space Consortium, Ariane, from their launch site at Kourou in French Guiana. Kincaid searched deeper into the database.

He was surprised to discover that the satellite had been launched only two days before. And it was currently highlighted on the DSP because its orbit was decaying, a further surprise. No one put a satellite up for only two days unless they had a very specific mission for it, or something had gone wrong and the decay was the result of a mishap.

Kincaid checked the decay as DSP continually updated his screen. TL-SAT-9-3 was coming down into the Earth's atmosphere in eight minutes. Kincaid stared at the red dot for a few seconds, then brought up a display underneath that showed its position relevant to the Earth below it. The satellite was currently passing over the eastern Pacific, heading toward South America.

Kincaid picked up a secure phone and called Space Command, asking for the officer in charge.

"Colonel Willis." The voice on the other end was flat, a result of the phone's scrambler.

"Colonel, this is Larry Kincaid from JPL. I'm currently following the data on a satellite you have decaying, TL-SAT-9-3. Do you a projected impact point?"

"Wait one," Willis said. "I have my people plotting it."

Kincaid knew that the staff at Space Command delineated four categories of objects in space. The first was a known object in stable orbit, such as a satellite or some of the debris from previous space missions. Each of those had a special code assigned to it and the data was stored in the computer at Cheyenne Mountain. There were presently more than 8,500 catalogued items orbiting the planet that Space Command tracked.

The second category was a known object whose orbit changed, such as when a country or corporation decided to reposition one of its satellites. The third was a known object whose orbit decayed, which was what Kincaid was looking at. When that happened Space Command put a TIP—tracking and impact prediction—team on the job to figure out where it would come down. TIP teams had been instituted as a result of the publicity after Skylab came down years before. The fourth category was an object that has just been launched and had yet to be assigned a code.

"Why's it deteriorating so fast?" Kincaid asked.

"It must have been planned to be brought down now," Willis said.

"For recovery?"

"Why else would someone bring a satellite down?" Willis asked, to Kincaid's irritation. Before he could retort, Willis had the information he'd originally asked for.

"She's coming down in western Brazil. We'll be able to narrow the location once it's down, but it's still under some flight control and the descent is being adjusted."

Kincaid watched as the red dot crossed South America. It suddenly disappeared.

"She's down," Willis said needlessly.

"At least it didn't strike a city," Willis said.

"It probably hit jungle," Kincaid said, noting the location where the dot had disappeared, the western edge of the Amazon rain forest. "Can you backtrack the satellite's orbit?" he asked. "I want to know if it passed close by either the mothership's orbit or the sixth talon's."

"Wait one," Willis said. He was back with the answer in less than a minute. "Negative. Closest it came to the mothership was over fifteen hundred kilometers. Farther for the talon."

Kincaid frowned. "All right. Forward all data on this to me. Out here."

He stared aimlessly at the computer screen for a long time. Then he cleared the screen and accessed the Interlink, the U.S. Department of Defense's secure Internet.

He checked his electronic mailbox. It was empty. Opening his file cabinet, he retrieved an e-mail that had been sent to him three days before. It was a short message:

```
Watch DSP downlink 0900-1200 MST.
Yakov
```

Kincaid hit the reply button on the e-mail. He typed:

```
Yakov
Watched DSP downlink.
Saw TL-SAT-9-3 come down.
Why is it important?
Kincaid.
```

Kincaid sent the mail. He waited. Ten seconds later, his computer announced he had mail. He opened the

box, only to find his message returned to him, undeliver-
able.

"Damn it," Kincaid whispered as he signed off the
Interlink. He sat back in his chair and pondered the
map that was now on his screen. After several moments
of thought, he went to work.

3

"Where are we going?" the man taking the depth readings asked Ruiz. The expedition had been going up this overgrown river branch for most of the day, and the men were very nervous. Ruiz had watched the sun the entire time, troubled about the direction it told him the boat was going.

"I don't know where the American is going," Ruiz said. He was standing on the bow of a beat-up, flat-bottomed riverboat, about forty feet long by fifteen wide. Two fifty-horsepower engines, coughing occasional black clouds, powered the boat.

The man was a peasant, recruited out of the ghetto, like the others. Only Ruiz and Harrison, the American, had any education, but Ruiz also knew that meant little this far inland. What was most important was Ruiz was the only one who had any experience upriver on the Amazon.

The rest of the expedition—six men Ruiz recruited off the streets—were scattered about the deck. Ruiz's dark scalp was covered with gray hair and his slight frame was tense, ready for action. He was a slight man with dark skin. He wore faded khaki shorts and no shirt, the muscles on his stomach and chest hard and flat. He wore a machete strapped to the left side of his waist, a short, double-edged dagger on the right. An automatic pistol was in a holster that hung off his belt, slapping his right thigh every time he took a step.

Ruiz had been upriver many times, but never on this particular tributary of the mighty Amazon. Given that there were more than 1,100 tributaries to the great river, 17 of them over 1,000 miles long, that wasn't unexpected. What was unexpected was to be this far to the south and west of the main river. Ruiz knew that very soon they would be in the Chapada dos Parecis, the first of the eastern foothills leading to the mighty Andes. The boat would not be able to go any farther, as they would face rapids and waterfalls in front of them.

He was amazed that the tributary was still navigable. The Amazon was almost a thousand miles away at Itacoatiara. To get from that major river to here, one had to travel on the Madeira for over five hundred miles, then branch south on a tributary.

This morning they had met the American at Vilhena, the regional capital for this part of Brazil, a small city sprawled on the riverbank. A fistful of cash had hired Ruiz's services and they had headed south and west from the town all day long, going onto progressively smaller branches until Ruiz had no idea where exactly they were and the water was less than twenty-five feet wide, the large trees from either side almost touching overhead and constant depth measuring being needed to prevent them from grounding themselves. The boat drew only two feet, but as the day had worn on, the amount of water between the keel and the bottom had gone from a comfortable five feet to a nerve-racking three. Already they'd had to pull the boat over three sunken logs.

Ruiz looked over his shoulder. Harrison was looking at his map and scratching his head. Ruiz climbed the few wooden steps to what served as the boat's bridge. He leaned close and kept his voice low.

"May I be of assistance?" The American was a very large and fat man, used to the easy life of the city.

Ruiz was a different breed of man from both the American and the street peasants. He was one of the few who made their living on the upper branches of the Amazon. Sometimes trading to remote outposts, other times guiding various expeditions and tours. Sometimes poaching. Sometimes capturing exotic birds and animals for sale on the lucrative black market for such creatures. Ruiz had also made some money off the illegal recovery and shipping of antiquities, particularly from countries west of Brazil, in the Andean highlands and mountains.

"We are on track," Harrison said.

"For where?" Ruiz asked.

Ruiz knew little about the American other than that he was from one of the many universities in the United States. He had said he was one of those who studied ancient peoples.

Harrison looked about at the thick jungle that surrounded them. He turned back to his guide. The American had paid good money. He had several plastic cases lashed to the deck, the contents of which were unknown to Ruiz when they were loaded.

"I am looking for something," Harrison said.

"I could help you if I knew what you were looking for."

"The Aymara," Harrison said.

Ruiz kept his face flat. He had won many a poker hand on the river with that look. "The Aymara are only a legend. They are long dead."

"I believe they still exist," Harrison said

"Senor, the ruins of Tiahaunaco, where the Aymara

lived, are in Bolivia. Many hundreds of miles from here. Many thousands of meters higher. We can never reach there by boat."

Despite not knowing exactly where they were, Ruiz was very interested. He knew they only had to turn around and go with the flow of the water and they would eventually reach Vilhena. But one of the reasons he had grown to love the river area were the fantastic stories his grandfather had told him. Of ancient cities hidden under the jungle. Lost cities of gold. Hundred-foot snakes. Strange tribes. And guiding someone like Harrison could lead him to a site to return to and plunder, something Ruiz had done more than once.

"How did Tiahuanaco appear so suddenly?" Harrison asked. He didn't wait for an answer. "And how did the Aymara disappear so abruptly?"

Ruiz had heard stories about both those events. "Kon-Tiki Viracocha."

Harrison paused and looked at Ruiz. "Yes. The strange white man who legend says founded Tiahuanaco. Some myths say he was from Egypt. Jorgenson sailed in his boat of reeds across the Atlantic to prove the ancient Egyptians could have made such a journey here to South America. He felt that the pyramids built at Tiahuanaco were so similar to those in Egypt that there had to be an ancient connection.

"And even before that," Harrison continued, "Jorgenson showed that the people of South America could have populated the Pacific, sailing his raft of balsa wood, the *Kon-Tiki*, west from Chile to the islands of the southwest Pacific. He speculated a worldwide connection between early civilizations, and he was laughed at despite his evidence and his expeditions. Now that we know about the Airlia, we know that he was right and there was a connection between the earliest human civilizations."

Ruiz was intrigued. He had read the papers about the aliens, but it had been hard to sort through all the conflicting accounts. "Jorgenson is at Tucume, on the Peruvian coast. He is digging at the pyramids he found there."

Harrison looked at his guide with more interest. "Yes. And now that we know Atlantis was real, his theories gain even more support. He was right, while those that scoffed at him are now the fools."

"Kon-Tiki Viracocha could have come from Atlantis?" Ruiz asked.

"It is possible. While others look in Egypt and at the ruins of the cities along the coast, what I am searching for here, deep in the jungle, is evidence of what happened to the people.

"Tiahuanaco is the key, not Tucume. Tiahuanaco once was a thriving city located on a mountain at over twelve thousand five hundred feet in altitude. It has a pyramid over seven hundred feet wide at the base and three hundred feet high. It ruled an empire that extended through the area we are now traveling, hundreds of miles from here to the Pacific Coast. But when the Incan Empire expanded south in A.D. 1200 and came across Tiahuanaco, the city was abandoned, the old empire gone. The people had to have gone somewhere. I think they went into the jungle."

"Why?" Ruiz asked.

"Why did they go into the jungle or why did they leave the city?" Harrison asked in turn. He didn't wait for an answer. "Something terrible happened to them. It had to have been very bad for them to give up their magnificent city. And why the jungle?" Harrison waved his hands around. "Where else would you go to hide?"

"Hide from what?" Ruiz asked.

"That I will know when I find the Aymara. But it must have been something very terrible."

"You think ancestors of the people of Tiahuanaco are still alive?"

"There have been many reports over the centuries of a strange tribe, far up the tributaries of the Amazon—a tribe where the members are white! To me that means they are the ancestors of Kon-Tiki Viracocha."

Ruiz rubbed a hand through the stubble of beard on his chin. "I have heard stories," he began, but he paused.

"What kind of stories?" Harrison pressed.

"Of a place. A very strange place. Where white men live. Have lived for a very long time."

"The Aymara? Their village?"

Ruiz shrugged. "People only speak of it in whispers. They call it The Mission. I have met no one who actually has seen the place. There are only rumors. It is said to be a very dangerous place. That anyone who sees it dies. I do not know where this place is. Some say it is deep in the jungle. Others say it is near the coast. Others say it is high on a mountaintop in the Andes."

"What is this Mission?" Harrison asked.

"It is said that the sun god, Kon-Tiki, lives there."

"What else?"

"I do not know any more," Ruiz said abruptly. He glanced down and noticed his fingernails were digging into the wood on the bridge shield.

Ruiz looked upriver. He knew it was just an illusion, but the river appeared to be shrinking, getting narrower every second. "Let me see your map, senor."

Ruiz took the sheet and stared at it. He placed an aged finger on the paper and traced a forty-kilometer circle east of the border of Bolivia and Brazil. "We are somewhere here." He shook his head. "There are dangers ahead. The river could close up on us. And there are other dangers. We should go back."

The last thing Ruiz wanted was to spend the night in this province with a naive American and a crew full of street thugs. They might not even be in Brazil anymore. They were far beyond the reach of civilization, and Ruiz knew that besides the wildlife there were other dangers that lurked in the jungle. Harrison was looking for a legendary white tribe, but Ruiz knew for a fact there were other lost tribes of headhunters and cannibals in this part of the world.

"The river will turn into a stream soon," Ruiz said. "The land will go up. There will be rapids. We must go back."

Harrison stared ahead. "I feel we are on the right path."

"It will be dark in a few hours," Ruiz said. "We should go back."

"We go forward as far as we can," Harrison said. He took the map. He slid his finger from the location Ruiz had them plotted to the west. "I think the Aymara are here somewhere."

Ruiz bit the inside of his lip but he said nothing, letting the purring of the two engines be answer enough as the boat continued upstream.

A half hour later, they turned a corner in the stream and the helmsman cut the engines. Ruiz reacted instinctively to the tangle of fallen trees that blocked the stream ahead, pulling his pistol out. He knelt behind the small wall, pointing his weapon ahead, searching for the ambush he expected to leap out of the foliage all around as he yelled for the men on the deck to be ready.

Nervous eyes scanned the jungle all around them,

waiting for the darts and arrows of the headhunters to come flicking out. But nothing happened.

Harrison was kneeling next to him. "What do you think?"

If there were any headhunters about, there was no doubt in Ruiz's mind that the boat's presence had long been detected and whispering was not needed, but he played along. "I do not know, senor." He peered at the trees. They'd been hacked down and pulled across the stream. Beyond he could see some smoke, maybe from a cooking fire. There was a small patch of thatched roof visible above the fallen trees. "There is a village there."

"An Aymara village?" Harrison asked.

This was headhunter territory, and Ruiz doubted it would be the Aymara. "I do not know."

"Can we get through the trees?" Harrison asked.

Ruiz took a deep breath. The stream had been blocked for a reason. Any fool could see that. "I will look, senor."

He stood and signaled for a couple of men to accompany him. He walked up to the front of the boat, then looked down. The water below was dark brown. He knew from the sounding it was about four feet deep. Ruiz slid over the side of the boat, the warm water embracing him.

The two men he had chosen looked nervous, and he didn't blame them. Death was all around them in the form of the jungle. The bottom under his feet was muddy. Ruiz pushed forward, holding his pistol above the water, as did the other two men.

They reached the block. Ruiz climbed up the tangled limbs and looked. A small village of about ten or twelve huts was in a clearing on the gentle bank that led down to the stream. There was no one moving about. A pile of smoldering logs on the right side of the village was the source of the smoke. There were also the remains of several huts that had been burned to the ground.

Ruiz frowned. The stream was also blocked on the far side of the village. What had the villagers wanted to stop? And where were they? Who had destroyed the huts?

He signaled for the two men to follow. He climbed along the logs until he was on the same shore as the village. He pushed through the undergrowth until he reached the clearing. Then he caught a scent in the air and stopped in midstep. He didn't recognize the smell, but it was terrible. He continued on.

Reaching the village, Ruiz first looked more closely at the pile of logs. He gagged as he now saw the cause of the awful smell. They weren't wood. They were bodies, piled four deep, smoldering.

He heard the two thugs begin praying to the Virgin Mother, and he felt like joining them. Ruiz went to the first hut and used the muzzle of his pistol to push aside the cloth that hung in the doorway. The stench that greeted his nostrils there was even worse than that of the burning flesh. The walls were spattered with blood. There was a body on the floor.

Ruiz had seen many bodies in his time, but this one did not look as if it had been killed by an explosion. However, that was the only thing he could think of that would cause the mangled flesh and the amount of blood splattered all around the interior.

Ruiz moved to the next hut, but paused as he heard Harrison's voice. "What is going on, Ruiz?"

"I do not know, senor." He looked back. Harrison was on the shore, walking toward him.

Harrison wrinkled his nose. "What is that stink?"

Ruiz pointed. "Bodies. Burning."

The American's eyes narrowed. "What has happened here?"

Ruiz felt fear now, an icy trickle running down his spine and curling into his stomach. He cared nothing for legends right now. He pulled aside the curtain to the next hut.

A family lay huddled together. All dead. Covered in a layer of blood. Ruiz forced himself to stare and take notice. Blood had poured out of all of them. From their eyeballs, their nostrils, ears, mouth, every opening. Skin that wasn't covered in blood had angry black welts crisscrossing it with open pustules.

Ruiz finally turned away. Harrison was staring. Ruiz grabbed his arm. "We must go, senor! Now!"

"We must look for survivors," Harrison said.

Ruiz shook his head. "There are none."

"We must check all the huts."

Ruiz frowned. "All right. I will do it. Go back to the boat. We must go downriver as soon as I get back."

Ruiz quickly ran to the next hut. It was empty. The next four held bodies, or what had once been bodies but were now just masses of rotting flesh and blood. In the next-to-last hut there was a person lying on the floor. A young woman. She turned her head as Ruiz opened the curtain. Her eyes were wide and red, a trickle of blood rolling like tears down her cheeks. Her skin was covered with black welts.

"Please!" she rasped. "Help me."

Ruiz stepped in, every nerve in his body screaming for him to run away. He knelt next to the woman. Her face was swollen and her breathing was coming in labored gasps. From the smell, there was no doubt she was lying in her own feces.

Suddenly the woman's hands darted forward and she grabbed the collar of Ruiz's shirt. With amazing strength she half pulled herself off the fouled mat, toward Ruiz's face. Her mouth opened as if she were going to speak, but a tide of black-red matter exploded out of her mouth into Ruiz's face and chest. He screamed and slammed his arms up, but couldn't break her grip. Struggling to his feet, he moved backward to the door, but the woman was still attached to him.

He jammed the muzzle of his pistol into her stomach and pulled the trigger until no more rounds fired. The bullets literally tore the woman in half, but even in death her hands held on. Ruiz threw his gun out the door, then pulled his bloodied shirt up and over his head and left it there, clutched in her dead fingers.

He staggered out into the clearing river, heading toward the block and the boat. "We must go back!" Ruiz screamed in the direction of the boat as he wiped at the blood and vomit on face. "We must go back!"

4

Yakov was seated on a stone block, his flashlight wedged between his large feet, pointing straight ahead. He had a camera in his hands and he shot several pictures of the flat stone set into the wall in front of him. Satisfied, he put the camera away. Then he pulled out a notebook and a pad of paper.

The notebook held copies of high rune symbols—the language of the Airlia—and the translation of those symbols, at least those Section IV had been able to make over the last fifty years, which was to say less than 25 percent of those they had found.

Slowly and carefully, Yakov began translating the runes on the stone. It was frustrating work and would have been impossible, except that Yakov had a very good idea of what he was looking at.

It was a record of history. Or, more appropriately, the end of a history for a people. Tiahuanaco had been founded in 1700 B.C. Historians agreed on that. But when the Incans began expanding their empire and came across the city in the thirteenth century, they found an empty place, devoid of human life. Sometime around A.D. 1200 this teeming city, home to several hundred thousand souls, and the empire it commanded for over 2,500 years, running along the Andes, down to the

Pacific Coast in the west and deep into the Amazon rain forest in the east, had simply disappeared.

What had happened to the people? It was a question no one had the answer to.

Except now, translating the stone as best he could, Yakov had that answer, and it was one he had feared to find. There were two symbols that he had seen before, at other places on the planet's surface, that he recognized all too well. It gave the reason:

The Black Death.

Rain lashed the enormous flight deck of the aircraft carrier, battering it with sheets of water so thick that visibility was less than a hundred feet. Despite not being able to see the forward end of the ship, Lisa Duncan was staring straight ahead through the thick windows of the USS *George Washington*'s bridge as if she could actually see the volcanic peaks of Easter Island. She knew that they were twenty miles from the island and even if the weather were clear, the land would be over the horizon. In the water around the flagship *Washington* were the other warships of Task Force 78.

A carrier task force was the most powerful military force the world knew. Centered around the *Nimitz*-class *Washington* were two guided-missile cruisers, three destroyers, two frigates, and two supply ships; under the waves, two *Los Angeles*–class attack submarines prowled the depths, while overhead planes in the CAP, covering air patrol, guarded the sky. One of those subs was going to make the attempt to get close to the island underwater and launch a probe.

The *Washington* itself carried the task force's most powerful punch in the form of its flight wing: one squadron (12) of Grumman F-14 Tomcats, three squadrons (36) of McDonnell-Douglas F/A-18 Hornets, 4 Grumman EA-2C Hawkeye surveillance aircraft, 10 Lockheed S-3B Vikings, 6 Sikorsky SH-60B Seahawk helicopters, and 6 EA-6B Prowlers. But at the present moment, Duncan knew this powerful force was impotent.

"Kelly?" she whispered under her breath toward the dark gray sky as if that person could hear her. The events of the past several weeks had shaken Duncan badly, and she felt a momentary wave of loneliness and weariness sweep over her as she thought of the others who had been with her when they tore the curtain of secrecy surrounding Area 51 asunder.

Deep under Rano Kau her friend Kelly Reynolds was trapped by the guardian computer. That Kelly was trapped because she had gone there of her own free will in an attempt to stop Duncan and Captain Mike Turcotte from defeating the Airlia invasion was something Duncan had thought long and hard about over the past several days, ever since Turcotte had destroyed the incoming Airlia fleet.

Thinking of Turcotte, Duncan's mind drifted south, where she knew he was joining the task force seeking to uncover the secret of Scorpion Base, where the mysterious STAAR organization had had its headquarters.

She could feel the power of the ship's engines vibrate up through the deck under her rubber-soled shoes. She knew she looked out of place on the ship's bridge, among all the sailors dressed in their uniforms. She could sense the military's inherent distrust of civilians from the moment she came on board. It was something she had experienced before and knew there was no way to counter.

"Ms. Duncan?"

The voice startled her. She turned toward the interior of the bridge where naval personnel bustled with the activity necessary to operate this floating city.

"Yes?"

A young ensign stood five feet behind her. "The admiral would like to see you in the commo shack."

Duncan followed the officer through the bridge and through a door at the rear. Shack was a bit of a simplification for the room she entered. Able to communicate securely anywhere on the planet, the "shack" boasted top-of-the-line equipment, including numerous direct uplinks to various satellites.

Admiral Poldan, the officer who had commanded the last failed strike against the guardian computer on Easter Island, had not been a happy man the past few days. He led a task force capable of devastating whole countries, but the alien shield that surrounded the island had withstood the best his fleet could send at it short of nuclear weapons. Duncan knew he was itching to throw that last punch, but UNAOC—for the moment—saw insufficient threat from the Easter Island guardian to authorize such a drastic move in the face of political realities following recent events.

Duncan nodded at the admiral, who was giving orders to one of his men. Done, he gestured for her to join him in front of a large computer display.

"The guardian is talking" was his greeting. "The National Security Agency is picking up alien transmissions."

"To who?" Duncan asked.

"The guardian on Mars."

"Was there a reply from Mars?"

The admiral nodded. "Yes. Yes, there was."

Duncan considered that piece of bad news. The nuclear attack on the Airlia compound on Mars via the *Surveyor* probe had been kept secret by the UNAOC for several reasons.

One reason had been not wanting to admit that the

attack had occurred under the direction of STAAR, an organization about which they still knew practically nothing. The fact that STAAR had placed the nuclear bomb aboard the probe prior to launch, two years before, indicated that organization had been far ahead of any government in recognizing the threat the Airlia posed, or that there was even an Airlia base on Mars, something that seemed to have eluded NASA for years.

There was also the issue that there was still a sizable percentage of the world's population that believed the Airlia represented good; that the destruction of the Airlia fleet was the most heinous act mankind had ever committed. The progressives, as they were called, felt that a remarkable opportunity for great strides in science—not to mention first contact with an alien race—had been destroyed.

Duncan had been hearing reports that a major reason Admiral Poldan wasn't given the green light to nuke Easter Island was a powerful progressive lobby in the UN. This lobby felt that the guardian computer under Rano Kau was irreplaceable. While that looked clear on the surface, Duncan was concerned that there was more to the progressive camp than was readily apparent. The plan by UNAOC to send up space shuttles to rendezvous with both the mothership and talon seemed a bit rushed to her. Her paranoia, justified in her investigation into Majestic-12, was still alive and well.

There was a growing movement in the progressive camp making an icon out of Kelly Reynolds. Nuking the island would undoubtedly kill her—if the nuke got through the shield—and UNAOC was very concerned that would bring about a martyrdom that might incur severe repercussions from the progressive camp.

Several countries, most notably Australia and Japan, had threatened to pull out of the United Nations to protest the preemptive strike against the Airlia fleet commanded by Aspasia.

Duncan had been as surprised as Mike Turcotte at the backlash in the wake of the destruction of the Airlia fleet. It wasn't that Turcotte had expected a parade down Fifth Avenue for his daring mission aboard the mothership, but he had not expected to be vilified in so many quarters. Nabinger's interpretations from the guardian computer under Qian-Ling in China had been greeted with much skepticism, given that Nabinger had never made it out of China alive and they had only Turcotte's word that Aspasia had been the enemy of mankind. The fact that the Airlia had destroyed a navy submarine near the foo fighter base had been explained away as an automatic defensive reaction by the guardian computer—as was the wall they now faced around the island ahead of them.

On the other end of the opinion spectrum the isolationists were pressing the UN to forget about the Airlia. They wanted Easter Island and the other Airlia artifact sites ignored. The isolationist thinking was that these artifacts had been on Earth since before recorded history—it had been only man's interference that had caused all the recent problems. In Duncan's opinion, the isolationists wanted to put the cork back in the bottle after the contents had already spilled out.

China had already pulled its representative from the United Nations and completely closed itself off from the rest of the world over the matter. The fact that the UN had launched a mission deep into China to uncover information in Qian-Ling about the Airlia had poured fuel on the fire. There were confusing intelligence reports that there was much fighting inside China, particularly in the western provinces where ethnic and religious groups were trying to break away from the central government using the uncertainty of the current world situation as their window of opportunity. Duncan, talking to several of her contacts in Washington, had heard rumors that the CIA and other intelligence agencies, particularly that of Taiwan, were aiding in this destabilization. So even as she had to concern herself with the alien situation, she knew she had to always take into account the fact that governments were going to act on their base, selfish interests first, and look at the larger, worldwide picture second.

The world had so anticipated the arrival of Aspasia and his ships that the sudden destruction of that fleet had created shock waves that were still echoing around the globe. Duncan had no doubt that she and her comrades had reacted correctly, but many didn't—obviously Kelly Reynolds had not felt that way.

Upon returning from China, Turcotte had relayed the Russian Section IV concern that STAAR was an Airlia front, part of one of the two warring factions that had been on Earth over ten thousand years ago. That was an entirely differently problem that was somehow connected to all the rest. There were many pieces to the puzzle, and so far Duncan was not sure how what she had went together. This new information that Easter Island and Mars were talking verified that all they had won was a respite.

"Can we break the guardian code?" Duncan asked.

"Negative. It's the same cipher they used before when they wanted to talk to each other and keep us in the dark. No messages of love and peace in binary to us." The admiral tapped the screen. "They're chattering back and forth at high speed and high data compression. A hell of a lot of information."

Duncan knew the admiral was worried. The extent of the Airlia's capabilities was not known. The foo fighter base north of Easter Island had been destroyed—at least all indications were that it had been, she amended now that it appeared the Mars guardian was still active—using a nuclear weapon. The talon ships had also been destroyed in orbit using nuclear weapons in conjunction with the ruby sphere that had been the mothership interstellar drive's power core. But what else might be uncovered remained to be seen, and like most of the military men she had encountered ever since they had cracked the secret of Area 51, the admiral was more than a little paranoid. She knew he would prefer to shoot first and figure it all out later.

"Aspasia must have left someone to mind the store on Mars," Admiral Poldan said.

"Or the guardian computer on Mars survived and is still functioning on its own," Duncan noted. "At least we destroyed their space fleet."

"Uh-huh" was the admiral's take on that. "But whoever—or whatever—is left on Mars survived a nuke strike."

"What about the *Springfield*?" Duncan asked, trying to focus attention on the immediate situation and the reason she was here. "Will the weather force a delay?"

"Weather doesn't affect a submarine," Poldan said. He pointed to a console where an Air Force officer was sitting. "We've got commo with it."

"Do you think this plan will work?"

Admiral Poldan shrugged. "The submarine itself is not attempting to penetrate the shield—if the shield extends underwater—which we hope isn't the case given that the foo fighter base wasn't shielded. We think the probe has a good chance of getting through."

"The foo fighter base probably didn't have a guardian computer," Duncan noted.

Poldan ignored that. "The probe is our best shot to get a look at what's happening on the island."

"No change in the shield?" Duncan asked.

"See for yourself." The admiral handed her several sheets of satellite imagery. He pointed at a dozen red spots in the lower left corner. "That's my fleet."

His finger moved to a black circle that dwarfed the fleet's images. "That's the shield. The NSA has tried every spectrum their satellites are capable of to try to see through, and nothing has worked. That computer is hiding something from us. And the longer we sit here on our butts and do nothing, the more time they have to do whatever it is they're doing."

"Ma'am!" a voice called out from the other side of the communications shack.

Duncan turned. "Yes?"

"NSA was doing an internal security check and they found an illegal tap in the Interlink from this area."

Duncan knew the Interlink was the Department of Defense classified Internet system. "And?"

"They backtracked the tap and it's coming from an uplink into FLTSATCOM from Easter Island. As far as NSA can determine, the guardian is into the DOD Interlink using some of the equipment we left behind when we abandoned the island."

"How long has it been in?" she asked.

"Over a day."

"And they're just letting us know *now*!" She turned to the admiral. "Shut the satellite down!"

"No can do." Admiral Poldan had listened to the exchange. "That FLTSATCOM is *our* only connection to headquarters."

"Admiral, you're letting the guardian into your Interlink and from there into the Internet. What the hell do you think it's looking for?"

"I have no idea," Poldan said stiffly.

Duncan stepped in close to the naval officer, who towered over her. "I don't either, Admiral, but I highly recommend you shut down that link before it finds what it's looking for—if it hasn't already. Unless, of course," she added, "there's a reason you want the guardian infiltrating the Interlink? What exactly are your orders, Admiral?"

Poldan stared down at her for a second. "I'll contact the NSA and have them shut the satellite down."

He had been sitting in the same place for many days, wrapped in a heavy sleeping bag with a white camouflage sheet covering his position. He was wedged behind a blown-down pine tree, the branches providing excellent overhead concealment, as they were thick and covered with snow from the previous night.

There was always snow here, even at the height of summer. This was the northernmost end of Novaya Zemlya, an island seven hundred miles long that separated the Barents Sea from the Kara Sea. The north tip of the island projected into the Arctic Ocean. It was 560 miles from Norway, north and west.

Archangel was the closest Russian city, over five hundred miles away. The ocean surrounding the island was ice covered year round. The weather was extremely unpredictable, with fierce weeklong storms common. A large portion of the island, south of this location, had been used by the Soviet government for years as a nuclear test site. This precluded anyone coming north by land, even if they could make it across the brutal terrain that had no roads. There were only two ways to this spot: by air or by icebreaker.

The man was on a steep mountainside, overlooking a cluster of buildings huddled around a landing strip between the base of the mountain and a glacier to the east. The ice-covered ocean stretched as far as the eye could see beyond the small level cove of land, caught between mountain, sea, and glacier.

He heard the other coming long before he saw him. The other was making his way through the thick forest, moving slowly in the thick snow. The first one didn't move, not even when the other stopped in front of him, breathing heavily and leaning on ski poles.

"I am Gergor," he said simply.

The other caught his breath and nodded. "Coridan," he introduced himself.

"Your trip went well?"

"It was difficult," Coridan allowed.

Gergor nodded. "That is why this"—he gestured at the complex—"is here. Not like the Americans putting their Area 51 in the middle of their country where civilians could drive up to the boundary."

"No one will drive here," Coridan acknowledged.

Gergor pointed to his right. "Rest there for a minute."

Coridan didn't do that right away. Instead he pulled a set of binoculars up to his eyes, letting the sunglasses he wore fall to the end of their cord. He scanned the compound. "How many people work there?"

"Forty."

"Security?"

"Half of them. The rest are scientists. This is the core of Section Four."

"It is smaller than I thought," Coridan noted.

"Most of it is underground. Those buildings are just quarters for the security force and supply sheds. That gray concrete building holds the elevator access to the main facility."

Coridan lowered the binoculars, revealing eyes that

were the same as Gergor's—elongated dark red pupils set against a lighter red eye. His hair was cut short and pure white. His skin, the little that was exposed, was pale.

"We are only two," Coridan noted. He threw his backpack down.

"I have had many years to prepare," Gergor said. "Do not worry. We are enough."

The two sat still for several minutes as Coridan caught his breath.

"It is time." Gergor pushed aside the white sheet and stood, snow falling off of him. He began walking down the hill. Coridan scrambled to gather his gear together.

Gergor was halfway to the Section IV compound by the time Coridan caught up to him.

"What are you going to do?" Coridan asked. "Knock on the front door?"

"In a manner of speaking," Gergor said. He pulled a slim black controller from inside his heavy coat. "Let us knock." He pressed the number one on the numeric pad.

Coridan staggered as the surface buildings erupted in violent explosions. When the smoke cleared, only the gray building that housed the elevator to the complex was still standing, the other buildings leveled.

"What did you do?" Coridan demanded.

"I told you I have had many years to prepare," Gergor said. He continued walking. "I believe they heard our knock. But I don't think they will open the door. So we must open it."

He pressed the second button on the controller. The steel door on the front of the gray building blew open with a flash. Gergor led Coridan inside.

Two large stainless-steel doors stood at the end of a

corridor. A security camera was above them, the light on it a steady red.

"The doors are six inches thick," Gergor noted as they walked up to them. "The shaft is eight hundred meters deep. There are emergency explosives planted along the shaft designed to go off and bury the entire complex."

Gergor smiled, revealing very smooth, even, white teeth. "Of course, I disabled the destruct long ago. I imagine someone down there is pressing a red button quite futilely, yet at the same time secretly relieved that it doesn't work."

"There will still be guards below," Coridan said.

"They will be dead guards," Gergor said. He walked to a vent shaft and ripped it open. He pulled a glass ball from inside his bulky clothes. A green, murky liquid filled it, glowing as if it were lit from inside. He dropped the ball into the shaft.

"It will take less than a minute," Gergor said.

Almost immediately screams echoed up the air shaft, horrible undulating cries of pain. As Gergor had promised, though, within a minute there was only silence.

"How do we get down?" Coridan asked.

"We ride," Gergor said, hitting another button on the remote.

The doors slid open.

"Will it be safe?"

Gergor stepped into the elevator and Coridan followed.

"It is safe now," Gergor said as he pressed the down button and they descended.

The elevator came to a halt, but Coridan did not open the doors. He waited, checking his watch, until finally he was satisfied the gas had dissipated. Then he opened the doors.

. . .

"There's Antarctica."

Turcotte looked over the pilot's shoulder, out the front windshield. Dark peaks, streaked with snow and ice, poked through the low-lying clouds, overlooking the ice-covered ocean.

"We'll parallel the shore, then punch in when we're closest to Scorpion Station," the pilot added.

UNAOC had confirmed the location of the secret base STAAR had been headquartered in with a flyby. The flyby had also noted that the foo fighter had blasted the surface over the base badly. It had been impossible to determine from that, though, whether Scorpion Base had also been destroyed. The American Navy had air-lifted an engineering unit to the site that had confirmed that the entranceway to the base was destroyed. The unit had begun digging, trying to get down the mile and a half of ice to the base.

As always, Turcotte knew, it was going to require someone on the ground to find out what the situation was. And, as he was used to in his military career, he was the person who got that honor.

Turcotte checked the map as they continued south and more peaks appeared along the coast. To the right was the Admiralty Range facing to the north; then the shoreline turned and headed south into the Ross Sea.

A single massive mountain appeared straight ahead, above the clouds, set apart from the others to the right: Mount Erebus, which actually formed an island just off the coast of Antarctica—Ross Island. Turcotte knew that McMurdo Station was on the far side of Ross Island, the largest man-made base in the continent. But where they were heading was far beyond that base, deep inside the continent.

Looking over his shoulder to the back of the Osprey,

Turcotte could see the Special Forces team in the cargo bay. He had no idea what they would find inside the base, so it was best to be prepared. The Osprey was a tilt-wing aircraft, capable of landing like a helicopter. A second Osprey followed them, carrying a HUMMV and a squad of Air Force Engineers to supplement the group already there.

Turcotte watched the slopes of Erebus come closer and then they punched into a thick cloud layer and all view was blanketed. The nose of the plane tilted up as the pilots made doubly sure they had plenty of sky between them and the mountain.

"The engineers have a beacon on the spot," the pilot said. He pointed at his control panel. "We're about two hours out." The pilot turned his wheel and the plane headed over the coast and toward the interior of Antarctica.

They crossed the shoreline mountain range, and as far as they could see in front of them was just a rippling white surface.

"Hey, Captain," one of the men in cockpit called out from his communications console. "Just got a message for you."

"Go ahead," Turcotte said.

"From a Lisa Duncan on board the *George Washington*. Says there is radio traffic between the guardian on Easter Island and Mars."

"Both ways?" Turcotte asked.

"Both ways," the man confirmed. "And also the guardian on Easter Island was into the Interlink and Internet for a while. They've cut off that link."

"Great," Turcotte muttered.

Turcotte went back into the rear and sat down on the red web seating along the inside skin of the plane. He was tired. Upon getting back to Earth after destroying the Airlia fleet, he had been whisked to Washington for an in-depth debrief. He'd had only the one day off, shared with Lisa Duncan in her mountain home, before starting on this mission.

Despite his weariness, he was grateful simply to be alive. He knew others who had not been so fortunate.

He could clearly see Colonel Kostanov from Russia's Section IV of the Interior Ministry—their version of Area 51. He had died on the slopes of Qian-Ling fighting off the advancing Chinese forces. Peter Nabinger was dead, his body unrecovered in the wreckage of the helicopter crash in mainland China. Kelly Reynolds was in the grasp of the guardian computer under Easter Island and had not been heard from since she radioed him to not destroy Aspasia. Von Seeckt was still alive, but barely, in the base hospital at Nellis Air Force Base outside Area 51. Of the original group that had uncovered the secret of that mysterious base, it looked as if only he and Duncan were still in the fight.

And from Duncan's message it appeared the fight would go on.

Kincaid threw the imagery down in disgust. Wherever TL-SAT-9-3 was, he wasn't going to be able to find it this way. The area he had had the spy satellite check showed only thick jungle. Using thermals or infrared wouldn't help on an inert piece of metal.

TL-SAT-9-3 had been swallowed up by the jungle.

Kincaid's computer beeped. He eagerly checked his e-mail, hoping he had another message from Yakov. When he had first received the e-mail message, Kincaid had checked in with Lisa Duncan and she had told him that Yakov was a Section IV operative. Given what had happened in China with Colonel Kostanov, another Section IV operative who had given his life so that Mike

Turcotte and Peter Nabinger could escape from Qian-Ling, Duncan had told Kincaid to take Yakov seriously and check out the information.

But the message wasn't from Yakov. Instead, it was from the CIA. He had asked for a check into the background of that satellite.

He read the short message: TL-SAT-9-3 had been launched by Ariana, the European Space Consortium, under contract to a civilian firm. No details about the satellite itself were available. The company that owned the satellite was called Earth Unlimited, and the report speculated that since that company dealt in mining, the satellite had been a ground-imaging sensor.

That didn't make sense to Kincaid. Why would they have brought it down after only two days if its job was to take pictures from orbit? He scanned the rest of the message, which gave some information about Earth Unlimited. He paused as something caught his eyes. Nestled among a listing of two dozen subsidiaries of Earth Unlimited, a name jumped out at him: Terra-Lei. The same company that had discovered the ruby sphere in the cavern in the Great Rift Valley.

Yakov listened to the hiss of static coming from the earpiece of the SATPhone for ten seconds before pushing the off button. He knew he had dialed the right number—it was the same number he had used for two decades—but he carefully punched it in once more. And again, his ear was filled with static.

In those two decades the other end had always been answered by the second ring. Yakov knew there could only be one reason it wasn't being picked up now—there was no one alive on the other end. Yakov had worked in the covert world long enough to know that, like an animal in the wild, a good operative had to adjust quickly and efficiently to any change in the environment they operated in. He didn't want to accept what his ear was telling him, but he did. He shut the phone off, tucked it into his backpack, and continued on his way, already making new plans.

5

The *Springfield* had listened as its sister ship, the *Pasadena*, had been destroyed by the foo fighters. Like their brethren on the fleet above them, the crew of the submarine felt no affinity for the Airlia or the alien race's machines. They would have much preferred loading a live torpedo in the tube and firing it toward Easter Island rather than the device that was currently being manhandled into the number one tube.

Sea Eye was developed to be a remote probe that the submarine could launch and use as a stand-off surveillance device. The housing for the device was a conventional MK-48 torpedo. Nineteen feet long by twenty-one inches in diameter, it fit perfectly into the firing tube.

Inside of the casing, the torpedo's propulsion system and wire-guidance spool remained intact. The warhead, however, had been removed and an array of surveillance equipment took its place.

The *Springfield* was currently at two hundred feet depth and cruising just on the edge of where the shield guarding Easter Island was plotted.

"We have a direct link to the *Springfield* and through her to the Sea Eye," the young lieutenant seated in

front of the computer informed Duncan. "They're closing on their launch point."

"How close will they get?" Duncan asked.

"The wire link is over eight kilometers long," the
lieutenant said. "They will get within two kilometers of
the shield to launch. That gives them plenty to work
with. The *Springfield* is taking a course that will follow
the shield around for the length of the mission. She's
running on minimum thrust and power. Stealth mode."

"Won't the shield react to the torpedo as a threat?"
Duncan asked.

"We're going to try to float the torpedo through, with
the power off," Admiral Poldan said. "Once it clears the
shield, we can activate it through the trail wire and take
a look."

"Two minutes to shield," the lieutenant announced.
He hit a button on his console. "Entry program is
loaded and ready to run."

Duncan looked once more at the imagery of the
shield. The guardian had made the shield opaque after
the last failed attack by Admiral Poldan's fleet. Up to
that point, it had been invisible. The best guess
UNAOC scientists had been able to come up with was
that the field that comprised the shield was similar to
the electromagnetic used by the bouncers—the small
Airlia atmospheric craft that Area 51 had had control of
for forty years. The fact that in all the years Majestic
had worked on the electromagnetic gravity drives of
those craft not a single clue as to how they actually
worked had been discovered told Duncan that the key
to the shield would not suddenly reveal itself.

"Torpedo launch!" the lieutenant announced.

The torpedo was spit out of the launch tube with a
gush of compressed air. It ran straight for two hundred

meters and then began curving to the left, approaching the shield.

When it was less than a hundred meters from the shield, the electric motor went dead. The torpedo's momentum kept it going forward.

The lieutenant checked the time. "Sea Eye is at the shield."

On board the *Springfield,* Captain Forster had also just been informed of the torpedo's status.

"Sonar?" he called out. "Anything?"

"Sea Eye is gone, as far as I can tell," the sonar man reported. "Snapped off, like a door shutting."

"So the shield blocks sonar," Forster summarized the first thing they'd learned so far from this mission. "Weapons?" he asked.

"All tubes loaded and ready," his weapons officer informed him.

"Intel?"

"Ten seconds until we power up Sea Eye again," his intelligence officer told him.

"Multiple targets!" the sonar man yelled. "Two eight zero degrees. Three hundred meters and closing."

"I got three clear objects!" The radar man's voice was overlaid on top of the sonar operator's.

Forster looked over the shoulder of his radar man. He recognized the signature. "Foo fighters!"

"Two hundred meters and closing."

"Intel?" Forster yelled.

"Sea Eye is on. All we're getting is a power feedback. Growing."

"One hundred and fifty meters," radar reported.

"They're using the wire to track us," Forster realized. "Cut wire. Complete power down!"

. . .

"Foo fighters?" Duncan had listened to the exchange in the operations room of the *Springfield* before the radio went dead after Forster ordered his ship powered down. "I thought we got them all."

The small, three-foot-diameter glowing spheres were the guardian's eyes and ears. Capable of moving through both air and water, their recorded history dated back to World War II when they had been spotted by Allied and Axis aircrews, following airplanes on their war missions.

A nerve was twitching on Admiral Poldan's cheek. "We nuked their base. We've got two subs watching that location and they've reported nothing."

"Then these had to come from somewhere else," Duncan said.

"Status on the *Springfield*?" Admiral Poldan demanded.

"She's powered down. Descending," one of his crewmen watching a screen responded.

"The foo fighters?"

"Staying between the *Springfield* and the shield. Holding."

"That alien computer knows we know how to fight them now. They're keeping their distance."

Duncan thought that was a bit optimistic of the admiral.

"How much water does the *Springfield* have under her?" Poldan snapped.

"Bottom is four hundred meters."

Poldan relaxed slightly. "She can bottom out and handle that depth."

"And then?" Duncan asked.

"She sits, so those damn things don't attack her."

"Until?" Duncan pressed.

"Until your goddamn politician bosses get off their asses and let us blast the crap out of the island. And destroy these foo fighters like we did the other ones."

Easier said than done. Duncan kept the words to herself.

"Five minutes out!"

The interior of the Osprey was crowded with men and equipment. As it banked, the tie-down cables strained, keeping the gear from rolling. Turcotte went forward and stuck his head in the cockpit, looking over the shoulders of the pilots, while he kept a tight grip on the door frame.

It wasn't hard to see where Scorpion Base was. About a quarter mile to the east of where they were landing, the surface of the ice and snow had been splintered by a powerful force that had dug out a quarter-mile-wide trench.

Turcotte returned his attention to more immediate matters as the surface below came up quickly, a rush of white. The plane was very low now, and the pilot banked hard left.

Turcotte looked down as they flew over. There were several prefab structures on the surface where the digging crew lived.

"Better go buckle up," the pilot said to Turcotte.

They roared over a snow tractor with a large red flag tied off to the top. A man on top of the tractor was holding a green flag pointing in a northeasterly direction. Turcotte went to the cargo bay and pulled the seat belt tight across his lap. His take on military seat belts had always been that their only purpose was to try to keep the corpse with the plane if it crashed.

Turcotte watched through the small window as the wings slowly began to rotate upward, slowing the plane's forward speed, while at the same time making up for the loss in lift from the tilted wings.

The plane bounced once, then was down. Turcotte could see the snow tractor had a flatbed trailer hitched to it and was heading toward them.

The silence as the pilots turned off the engines was as shocking as any loud sound. They'd lived with that noise for eight and a half hours on the flight down here from the USS *Stennis*. As his senses adjusted, the steady whine of wind bouncing off the skin of the plane became noticeable. With the airplane's heater off, the interior temperature immediately started dropping.

Turcotte cinched his hood on his Gore-Tex parka. He made sure all his gear was secure before finally pulling the bulky mittens on over his hands.

For this trip, Turcotte had pulled his cold-weather equipment out of the duffel bag that traveled everywhere with him. He was wearing a Gore-Tex camouflage parka and overpants over Patagonia Pile jacket and bib pants that zipped on the sides. He had polypropylene underwear next to his body to wick away any moisture from the skin. Large boots—Turcotte referred to them as Mickey Mouse boots—covered his feet. Despite all the advantages in technology over the years, this outfit was little different from what he had worn for cold-weather training five years earlier. The boots were the same soldiers had worn twenty years earlier. Turcotte was always disgusted with the way the Pentagon would spend billions on a new jet but wouldn't spring to get the soldier a warm boot.

The back ramp cracked open and the blast of cold air slammed into Turcotte's lungs. The air on the tiny parts of his face that were exposed hurt. His skin automatically rebelled, trying to shrink from the pain of the cold, and he felt his muscles tighten as if he could make him-

self smaller and that would in some way make him
warmer. He tried to force his body to relax as he walked
toward the tractor.

The tractor roared up, treads clattering, placing the
trailer alongside the plane. The driver, looking like a
bear in his garments, waved down at them, pumping his
fist. There were several drums on the trailer, and the
crew of the plane began refueling.

"Let's off-load," Turcotte called out.

Once all the equipment was off the aircraft, Turcotte
climbed into the cab of the tractor. The other members
of the party climbed on board and all grabbed on for
dear life as the driver threw the tractor into gear and
roared off toward the site of Scorpion Base.

"Welcome to hell," the driver said.

Turcotte didn't say anything. His gaze was focused on
the thrust-up ice not far away.

Ruiz buttoned his pants and threw several bills on the
ground. The whore scooped them up and they disappeared into the robe she wore. She hadn't even bothered to take it off for their brief coupling, simply hitch-
ing it up at her waist. Prostitution was not exactly an art
form this deep in the Amazon basin. Vilhena was the
district headquarters for this province, an area bigger
than the state of Texas in western Brazil. Ruiz had been
very glad to see the small town, population of less than
five thousand, appear earlier today after backtracking
downstream all night from their gruesome discovery the
previous day. Vilhena was remote, but it was the known
world.

Ruiz walked out of the house made of cast-off card-
board and squinted up at the sun. It was good to be out
from underneath the gloom of the triple-canopy jungle.

"There you are!" A man who had been on the boat

ran up. "The American wants to see you. He is at the governor's office."

Ruiz frowned. "What for?"

"How should I know?" The man pointed at the hut with a knowing smile. "How is she?" He didn't wait for an answer, disappearing into the black hole of the doorway, already tugging at his pants.

Ruiz walked toward the provincial headquarters, wondering why the American would want him. A policeman lounging in the shade didn't even acknowledge Ruiz's approach. He walked down the hallway until a sign on the door indicated he was in the right place. He knocked once, then entered.

Harrison was standing across the desk from the provincial governor, a slight, unkempt man whose primary responsibility was making sure taxes on river traffic were collected, taking his cut, then forwarding it downriver.

"Senor Avilon." Ruiz nodded respectfully toward the governor.

"Tell him!" Harrison yelled.

Ruiz glanced at Avilon.

Harrison grabbed Ruiz's arm. "Tell him what we saw!"

"I don't—" Ruiz began.

"The village. The dead people!" Harrison was shaking Ruiz's arm.

"Mr. Harrison tells me you came across a village yesterday," Governor Avilon said. "He says everyone there was dead."

"They were all dead," Ruiz acknowledged.

"Indians?" Avilon asked, and Ruiz knew where this was headed.

"Yes, senor."

Avilon spread his hands on the top of his desk and gave a wide smile at Harrison. "My friend, many strange things happen upriver. If I told you half the stories I hear every week, you would be amazed."

"The village—" Harrison began, but the governor cut him off.

"Is all dead, correct?"

Harrison nodded.

"Then there is nothing I can do."

"Something killed those people!" Harrison sputtered.

"Of course something killed them," Avilon agreed. "People die in this part of the world all the time. If you will excuse me, I have much work to get done."

"Tell him about The Mission!" Harrison suddenly said.

Avilon had stopped pretending to work. He was staring at the American with hard eyes. They flickered over to Ruiz, fixing him. "What of this Mission?"

Ruiz spread his hands and put a stupid smile on his face. "I do not know what he is speaking of, Governor."

The governor pointed at the door. "Go home, Mr. Harrison. There is nothing here for you."

"You must block the river," Harrison said, "to keep this death from spreading."

"No one goes up there except fools like you," the governor said.

"You must quarantine this town," Harrison insisted.

"I am very busy," the governor growled. "It is time for you to leave."

Ruiz walked out the door, pulling the protesting American with him.

"Why won't he do something?" Harrison demanded as they stepped out into the street.

"Because he does not think they are people," Ruiz said.

"What do you mean?"

"They're Indians. Natives. People like the governor, they consider the ones who live in the jungle to be less than animals. They die, no one here cares."

"They're human beings," Harrison said.

Ruiz looked more closely at the American. "There is nothing to be done," Ruiz said. He had a pain in his left temple. The beginnings of a headache.

"That is where you are wrong," Harrison said. He walked off toward the river.

"See and know and understand that the end of the world is near." The voice was deep and full of power. "Mankind's crimes are too great! Death will come. Nation will fight against nation. A monstrous plague will purify, and only those true of heart will be saved." There was an echoing silence before the voice continued. "Do you believe?"

"We believe!" a hundred voices echoed back.

"Do you believe?" the man repeated, his voice testing the people massed on the floor of the auditorium. The lights were turned low, only a spotlight blazed, centered on the screen behind the speaker, ten feet above his head. The light outlined a ten-foot-wide circle that had a representation of a small blue and white Earth in the center. Coming out of the Earth were lines that led to bright silver stars that made up the circumference of the circle. It was a symbol that was becoming more and more familiar around the world: the sign of the progressives.

"We believe!" The people shouting back were all dressed in brown pants and shirts.

"Ours is the only way. Our path is the path of enlightenment and the future," the speaker continued. The auditorium was in the center of Melbourne, but the meeting had all the aspects of a church revival in the Deep South of the United States.

"It is not a path for everyone," the man continued. A placard on the front of the podium identified him as Guide Parker. He was a dignified-looking man, with thick white hair framing a patrician face. "It is a path only the chosen can be led to. I have been designated to guide you there. If you believe and trust in my guidance, you will survive the coming darkness!"

"We believe!" the audience screamed back. "We trust you!"

Parker's voice lowered, becoming even deeper. "Your trust must be absolute. The darkness will take all who do not trust and believe! It will consume the disbelievers. It will consume the enemy of those who came from the stars and tried to help us. We must ask for forgiveness of man's sins against the stars and our own planet. To be helped we must be true. We must believe. Do you hear me?"

"We hear you!"

"Mankind will be blotted from the face of the ground. But we—we have found favor and grace for our belief. We are the righteous. We will be taken up and protected, and then freed once more to populate the world."

A nerve on the side of Parker's face twitched and his eyes lost their focus for the slightest of moments. He raised a hand to the side of his head as a spasm of pain passed through his brain. Then the face was calm once more. He smiled. "We will take action soon. You must be prepared or else the darkness will take you!"

Around the world, in a dozen other rooms like this one, a similar sermon was being preached.

·   ·   ·

There was no doubt that the wreckage was American—the Chinese lieutenant could still see the "U.S." painted in black on a section of the tail boom. He spit in the direction of the marking. Foreigners, invading the sovereign borders of his country. China had been neglected on the power scene of the world for too long. Its place was at the top, not second to anyone.

He kicked aside a piece of metal as he stepped into what had been the main compartment. The Chinese lieutenant pulled the notebook out of the dead man's hand. He ignored the corpse as he thumbed through the pages. He noted the drawings of the high runes and the photos. The English writing scrawled on the last page he didn't understand, but there were those in intelligence who could translate it. The one thing he could recognize was the English word for the tomb that the foreigners had invaded—Qian-Ling!

He yelled for his radioman. The sergeant ran up, holding out the handset for the radio on his back.

The lieutenant got in contact with the helicopter that was still quartering the area after dropping them off. He ordered it to return to pick them up so that he could take this most important of discoveries back to headquarters.

Ruiz rubbed his crotch. His testicles ached. It was not the first time he'd had trouble in that part of his body. He knew the source. That whore from earlier, although he'd never had a reaction this quickly.

Ruiz cursed. The ache was under his skin, and no amount of scratching was going to make it go away. He checked his watch. He was going to have to get the cure.

Ruiz walked away to the Vilhena Mission Hospital. A rather ostentatious name for a few shacks sitting off to the side of the Catholic Church that didn't even have a doctor in attendance. The hospital was administrated by missionary nuns. The primary problems they saw were malnutrition, but they also dealt with every possible type of injury and illness in a country where there was an average of only one doctor per ten thousand people, the ratio ten times worse over a thousand miles from the major cities on the east coast.

All day long people were lined up outside the hospital. Some had walked many days out of the surrounding countryside to get there. Ruiz took his place in line.

The young nun working the reception table asked him a few questions. Her face didn't register anything as Ruiz explained that he had a venereal disease.

The nun gave him a piece of paper, and he walked over to another table where an older sister held court with a shiny hypodermic needle. She looked at the paper, dipped the syringe in a dish of warm water, then drew out the appropriate medicine from a vial on the shelf behind her. She jabbed the needle into Ruiz's buttock and pulled it out. He was done.

As he walked away, the nun dipped the syringe into the warm water, pulled up and down on the plunger to clear out the inside, then checked the piece of paper from the next client, a young boy with an infected hand. She picked up the appropriate vial and gave him a shot, looking up with tired eyes at the line of people behind the young boy. It was going to be a long morning.

Ruiz walked back to the boat tied up on the river and decided to get some sleep. He did not feel well at all, and surely the American had nothing planned for today. He was probably still trying to find a radio so he could tell the world the tragedy of the village of dead Indians. Ruiz chuckled at that.

He noted that one of the small plastic cases that Harrison had had on the rear deck was gone, but there was no sign of the American. Ruiz curled up in the shadow of the boat and pulled a poncho up over his head, slipping into a very uneasy slumber.

6

Turcotte stood on the edge of a twenty-foot-wide section of buckled ice. Behind him he could hear the second Osprey landing, the tilt wings rotating upward so that the large propellers brought the craft to a hover.

The second one settled down next to the first and the back ramp lowered. The scientists and engineers from UNAOC waddled off, swathed in heavy layers of protective clothing. The tractor had gone back for them.

The lead engineer came up next to Turcotte. He'd been here four days, and the skin on his face was already cracked and blistered from the cold, like the ice that surrounded them.

"That damn foo fighter did a number on the surface." Below them, in the center of the trench, the ice had been melted, then refrozen, forming a glassy surface.

"How about the base?" Turcotte could see his breath forming puffs of white, the moisture immediately freezing.

"A mile and a half of solid ice is pretty good protection. We're not sure, but we think it should be in good shape." He pointed at the jagged gash in the surface. "The foo fighter used some kind of beam. Blasted down about fifty meters, and the shock wave went much farther."

"How far are you from getting in?"

The engineer tapped Turcotte on the arm and led him toward a plowed track in the ice and snow.

"By the time we get down there, they should be ready to punch through." The engineer pointed to the right. A twenty-foot-wide cut had been made in the ridge of blasted ice. Turcotte followed him to it. The cut continued down at a thirty-degree slope until it centered over the re-formed ice. A large, two-story metal hangar had been built there. Turcotte held on to a rope as they slithered down to the hangar.

He could hear the steady roar of several generators as the engineer held the door open for him. Turcotte stepped inside, and the noise was even louder. The engineer threw his hood back.

"I'm Captain Miller," the man introduced himself.

"Mike Turcotte."

It was only slightly warmer inside. Miller pointed to what looked like a mini oil rig in the center of the shed. "We've been drilling for four days nonstop. Since it's so deep, we had to put in three intermediate staging areas on the way down."

Miller led Turcotte up the metal stairs to the first-level platform. Turcotte looked into the fourteen-foot-wide shaft—a white tunnel as far as he could see, straight down. Several black cables were stretched along one side of the shaft.

"We reached the proper depth an hour ago. My men went horizontal, toward the base, and they've reached the edge of the cavern the base is inside. They're waiting on us."

A steel cage rested on the platform. "Ready to go down?" Miller asked.

Turcotte answered by getting inside the cage. Miller joined him, pulling a chain across the opening. He gave hand signals and a crane operator lifted them over the shaft.

With a slight bump, they began descending, the steel cable attached to the roof playing out. It took fifteen minutes to reach the first staging area. The open space suddenly widened to a chamber forty feet wide and thirty high. Another derrick was wedged to the right of where the basket touched down. The chamber was eerie, the walls white ice, the light from the spotlights reflected manyfold. Turcotte felt as if he had entered an entirely different world from any he had ever known.

Two men stood by a heater set on a pallet, warming their hands. "Hey, Captain."

"Going down," Miller said, leading Turcotte over to another cage dangling above the other shaft. They stepped on board and the men turned on the winch, lowering them. Stage 2 was reached after ten minutes, and the process was repeated.

"Metal soundings we took this morning indicate we're right next to the base," Miller said as they descended. He shook his head. "Those guys who got the bouncers out of there in the fifties did a hell of a job. They had to cut a shaft wide enough to fit the bouncers and put in enough stages to lift them out. We tried to find the original shaft, but the explosion from the foo fighter must have filled it with debris and shifting ice."

Turcotte knew Scorpion Base was a part of the history of Area 51 even though it was half the world away. When Majestic found the mothership in the cavern in Nevada's desert, there were two bouncers alongside. Also inside the massive cavern that held the mothership, they found tablets with strange writing on them. It was now known that the writing was the high rune language that had developed out of the Airlia's own language by early humans, but at the time Majestic had been able to make little sense of the markings. The tablets with the mothership had been warnings against engaging the ship's interstellar drive or risk detection by an alien enemy, but that had not been discovered until Nabinger had interpreted the runes. Although Majestic's scientists could not decipher the symbols on the tablets, there were drawings and maps that could be understood.

There was no doubt that much attention was being paid to Antarctica, although the specific location was not given. Just a general vicinity on the continent. Majestic eventually broke it down to an eight-hundred-square-kilometer area.

However, those discoveries were made during World War II, and resources were not immediately available to mount an expedition to Antarctica, although after the war it was discovered that the Germans had made some efforts to explore the seventh continent.

The Germans had been big believers in the mysterious island of Thule. A version of the legend of Atlantis, Thule was supposed to be an island near either the North or South Pole where an advanced, pure civilization had existed in prehistory. The Germans had sent U-boats to both ends of the Earth, even while waging war, to search for any clue to the island's existence.

In 1946, as soon as the material and men were available, the United States government mounted Operation High Jump. It was the largest expedition ever sent to Antarctica. It surveyed over 60 percent of the coastline and looked at over half a million square miles of land that had never before been seen by man, but it was all a cover for the true nature of the mission—to find the Airlia cache.

Finally, right in the middle of the great wasteland of Antarctica, the searchers picked up signs of metal buried under the ice. Turcotte could see Von Seeckt, the old German and a member of Majestic-12, speaking as he had told Turcotte all this shortly after he joined Nightscape, one of the security forces at Area 51.

The cold air came off the ice around the cage, and Turcotte remembered Von Seeckt describing the unique nature of the seventh continent. The ice layer was three miles thick in places, and so heavy it pressed the land beneath it below sea level. If the ice were removed, relieved of the pressure, the land would rise up!

Despite intermittent attempts, it took nine years before Majestic could get another serious mission launched to recover the bouncers. In 1955 the Navy launched Operation Deep Freeze, under the leadership of Admiral Byrd, the foremost expert on Antarctica. As a cover, the operation established five research stations along the coast and three on the interior.

The first plane to land at this site fixed the position of the metal under the ice, but the crew was killed when a storm blew in and froze them to death.

Scorpion Base was the ninth base established, under a tight veil of secrecy. Von Seeckt himself went there in 1956 after engineers spent all of 1955 drilling the same ice that Turcotte was now going down through. In 1956 they broke through into a large cavern inside the ice.

Inside were seven bouncers lined up. It took Majestic three years to bring the bouncers to the surface. First the engineers had to widen the shaft to forty feet circumference. Then they had to dig out eight intermediate stopping points, in order to bring them up in stages. Then it was necessary to tractor the bouncers to the coast and load them onto a Navy ship for transport back to the States. Actually being here, Turcotte realized what a fantastic engineering job those men had done decades before.

But Von Seeckt had also told him that once the bouncers were recovered, Scorpion Base had been closed. As far as Majestic had been concerned, the base was no longer an issue.

But Majestic had also heard rumors over the years about the existence of another secret government organization called STAAR. And Major Quinn at Area 51 had tracked back communication between STAAR operatives and this isolated location.

"Staging area four," Miller said as the cage stopped on an ice surface.

Turcotte looked around. The shaft dug out of this staging area was horizontal. About forty meters down the tunnel, a cluster of men were waiting next to several large drills.

Miller led the way. Large lights were rigged, their output reflecting off the cut surface.

As he waited, another cage came down, disgorging the six Special Forces men with their weapons.

Miller watched them approach with a questioning look.

"We don't know who or what is in there," Turcotte said as he deployed the men behind the engineers.

"We're ready whenever you are," Miller said.

"Go ahead," Turcotte ordered. The sound of the drills drowned out any possibility of further conversation as Miller gave the order.

After a minute the whine of the drills suddenly went lower. One of the men, covered in ice shards, was waving for Captain Miller. "We're through!"

Miller ordered his men to pull their gear back, leaving the end of the tunnel open. Turcotte walked forward, the team behind him. He pulled off his right mitten, keeping on the thin glove he wore underneath, and slipped his finger in front of the trigger of his sub-machine gun.

There was a small opening in the ice, about four feet high by three wide. Darkness beckoned beyond it. Turcotte took a flare out of his backpack, lit it, and tossed it through. The sputtering light was a halo in the darkness.

Turcotte stepped through. As far as he could see in the limited glow of the flare, there was open space.

"Miller!" Turcotte yelled over his shoulder.

"Yes?"

"Can you get some light in here?"

"One second."

The rest of the Special Forces team stepped through, deploying around Turcotte, the sound of their feet moving on the ice echoing out to some great distance.

A bright light flashed on behind Turcotte, a powerful searchlight spearing through the dark.

"Jesus!" one of the Special Forces men muttered.

The light went for almost a half mile before touching the far wall of the ice cavern. Like a toy town set on the icy floor, a small group of buildings sat in the center of the cavern about two hundred meters ahead.

Turcotte waved the men to follow him as he headed for the nearest building.

Lisa Duncan was slammed back as the catapult pulled the E-2C Hawkeye down the deck. Her stomach flipped as the plane dropped off the front end of the flight deck. The nose of the plane lifted and it began climbing through the rain.

The pilot banked the plane hard as he turned toward the south. Duncan looked over her shoulder at the *George Washington,* then the carrier was gone in the mist.

She settled back in her seat. She felt slightly guilty. It would have taken only several more hours for Turcotte to return to the *John C. Stennis* and catch a flight to the *Washington,* but she didn't want to wait. According to flight ops, she would land on the *Stennis,* its battle group in the South Pacific about a thousand miles east of New Zealand, just thirty minutes after Turcotte returned from Antarctica. Once she linked up with him, they could formulate the next step before she left for Russia. The fact that foo fighters were active, although sticking close to Easter Island, was unsettling. It also bothered her that the guardian had been into the Interlink for a day before anyone at the NSA noticed. She found that very hard to believe.

"Can you connect me with the NSA?" she asked the crewman seated next to her.

"Yes, ma'am," he replied.

While she waited, she felt a vibration on her thigh. She pulled her SATPhone out of her pocket and flipped it open.

"Duncan."

"Dr. Duncan, it is my pleasure to speak with you."

Duncan tried to place the man's voice but couldn't. Her SATPhone number was classified and only a few people had access to it.

"Identify yourself."

"That is not important, Dr. Duncan. I am unimportant."

"Then I guess I don't have a need to speak to you," Duncan said.

"If it matters to you, for the purpose of this conversation, you can call me Harrison."

"And what can I do for you, Mr. Harrison?"

"The shuttle launches. Why is UNAOC in a rush to get back to the mothership?"

That was a question Duncan herself had.

"There is danger there," Harrison said.

"What kind of danger?"

"The same danger there always was," Harrison said. "The mothership's drive must not be activated."

"The ruby sphere was destroyed," Duncan said.

"Do you think there was only one?"

Again Duncan had no answer.

"Why do you think there is a rush to get to the mothership?" he asked once more.

"I don't know," Duncan said. "Why don't you tell me."

"There is a plan. It must be stopped."

"Whose plan?"

"The guardian. Aspasia's guardian. There is much you don't know. Majestic did not uncover the guardian computer they brought to Dulce in Temiltepec."

"How do *you* know that?"

"Look to the south, Dr. Duncan. Look to the south. If you find where it came from, you can find the history, and history is most important."

"Where did the Dulce guardian come from?"

"I don't have much time. There is danger," Harrison said. "The Black Death is coming once again."

"What are you talking about? Who are you?"

"I will send you proof. Then you must act before it is too late. It is already too late for me. I am violating an oath in speaking to you, but we underestimated what would happen and how quickly it would come. There was interference."

"Who is 'we'? What are you talking about?" Duncan asked, but the connection was cut.

"Must you kill?" Che Lu asked.

Lo Fa spit into the bush he was hiding behind. "Old

woman, I do not tell you how to dig in those old places you root around in. Do not tell me how to do my business. You told me to have my people find this place. We have found it—but the army was here first. If you want what is there"—he pointed to the wreckage of the American helicopter—"then we must get rid of the army people."

"There has been so much killing," Che Lu said, but it was an observation, not an argument. She knew the old man was right. This was his business, and the stakes were too high to take chances.

They heard the incoming helicopter, and Lo Fa gave his final orders. Two of his men dashed to the left, an RPG rocket launcher in the backpack of one of them. Lo Fa led the way to the right, closer to the crash site and the two Chinese soldiers. Che Lu followed. She had done the Long March with Mao; she could walk a little farther before her days were done.

Che Lu was seventy-eight years old, bent and wrinkled with age. Her eyes, though, were the same they had been when she had walked across China, six thousand miles, as a young girl—bright and sparkling, without the need of glasses to aid her vision. She was—had been— the senior professor of archaeology at Beijing University. Now she knew she could never go back to Beijing. Even here, far in the western provinces, they had heard of more rioting in the capital city, of students again being gunned down in the streets. But this rebellion did not look as if it was going away as quickly as the one in 1989. Not when men like Lo Fa were picking up arms in the countryside.

Lo Fa was a bandit. Or had been. Che Lu found it amusing that while she had lost her prestigious position as a professor, events had changed Lo Fa's status from bandit to guerrilla.

She paused in her thoughts as a rocket flashed out of the trees and hit the incoming helicopter square-on. The aircraft careened over, blades splintering treetops, before crashing into the ground.

The Chinese Army lieutenant and his sergeant stared dumbfounded at the burning helicopter for a few seconds, then they turned and ran in the opposite direction. Directly into Lo Fa's ambush. They were both cut down in a quick burst of automatic fire. It was all over in less than thirty seconds. Che Lu had seen much violence in her life, and it never failed to amaze her how quickly death could come. She had lived many years, and she always wondered why certain people—like the soldiers who had just died—would never have the opportunity to live as many years as she had been given. She did not know whether it was simply random chance or if there was a higher power that determined the course of things. Or if it was both.

The longer she lived, the more she realized how little she knew. Discovering the alien artifacts inside of Qian-Ling the previous week when she had entered it on an archaeological dig had certainly proven that truth once more. It was just as well that she would not be back at the university, because she knew that everything she had taught was now questionable. The entire history of mankind was going to have to be rewritten.

Che Lu arrived at the wreckage of the American helicopter. She looked down at the dead men. Lo Fa grabbed the leather notebook and presented it to Che Lu.

"We must be away quickly," Lo Fa hissed as Che Lu opened the notebook.

She pointed at Professor Nabinger. "You must bury the American. He was a good man. And he gave us the key to Qian-Ling." She shook the notebook at Lo Fa.

"Crazy old woman," Lo Fa muttered, but he yelled commands to quickly do as she wished.

There was a part of Kelly Reynolds that was still her own. That the guardian couldn't touch. It wasn't a large part of her mind, but it was enough for her to still have an "I." A self.

And that self, even while the guardian's golden tendril was weaving its way through her brain, was able to go in the other direction. The mind connection from the guardian, as Peter Nabinger had learned when he "saw" the destruction of Atlantis while in contact with the Qian-Ling guardian, was a two-way street. While the guardian learned from her, Kelly was able to catch bits and pieces from it.

She saw the long column of men pulling on fiber ropes. Women between the men and the object they were pulling, placing logs under the front end of the stone so it could roll. Slowly being pulled over the logs was the greatest of all the Moai, the stone figures that the people carved.

Rapa Nui, they called their island. It would be westerners who would name it Easter Island. The stone they were pulling had already been shaped into the long-eared, long-faced, head shape and weighed over ninety tons. It had been carved out of the flank of Rano Raraku, one of the two volcanoes on the island.

The other volcano, Rano Kao, was forbidden to the people except to worship in the sacred village of Orongo. Also, every year, the cult of the Birdman held its festival, where young men would climb down the side of the volcano, jump into the sea, and swim to the small island of Moto Nui off the coast. The first one to return with a tern egg would be the Birdman for the following year.

Kelly could hear the people chanting in unison as they

pulled the stone. Their destination was several miles away,
the shoreline, where they would place the statue into the
ground, the frowning face pointing out to sea.

Kelly now understood the statues. Why these people
went through such great efforts. To carve them, to haul
them miles to the shore, to place them on their altars. They
were warnings. To other people. To stay away.

"Someone was here not too long ago." Turcotte
picked up a frozen cup of coffee from the table. He
turned it upside down. There was a date stamped on the
bottom—1996—thirty years after Majestic had shut
down the base. There was sophisticated communications equipment—top-of-the-line satellite systems and
modern computers in the commo room.

"But they're not here now," Captain Miller said.
"Must have beat the foo fighters' arrival."

Turcotte walked out of the room he was in and along
a corridor. He pushed open the door, stepped inside,
then stopped in shock. The large room held ten large
vertical vats that were full of some amber-colored liquid. Turcotte had seen this before—at the bottom level
of Majestic's biolab at Dulce. He stepped closer to the
nearest vat. It had something in it.

Turcotte stepped back as he made out a body inside.
There were tubes coming in and out of the body, and
the entire head was encased in a black bulb with numerous wires going into it. He pulled off his glove and carefully touched the glass—it was very cold, the liquid inside frozen.

"What the hell is that?" Miller asked.

"STAAR," Turcotte said.

"What do you mean?

"I think this is how they get new recruits."

·   ·   ·

Through night-vision goggles, Toland continued to scan the forty-foot section of trail that was directly in front of his position. He knew the exact placement of every one of his eighteen men and their weapons. All they had to do was fire between the left and right limits of the aiming stakes they'd carefully pounded into the ground during daylight and the kill zone would become just that to the party approaching their location.

Toland had chosen this spot because it was where the trail ran straight, with a steep slope on the far side. Anyone on the trail would be caught between the weapons of Toland's men and the slope, which was carefully laced with some of Faulkener's "specials." The trail ran through the only pass in a hundred miles where people could cross from the eastern, inland slope of the Andes in Bolivia to the western. The terrain was low enough on this eastern approach to be just below the tree line, steep and heavily vegetated. Farther up the pass there was snow on the ground.

The mercenaries had flown separately on commercial flights into La Paz the previous day and assembled at the airport. Toland had hired several trucks to take them as far as the roads would go into the Andes. From there Toland had led his men on foot through the pass.

Toland heard someone moving behind him. He assumed it was Faulkener, his senior NCO, and that was confirmed when Faulkener tapped him on the shoulder. "Andrews has a message on the SAT. He's copying it down."

Toland twisted his head and looked over his shoulder into the thick jungle. Andrews was back there with the satellite radio, their lifeline.

No time for it, Toland realized as he heard noise coming down the trail. He returned his attention to the matter at hand. There was the sound of loose equipment jangling on men as they walked; even some conversations were carried through the night air.

The point man came into view. Jesus, Toland swore to himself, the fool was using a *flashlight* to see the trail. And not even one with a red lens! It looked like a spotlight in the goggles. Toland adjust the control and looked for the rear of the column.

There were thirteen men and two women in this group. There were more shovels than weapons scattered among them. They were also carrying two of their number on makeshift litters—ponchos tied between two poles.

Toland pulled off the goggles, letting them dangle around his neck on a cord. He fit the stock of the Sterling submachine gun into his shoulder. His finger slid over the trigger. With his other hand he picked up a plastic clacker.

The man with the flashlight was just opposite when Toland pushed down on the handle of the clacker. A claymore mine seared the night sky, sending thousands of steel ball bearings into the marching party at waist level.

As the screams of those not killed by the initial blast rang out, Toland fired, his 9mm bullets joining those of his men. The rest of the marchers melted under the barrage. A few survivors followed their instincts instead of their training and ran away from the roar of the bullets, scrambling up the far slope, tearing their fingernails in the dirt in desperation.

"Now," Toland said.

It wasn't necessary. Faulkener knew his job. In the strobelike flashes from the muzzles of the weapons, the fleeing people were visible. Faulkener pressed the button on a small radio control he held in his hand and the hillside spouted flames. A series of claymore mines, which Faulkener had woven into the far slope at just the right angle to kill those fleeing and not hit the ambushers on the far side of the kill zone, wiped out the few survivors.

"Let's police this up!" Toland called as he stood.

He pulled up his night-vision goggles and watched. Faulkener took up position at the other end of the kill zone. Toland's mercenaries descended like ghouls upon the bodies, hands searching. A shot rang out as one of the bodies turned out to be not quite dead.

Toland checked the bodies with a red lens flashlight. Various faces appeared in the glow, frozen in the moment of their death. Some of the faces were no longer recognizable as human, the mines and bullets having done their job.

As he got to the one of the bodies that had been carried, he saw a female's face caught in the light, the eyes staring straight up, the lips half parted. He could tell she had been beautiful, with an exotic half-Indian, half-Spanish look, but she was covered in blood now and there was a rash across her face—broad black welts. Toland walked over to the other makeshift stretcher. The body in there was in even worse shape. There was much more blood than the round through the forehead would have brought forth. The same black welts across the face. Toland reached down and ripped open the man's shirt. His body was covered with them.

"Let's get a move on!" Toland yelled out. After five minutes, the men began to file by, dropping whatever they'd found in front of him. A stack of plastic-wrapped packages soon covered the sheet.

Toland stabbed one of the packages with his knife. Coca paste poured out of the hole. "Shit," he muttered. He looked up at Faulkener. "It isn't here."

Faulkener shrugged. "We were told to stop anyone coming out and find a metal case. What now?"

Toland pointed to the east, down the pass. "We do what else we were told to."

The patrol began moving toward the border with Brazil.

Turcotte headed back for the Osprey. He'd left Captain Miller in charge of Scorpion Base. Besides the bodies in the vats, there was little else to indicate anything about STAAR. There were several computers in an area that had obviously been a command-and-control center. Turcotte had the hard drives of those computers with him, and he would give them to Major Quinn at Area 51 for analysis.

Miller was also supposed to remove at least one of the bodies from its vat. That task was going to be harder than it appeared, given that the liquid inside the tank had frozen also. They were going to have to thaw the entire thing out. Turcotte gave the order for the plane he had come in on to head north.

As the Osprey took off, he looked at the hard drives he had with him. He doubted that STAAR had been stupid enough to leave anything of importance on them, but one never knew. He'd seen some very smart people do some very stupid things over the years when they were in a rush, and with the foo fighter bearing down on their location the STAAR personnel would have been in one hell of a rush.

The mystery of STAAR would remain a mystery. For a few days longer, at least.

"Major Quinn, this is security," the voice came over the tiny receiver fitted into the Air Force officer's left ear.

Quinn's station was set on a dais that overlooked the Cube. Since the discovery that the two STAAR bodies weren't quite human, the entire facility had been shut down, bringing outraged cries from the media that had descended on the place after the "outing" of the mothership and bouncers by Duncan and Turcotte.

Quinn was actually happy they were closed off to the outside world. His years of working for Majestic-12 had left him ill-prepared to deal with the reporters who had tried poking their noses into everything. UNAOC and Washington both felt the STAAR story needed to be kept under wraps for now, and for that Quinn was grateful.

"This is Quinn," he replied into the small boom mike in front of his lips. "What is it?"

"We've got an intruder."

"Location?"

"Well, sir, he just drove up to the main gate."

"Turn him over to the local authorities," Quinn said irritably.

"He's asking for a Larry Kincaid and a Lisa Duncan, sir."

Quinn pursed his lips. "What's his name?"

"He refuses to give it, sir. But he's not American. He says he's from Russia. From something called Section Four."

"Bring him in."

7

"Mike." Lisa Duncan wrapped her arms around him and squeezed tight.

Turcotte returned the hug, half lifting the much smaller woman off the flight deck. They stayed that way for a few seconds, then Duncan was the first to let go, conscious of the eyes watching them.

"Come on." Turcotte gestured toward a hatch in the island on the right side of the flight deck. The *John C. Stennis* was a sister ship to the carrier Duncan had left; a *Nimitz*-class carrier, the top of the line of the U.S. Navy. The class of carrier was not only the largest warship afloat, it was considered the most powerful weapon on the face of the planet, carrying over seventy warplanes capable of launching weapons up to and including nuclear warheads.

The *Stennis*'s flight deck was 1,092 feet long and 252 feet wide. The plane Duncan had flown in on was already disconnected from the landing cable and being towed to the large elevator that would bring it to the deck below for service. F-14 Tomcats and F/A-18 Hornets crowded the deck, jammed in tight.

Turcotte led the way to a conference room just off the communications shack that the captain had reserved for his use. Turcotte had arrived on the *Stennis* a half hour before from his Antarctic expedition, only to learn

that Duncan was en route and that the Easter Island
Task Force was in a communications blackout owing to
the NSA shutting down the FLTSATCOM satellite.

As Turcotte poured them both a cup of coffee, Lisa
Duncan took off her leather jacket and put her briefcase
on top of the conference table.

"Nothing from Easter Island?" Turcotte asked.

"The Sea Eye torpedo went through the shield. But
that's the last we've heard from it. The *Springfield* cut
the wire."

"And the *Springfield*?"

"Sitting on the bottom, just outside the shield. Three
foo fighters are around it."

"Where did they come from?"

"I'd say from Easter Island. Maybe the guardian
made some."

"Made some," Turcotte repeated. "That's not good.
How long can the sub just sit there?"

"Months if necessary," Duncan said.

"I wonder what the hell is going on with Kelly,"
Turcotte said. "I'm sure she was in contact with the
guardian."

Duncan accepted the coffee and took a drink. She
wrapped her fingers around the mug, feeling the
warmth. "She could be dead."

"She could be, but I don't think so. I think the guardian would find her too useful."

Duncan didn't like dwelling on that, so she changed
the subject. "I got your report on Scorpion Base."

"I'm having the computer hard drives forwarded to
Major Quinn at Area 51. Maybe his people can pull
something out of them. We'll have to wait on the bodies
until they can thaw those tanks out and remove them."

Lisa Duncan held up a sheaf of faxes she'd received
in flight. "This is only a partial listing of what the guard-

ian got into on the Interlink and Internet before it got cut off."

"Anything significant?"

Duncan snorted. "Yeah, everything's significant. Classified-weapons programs. Research information. It accessed the skunkworks and got performance data on all the classified-aircraft programs. It completely went through NASA's database and got everything on the space program. Department of Defense records."

"A recon," Turcotte summed it up.

"Exactly."

"But for what purpose?" Turcotte mused. "Simply to gather information, or does it have something planned?"

"Probably both," Duncan said. "The guardian also went into the Internet."

"And?"

"NSA is still trying to track everything it did. But the disturbing thing is that it appears the guardian sent some e-mail messages."

"To who?"

"NSA hasn't tracked that down yet, and they're not sure they're going to be able to as the addresses no longer exist."

"What were the messages?"

"They were encoded. NSA is still trying to break the code." Duncan shoved the papers aside. "There's more."

Turcotte rubbed his eyes. "What?"

"I got a strange call." Duncan told him of the brief conversation with Harrison.

"Anything on this Harrison guy?"

"I've had Major Quinn check. Nothing."

"And his claim that Temiltepec was not the site the guardian was found at?"

"Major Quinn's got someone checking on that, but Majestic didn't keep very good records the last year and a half at Area 51 on all that—it was all at Dulce."

"And the shuttles?"

"NASA is doing a dual launch. One shuttle from Cape Kennedy, the other from Vandenberg Air Force Base. The *Columbia* will rendezvous with the sixth talon. The *Endeavour* will go to the mothership. I talked to Larry Kincaid about it and he says UNAOC has put a blanket of secrecy over the whole thing, but his opinion is that the whole operation, starting with the dual launch, to trying to make the rendezvous, is very dangerous and he hasn't really heard a good reason why there is such a rush to accomplish this."

"What about the possibility there is another ruby sphere, like this Harrison guy suggested?" Turcotte asked. "Could UNAOC have uncovered another one and kept it a secret?"

"I doubt it," Duncan said, "but it's possible."

"Why is the mothership so important right now?" Turcotte asked. "What's this plan that Harrison mentioned?"

"I have no idea," Duncan said. "There's other news out of Area 51."

"What?"

"I don't know yet. I just got a call while flying here. Major Quinn and Larry Kincaid are on their way here on a bouncer. Should be arriving any minute."

"Why are they coming here?" Turcotte asked. "Wouldn't it have been easier to videoconference?"

"I don't know," Duncan said. "Quinn sounded very weird. We'll find out when they get here."

"Let's take a walk while we wait," Turcotte said. He led the way, along a walkway just below the flight deck, toward the bow of the ship. They stood together at the very front of the *Stennis,* underneath the leading edge of the flight deck. Turcotte could feel the spray as the bow cut through the water and the ship made flank speed to the north. He reached out and gave Lisa Duncan a hand as she stepped over a cable and joined him.

It was dark, but the phosphorescence of the algae being churned up glowed below them. Turcotte could feel the power of ship, its engines at full power, the propellers cutting the water, moving over 100,000 tons at forty miles an hour.

"I talked to UNAOC headquarters in New York and to the National Security Adviser at the White House on my way here," Duncan said, "to get a feel how things are going. And to try to find out about the shuttle launches and the ruby sphere."

"And?" Turcotte sensed her reluctance to speak. But he'd done some thinking on the way up from Antarctica and he had a good idea what was coming.

"From the former, like talking to a brick wall. I didn't tell them much, just tried to feel things out."

"What a surprise," Turcotte said.

"UNAOC is lying low," Duncan said. "The backlash against the destruction of the Airlia fleet took them by surprise."

"But they're still planning on launching space shuttles to hook up with the mothership and talon, right?"

Duncan nodded. "I know. Something strange is going on."

"I recommend we look at UNAOC like we used to look at Majestic-12," Turcotte said. "Don't run anything by them, don't ask them for anything."

"But they supported us against the Airlia fleet," Duncan protested.

"After the fact," Turcotte said. "And now they've changed their tune." Turcotte let the silence play out.

"All right," Duncan agreed to his proposal.

"What about our government?"

"Split."

"Great."

"Politics, Mike," Duncan explained. "The progressives are growing stronger every day. And then there's the isolationists."

"So we're on our own?" Turcotte asked.

"I can get us some help if we need it." Lisa turned to face him and took his hands in hers. "I also wanted you to know that I'm going to need you for whatever comes up."

"Who else?" Turcotte felt the sea breeze on his skin. He drew in a deep breath through his nose, his nostrils flaring as the scent of salt water filled them. "There." He pointed down to their left. "See them?"

Duncan looked.

There was a flash of something white against the phosphorescent glow.

"Dolphins," Turcotte said. "They're playing."

But Duncan's attention was elsewhere. Turcotte followed her gaze toward the horizon. A silver bouncer was coming in fast and high, dropping altitude as it closed on the carrier.

"Time to go," Duncan said.

Turcotte was trying to assimilate all the new information that Duncan had just given him. "Give me a few minutes alone, Lisa."

"Mike—"

He placed a finger on her lips. "Give me a few minutes alone to think, then I'll join you in the conference room and we can try to figure out what's going on. Okay?"

"Okay."

Turcotte stood perfectly still, feeling the wind in his

face, the smell of salt water. He remembered as a child going to the rocky coast of Maine with his family on their rare vacations. After entering the military he'd been shocked the first time he'd gone to a real beach, where the shoreline wasn't rock and the water wasn't freezing. But despite the discomforts, there was something about that coastline that called to him, like the mountains meeting the sea.

Turcotte pulled himself out of his musings and headed into the interior of the *Stennis*. He wove through numerous passageways until he arrived at the conference room that had been set aside for Duncan's use.

There were three men in the room along with Duncan. Two of them Turcotte knew—Major Quinn and Larry Kincaid. The third was a rather impressive stranger, almost seven feet tall and wide as the door Turcotte had just come through. A thick black beard, streaked with gray, adorned a red face. The man looked tired, his eyes red with large dark bags under them. His face was weather-beaten.

"Mr. Yakov," Duncan began, "this is Captain Mike Turcotte."

"Just Yakov will do." His voice was a rolling deep bass with a heavy accent. Turcotte's hand was lost inside the other man's massive paw. "Do you have anything to drink?"

Duncan reached for the water carafe on the desk.

"Something real to drink," Yakov corrected her.

"I'm sorry," Turcotte said, "but our Navy is dry."

"Ahh!" Yakov snorted with disgust. "No place, especially a ship, should be dry."

"Yakov is from Section Four," Duncan explained as they all took their seats around the small conference table. Turcotte knew that Section IV was Russia's secret UFO investigative group.

"Are we secure?" Yakov cut off Duncan before she even got started.

"Yes," Duncan said.

"I don't mean the room," Yakov said, "I mean the people." Yakov leaned forward. "Section Four was just destroyed, so you must excuse me if I am not overly trusting."

"Why do you think it was destroyed?" Turcotte asked.

"I cannot communicate with it. I checked with Moscow. The base has missed its last two scheduled contacts. I had to call the KGB to check that. Then my SATPhone indicated I was being traced—backtracked through the satellite links. That made me—how do you say—nervous. I cut the connection."

"They missed their contacts, but how can you be sure it was destroyed?" Turcotte asked.

Major Quinn spoke up. "After Yakov told me where it was, I had one of our satellites take a picture. The base is destroyed."

"Who did it?" Turcotte asked.

Yakov shrugged. "That is a good question. I do not know."

"I doubt that," Turcotte said, which earned him a quick glance from Yakov but no elaboration.

"Why did you go to Area 51?" Duncan asked.

"We never trusted anyone—particularly the KGB— at Section Four. With it gone my list of those I could trust has shrunken dramatically." Yakov shrugged. "I talked to you before, Dr. Duncan. And you, Captain Turcotte, I understand you knew Colonel Kostanov?"

"Yes."

Yakov's dark eyes bored into Turcotte's. "I understand he died bravely in China."

"Colonel Kostanov was very brave."

"I suppose I must believe that you can judge that. You are the slayer of the Airlia in space. That was a brave act. And you are a—what do you Americans call it—a Green Hat?"

"Green Beret," Turcotte corrected, although he was sure that Yakov had to know the proper term.

"Yes, that is it. I saw the movie. John Wayne. Very impressive. Except when he jumped out of the airplane without hooking up his parachute. Hollywood stuff. And when do colonels go into combat? Every colonel I know hides behind a desk or far behind the front lines."

"Colonel Kostanov did not hide," Turcotte said.

Yakov's cheerful face sobered. "No, he didn't. I will take your word, Captain Turcotte, on the fate of my friend."

"Back to Section Four," Duncan said. "Your base?"

"Ah, *Stantsiya Chyort,*" Yakov said. "That is what we call our Area 51. The Demon's Station. The official name was something I've forgotten—something a bureaucrat made up. But Demon's Station will do, will it not? Much more imaginative than Area 51, would you not agree?"

"I suppose," Duncan said.

"You suppose?" Yakov laughed. "Of course it is better. And much better situated. You think Area 51 was remote, you should have seen *Stantsiya!* It was the asshole of the world. Nothing within hundreds of miles except nuclear test ranges. And you don't want to spend much time wandering through those, eh? But now it is gone," he said simply.

"I think you know who attacked it," Turcotte said.

Yakov shrugged. "That brings me back to my question of whether all of you can be trusted."

"You're going to take our word?" Turcotte asked.

"I will take your word and Dr. Duncan's word based

on what you have done. But even then, I warn you, you can trust no one."

"Including you," Turcotte said.

"Ah, yes, including me. I see bad everywhere. I am paranoid. All Russians are paranoid. And remember, just because you are paranoid it doesn't mean they aren't out to get you."

"If we don't trust each other," Duncan said, "then we might as well end this conversation right now."

The silence played out for several seconds before Yakov broke it. "I think *Stantsiya Chyort* was destroyed because of that electronic mail message I sent to Mr. Kincaid. I think Section Four had been infiltrated long ago, and I warned my superior. He did not believe, or he was one of them. I do not know. That is why I had to contact your Area 51, because this is more important than my country or your country. And events proved me right."

"Let's slow down," Turcotte said. "Start from the beginning." Turcotte turned to the scientist from JPL. "What was Yakov's e-mail?"

Kincaid spoke for the first time. "It only said to check out the DPS system for a certain time period."

"DPS?" Turcotte asked.

Kincaid quickly brought them up to speed on what the Space Command system looked for and what he saw that night.

"Yakov." Duncan turned to the Russian. "Why did you have Mr. Kincaid check the DSP?"

Yakov spread his hands. "What did he see?"

"A satellite went down in South America," Duncan said. "Why is that important?"

"A satellite from a company called Earth Unlimited, correct?" Yakov said.

Major Quinn nodded. "Yes. And Earth Unlimited is the parent company of Terra-Lel."

That clicked in Turcotte's brain. "The ruby sphere."

Kincaid nodded. "We never found out how Terra-Lel found the cavern or the sphere."

"No," Turcotte said, "UNAOC hasn't found out. *We* haven't tried to find out."

The hint of a smile played across Kincaid's lips. "Well, Major Quinn and I have done some digging." He glanced over at Yakov. "I don't know if our Russian friend knows this or not, but Earth Unlimited launched not only this satellite but two previous ones."

"And," Quinn interjected, "they have four simultaneous launches planned shortly. They're going to use every launch platform Ariana has at Kourou."

"What are they doing?" Duncan asked.

"That we haven't figured out yet," Kincaid said. "At first I thought they might be trying something with the mothership or talon, but the flight paths of the satellite came nowhere near either craft."

"What is Earth Unlimited?" Turcotte asked. "How did they know about the ruby sphere?"

"Well," Quinn drawled the word out, "that's a couple of good questions. Another interesting question would be what was Earth Unlimited's connection to the facility at Dulce?"

"What?" Turcotte snapped.

"A subsidiary of Earth Unlimited was the primary Defense Department Contractor for the construction and continued operation of the biolab at Dulce," Quinn said. "A contract let through the Black Budget."

"But—" Turcotte turned to look at Duncan. "What the hell is going on?"

"Maybe our Russian friend knows," Duncan said.

All four sets of eyes turned toward the largest person in the room.

Yakov reached out and took the carafe of water. He poured himself a glassful and took a drink. He grimaced as he tasted the water. "We knew Earth Unlimited was associated with Terra-Lel, the company that was involved with the ruby sphere in the Great Rift Valley. We were interested in Terra-Lel's compound in Ethiopia for a long time, as Colonel Kostanov must have told you. Section Four even sent a team to try to infiltrate it, but they were attacked and stopped.

"We also knew about the previous launches by Earth Unlimited from Ariane's launch site at Kourou. When I requested that our own space-tracking satellites keep—how do you say? tabs?—tabs on any future launches, I started to get information back that someone was looking back in my direction. Wanting to know why I wanted to know about these satellites. That's what caused me to warn my boss and to electronic-mail your Area 51."

"Is Ariane in on it?" Turcotte asked.

" 'In on it'?" Yakov repeated. "I think not. Cash rules. Do you know how much Earth Unlimited is paying for those four rockets to go up at the same time? One point two billion dollars. That's on top of the nine hundred million they've already spent for the three previous launches. People's vision tends to get very blurry when that much money is involved.

"I have no evidence the European Space Consortium is aware of what Earth Unlimited is trying to do, but it would also not be the first time I have been proven wrong. They are everywhere."

"They?" Turcotte asked.

Yakov ignored Turcotte and turned to Kincaid. "Since you have had some time to check on things, perhaps you know something more?"

"I've found out a little bit," Kincaid said after Duncan indicated for him to go ahead. "I had a DOD satellite do a scan of the area the satellite went down in, looking for the payload. We didn't find that, but something strange came up. Take a look at this." He put a sheet of colored paper on the table.

"What are we looking at?"

"Thermal imaging of the region where the Earth Unlimited payload went down," Kincaid said.

"And?" Turcotte saw various hues of blue and green.

"Lower right quadrant," Kincaid said. He slid a second image to the center of the table. "Next shot is a zoom on that area."

A new image appeared on the screen. Two areas were circled in yellow. One was full of tiny blue spots. The other had red dots.

"That's two villages," Kincaid said. "The blue dots are dead bodies. Recently dead and cold."

"My God," Duncan exclaimed, "there must be a hundred of them."

"I don't get it," Turcotte said. "Are they connected to the rocket that went down there?"

"I think so," Kincaid said.

"How?" Turcotte asked.

"I don't know," Kincaid admitted. "It just seems like too much of a coincidence. And what's even more bizarre is the other village, where all the people show up dark red. The shade indicates the average body temperature is over 101 degrees Fahrenheit."

"Everyone in the village is hot?" Turcotte asked.

"Looks like it," Kincaid said. "If I hadn't gotten the tip from Yakov, no one would even have looked in this area."

"But we don't know exactly what we're looking at," Turcotte pointed out.

"Not yet," Kincaid said.

"What are we looking at?" Duncan addressed the question to Yakov.

"The end of the world," Yakov said. "To be more specific, the death of every human being on the face of the planet who is not a puppet of the Airlia."

Turcotte glanced at Duncan. She returned the look, which said that they didn't know the how or why yet, but they believed Yakov.

Yakov picked up the imagery, then put it back down. He looked around the table. "Have any of you heard of something called The Mission?"

When there was no response, he continued.

"Have any of you heard of the Guides?"

Another silence.

"Your Majestic-12, they were what we call Guides."

"What do you mean?" Turcotte asked.

Yakov tapped the side of his large head. "Their mind was affected by a guardian computer. You know of STAAR. It was founded by your government the same time as Majestic-12, but its mission was to prepare for actual encounter with aliens. But STAAR was just a cover for an organization that had existed already. The Guides are Aspasia's version of STAAR. Not the same, but they, too, work for the aliens. I can only tell you the little I know, and the little I guess from that little I know."

Turcotte found the Russian's way of speaking interesting. He also understood the man's paranoia, given what had happened ever since he'd been involved in this entire Area 51 mess.

"The Mission is an organization, not a specific place. It moves. It is the headquarters for the Guides. I do not know its exact makeup or much about it at all.

"We believe it is now in South America. How long it

has been there, I do not know. I know it is the place behind this satellite that came down. You could call this company Earth Unlimited's headquarters, although I think that is just the front they use to work in the world now. I think The Mission has existed for a very long time. It is the source for what came from the satellite and killed those people in your thermal imagery."

"And what is that?" Turcotte asked.

"The Black Death."

8

The Guide Parker sat alone in the darkness, staring at the screen of his laptop. A trickle of sweat ran down his forehead, along his left temple, and onto the hard floor.

There was knock on the door to his room. He swung his chair around, wincing in pain. He closed his eyes for a few seconds, then called out.

"Enter."

A young woman in her early twenties cautiously stepped into the dimly lit room, only a pair of candles and the screen supplying light.

"Guide Parker?"

"Yes, my child." Parker's voice was low and soothing.

The woman stepped forward. "I . . ." She paused.

"Go ahead," Parker said. "You must speak freely."

"I want to believe," she said.

"I know you do."

"The Airlia—" she began, then stopped.

"Go ahead. Speak freely."

"The Airlia aren't human. How can we be sure . . ."

Parker smiled reassuringly. "If they were human, there would be no reason to believe. The Airlia are more than human. For us to become more than we have been, we must follow them. Meet them—if we could have before UNAOC took its sacrilegious action. But we still have their technology to take us to the stars. To help us rise above the disaster we have inflicted upon ourselves on this planet. It is the path we must take. It is the only path that will take us out of dirt-locked existence. But to take that path we must be prepared to serve."

The young woman nodded, but her eyes still wouldn't meet Parker's. "I understand . . . but the talk of doom, of death for the nonbelievers. I don't know if . . ."

There was only the faint sound of the candles flickering for several seconds before Parker spoke, his voice softening. "Do you know the story of the Great Flood?"

The young woman nodded.

Parker reached out and took her hand. "Another Great Flood is coming. Not of water, but just as deadly. And the chosen ones will have to rise above the flood to survive. If you believe, you will be saved. If not . . ." He didn't finish the sentence, and when he spoke again, he pulled his hand away and his voice hardened.

"Do you understand free will? Everyone on the planet knows of the Airlia now. They cannot claim ignorance. Everyone has a choice. It is our job to tell people of their choice. But it is their choice, just as it is *your* choice." Parker's voice slowly changed timbre and the room seemed to close in. "But once the choice is made, each person must bear responsibility for their actions. And the weight of that responsibility if they choose wrong will be most dire!"

Yakov leaned back in his seat, and they could all see how weary he was. It was as if after making his pronouncement of doom, he had lost what little energy he had left. "I don't know where to begin. I've told you there are these Guides. People who have been directly affected by a guardian computer and do the bidding of the aliens. They are not many in number, since access to the guardians is very limited. And then there are the STAAR. Humans who are cloned."

"Not just cloned," Major Quinn interjected.

Yakov raised his eyebrows at that.

"Go ahead, Major," Duncan said. She wanted to give Yakov a chance to get his energy back. She also wanted a chance to think. First this stranger, Harrison, calling about Black Death, and now Yakov using the same term.

Quinn ran a hand through his thinning blond hair. His thick, tortoiseshell glasses reflected the lights inside the room. "We did an autopsy on the two STAAR personnel."

"And?" Duncan prompted.

"They're not human. Not exactly."

Turcotte glanced at Duncan before speaking. "How are they not exactly human?"

He remembered Kostanov telling him that Section IV had captured a STAAR operative in the early nineties, and that Russian scientists had discovered that the man was a clone. But a clone was still human. Turcotte had assumed that the bodies in the tanks at Scorpion Base were human clones; this shed a different light on that assumption.

"We're not sure exactly," Quinn said. "UNAOC pathologists and other scientists are still working on the bodies, but the first thing we noticed was that their eyes were red with elongated pupils. They'd been wearing cosmetic contacts and, of course, the sunglasses. Red eyes are definitely not human."

Turcotte remembered the holographic figure that had guarded the passageway in Qian-Ling. It had had the same type of eyes. "They're Airlia?"

"We think they are a mixture of Airlia and human genetic material," Major Quinn said.

"Any indication of cloning?" Turcotte asked.

Quinn nodded. "Both bodies' genetic material are almost identical. That indicates they either are twin sisters or else they were—shall we say 'developed'?—out of the same genetic material. So, yes, cloning is a very real possibility.

"The scientists are still working to determine what the exact percentages are, but it appears they are mostly human. However, we do have to assume that the Airlia were capable of surviving unaided on this planet, given that they established a base here and kept it going for several millennia. Plus the figure you saw in the holograph was shaped roughly like a human. Their genetic background can't be too far off from ours."

"Interbreeding?" Duncan wondered out loud.

"It's possible," Quinn said. "The scientists think it's more likely, though, that the Airlia played with human DNA, mixing in some of their own, and came up with these STAAR people."

Yakov shook his head. "The STAAR operative we captured did not have these eyes. He was a perfect clone, one hundred percent human."

Quinn raised his hands to indicate it was beyond him. "I'm just telling you what we found."

"Did you see this body?" Duncan asked.

Yakov turned in her direction, his eyes narrowing. "No." Before she could say anything else, he raised his hand. "Point taken."

"Maybe the ones you examined at Area 51 were sleeping like the Airlia on Mars," Turcotte said.

Duncan shook her head. "No, they've been awake at least since 1948. When Majestic got formed, STAAR was also formed as the Strategic Advanced Alien Response team, but as Yakov says, I think it existed before that."

"Zandra told me that STAAR existed in case of alien attack, but now that we know they were part Airlia we know that's a bunch of bull," Turcotte said.

"Maybe not," Duncan interjected. "Maybe they were to guard against a specific alien attack?"

"Against Aspasia?"

"Zandra didn't seem too keen on him coming here in the talons," Duncan said.

Turcotte considered that. "That means STAAR was Artad's version of the foo fighters and guardian. Left here to keep a watch on things, to make sure the truce between Artad's faction here on Earth and Aspasia's on Mars was maintained."

"That's possible, but we need to know more," Duncan said.

"We've only got the two bodies," Quinn said. "We're still working on them."

"You'll have more bodies soon," Turcotte said. "We found ten at Scorpion Base. I'll have them shipped to Area 51 once the engineers unfreeze them."

"That might help," Quinn said.

"No further intelligence on STAAR itself? Where the rest of it went?" Duncan asked.

"UNAOC has contacted the intelligence agencies of every country and requested any information they have, but the response has been slow. Nothing significant so far."

"UNAOC has no idea where STAAR is now?" Turcotte pressed.

"None."

"What do you know of STAAR?" Duncan asked Yakov.

"STAAR is one of the many names that group has

gone under," Yakov said. "STAAR is the enemy of The Mission and the Guides. Artad versus Aspasia. The two warring alien groups in their civil war."

"Great," Turcotte muttered.

"All right," Duncan said. "Yakov, you said this thing in South America is the Black Death. What is it and how do you know that?"

"History." Yakov poured himself another glass of water and downed it quickly. "I should have said another Black Death."

"Another?" Turcotte was looking at the imagery of the dead village.

"The Black Death we know from history books devastated the world in the fourteenth century like nothing before and nothing since," Yakov said. "I have done some research on it, because I believe it, too, was caused by the Guides."

"No." Duncan shook her head. "The Black Death was *Yersinia pestis,* the bubonic plague. It was spread by fleas on rats."

"Yes, that is how it was spread," Yakov agreed, "but what caused it? What started it? Where did it come from? Historians still aren't certain. The first Western recorded instance of the plague was during the reign of the Emperor Justinian in A.D. 542. Why did it not devastate the world then as it would eight hundred years later? I believe that someone was experimenting, working with the organism that causes the plague. Plus, they might not have had orders to use it then."

"They?" Turcotte asked,

"The Guides. The Mission. It is most commonly accepted that the Black Death as we call it in human history started in China in 1346. China, my friends. How did it get from Rome to China in those intervening years? And I believe we all agree that the Airlia had a presence in China. Some of you were inside of Qian-Ling. I think there was more going on with the Airlia in China, though, than just the guardian in Qian-Ling. I think there was a presence from both sides of the Airlia civil war in ancient China.

"The Black Death spread from China along the Silk Road through Mesopotamia and Asia Minor. In January of 1348, the plague reached Marseille in France and Tunis in Africa. By the end of 1349 the Black Death's deadly fingers had reached all the way to Norway, Scotland, and Iceland, blanketing Europe and reaching even into my own Russia.

"Less than ten years after it started, it had killed over half of Europe's population. The mortality rate of those infected ranged between seventy-five and ninety percent. The final toll is estimated to be 137 million dead. This is at a time when the entire world's population was less than five hundred million people. Can you imagine the devastation? The Black Death was probably the greatest event in mankind's history."

"But man survived," Turcotte noted.

"Maybe the goal then wasn't to wipe mankind out," Yakov said, "but simply to clean out the ranks. Historians acknowledge that while devastating in death toll, the Black Death was very instrumental in getting Europe out of the Dark Ages. It is very simple economics. There were fewer workers, the wages had to go up, and conditions got better for workers. Poor farm areas were abandoned as the surviving farmers took the better land. Oh yes, it was a great boost for civilization. Maybe that was the goal."

"A rather brutal means to an end," Larry Kincaid said.

"Do you think these things, these aliens, care anything for us other than as a means for their own end?"

Yakov asked. "I believe they use the Black Death—biological warfare, if you like—whenever they see a need to control the human populace. I think destroying Aspasia and his fleet has told them that they not only need to control us, but need to wipe us out completely this time."

"This isn't the Dark Ages," Duncan said. "Using just—"

"The Black Death in history books isn't the only time a Black Death was used against mankind. I just came from South America," Yakov said. "An ancient city called Tiahuanaco. The heart of a great empire—the Aymara—that stretched across the continent for thousands of miles and had a population in the hundreds of thousands. The Aymara empire disappeared around A.D. 1200. It was simply gone. What happened? No one knows. But I went there, deep into the Pyramid of the Sun, and found high runes, written by the last priests." He reached into his pocket and pulled out a photograph. He tossed it on the conference table.

"The Black Death. That's what those runes in the center stand for. I know because I've seen it in other places. The Black Death killed everyone in the Aymara Empire, wiped it off the face of the earth.

"Before South America I was in Southeast Asia. In Cambodia. Historians have always wondered what happened to the ancient Khmer Empire. From the ninth to fifteenth centuries it was the greatest kingdom in Southeast Asia. Then it, too, suddenly disappeared.

"Did you know that Angkor Wat, the temple in the center of the ancient Khmer city of Angkor Thom, is the largest temple in the world? There's more stone in that temple than was used in the building of the Great Pyramid. It was a great empire, a great civilization. I traveled there, braving the mines, the Khmer Rouge, the warring parties. And deep inside a hidden chamber in Angkor Wat, I found a panel with high rune carvings. The last record of another dying culture. And at the center was the same symbol—the Black Death.

"I think that whenever the guardians are tired of the humans around them, or need to stop our development in a certain direction, or direct it, or simply need a tactical victory in their civil war, they use the Guides to develop a biological weapon that cleans the slate, as you say in English. I think they are now ready for such another time, except on this occasion, I think they are ready—and have the technology—to clean off the entire planet."

"I don't understand," Duncan said. "You say on one hand the Guides want to move society forward even if they use rather brutal means, and on the other they want to destroy it. Which is it?"

Yakov raised his hands in a helpless gesture. "I do not know what their ultimate goal is, so I cannot explain their actions. I agree that they do not make sense at times."

"You say The Mission—the Guides—are behind this," Turcotte said. "How do you know?"

Yakov shrugged. "It is, how do you say, a theory of mine."

Turcotte sensed the other man was holding back. "What makes you think the Black Death is back?"

"This village being destroyed." Yakov tapped the last imagery. "This tells you something is killing people. Majestic-12 was infiltrated by Guides. Your facility at Dulce was part of Majestic-12; in fact, it was the place the guardian computer that took over your Majestic people was brought to. And what went on there?" He didn't wait for an answer. "You had some of your Operation Paperclip people. Nazi scientists. But those at Dulce were the biological and chemical warfare people. The ones who made the gasses in the camps. Who tested diseases on prisoners."

None of the Americans in the room said anything, knowing that what Yakov was saying was one of the ugly legacies of the Cold War.

"General Hemstadt," Yakov said. "Is that name familiar?"

"He was the German who was at Dulce," Duncan said.

"But he did not die when Dulce was destroyed," Yakov said.

"How do you know that?" Turcotte demanded.

"The digging at Dulce has been stopped, hasn't it?" Once more Yakov didn't wait for an answer. "Maybe someone doesn't want what was going on there to be discovered," Yakov said. "But not because of what was there, but because what was there is now at The Mission with General Hemstadt."

"I know of no Majestic facility in South America," Major Quinn said.

Yakov shook his head. "Don't you understand? This is not about America. Or Russia. These Guides care nothing for countries. In fact, they like the fact that humans fight among themselves and have split the world into portions and stare across imaginary borders at other humans with distrust. Very convenient, don't you think?

"This is a *world* problem. The Mission—I don't even know exactly where in South America it is. All I know is that your Dulce facility was not the only one working on diseases. We had our secret labs in Russia. And who knows if someone from there isn't now at The Mission along with Hemstadt and others."

"How do you even know there is a place like this Mission?" Turcotte asked.

"It is no coincidence that General Hemstadt ended up there," Yakov said. "I believe The Mission was founded many centuries ago. It is not a specific place, because what little I have learned says it has changed location over the years.

"When our troops overran Berlin at the end of the Great Patriotic War, we uncovered many documents. I have spent the last two years trying to find those documents and other material recovered. Some of it the KGB kept, and I have not been able to get access to it. But some of it I was able to find, and I uncovered some mention of The Mission. What I found strongly indicated that The Mission was involved with the Nazis during World War Two.

"Think of the work on biological weapons at Dulce and in my country and other countries. The fact that key personnel working at those facilities have disappeared. The fact that The Mission was a refuge for Nazis. The fact that Earth Unlimited launched this satellite and plans more launches—what better way to spread a plague than raining it down from above?"

"But why would these Guides want to do this?" Duncan asked.

Yakov gave a bitter laugh. "Why? I already told you I don't know their ultimate goal, but I would say right now, perhaps vengeance? You destroyed the fleet. Killed Aspasia. But they still want to win their millennia-old war. Humans have been a pawn in this war as long as it has been going on. If I were the surviving Airlia on Mars controlling the guardian and thus the Guides, I would want to get rid of the opposition in the same manner they have done many times in the past. I believe you would agree we have not only become dispensable, we have become quite an irritant."

"The only way to find out what exactly is going on"—Duncan tapped the satellite imagery—"is to go here and get a sample of whatever killed these people. And we need to find The Mission."

"There must be a quicker way," Coridan said.

Gergor pulled his pack off and put it down in the snow. "You know there is no quicker way here. Once we get to the southern shore, we can travel more quickly."

The land around them achieved something Coridan had not thought possible—it was even more desolate than the terrain around the Section IV compound on the north end of the island. Whatever vegetation that had once struggled to live here had been blasted away over years of nuclear testing. They had been moving nonstop and were thirty miles south of Section IV, having crossed the first mountain range with great difficulty, but Gergor knew his way.

"How hot is this place?" Coridan took his own pack off and sat on it.

Gergor laughed. "You worry too much. Even though the ban went into effect, that doesn't necessarily mean it was followed. The Russian military has tried to slip a few tests through here and there. In 1997 researchers recorded what seemed like a nuclear explosion on this island. The Russian government managed to convince them it was an earthquake. The other countries wanted to believe that—what else could they do?—so they believed."

"Was it a nuclear test?" Coridan was looking about nervously.

"Oh, yes. I saw the mushroom cloud."

"Then this is hot."

Coridan had brought the conversation full circle.

Gergor momentarily stopped what he was doing. "Yes, it's hot. Worse than the nuclear weapons, Minatom, the Russian atomic agency, has been surreptitiously slipping in spent fuel here for many years. This place is an environmental disaster. But what do you expect? People are hardly better than the animals."

"I expect not to kill myself stupidly," Coridan said.

"You think you have a right to your life? Your body, your life, belongs to The Ones Who Wait. As does mine. We do as we are ordered."

"We did not wait in destroying Section Four," Coridan noted.

"There is a reason for everything," Gergor said cryptically.

Coridan snorted. "We did not find what we needed. And we killed many in accomplishing that failure."

"We succeeded in one way," Gergor said. "We know one more place where it isn't. Plus we did get something worthwhile out of there."

He returned his attention to the object he had pulled out of the pack. It was a black sphere, fourteen inches in diameter. The surface was completely covered with very thin lines shaped like hexagonals. Gergor pulled his gloves off, ignoring the bitter-cold wind. He turned the sphere in his hands, looking carefully at the very faint high rune writing on it, then pressed down on the top. A red inner glow lit the globe, highlighting the high rune hexagonals. Three panels on the bottom opened, extending short legs.

"What are you doing?" Coridan was shivering, now that the heat produced by moving was gone and the cold wind was biting through his outer garments.

"It would be stupid to carry this thing all the way only to find out it doesn't work," Gergor said. He had put the sphere down on top of his pack and was reading the markings.

He pressed. There was a low humming noise. Around the center of the sphere were eight hexagonals. One blinked red, then turned black. The next one did the same. Then the next.

But the fourth one blinked red and continued blinking. Gergor looked up at Coridan even as the fifth, sixth, and seventh ones all went black. The eighth, and final, hexagonal blinked red, then went down to a steady orange flash.

Coridan reached forward with a gloved finger and touched the one hexagonal that was a steady red. "How can that be?"

Gergor turned the sphere off and began repacking it. "You know what that means."

"But I thought they were all destroyed."

"You thought wrong."

"UNAOC is launching the American shuttles to—"

"I know what UNAOC has planned," Gergor interrupted.

"We have to tell Lexina. She has to know this!"

Gergor had his rucksack back on his back. "We will, but we can't signal out of this area. When we get to the aircraft, we will call her."

"Why couldn't you have put the aircraft on this side of the test area?"

"Because security was the primary consideration," Gergor said.

Without a backward glance at the other, Gergor skied into the test range.

Ruiz stared at his arm. A deep trace of black welts crisscrossed the skin. His head was pounding, his throat and mouth were dry, even though he'd just drained a canteen full of water.

He heard deck boards creak. Lifting his head off his chest, he saw Harrison leaning over the plastic cases.

"Senor!" Ruiz croaked.

Harrison slowly stood and turned. Ruiz wasn't surprised to see the man's skin had a faint trace of the same welts. The American had a case in his hands. He walked over to the bridge shield and put the case on it.

"Ruiz." Harrison nodded.

"We have it—what the villagers had?"

Harrison nodded.

"Did you know?" Ruiz asked.

"I suspected this might come, but it's happening faster than I expected."

"You weren't looking for the Aymara," Ruiz reasoned out loud. "You were looking for that village. For this—" He held his arms up.

Harrison paused, then nodded. "Yes."

"Who are you?" Ruiz asked. "You are no university professor."

"I am a Watcher," Harrison said.

Ruiz staggered, bending over double and vomiting over the side of the boat. When he looked up, Harrison had a videocamera in his hands, the lens pointed at Ruiz. He pulled out a tripod and set the camera on it, locking it down, then adjusting the focus.

"What are you doing?"

"We have to let others know the threat."

9

The patrol looked like a party of ghouls as the sun revealed details. Most of the men were splattered with dried blood and all were covered in mud. They'd made good time in the darkness, following the pass down from the site of the ambush. The stream in the center of the ravine had grown larger as they went lower, until now it was almost a river.

Steam was rising off the surface of the water, mingling with the trees that hung over it. The foliage almost touched in the middle overhead, making the band of water a dark tunnel with splotches of light playing along the surface.

"All right. We'll break here," Toland called out. Daylight revealed him to be more than just a voice in the dark. He was a tall, thin man, his hair completely white—unusual for a man of thirty-six, but not for someone in his line of work.

Faulkener placed out flank security on either side and the rest of the men slumped to the ground, exhausted. Faulkener was the opposite of Toland in body type: short and stocky with heavily muscled arms and legs. He'd been the heavyweight boxing champion of the regiment before Toland.

"I suggest everyone take a bath and get cleaned up," Toland said.

"Hell, we're just going to get dirty again," one of the new men replied, pulling his bush hat down over his eyes. Those who had served with Toland before were already beginning to strip down.

"Yes, but cleanliness is very important," Toland replied, keeping his voice neutral.

"I'll clean when I get out of this pigsty of a country," the Australian joked.

Toland pulled the bolt back on his Sterling, the sound very loud in the morning air. "You'll clean now."

The Australian stared at him. "What the hell, mate? You queer or something?"

"I'm not your mate. I'm your commander. Take your clothes off, put them on the riverbank, then get in line." He centered the muzzle of the submachine gun on the man. "Now strip."

Soon there was a line of naked men standing waist deep in the water. The white ones had farmer's tans, their torsos pale, their faces and forearms bronzed from the sun. Toland and Faulkener went through the men's clothes and gear, very slowly and methodically.

Toland held up a plastic canteen and shook it. He turned it upside down. No water came out. He took his flashlight and peered in. "Ah, what do we have here?" Toland asked. He drew a knife and jabbed it into the canteen, splitting the side open. A plastic bag full of brownish powder fell out.

"Whose gear?"

The men all turned and looked at one of the Australians who had just joined them for this mission. The one who had complained about taking a bath. "Come here, mate," Toland called out with a smile.

The man walked out of the water, his hands instinctively covering his groin. "I told you no drugs, didn't I?" Toland asked.

"I didn't—"

The first round caught the man in the stomach, and Toland casually raised his aim, stitching a pattern up the chest. The man flew backward into the river, arms splayed, blood swirling in the brown water.

The men redonned their clothes and gear. "Make sure you drink upstream from that," Faulkener advised the men, pointing at the body of the Australian, which was slowly floating away downstream. "We'll rest here for a few hours."

Toland retired to the shade of a tree. Faulkener joined him there and handed him a sheet of paper. "The message Andrews received last night."

Toland looked at it—a long list of letters that made no sense. "They encoded it. Must be getting worried about someone listening in."

Faulkener didn't reply. He took his knife out and began sharpening the already gleaming edge.

Toland retrieved a Ziploc bag from his breast pocket. Inside it was a small notepad. He turned to the eleventh page—equaling the day of the month they received the message on—and began matching the letters of the message with the letter on the page. Then, using a tri-graph, a standard page that had three letter groups on it, he began deciphering the message. It was slow work, made more difficult by the need to figure where one word ended and the next one began. After twenty minutes he had it done:

```
TO TOLAND
FROM THE MISSION
LINK UP WITH PARTY
VICINITY PACAAS NOVOS ACROSS BORDER
IN BRAZIL
AT COORDINATES SEVEN TWO THREE SIX
```

```
FOUR EIGHT
  IN TWELVE HOURS
  FOLLOW ALL ORDERS OF PARTY TO BE MET
  BONUS ASSURED
  A MILLION A MAN
  TIME IS OF ESSENCE
  CONFIRM ORDERS RECEIVED
  END
```

Toland pulled out his map and looked at the coordinates. About fifty kilometers north and east. He handed the message to Faulkener.

"Why don't they just drop this party off at one of these dirt runways in-country?" Faulkener asked.

"The Americans have this area blanketed with radar. To track drug runners. Whatever The Mission is up to, they must want to keep it secret."

Faulkener looked at the map. "It's a long walk and not much time. What's the rush?"

"We can do it." Toland rubbed the stubble of his beard. "I wonder what they want us to do after we link up with this guy?"

Faulkener nodded toward the merks. "Some of these boys won't want to go farther into the jungle."

Toland laid a hand on the stubby barrel of his Sterling. "Anyone says anything, they can talk to my complaint department. We move out in fifteen minutes."

"They are afraid." Lo Fa lowered the binoculars. "But they are many. More than we have here."

"Are you afraid?" Che Lu asked.

Lo Fa laughed. "Mother-Professor, I am not one of your stupid students to be manipulated so easily by your words."

He pointed to the west, where the bulk of Qian-Ling

was highlighted against the setting sun. It rose out of the countryside, over 3,000 feet high, so large it was hard to imagine that human hands had made the mountain. And it was not a mountain, but a tomb, a monument built before the birth of Christ to honor the Emperor Gao-zong and his empress, the only empress in the entire history of China.

Or at least that was what Che Lu had thought. Now she wondered why it was really built and who was behind the building. The man-made hill dwarfed even the Great Pyramid of Giza, making it the largest tomb in the world. The amount of labor needed to move that amount of dirt and rock was staggering to conceptualize. Trees and bushes had taken root on the mountain, and it looked almost natural except for the symmetrical shape. Around the tomb were various statues, particularly on the wide road leading up to it, where rows and rows of statues were lined, to symbolize all the people and officials who had come to honor the funeral procession of Gao-zong when he was buried in A.D. 18.

What Lo Fa was pointing to, though, was not the tomb or the statues, but the soldiers, tanks, and trucks surrounding the tomb.

"They fear to enter, but they will kill us to keep us from doing so," Lo Fa said. "And your ridicule will not make me throw myself under the treads of one of their tanks. I have not gotten to be this old without a little bit of common sense."

Che Lu shook Nabinger's notebook in front of Lo Fa. "But we have to get in."

Lo Fa squatted. His guerrilla band was spread out around in the grove of trees they were hiding in. They were five kilometers from the tomb, having force-marched here after recovering the notebook.

"I came here because you insisted," Lo Fa said. He

looked around to make sure none of his men were listening. "I came because I respect you, Che Lu. We made the Long March together."

Che Lu looked at her comrade in surprise. In all their years he had never called her by name.

Lo Fa continued. "But if I am to go further, if I am to ask these men to go further, I must know why. I must know what is so important about this old tomb. What was so important for the Russians and the Americans to send men to die getting into and out of it? Why does the army flutter about like moths around a fire—attracted but scared of the flames?" He leaned close, his wrinkled face close to hers. "Tell me about Qian-Ling."

Che Lu rested her back against the rough pack she had carried. She was not young anymore. Her body ached from the march. "You have a right to know, old friend. I will tell you as much as I know and as much as I can guess. But the truth is inside, and that is why we must get in.

"There is more in Qian-Ling than a tomb." She proceeded to tell Lo Fa what she had discovered on her last trip inside—the hologram of the alien that warned in the strange tongue in the central corridor that led to the lowest chamber; the beam that had cut one of her students in half that guarded the way beyond the hologram; the large chamber full of containers that she suspected were Airlia machines and equipment; and through it the chamber holding a small guardian computer.

"But it is the lowest chamber, the one we were not able to get into, that is the key." She held up the notebook once more. "Professor Nabinger could read the high runes. He made contact with the guardian computer inside Qian-Ling. In here he wrote some of what he knew before he died."

Lo Fa waited, his dark eyes meeting hers.

"In the lowest chamber"—Che Lu's voice quavered—"in the chamber, according to Nabinger's writings, I believe there are aliens—more Airlia. Along with their leader Artad. Waiting to awaken."

Lo Fa spit. "So?"

Che Lu was indignant. "So? So! What—"

Lo Fa hushed her. "Shh. Listen to me, old woman. Why would you want to go down there? Why would you want to waken these sleeping beings?" He pointed up. "I have not been ignorant. Others of these woke on Mars. They came here to destroy the planet. Their dead ships circle our world."

Che Lu smiled. "Because these ones"—she pointed at the fading bulk of Qian-Ling—"these ones are the ones who saved us long ago. And maybe they can save us again.

"And there is more down there than just the aliens. According to what Nabinger was able to decipher, there is the power of the sun. Power, Lo Fa. Would you not agree our people need power now? Maybe they can give us the power we need to defeat the government and bring China back the glory it once was! Because if Artad and other Airlia are in Qian-Ling, does it not make sense that the Airlia were instrumental in making China the Middle Kingdom so many years ago?"

The twenty-foot-high pyramid that housed the guardian computer under Rano Kau was now the core of a bizarre structure of which Kelly Reynolds's body was just one part. Metal arms reached out of the side of the pyramid, made out of parts cannibalized from the material UNAOC had left behind.

Microrobots scurried about the cavern. A line of them went up to the surface through the tunnel

UNAOC had drilled. They carried small pieces of stone and returned on the opposite side, each one carrying something taken from the surface, like an army of ants returning from a feast. Most of them brought their scraps to a line of differently shaped microrobots that were aligned along the wall. Taking the raw material brought to them, these made more of their own kind, shaping the various material into bodies, computers, and energy packs.

There were several types of microrobots. The carriers, about three inches long, had six metal legs, and two arms for grasping and holding that could reach forward, then rotate back and hold whatever they picked up on their backs. The makers, six inches long, had four legs and four arms. The arms were different on each, depending on what function they served in the production line.

Another type of microrobots disappeared into a hole in the floor of the cavern—the diggers, with eight legs spaced evenly around a central core body that was two inches wide and eight long. At the very front each one had a set of small drills on very short arms. Those diggers coming out of the hole each carried a small piece of rock. They dumped it in front of the carriers, who picked up a piece and headed for the surface.

The hole was already four hundred feet deep—the goal, a plasma vent two miles down. The guardian needed more power, because this was only the beginning and the UNAOC generators had gone off-line, running out of fuel. The fusion plant that had been left by Aspasia to power the guardian was low on power and needed to be supplemented.

Some of the UNAOC computers were now hardwired into the guardian. Across the monitors information flashed, faster than a human eye could follow as the alien computer sorted through what it had learned from its foray into the human world via the Interlink/Internet. Already it was putting some of that information to use, but there was so much more.

And it maintained its link to Mars, to its sister computer deep under the surface and the alien hands that controlled that computer.

A metal probe came out of the golden pyramid. It hovered overhead, then approached Kelly. It halted an inch from the center of her back. A thin needle came out of the end of the probe. It punched through skin, into her spine. Wrapped in the golden glow, with wires and tubes spun around her body, Kelly Reynolds twitched, like a person experiencing a bad nightmare. The needle came back out, retracted into the probe, and was then pulled back inside the guardian.

Kelly shivered for several moments, then the body relaxed and became one with the guardian once more.

Turcotte knew Duncan was on the satellite radio, arranging for some assistance through her own private network. He had something else on his mind.

He found Yakov sprawled in a chair in the cabin that had been provided the Russian. A bottle of clear liquid rested on a table nearby.

"My friend!" Yakov said as Turcotte came into the cabin. "A toast to fallen comrades."

Turcotte took the glass. He raised it to his lips and took a drink. The fiery liquid burned as it went down. "Where did you get this?" Turcotte asked when he could speak.

"Ah, I am a man of many resources," Yakov said. "Your navy says it has no alcohol on its ships, but they are men too."

Turcotte sat down across the Russian. "You say this

group, The Mission—its Guides—have been around for a long time."

"A very long time." Yakov nodded.

"Then they've been active and not just watching throughout the course of human history."

Yakov nodded once more. "It appears so."

"You also said the Nazis were involved with The Mission."

"Yes."

"There's someone who might know something about The Mission. Someone who had been to Dulce and knew Hemstadt."

Yakov poured another drink. He tilted the bottle toward Turcotte, who shook his head. "Ah yes. Your Dr. Von Seeckt is still alive, is he not?"

"Is there anything you don't know?" Turcotte asked.

"There is a terrifyingly large amount I do not know," Yakov said. "What I don't know wakes me in the middle of the night sweating with fear."

"I've got Major Quinn setting up a video-conference link to Von Seeckt's hospital room."

Yakov lumbered to his feet. "Let us talk to your Nazi doctor, then."

They went to the conference room where Quinn was waiting.

"I've had one of my people from Area 51 go to the base hospital at Nellis Air Force Base," Quinn said. "We're all set. This is being relayed through Area 51 to us over a secure network."

Turcotte and Yakov sat down in front of the laptop computer. A small camera was clipped on top of the screen pointing at them. The screen snapped alive with an image. An old man lying in a bed, his skin wrinkled and worn, the eyes half closed, peering straight ahead at the camera that must be near the foot of the bed. A microphone was clipped to the old man's sheet, just below his chin. Turcotte could see the tubes running into the man's arms, and he marveled that he was still alive.

"We're all set," Quinn said. "I talked to his doctor. He's got quite a bit of medication in his system, so he might not be too coherent."

"Dr. Von Seeckt," Turcotte said. "This is Captain Turcotte."

"Good day, Captain," Von Seeckt replied in German, his voice just a whisper, amplified by the mike.

"I need some information," Turcotte said in the same language.

Von Seeckt muttered something unintelligible.

"Dr. Von Seeckt!" Turcotte raised his voice, trying to reach the other man's mind. A hand moved the small mike closer to the old man's lips.

"Death," Von Seeckt whispered. "The shatterer of worlds."

Turcotte had heard the old German say those words before—the first time he met him, on a flight out of Area 51. It was a quote from Oppenheimer upon viewing the detonation of the first man-made atomic bomb at Trinity test site in New Mexico. Von Seeckt had been there, and his presence put an asterisk on the term "man-made" for that first explosion, because Von Seeckt had brought with him from Egypt an Airlia-made nuclear weapon.

The Nazis had interpreted enough of high rune symbols from a stone artifact under the water near Bimini—the apparent site of Atlantis, the Airlia main base—found by one of their submarines, that had pointed them to a secret lower chamber in the Great Pyramid of Giza. Von Seeckt, a young scientist of the Third Reich, had been picked to accompany the military team that traveled to Egypt, even as war raged across the desert and the Desert Fox, Rommel, closed on the British forces.

Breaking through a wall in the pyramid, the Germans found a black box that they couldn't open. They took it with them, but in their attempt to return to their own lines were ambushed by the British and Von Seeckt and his box captured. Eventually the radioactive box—along with Von Seeckt—ended up in America as part of the Manhattan Project, because when they finally opened it, they found a nuclear weapon that gave the American scientists great insight into what they were trying to do.

"Doctor, I need some information," Turcotte repeated.

The old man's eyes blinked, trying to find who was speaking. "I took a vow. An oath."

Turcotte knew he had to get through to the old man. "Why do you obey?" Turcotte snapped in German.

Von Seeckt's voice firmed up. "From inner conviction, from my belief in Germany, the Führer, the Movement, and the SS!"

Turcotte could sense Yakov stir next to him, uncomfortable with what he was hearing. While World War II was certainly significant in American history, Turcotte knew the Russians, with over 20 million dead and half their country devastated, held a far harsher memory of that war.

"Hitler is dead," Turcotte hissed. The words Von Seeckt had spoken had been his vow, taken when he'd joined the SS over fifty years earlier. "He's been dead over fifty years. You are in America now. You've been here since the middle of the war. And you must tell me what I need to know!"

Von Seeckt's eyes were wide open now. They focused on the screen at the foot of his bed. "Captain?"

"Yes."

"Orders. I had to follow orders."

"I need you to think," Turcotte said. "Back to when you were in Egypt in the war. After you left the Pyramid with the black box."

"The desert," Von Seeckt whispered. "It was cold at night. I was not ready for that. It surprised me. Very cold. Always in the desert. Why have I always been in the desert?"

"When you were ambushed in the desert," Turcotte said, "was it just chance or did the British know?"

"Know?" Von Seeckt repeated, still speaking German. He blinked. "What have you discovered?" he said in English.

"You told Major Quinn that you had heard rumors of STAAR," Turcotte said. "That you believed it might not be made up of humans. But you also told him that it did nothing. That it just existed until recently taking action. But I don't think that's so. I think STAAR or a group like it has been acting all along, manipulating things, and I think it might have had a hand in your patrol getting ambushed and the Airlia bomb going from German to Allied hands."

Von Seeckt stared at the camera, then his head nodded ever so slightly. "I always thought it was strange. Such a coincidence. We thought we were betrayed by our Arab guides, but the British killed them also, which was rather brutal for those so-called gentlemen. And they were not regular soldiers. I—who had seen the SS stormtroopers—knew these British were special commandos. What were they doing at just the right spot in the desert at just the right time?"

"So it is possible that the British were tipped off?"

"It is possible," Von Seeckt agreed. "But so many things are possible. Who knows what the truth is?"

"I think you know more than you have told us," Turcotte said.

Von Seeckt didn't say anything.

"How did General Gullick and Majestic learn of the dig in Temiltepec?" Turcotte knew that was the event that had suborned the members of Majestic-12 and, if Yakov was to be believed, turned them into Guides. When Majestic uncovered the guardian computer and brought it back to Dulce, it affected the minds of those in charge, particularly Gullick, and led to the attempt to launch the mothership that Turcotte and the others had narrowly averted.

"Intelligence," Von Seeckt said. "Kennedy, our CIA representative, forwarded a report about Jorgenson's dig there and the discovery of something strange."

"Bullshit," Turcotte snapped. "I've had Major Quinn check both the CIA and Majestic records. A lot of them have been destroyed, but what is there suggests the guardian pyramid wasn't uncovered until *after* Majestic's team got there. And they knew exactly where to dig. What isn't in the records is how they got that information."

"I do not know," Von Seeckt said.

"Again, bullshit. You were part of Majestic. You've played this 'I don't know' game long enough." Turcotte wished he could reach through the screen and wrap his hands around the old man's scrawny neck. He had to give the old man credit that he had helped them stop the flight of the mothership, but with Yakov's new information, Turcotte wasn't so sure that Von Seeckt had acted out of altruism.

Shortly after first meeting, Kelly Reynolds had told Turcotte how the place Von Seeckt had worked at—the V-1 and V-2 rocket site at Peenumunde—prior to going on the mission to Egypt had used slave labor from the nearby concentration camp and how thousands had died in those factories and camps. But Von Seeckt had conveniently claimed ignorance of that also at first.

"And I've also received information that the guardian was not found at Temiltepec," Turcotte threw out.

Von Seeckt shook his head. "I have told you all I know. I was told it was Temiltepec."

"You're lying."

"What difference does all this make now?" Von Seeckt sounded very tired. "I understand the Airlia fleet was destroyed. Why are you delving into these things?"

"Because this group is still around somewhere and we need to know more about it. And I think this group had something do with Majestic recovering the guardian wherever they found it." Turcotte saw no reason to divulge to Von Seeckt the information about the Guides or The Mission yet.

"No. I know nothing of such a thing."

"Then tell me about Dulce," Turcotte said.

"I told you already that I only went to Dulce once. That Dulce was the province of the others."

"The other Nazi scientists brought to the United States under Operation Paperclip to work for our government," Turcotte clarified. "But what exactly were they doing there? What was on that lowest level where the guardian computer was stored?"

"I do not know. I never—"

"What was there?" Turcotte cut the old man off. "You do know! Tell me!"

"All they told me was that they were doing experiments. It is what Nightscape picked up the people for."

"No." Turcotte shook his head. "Nightscape kidnapped people, but they were brainwashed on the level above, the level where we found Johnny Simmons."

"Yes, the abductees who were returned with their

disinformation. Did you ever wonder what happened to the abductees who never came back?" Von Seeckt asked. "All those people who disappear every year and are never seen again?"

"They went to the bottom level at Dulce?"

"I am sure some did," Von Seeckt said. "The Paperclip people who worked there, they were most ruthless. They had experience in the camps. Even in your great democracy such things go on."

Turcotte ignored Von Seeckt's barbs. "What was going on in the very bottom level? Where the vats holding those people were? I saw vats like that at Scorpion Base. It was how STAAR 'grew' their own agents. Agents who we now know were Airlia/human genetic combinations. What was going on at Dulce? Were they doing that? Or were they doing something else? Biological-warfare experiments?"

"I don't know." Von Seeckt turned his head.

"What about General Hemstadt?" Turcotte asked.

"He had cold eyes," Von Seeckt murmured. "No life in them."

"Was he working on biological warfare?" Turcotte pressed.

Von Seeckt said nothing.

"The Black Death," Yakov growled.

Von Seeckt turned back toward the camera. "Who are you?"

"The Black Death," Yakov repeated. "Have you heard of it?"

"Rumors," Von Seeckt whispered.

"Rumors of the Black Death?"

"Just rumors. A weapon."

"The Mission." Yakov spit the two words out.

Turcotte noted that that brought a reaction. Von Seeckt's eyes widened.

"Tell me about The Mission," Turcotte pressed.

"I don't know—"

Yakov cut the old man off. "Do not lie to us! Hemstadt went there, didn't he?"

Von Seeckt wearily nodded. "When I heard he left Dulce, I knew something was wrong. It was a month before General Gullick wanted to fly the mothership. I wonder now if they were connected. I also feared that Hemstadt wanted to use the bouncers. To spread whatever he had been working on in the lab at Dulce."

Turcotte stared at the screen. Von Seeckt had slumped back on his pillow, his eyes closed.

Turcotte cut the connection. There was so much that wasn't clear. If Majestic had been infiltrated by the Guides—or STAAR—then that put a whole new light on many things that had occurred. It also put a new light on the destruction of the Dulce facility by the foo fighter. Maybe the target of the foo fighter had been more than just the guardian? Maybe the foo fighter had taken out the Dulce facility to destroy whatever Hemstadt was working on? But the foo fighter had been controlled by the guardian. Had they taken out Dulce to cover the trail? To protect The Mission? The more Turcotte learned, the less he understood.

10

The traveler walked the dusty path, a solitary figure in a very inhospitable land. The person was tall, wrapped in gray robes that were worn and dirty. A hood covered her face, the only indication of her sex being the slight curve at bosom and hips. She had a large pack on her back that she carried easily.

The path could barely be called that. She had picked it up thirty miles southwest of Nairobi, the capital of Kenya. She had not seen a human in the four days since starting her journey. At times the path was so overgrown, she used the machete strapped to her waist to cut through. But always she pressed on, even moving at night, resting only a few hours out of each twenty-four-hour cycle. She wished there were another way, but by foot was the only means of finding where she wanted to go. The trail was ancient, and modern means would not work to follow it.

The path ran along the Great Rift Valley. The longest, continuous crack on land on the surface of the planet, the valley ran from southern Turkey, through Syria, between Israel and Jordan where the Dead Sea lay—the lowest point on the face of the planet. From there it formed the basin of the Red Sea. At the Gulf of Aden the Rift Valley broke into two, one part going into the Indian Ocean, the other inland into Africa, the track the woman was currently on.

To her west, she knew the Rift Valley framed Lake Victoria, the world's second-largest freshwater lake. Ahead of her, it went south for hundreds of miles through the rest of Kenya, into Tanzania, before ending somewhere in Mozambique. The Rift Valley made California's San Andreas fault look like a child's scratching on the face of the planet, while this split was the work of a god.

The land she passed through was tumbled and broken. A river ran through the lowest part, surrounded on both sides by high, tortuous mountains. The path roughly paralleled the river. The sun beat down on the land, raising the daytime temperature easily over one hundred. She relished the heat even though it was difficult to adjust to, as she had spent the past twenty-two years under the ice in Antarctica. To those she had worked with there, she had been known only by the name Lexina, the head of STAAR. Since they had fled Scorpion Base, her small group had scattered across the globe to continue their tasks, but as always, it seemed as if all they were doing was reacting.

Lexina paused as she turned a bend. She scanned the terrain until she saw the anomaly in the growth near the trail. Drawing her machete, she cut through the weeds and cleared away the vegetation. A weathered stone obelisk, five meters high, slowly became visible. It was on the side of the path, half obscured with weeds, the stone itself worn with the passing of many years.

Long, pale fingers reached out and traced the markings on the stone. It was the third such obelisk she had passed in the last few days.

They were markers, border stones from the ancient Empire of Axum. The top half of the stone was covered with Ge-ez, the official language of Axum. Lexina could read it—indeed, it was not a dead language, as it was still in use among a few monks of the Ethiopian church.

Axum was accepted by historians as one of the earliest empires in the world, founded around the first or second century before the birth of Christ. The empire covered most of what was now Ethiopia and Kenya. It traded with Greece and Rome during its heyday, while at the same time reaching to the east to India and even China.

Lexina also knew it was an empire few people had heard of. Mostly because it was here in Africa and because it was an empire of dark-skinned people—not the most popular subject around the world's history courses. But at its height, Axum rivaled any of the kingdoms it traded with—Rome, China, India. And it had a most interesting history. Like many early peoples, the people of Axum worshiped a sun god. Even long after Christianity came to Axum, the Queen of Sheba was reported to be a sun god worshiper. Although she was known to most in the present day as the Queen of Sheba and her visit with King Solomon was well recorded, Lexina and those who knew the history of Axum knew her official title was Queen of Sheba and Axum.

This marker made mention of the queen, and her borders, but it was the bottom half of the marker that interested her. She could make some sense of the writing there also—the high rune language.

The markings indicated she was on the right path.

She pulled a small headset out of a fold in her cloak. The mike was voice-activated, the cord connecting it to a very small but powerful transmitter in her pack.

"Elek?"

She waited a moment.

"Elek?"

"Yes?" The voice on the other end was crystal clear, relayed through the earpiece.

"I have found another stone," Lexina said.

"The path is still good?"

"Yes. Anything further on your mission?"

"I am arranging transportation and mercenaries. That is proving to be difficult, but not impossible."

"We are running out of time," Lexina said.

"I will be ready to move on schedule."

"That may not be good enough. You must find the power."

"The power will be no good without—"

"I know," Lexina snapped. "Do you have any further information that could help my quest?"

"Nothing yet."

"Coridan and Gergor?"

"They have done what they were ordered to."

"Did they find it?"

"No."

"I will check with you later."

She took the headset off.

Lexina continued. As the path went up over a rise, she stopped. Far in the distance was a shimmering white cloud. She stared at it for several minutes, but it didn't move. She pulled the hood back. Her face was pale and smooth, the white hair cut tight against her skull. She wore black wraparound sunglasses.

She pulled the sunglasses off for a moment. Red, elongated pupils narrowed as the bright sun hit them, but she wanted a clear look. She knew the white wasn't a cloud but snow, the very top of Mount Kilimanjaro, rising 19,340 feet above the plain that surrounded it. Her destination, according to the markers, was to the west of that landmark. She put the glasses back on.

·   ·   ·

"My men have gone completely around the tomb and checked all the approaches. The army is too strong. They have tanks, we have rifles. They have helicopters, we have grenades." For Lo Fa that was a speech. He had spoken in a low voice, so that only Che Lu could hear him.

The small grove that sheltered the group's base camp had filled up. The men's women had arrived, bringing their children. Che Lu had not realized how extensive the rebellion was. Wandering the camp, she heard tales of villages being burned, people slaughtered.

The population in this part of China differed somewhat ethnically from the east, but more important, Islam was the religion of the majority of people. The central government had long waged battle against that religion as its practitioners looked westward rather than east.

Che Lu had seen many refugees in her life and the sight never failed to depress her. They were people who had lost everything but their spirit and what they carried on their back. Having lived through all of China's modern history, she found it particularly ironic that the government in Beijing, which had been founded by those she had been with on the Long March—refugees to the extreme—were now inflicting the same situation on their own people.

Che Lu returned her attention to Lo Fa, who had accepted a tin of stew from a young girl. Che Lu had been reading Nabinger's notebook while the guerrillas did their reconnaissance.

"Has the army entered?" she asked.

"No. Remember, they sealed the entrance you went in. The only opening right now is the way you got out, on the top. They have rigged explosives around it and have guns trained on it, as if they fear someone coming out more than they consider going in themselves. They fear the tomb."

Che Lu knew a westerner would find such a reaction by an army to be strange, but the Chinese people had different beliefs and values from those in the West. What checked the army from going in were several factors. One was an ingrained respect for ancestors—thus any entry into a tomb was viewed as a terrible crime. Another, though, was fear of the unknown. The army had to know by now that there was more to the tomb than just the graves of Gao-zong and his empress.

"So they wait and do nothing," she said.

"They keep us from getting in," Lo Fa replied. "That is something."

She held up Nabinger's notebook. "I have discovered some interesting information."

"What is that?"

"Shi Huangdi."

"The First Emperor. The Son of Heaven." Even Lo Fa knew who that was, as did every Chinese.

"Yes. The emperor who unified China. Who pulled together the Great Wall."

"What about him?" Lo Fa asked.

"I think he is in the tomb."

Lo Fa considered the old woman. "How can that be? The tomb holds Gao-zong and his empress. Gao-zong was of the Tuang Dynasty, well after Shi Huangdi."

Che Lu shrugged. "That is what some of the notes that Professor Nabinger transcribed indicate. I do not know how it can be, but also remember that Nabinger told me that part of the Great Wall had been built in the form of an Airlia high rune. Since Shi Huangdi was responsible for most of the Great Wall, it must be that he was somehow connected with these aliens."

"Ahh . . ." Lo Fa shook his head. "This is crazy talk.

Aliens. The Wall built to signal to space. Flying saucers." He looked away.

Che Lu felt sorry for her old friend. His world, the world he had grown up in and lived in for over seven decades, was being thrown on its ear. The rulers in Beijing were all old men like Lo Fa, and she knew they were having an even harder time accepting the new reality, especially since they had so much more to lose than her friend.

"Just think," Che Lu pressed. "If we discover the link between Shi Huangdi and the aliens, it may mean we were indeed the central kingdom. The source of civilization. Not the way we had always thought, but still in a way. Perhaps we were the chosen of the Airlia, the humans picked to be their special people.

"Nabinger told me some things," Che Lu continued. "When they found the ruby sphere in the great cavern in Africa, they found a stone marker. It talked of Cing Ho."

"Who is that?"

"I thought he was nothing more than a legend. A made-up tale. According to the story, Cing Ho was a sailor, the admiral of a fleet that sailed from China, through the Straits of Malacca, past India, to Africa and the Middle East. He did this long before the Silk Road was open to Rome, before the birth of Christ."

Lo Fa pulled some tobacco and paper out of a pouch and began making a cigarette. "So?"

"So? First, if Cing Ho was real, it means there was a Chinese sailor traveling farther than any explorer of his time. According to history, we did not use the compass for navigation until A.D. 1120, although there are records of magnetic pointers being used thousands of years earlier in the emperor's courts for divining purposes. But maybe Cing Ho did use a divining compass to navigate to the Middle East. And, if he was the one who placed the ruby sphere in that cavern, as the stone indicates, then he had some connection with the Airlia."

"So?"

Che Lu could not tell if her old friend was trying to antagonize her or not. "Then we—China, the Middle Kingdom—are central to all of this."

"We do not know what *this* is," Lo Fa noted.

"If we get in the tomb we can find out," Che Lu said. "What is interesting to me is the thing that destroyed China as a world power was our unwillingness to go outside of our borders in the last five centuries. The last time we made any attempt to was in 1405."

"Are you giving me a history lesson?" Lo Fa asked.

Che Lu ignored the sarcasm. "In 1405, over twenty thousand men and three hundred seventeen ships led by Zheng He left China and traveled west, following the route Cing Ho took over two millennia previously." She thumped Lo Fa on his skinny chest. "They went to the Middle East. To northeast Africa. And then they came home and China never again mounted any sort of expedition. And the question I have, old man, is what were they looking for? And did they find it? Is that why they came home? Or did they fail? If they did find whatever it was that Cing Ho removed so many years ago, is it now inside the tomb in front of us? Or did they take something with them like Cing Ho did? I believe the answer lies inside the tomb."

"This thinking is all fine and well," Lo Fa said, "but it will not get us in the tomb."

Che Lu ignored the comment. "Shi Huangdi," she whispered.

"What of Shi Huangdi, old woman?"

"There are many legends surrounding Shi Huangdi," Che Lu said. "He has been called the Yellow Emperor, among many other titles. It is said when he was born there was a great radiance in the sky, coming from the region of Ursa Major. In his biography it is written that when he met the Empress of the West in the mountains of Wangwu, they made something together."

"A child?" Lo Fa said with a smile.

"No. Twelve large mirrors."

Lo Fa was interested despite himself. "Who was the Empress of the West?"

"I don't know."

"Well, what about these mirrors?"

"I also don't know much about that," Che Lu admitted. "In conjunction with the mirrors, there were things called tripods. These tripods pointed the mirrors to the heavens. Zao Ji wrote about the tripods of Shi Huangdi in a text I have read. There are many rumors about these tripods and mirrors in ancient texts, enough that I have to believe there is a truth underneath.

"They were supposed to be able to manipulate gravity. To emit loud noises. To look at the stars. And Shi Huangdi was supposed to be able to control the thunder. Perhaps through these devices."

"Interesting legend," Lo Fa said.

"You have heard of Chi Yu, have you not?" Che Lu asked.

"Who?" Lo Fa's voice quivered slightly, and Che Lu knew he had heard of that legend. Perhaps told by his mother, to scare him into going to bed as a young boy.

"While Shi Huangdi ruled in the north, Chi Yu was the name of the ruler in the south. But Chi Yu was different. Not a man, according to legend, but a metal beast. With many arms and legs and eyes. Who could fly about the countryside." Che Lu pointed to the mountain tomb. "The answer to many mysteries lie inside, Lo Fa."

Lo Fa spit. "That may be, old woman. But all your legends still won't get us inside."

"Can you get me a radio?" Che Lu asked. "One that speaks to the satellites?"

Lo Fa nodded. "I think I know where one is. It will take some time."

"You get me a radio," Che Lu said. "Then I can call for help."

"Who will help us?" Lo Fa asked.

"I will ask UNAOC."

Lo Fa laughed. "They will not try again."

"I can only ask. If they do not give us help, then it is up to me alone."

"I will get the radio."

"What's the plan?"

Lisa Duncan was startled. She had not heard Mike Turcotte walk into the conference room with Yakov. She pointed for them to take seats at the table.

"I sent Major Quinn and Larry Kincaid back on the bouncer to Area 51. I contacted a friend of mine at USAMRIID—the United States Army Medical Research Institute of Infectious Diseases. She's promised me some help. A bouncer will pick her people up and bring them to us along with some special gear. Once they get here, you go south with them and find out what exactly is going on."

"And then?" Turcotte asked.

"We try to stop this."

"An optimist," Yakov said with a dry chuckle.

A madman working in a wax museum could not have produced a more gruesome scene. The bodies were twisted into grotesque shapes. Mouths were open; silent lips that would never know the passage of a final scream were pulled wide over fangs. Chests had been sliced opened, red blood frozen and caught hanging like threads of red. The eyes were the worst. Black orbs staring aimlessly out, framed in red blood like cheap eyeliner that an epileptic makeup artist had applied.

Steve Norward didn't like dealing with frozen bodies. Not out of any sense of aesthetics, but because frozen objects had pointy parts and pointy parts make holes in gloves and flesh. And this frozen locker was hot. As hot as any place on earth. And hot plus a hole in the protective suit he wore equaled dead.

Inside his suit, Norward was a large man. He just barely made it inside the Army's weight standards every time his annual PT test rolled around, and that was only after careful dieting and some fudging by the unit first sergeant on both the scale and height recorded. The philosophy around USAMRIID was that they weren't going to have one of their own separated from the army just because of some stupid rules that had nothing to do with the capability to do their job.

Norward had light hair and a wide, cheerful face that belied a man who was handling dead bodies. Very carefully, he rolled a cart under one of the monkeys. He pushed a button, and the chain that had held the body lowered the carcass until its entire weight was on the cart. Carefully he unfastened the meat hook that was jammed through the monkey's back from the chain, leaving the implement in place.

Norward slowed his breathing. His faceplate was fogging up and the air inside his suit was getting stale. He rolled the cart out of the refrigerator room and shut the large steel door behind him. Then he went down the corridor to the necropsy room, where he plugged in the air hose for his suit to a wall socket. The familiar sound of fresh air being pumped filled his ears and the mask cleared. The sound was as comforting to him as the whine of a smoothly running engine was to a pilot.

He locked the wheels on the base of the cart so it wouldn't move. Every action was slow and deliberate.

Norward pulled extra-large surgical gloves over the space suit gloves, then glanced at the second living occupant of the room and pointed at the monkey. "On three."

The other person had the name Laniea stenciled on the chest and a woman's voice echoed over the radio to confirm she understood. "On three."

"One." Norward and Laniea each grabbed one end of the monkey. "Two. Three." They lifted the body and placed it on an operating table, handling it as delicately as they would a bomb, which in effect it was. The monkey was dead, but there were things inside it that existed in a netherworld between life and death, waiting on other living flesh to devour just as it had devoured that of the monkey's.

"It'll take a couple of hours to defrost," Norward said. "We'll do the cutting on this one at thirteen hundred."

"All right," Laniea acknowledged. She was tiny inside her oversized suit.

Norward turned to the other table, where a second monkey lay. They had taken it out of the freezer the previous evening. Norward picked up a scalpel and handed it to Laniea. "Welcome to Level Four. Your first patient, Doctor."

He couldn't see Laniea's face as she bent over the corpse. "Thank you, Doctor." She pressed the blade into the monkey's stomach and sliced. The interior cavity was full of pooled blood.

Norward watched his subordinate as she worked, making sure that she was noting all key abnormalities, although most were not hard to spot. The kidneys were totally gone. The liver was yellow, and part of it had dissolved.

He took the samples she was cutting off and placed them onto glass slides, the only glass allowed on Level 4. When she indicated, he took a pair of large clamps and cracked the monkey's chest, holding open the rib cage for her to work.

There was a crackling noise in the air, and Laniea was startled. She froze and looked at Norward, trying to guess what the cause was. "Voice box," he mouthed to her, looking up at the ceiling. She looked relieved. Any break in the routine was scary down here.

The speaker crackled again, and this time he recognized a woman's voice, the commander of the USAMRIID, Colonel Carmen.

"Dan, we have a development in South America."

A development, Norward thought, his pulse skipping a beat.

"I need you to look at something," Carmen's voice continued. "ASAP."

Norward unplugged his air hose and moved to the air lock. He stepped in. His mask was fogging badly. "Got to have control," he whispered to himself, slowing his breathing. The lock cycled and he stepped through. He ripped off his boots, then stepped into the next chamber. He pulled a chain and the suit was hosed down. He waited impatiently as the shower ran through its sequence. There was no way to make it go quicker. Not if it was going to ensure that anything that might be on his suit was gone.

A development. The word echoed through Norward's consciousness. He was coming out of one of only two biohazard Level 4 labs in the country. The other one was at the Centers for Disease Control—CDC—headquarters in Atlanta. The people who worked at both USAMRIID and CDC around Level 4 agents knew that a development usually meant someone had died and that more people were going to die unless they intervened quickly and effectively.

It was obvious to most people why the CDC had such an interest in disease. It was less obvious why the Army ran one, except to students of military history. Even in the relatively modern times of the last century, more soldiers died of disease than in battle. Whenever masses of men gathered together, pestilence was never far away.

The shower finally shut down. Norward walked into the staging area and took off his suit. He rapidly threw on his Class B uniform and went to the elevator, still tucking the light-green shirt in.

The door opened and he rode it up to ground level. When the door opened, Colonel Carmen was waiting, dressed in sweatpants and a faded green surgical shirt—her normal work uniform. "This way," Carmen said. They went directly to her office. Four other people were gathered there: the other top experts in the office on bio-agents.

"We've already looked at this." She handed him the satellite imagery forwarded from Area 51. "First image was taken yesterday. The second one is today's."

"Oh, God," Norward muttered as he saw the blue dots in the one village, then the red in the next. He knew what those temperatures meant. The second image showed the spread.

"That was our conclusion," Colonel Carmen remarked dryly.

Norward looked around the room and then focused on one man. "What do you think, Joe?"

"It's South America, so it's not likely to be Ebola," the man said. He was dressed casually in cut-off jean shorts and T-shirt. He appeared to be in his mid-thirties, but Norward knew that Joe Kenyon was only twenty-eight. He'd had a tough life. He had black hair hanging down to his collar, and framing his face was the outline of a two-day beard—Norward wondered how Kenyon always managed to look forty-eight hours from his last shave.

Kenyon was a civilian on contract with USAMRIID. Inside the tight community of scientists that dealt with deadly infectious diseases, Kenyon was known as a virus cowboy. Someone who traveled around the world looking for microscopic bugs that killed. Corralled them. Brought them back to Level 4. Then tried to take them apart to find a way to beat them.

Kenyon was the resident genius on Level 4 bio-agents at USAMRIID. He had a Ph.D. in epidemiology and six years' experience in the field. "There's no way we can tell without going there and taking a look-see."

"What's in this area?" Norward asked.

"Small villages scattered about the jungle," Colonel Carmen said. "They make their living harvesting coca leaves and making paste for shipment to drug dealers."

Norward checked the two photos against each other. "This thing is moving fast. How is it getting transmitted?"

"We won't know that until we get there," Kenyon said.

"Who's calling us in on this?" Norward asked.

Colonel Carmen sat behind her desk and steepled her fingers. "That's the hard part. We haven't officially been called in. This is coming from, let us say, unofficial channels. There's a bouncer en route to our location to pick you guys up, link you up with some other people, and take you to ground zero."

"A bouncer?" Norward frowned. "I don't—"

"The less questions you ask right now, the less I have to tell you I don't know," Carmen said. She pointed at the imagery in his hands. "Let's deal with that first. God knows what it is, but it's spreading fast. Be ready to move in thirty minutes."

"That's the spot," Faulkener said.

Toland looked at the border crossing. The rest of the mercenaries were farther back, hidden in some low ground. There was only the faint impression of a rough road cutting across the ground. No border post. No sign that there was even an international border between Bolivia and Brazil.

"We'll keep surveillance on it," Toland said. "I wouldn't put it past The Mission to have a trap set for us now."

Faulkener turned to him. "Who exactly is The Mission?" The two had always worked for The Mission using a cutout, never meeting their occasional employers face-to-face.

"I've heard they're Germans." Toland spit. "Nazis. Hiding in the damn jungle all these years."

"I don't like working for no Nazis," Faulkener said.

"You want the money or not?" Toland said. "After this job we can retire. Quit and live in style."

Faulkener's silence was answer enough. Faulkener glanced toward where the other men were. "Some of the men are sick. Justin is in real bad shape. He's throwing up blood."

Toland had been thinking. "All right. I've changed my mind. I think it's better for us to go small. Let those go who want to and get rid of all that are sick. We'll keep about four good men who you trust. Whatever this guy we're to link up with is coming after, it's worth five million to The Mission. And after we get him where he wants to go," Toland added, "we'll have both the guy and whatever it is."

11

Area 51 had become the hub of UNAOC's scientific center to investigate the Airlia. The choice had been made early for UNAOC because of the presence of the mothership and bouncers, but since the unveiling of that to the public, the site had expanded even further and Major Quinn, despite his relatively low rank in the military, was in charge.

Area 51 was the unclassified designation on military maps for a training area on the Nellis Air Force Base. Every military post had its land broken down into training areas, usually designated by numbers or letter. But Area 51 had developed into much more than a training area. For decades it had housed a top-secret installation burrowed into Groom Mountain. Next to the mountain lay the longest runway in the world. From that runway not only had the bouncers flown, but the skunkworks had tested all the latest top-secret aircraft, from the Stealth fighter to the still-classified Aurora spy plane.

Only a few of the facilities were aboveground. Most of the core of Area 51 was built into and below the side of the mountain next to the runway. Besides the mothership hangar that had been found, another large hangar had been hollowed out over the years to house the bouncers.

Majestic-12 was the committee that had been designated to run Area 51 and oversee the secrets it contained. Over the years it had turned into a world of its own, ignoring current administrations and believing itself to be above the law. That had all come to a crashing halt several weeks earlier.

Quinn now knew that the members of Majestic-12 had been mentally taken over by the guardian computer uncovered at a dig in Temiltepec and brought back to MJ-12's other secret site at Dulce, New Mexico.

When MJ-12's secrets were finally exposed, Area 51's shroud had been torn asunder. The media had descended on the site, shooting images of the massive black mothership resting in its newly dug-out cavern and the bouncers being put through their paces by Air Force pilots. What had once been the most secret place in America was now the most photographed and visited.

But the discovery of the true nature of the STAAR bodies had brought a shadow into the new light. The information about the Airlia and STAAR had been deemed by UNAOC to be too inflammatory, and Quinn found himself once again guarding secrets.

That was a task much more difficult than it had been to keep the secret when Area 51 was spoken of only as a myth. He had reporters all over the complex now, and the best he could do was keep them out of the Cube and the autopsy area.

The underground room housing the Cube measured eighty by a hundred feet and could be reached only from the massive bouncer hangar cut into the side of Groom Mountain via a large freight elevator that allowed Quinn to control access.

Quinn sat in the seat in the back of the room that gave him a full view of every operation now in process. In front of him, sloping down toward the front, were three rows of consoles manned by military personnel.

On the forward wall was a twenty-foot-wide-by-ten-high screen capable of displaying any information that could be channeled through the facility's computers.

Directly behind Quinn a door led to a corridor, which led to a conference room, his office and sleeping quarters, rest rooms, and a small gallery. The freight elevator opened on the right side of the main gallery. There was the quiet hum of machinery in the room, along with the slight hiss of filtered air being pushed by large fans in the hangar above.

A man walked into the control center and took the seat next to Quinn. He looked out of place among all the short-haired military personnel in the room, sporting long black hair, tied in a ponytail that went a quarter of the way down his back. Rimless glasses were perched on a large nose, below which a Fu Manchu mustache drooped.

"What do you have, Mike?"

Mike reached up and twirled the left part of his mustache. "All of the drives recovered from Scorpion Base were wiped clean."

"Damn." Quinn sat back in his chair.

Mike shook his head. "Oh, no! That doesn't mean there's nothing there."

"I don't understand," Quinn said.

"When you wipe a computer drive clean, that doesn't mean it's totally clean. There's always residual information. Like a shadow remaining after the object that caused it is gone."

Quinn had reversed his position, now leaning forward. "What have you got?"

"Nothing coherent yet," Mike said. "I'm cleaning it up, but it takes time. It's like putting a puzzle together piece by piece, except you only have a few pieces of each piece rather than the whole piece."

Quinn blinked, then gave up trying to figure it out. "What do you think you have?"

"I think we have some information about STAAR's personnel. Also, there's some intriguing stuff in one of the drives that the report indicates was hooked to a satellite radio. I think it might help us decrypt the Airlia messages going between the guardians."

"Anything else?"

Mike frowned. "Well, it's hard to say, but it looks to me like these people . . ." He paused and looked at Quinn questioningly.

"STAAR," Quinn filled in.

"Yeah, STAAR, well, they were trying to decode something themselves. Actually, it looks more like they were trying to recover some information from a database, much like I'm trying to do with their hard drives."

"What was their source for this database?"

"I don't know, but I don't think it's among the stuff recovered from the base in Antarctica."

"How close are you to getting any coherent information off the hard drives?" Quinn asked.

Mike shrugged. "Days. Weeks. Maybe never. It's hard to say."

"Have you recovered anything?" Quinn asked.

"A couple of things. First, they were doing a keyword search."

"The keyword?"

"Ark."

"Ark?" Quinn repeated. "What kind of ark?"

"I don't know."

"And the other thing you found?"

"There was a file pulled from a bunch of sources, and I'm getting ghost images off some of it. Some sort of historical research."

"On what?"

"Something called The Mission. With a capital *T* on the *The*."

"Anything solid?"

"I should have something shortly on that part of the hard drives."

Quinn pointed a finger. "Get back to work."

"How the hell are we getting out?" The man who asked the question had one hand wrapped around a steel cable that ran the length of the plane's cargo bay. His legs swayed as the low-flying cargo plane followed the contour of the earth outside. He wore camouflage fatigues with no marking or rank insignia—like the rest of the thirty men inside the plane. He was a former French Legionnaire who called himself Croteau.

Elek looked up from the satellite images he had been studying, his eyes hidden behind the black glasses. "Do not worry about that. I will take care of it."

"Do I look stupid?" Croteau asked. "I don't trust anyone when it comes to getting my ass out of the frying pan. And the middle of China is the damn fire."

Croteau looked at the other mercenary leaders inside the aircraft. They were nodding their heads, agreeing with him. The money was good, no doubt about that, now fifty thousand a man, but as every mercenary knew, dead men couldn't spend good money.

The plane was low to the ground, flying north of Afghanistan, heading toward the Chinese border. Croteau was a little surprised that they had made it this far without being challenged by some country's air force, but Elek seemed to have no concerns about that. They'd landed at an airfield in Turkmenistan, one of the new former Soviet Bloc countries, and the plane had been refueled by the ground crews there. Croteau had always known that money could buy a lot of cooperation, but the extent of this Elek fellow's influence seemed to transcend national boundaries.

"Plus how are we going to get past the Chinese army?" one of the other merk leaders, a man named Johanson, a former South African officer, asked. "They got the place surrounded."

"We jump right on top of the tomb," Elek said.

"And get our asses shot off coming down," Croteau said. "You know what kind of target a man hanging in the harness makes?"

"There will be no one shooting at you." Elek held up a small glass ball. There was a murky green liquid inside that seemed to glow. "This will take care of everyone on the ground."

"What is that?" Croteau demanded.

"Nerve gas. Developed by the Russians, tested and perfected in Afghanistan," Elek said. "It works within twenty seconds and dissipates within sixty. Before we jump, we drop the gas. Everyone on the ground will be dead by the time we land, and the gas will be gone also."

"Jesus," Croteau exclaimed. "You use that stuff, we'll have every agency in the world after our ass."

"You are stupid," Elek said. "No one will care what happens in western China. And no one will know what happened."

"No way," Croteau said. "I'm not—" He froze as Elek held the glass ball under his nose.

"Yes, you will," Elek said, "or I will drop this right here. The cabin is on a separate pressure system, so the plane will continue, but all of you will be dead."

"You're bluffing," Croteau said. "You'll die with us."

"I've already been injected with the antidote." Elek tossed the ball in the air, every eye following it, then caught it. "It does not scare me. But it should scare you. It is a most horrible death. Your brain cannot send any impulses to any part of the body. Your lungs stop working, your heart stops beating. But the impulses coming into the brain, those you feel."

Croteau swallowed. "All right. We jump."

Turcotte walked forward along the flight deck, avoiding the bustle that was the normal activity of the aircraft carrier. He turned and watched as an F-14 Tomcat came in for a landing, going from a forward speed of almost two hundred miles an hour to a complete halt in less than a couple of seconds. The intricate choreography of action that followed the landing was just as amazing, as flight personnel unhooked the plane, towed it away, reset the landing cables, and prepared for the next incoming plane in short order.

He turned his back on the ship and looked forward. The weather was clear and he could see to the blue horizon where the water met the sky. Looking over the edge of the flight deck, he could see that dolphins still splashed along the bow. Whether they were the same he had seen earlier or new ones to pick up the sport, he had no idea.

"A penny for your thoughts?"

Lisa Duncan had her leather jacket zipped up tight against the salt breeze. A briefcase was in her left hand. Turcotte knew they both had to leave shortly, going in different directions once again.

"I'm not sure they're worth that much," he said as she joined him.

"I think they are."

Turcotte looked out to sea. "I don't know. Seems like everything's been moving so fast that it's hard to think. Always something else to do that seems to take precedence."

"Precedence over thinking?"

"You know what I mean," Turcotte said. "Real thinking. Going a level below."

Duncan slipped her right hand into his left and squeezed. "And what's a level below?"

"I'm not sure I want to know," Turcotte said, hoping she would change the subject, but she said nothing.

Finally, he spoke. "I guess I wonder why."

"Why?" Duncan repeated.

"You know, what's the meaning of it all. You know we've been so focused on who and what and where and when, and we hardly know any of those, but it's the why that's the key to everything."

"I'm not sure I follow."

Turcotte struggled to find the words that would make concrete the thoughts that had been swirling about in his head.

"You know what happened in Germany," he started.

"Something you were involved in?"

Turcotte nodded.

"The incident in the café?"

That was a delicate way of putting it, Turcotte thought. He'd been assigned to a classified counterterrorist unit in Berlin. A unit that, once the Wall fell, spent most of its time trying to keep a lid on the piles of weapons from the former Soviet Bloc. It was a joint U.S.-German team. Handpicked men from the U.S. Special Forces and the Germans' GSG-9 counterterrorist force. Their orders were to fire first and ask questions later, especially when they were dealing with weapons that could kill hundreds, if not thousands.

On his last mission before being assigned to Nightscape at Area 51—indeed, Turcotte knew it might well have been because of what happened on that mission that he received the Area 51 assignment—intelligence had received word that some IRA extremists were trying to buy surplus East German armament—SAM-7 shoulder-fired antiaircraft missiles.

The supposition was that they would shoot down a Concorde taking off from Heathrow. The weapons were being transported when Turcotte's team went to interdict.

They set up an ambush, but the terrorists stopped in a *Gasthaus* just before the ambush point. Getting antsy, the team leader took Turcotte with him to check it out.

With silenced MP-5 subs slung inside their coats, they walked in the combination bar and restaurant. The place was full of people. They saw two of their targets sitting in a booth, but the third was nowhere in site.

And Turcotte's partner froze, his unnatural demeanor catching the attention of the Irishmen. All hell broke loose. Turcotte and his partner exchanged fire with the two in the booth, killing both.

But the third man tried to run out of the bar, and Turcotte's team leader fired at him in the middle of a crowd of civilians also trying to escape. Turcotte could feel Duncan's hand in his, her skin against the knotted tissue on his right palm—a scar that had formed from the burn he'd gotten when he'd grabbed the gun out of his team leader's hands by the barrel, the red hot steel burning the flesh.

It was only later that Turcotte found out the body count. Four dead civilians. Including a pregnant, eighteen-year-old girl. To add insult to injury, the powers that be had tried to give Turcotte a medal for the action. Something had snapped in Turcotte after that, and he wasn't sure he had ever put whatever it was back together.

"Mike?" Duncan's voice indicated her worry over his long silence and his mood. "What about Germany?"

"Nothing," Turcotte said. He felt very tired.

"Don't give me nothing," Duncan said.

Turcotte sighed. "Those guys I killed in Germany. The IRA gunmen. Their why. Their motivation. I've thought about it a lot. They thought they were right. They thought their cause was just and were willing to pay any price to further that cause. Do anything, even if it meant killing innocent civilians."

"Oh, come on," Duncan said. "You can't be comparing—"

"You said you wanted to know what I was thinking," Turcotte said, harder than he intended. "Then you need to listen."

Duncan lapsed into silence and waited.

"Okay," Turcotte said, still trying to find the words. "The thing is these guys here on this ship. They wear American uniforms. This ship took part in the Gulf War. Bombed the crap out of Iraq. Killed a bunch of Iraqis. But those Iraqis believed in what they were doing, just as much as these sailors and pilots believed in what they were doing. And that's the way it's always been. You know—God was on both sides. How come one side ends up winning, then?

"I guess the why I'm wondering is what's behind it all? I've been reacting to this Airlia thing with the basic philosophy that they aren't us—humans, that is. But is that so much different than being an American and thinking an Iraqi is different? I don't know. Now Yakov is here telling us that it's more about a long battle among us—humans—than the aliens."

"But the aliens are manipulating us," Duncan said. "STAAR isn't exactly human, and these Guides—like Majestic-12—their minds have been manipulated by the guardian."

"So they're just pawns?" Turcotte asked. "What are we? We can't even go to UNAOC or our own govern-

ment for help now. We can't trust anyone, as Yakov
says. I was paranoid when I was working Special Operations, but this is ridiculous. There's got to be something
more. Something different."

"Why?"

The word caught Turcotte by surprise. "What?"

"I'm asking the same thing you started this with,"
Duncan said. "Why does there have to be something
more? Something on another level?"

Turcotte blinked. "Don't you think there has to be a
purpose to all this? All our efforts?"

Duncan spread her hands. "There might be. I don't
know what it is right now except we have to do the next
right thing."

A small smile crossed Turcotte's lips. "The next right
thing. I like that."

They stood there in silence, the ocean breeze of the
mid-Pacific cool against their faces.

"There's something else," Duncan finally said.

"Yes?"

"Yakov."

"What about him?"

"Do you trust him?" Duncan asked.

"He told us not to," Turcotte said.

"I agree with him," Duncan said.

"Why?"

"I spoke with Larry Kincaid and Major Quinn privately before they left, while you and Yakov were talking to Von Seeckt. Kincaid did a check on the Earth
Unlimited satellite's path prior to coming down, backtracking through Space Command's database."

Turcotte waited.

"While it didn't get close to the mothership or the
talon, he found the point at which the satellite's orbit
abruptly began to change and deteriorate. It was over a

place called Sary Shagan in central Asia. That's Russia's primary ABM and ASAT research test site. ASAT stands for antisatellite. There have been reports from both the U.S. and NATO countries of their satellites that pass over that site being interfered with. Some suspect a low-power laser. Others, electronic jamming."

"So you're saying this satellite was interfered with by the Russians?"

Duncan nodded. "Kincaid definitely thinks so. Quinn has tried tapping into the intel network reference at the Ariana Launch Site at Kourou—the point of origin of the satellite—and he wasn't able to find out much, but one thing he did learn was that this specific satellite was supposed to stay in orbit another day, then come down for an ocean recovery in the South Atlantic—just like the previous two Earth Unlimited satellites.

"The satellite had its own maneuvering rockets, and the DSP tapes show they fired during the descent, so Kincaid thinks the Russians damaged it, then The Mission brought it down as best they could, given it was going to come down anyway."

Turcotte looked out to sea and considered that information. "So the Russians interfered with the satellite and The Mission brought it down early and not in its recovery zone. And maybe Section Four getting destroyed was in retaliation for that. If Yakov is telling the truth and it was destroyed. Perhaps Yakov knows more than he's telling us."

"That's the way I see it. Maybe he made a mistake and he's here to get us to clean it up for him since he doesn't have the resources anymore."

"But the good thing is that this plan of Earth Unlimited, whatever it is, got screwed up."

"Yeah," Duncan acknowledged. "But the bad part is that maybe this satellite wasn't supposed to come down on land. Maybe something was in that satellite that wasn't supposed to get out. And now it's out and everything's out of control."

"Jesus," Turcotte said. He rubbed his forehead. "So perhaps The Mission isn't on top of the situation either."

"Or Yakov is lying and there is no Mission," Duncan suggested.

"Or Yakov is one of them."

"Them?"

Turcotte laughed, not from humor, but rather futility. "STAAR. Guides. Section Four. The KGB. Hell, he could be a double, working for the CIA. Who the hell knows? Or he could be what he says he is. It doesn't matter," he finally decided. "Those people are dead in South America, and we've got to find out what the hell was on that satellite, whether it was the Black Death or something else."

"While you're going to South America," Duncan said, "I need to go back to the States to do some checking."

"On what?"

"First, I have to stop at Vandenberg Air Force Base. One of the shuttles is being launched from there. I still work for the President, and he wants me there for the launch. I also want to get an idea of what the UNAOC people involved in the talon and mothership missions are up to. Then I want to go on to Area 51. I think that's the best place to coordinate everything from once you find out what is going on. Plus I want to see if I can't find out any more about Dulce and Temiltepec."

Turcotte nodded. "All right. I'll return with Yakov to Area 51 once we do our recon."

•   •   •

Since getting his marching orders Norward had been on the move, gathering equipment and packing. To go to the target site and collect what was necessary—without becoming infected themselves in the process—they needed specialized gear. They would have to take biosafety Level 4 precautions with them.

Norward had let Kenyon take charge. The other man had much more experience in traveling and going places. In fact, Norward was now counting his blessings that Kenyon had gone on the "jaunt" a couple of years before. The jaunt was part of the lore at the Institute, and Norward had heard more than a few stories about it.

There were two things that were of primary importance to be discovered when a new biological threat appeared. The first, of course, was to determine exactly what it was. To isolate it. The second was to find out where it came from. With those two facts, they at least had the basics needed to try to defeat the bug.

Two years earlier a virus had erupted out of southern Zaire. Of course, since southern Zaire wasn't a media hot spot, the word got out slowly. The disease burned along the Zaire-Zambia border with a kill rate of over 90 percent of those infected. Thousands upon thousands of people died.

After two weeks ripping through the countryside, the virus made a toehold in the Zambian city of Ndola. The Zambian president had the city cordoned off by troops. Roads were blocked, the airport was shut down, and travel was prohibited. The president was prepared to lose the city to save the country.

And just as swiftly as it had appeared, the virus went away. The last of the victims died and their bodies were burned. Life went back to normal along the border, except for the forty thousand people who had died. But forty thousand dead in Africa barely made a blip on the world media. Except for those at the Institute.

From Zairean doctors, they managed to get samples of the virus in the form of frozen tissue samples sent by plane. They quickly isolated the deadly virus. It was a filovirus, a cousin to Marburg and the two Ebolas. But it wasn't any of them, and for lack of a better name, the new virus was christened Ebola3. A filovirus was derived from the Latin—thread virus. If they had not already seen Marburg and Ebola at the Institute, they might not have so quickly caught on to Ebola3, but as soon as the strange, thin, elongated forms showed up in the electron microscope they zeroed in on it.

They had Ebola3, but they didn't know anything else about it other than it killed and killed well. So Kenyon proposed to go track down where the virus had come from. He took a trip to Zaire and investigated. Like a detective, he backtracked the line of death that the few survivors remembered. Kenyon found that Ebola3 had probably originated not in Zaire but somewhere on the southeast side of Lake Bangweulu in Zambia. He hired a small plane pilot to fly him up there. They flew over mile upon mile of swampland bordering the lake. It was a dismal-looking place, full of wildlife and little visited by man. Kenyon tried to get the pilot to land at a small town on the edge of the swamp they overflew, but as they descended, the odor of rotting corpses was so great they could smell it in the cockpit of the plane and the pilot refused to land.

Kenyon came back to the Institute and proposed an expedition to Lake Bangweulu to find out the birthplace of Ebola3. His justification was that if it had come out once, it might come out again, and the next time it might not go away. Forty thousand dead and a 90 percent kill rate made for a very effective argument. The funds were appropriated, and Kenyon went back to Zambia with a team of experts and the proper gear to work with Level 4 bio-agents in the field. Something that had never been done before.

They went into the swamp and, after two weeks of searching, found an island where Kenyon suspected the disease might have originated among the local monkey population. A few local survivors told him that swamp people went to that island occasionally to capture monkeys for export to medical labs for experimentation. That might help explain how the disease got out of the swamp, Kenyon reasoned. They suited up and went onto the island as if it were hot. But they found nothing, and eventually Kenyon had to order them to pack up and head back.

Kenyon never found out where Ebola3 came from; thus the nickname "jaunt" for the entire exercise. But he had learned a lot about taking a Level 4 lab to the field, and for that Norward was now very grateful because most of the equipment on the second helicopter was prepackaged gear that Kenyon had used on the jaunt. Kenyon had used his expertise to put together easily movable equipment that they had stored at the Institute. If ever there was a need to go virus hunting again, Kenyon had wanted to be ready.

And now they were off hunting. Several dead villages in the Amazon highlands didn't necessarily mean they had another Ebola3 on their hands, Norward knew. But if they did, at least they wouldn't be starting from scratch preparing this expedition.

In the past several decades Ebola3, Ebola, and Marburg had broken out occasionally in Africa and killed with ruthless efficiency—or propagated with amazing strength, depending on one's outlook, Norward thought. Then it had disappeared. There was still no vaccine for those known scourges—never mind something new. It was a sore point at both USAMRIID and the CDC in Atlanta that they hadn't broken any of the filovirus codes. The only thing they had accomplished in the past several years was to come up with a field test to determine if someone had Ebola or Marburg.

But South America was something new. And the bouncer—Norward wondered how that was involved. Was it simply being used because of the time rush? And Colonel Carmen indicating that this trip was occurring outside of official channels added to the mystery.

"Here's our ride," Kenyon said.

The bouncer came in low over the grounds in front of the main building for USAMRIID. The gear that they would need was piled next to them. Norward marveled as the alien craft came to hover, then silently touched down on the lawn.

An Air Force officer came out of the top hatch.

"Major Norward?"

Norward nodded. "Yes."

"We've got your ride." He looked at the lab gear. "Might take us a couple of minutes to get your stuff loaded. This whole thing is kind of unorthodox, but we'll get you out of here as fast as we can."

"How long will it take us to get to the target area?" Kenyon asked.

"We have to stop at the *Stennis* first to pick up a couple of passengers."

Kenyon shook his head. "We don't have time for any side trips."

"What's the big rush?"

"In an hour," Kenyon said, "certain viruses can replicate themselves almost a million times. That is the rush."

12

Inside the *Springfield* the crew waited. The three foo fighters were still on station. Captain Forster was prepared to wait until he was just about out of oxygen—two months—before doing anything. He'd heard the *Pasadena* destroyed by the foo fighters and he had no desire to share that fate.

The bottom line, though, was that the ball was in the court of the politicians, and Captain Forster knew that he might well have to get close to running out of oxygen before any decision would be made. If it was up to Admiral Poldan, commanding the carrier task force just twenty miles away, Forster knew there would be nukes hitting Easter Island until there was no longer an island. But the ball was not in the military's court.

On Easter Island, Kelly Reynolds's body had all but ceased functioning, held in the field by the guardian. Her mind, though, was still alert. And she still saw images, slices of the past.

The largest statue of all, over seventy feet in length and two hundred tons, lay among four hundred other unfinished statues on the side of Rano Raraku. But there were no people to raise it in warning.

The last Birdman had violated the law. People had

come from over the sea. From the rising sun, ignoring the warning of the Moai statues along the shore. They had talked to the Birdman, then left. He had gone inside of Rano Kau. He was gone for five days, and when he came back the people had split—those who remembered why they were here on one side against the blasphemers who followed the Birdman.

The latter began tearing down the statues, destroying the warning signs. The former fought them. The bloody civil war raged, but then the Black Death came and killed both sides indiscriminately until all traces of the old ways, the stones, the writing of high runes on the rongo-rongo *tablets, all was gone.*

The Guide Parker accessed his e-mail. There was only one message waiting and he knew where it was from, given that his address was available to only one place.

As he reached forward to move the mouse to open the message, he noticed his hand was shaking. He tried to steady it, but his nerves were unable to do that. With difficulty, he opened the message and read it.

The timetable had been moved up. There was no explanation, nor was one required. The orders were succinct and to the point. Parker sent his acknowledgment.

Duncan, Turcotte, and Yakov were walking up a steel staircase toward the flight deck when a crewman stopped them.

"Dr. Duncan?"

"Yes?"

The crewman held out a computer disk. "This just came in for you over the secure Interlink with Area 51."

"Is the bouncer due in soon?" Turcotte asked.

"Yes, sir. Five minutes out."

"Escort the passengers to the conference room," Duncan said.

Duncan took the disk and she, Turcotte, and Yakov retraced their steps.

"What now?" Turcotte asked.

"I don't know." Duncan turned on her laptop and slid the disk in. She accessed her A drive. "It's an AVI."

"A what?" Turcotte asked.

"A video that can be run on a computer," Duncan said.

"On a computer disk?" Turcotte shook his head. "Guess I'm just technologically impaired. Who's it from?"

"Major Quinn." Duncan was working on the computer. She looked up. "He received it from Harrison."

"Your mystery man," Yakov said.

They heard footsteps in the passageway. The door opened and the two USAMRIID men walked in. The introductions were quickly made.

"What do you have?" Kenyon immediately asked.

"Nothing more than I sent Colonel Carmen," Duncan said. She gestured at Yakov. "He believes we have another version of the Black Death."

Norward frowned. "The plague hasn't been eradicated—there was an outbreak in India just last year—but it's not the threat it once was. We can handle that. And the plague doesn't kill as quickly and thoroughly as the imagery we've seen."

"Something with an *effect* like that of the Black Death," Yakov amended, "not necessarily the same thing."

"I think we'll have a better idea in a second." Duncan was still at her computer. "I've got a video here from South America. Gather round."

Once everyone could see the screen, she hit the button to play the video. A man was standing on the wooden deck of a ship. His skin was covered with black lines.

The man staggered, then went down to his knees vomiting blood and going into convulsions. A second figure appeared, holding something in his hands. The first man gave a strange, choking sound. He vomited a vast quantity of dark red blood.

The second figure leaned over and put his hand into the man's mouth, sweeping around with his fingers, trying to clear it out. He wiped off a mass of black goo onto the first man's shirt, then put the tip of a tube inside the man's mouth. The man violently threw up again. This time it was a mass that went around the tube and splattered into the first man's face and over his chest.

"Breathing tube," Kenyon said. "The vomit and blood must be blocking the throat."

"He's not gloved or masked," Norward whispered in horror.

"Look at his arms," Kenyon said. "Same black tracks. Not as advanced. He's got it too."

The man got the breathing tube stuck in the other's neck. He looked over his shoulder at the camera. "My name is Harrison."

The voice sounded tinny coming out of the small speakers of the laptop, but Duncan recognized it as the same one from the phone.

"This is my guide, Ruiz. Two days ago we came across a village where everyone was dead from this." Harrison pushed the tube farther in. Ruiz's chest began rising and falling. "All right. He's got air," Harrison said. He reached inside an aid kit and pulled an IV out. "But he's lost so much blood, he's going into shock. He'll be dead if I don't get something in him."

There was a horrible tearing sound from inside Ruiz that those inside the conference room could clearly hear.

"What was that?" Turcotte asked.

"His guts," Kenyon said.

More blood came up out of Ruiz's mouth, around the tube. There was material mixed in the blood.

"That's what we heard tearing." Kenyon might have been discussing last night's basketball game. "His insides are disintegrating."

The needle hadn't taken, and blood was seeping out around the hole. Harrison tried again, with the same result.

"Needle won't work," Kenyon said succinctly. "The blood has lost its ability to clot. All he's doing is opening more wounds."

Ruiz's eyes flashed open. It looked to Turcotte as if he was trying to speak, but the tube prevented that. More blood and guts poured out. Then Ruiz's head flopped back and his eyes rolled up.

Blood had poured out of every orifice, pooling on the deck beneath him. Harrison faced the camera. He seemed unaffected by the other man's death. "Now you want all I can show you, don't you?"

He reached into the aid bag and pulled out a scalpel.

"What is he going to do?" Yakov asked.

Kenyon was nodding. "Good, very good."

Harrison placed the tip of the scalpel on the center of Ruiz's chest.

"Who is this guy?" Norward asked.

"We don't know," Duncan said.

"He seems to have an idea of what he's doing," Norward commented as Harrison slid the blade through flesh. Ruiz's stomach was full of black blood with traces of internal tissue mixed in it. Harrison reached through the goo with his hand, pulling up dripping internal organs.

"God," Duncan whispered. "I've never seen anything like that."

"His kidneys are gone," Harrison said to the camera. He pulled something up. "That's his liver." It was the color of urine and partly dissolved. Harrison put it back down on top of the mass of blood and guts that had been Ruiz. He looked up at the camera. "I don't know exactly what killed this man, but I hope the people who might know are watching this."

Harrison stood and pulled a poncho out of a pack. He draped it over the body, then raised his arms toward the camera. They could see the black welts crisscrossing the skin. "Please hurry."

The screen went blank.

Norward looked around the room and then focused on his partner. "Ebola?"

Norward knew there were now three varieties of the deadly Ebola virus: Ebola Sudan, Ebola Zaire, and Ebola3. Zaire had a kill ratio of 90 percent of those infected, the Sudan variety not too far behind. It might not be a virus, Norward hoped. It might be nothing—but he knew nothing didn't kill like that. It had to be something.

"No." Kenyon was certain.

"South America." Norward recalled what he had been thinking on the flight to the carrier. "What about Bolivian Fever?"

"No."

"Venezuelan equine encephalitis crossing over to humans?" Norward desperately wanted it to be an enemy they knew something about.

"No." Kenyon tapped the computer screen. "Where was this shot?"

"Western Brazil, near the border with Bolivia," Duncan answered. "The town of Vilhena."

"Is the town quarantined?" Norward asked.

Kenyon laughed. "Come on, man, get real. We just saw this. They don't have a clue there, although whoever did the quick autopsy for our benefit, he's smart. This Harrison fellow definitely has a good idea what he's got there. The only ones who really know right now are us. And from this, well, we really don't know too much, either."

"Have you ever seen this before?" Norward asked, aware that the others were waiting on their words.

Kenyon shrugged. "I didn't see a damn thing other than a crash and burn."

A crash and burn was the Institute's term for the final stages of a victim carrying a deadly agent. The bug had taken over the body and consumed it and was ready to move on, having killed its host.

"Could it be Ebola3?" Norward asked, referring to the fourth of the deadly filoviruses to come out of Africa.

"I doubt it." Kenyon scratched his chin. "Only way we're going to find out for sure is to go there."

"Go there?" Turcotte shook his head. "How do we keep from getting infected ourselves?"

"We go in suited," Kenyon said. "Let's go—time's awasting."

"How do you work it?" Che Lu stared at the strange piece of machinery. She did not want to ask Lo Fa about the red stains on the radio's metal.

Lo Fa shrugged. "I do not know." He pointed. "The instructions are written on it, but they are in Russian."

"Russian?"

"It was carried by the team of Russians who went

into Qian-Ling. The army took it off the bodies. I took it off the army."

Lo Fa called to one of his men. A young man, barely more than a child, came up.

"Can you read the Russian?" Lo Fa asked.

The boy nodded.

"Can you work the radio?"

The boy ran his fingers over the writing, his lips silently moving. "I think so," he finally said. He pulled a small satellite dish out of a canvas pack attached to the radio. He flipped open the leaves, putting the small tripod on the ground. He hooked a cable from the antenna to the radio, then flipped a switch. He took a handset that looked like a phone off the side of the radio and extended it to Che Lu. "You may dial the number you wish to call."

Che Lu was amazed. "That is all?"

The young man shrugged. "That is what it says."

Che Lu carefully punched in the numbers that she had been given by Turcotte.

Lisa Duncan took two ibuprofens, washing them down with a swig from her water bottle, trying to tame a pounding headache. Once again, she and Mike Turcotte were going in different directions. While Turcotte and Yakov had just taken off in the bouncer with the two USAMRIID men for South America, she was heading for sunny California.

The pills had barely gone down when her SATPhone rang. She pulled it out of her pocket.

"Duncan."

The voice on the other end was hesitant and the accent was heavy. "I am trying to find a Captain Turcotte."

"Who is this?"

"Professor Che Lu. Ms. Duncan, Captain Turcotte

spoke well of you and gave me this number to call in
case of emergency."

Duncan's hand gripped the phone tighter. "Where
are you?"

"About five kilometers from Qian-Ling. I have Professor Nabinger's notebook."

"And Peter?"

"We buried him."

Duncan let that sink in. Even though there had been
little doubt Nabinger had died in the helicopter crash,
the reality of the words had a weight she had not expected.

"We paid him as much honor and respect as we
could," Che Lu added.

"I appreciate that."

"His notebook has some important information in
it," Che Lu said.

"The secret to the tomb?"

"I believe it talks about the lower tomb, but it does
not say exactly what is in there. From what he wrote, I
guess there may be more Airlia in there. It also talks
about power—the power of the sun."

"A ruby sphere?"

"I do not know," Che Lu said. "It does mention that
a key is needed to enter the lowest level."

"What kind of key?"

"I do not know. There is some more information in
the notebook written in high runes that I have not been
able to translate yet. It is possible that the key is already
inside, perhaps in the large cavern with all the Airlia
equipment. Or the key may lie inside of the guardian.
The word *key,* as indicated by Nabinger himself in his
last notes, could also mean just a code word. Or a pattern of codes to be used on the hexagonal control
panel."

Duncan sighed. As usual nothing was clear when dealing with the Airlia. "Can you get in Qian-Ling?" she asked. She had seen the satellite imagery from the NSA and the ring of PLA troops around the tomb. Still, Che Lu had gotten inside once before. And away.

"Getting in may be possible," Che Lu said. "It is the getting out that may be impossible. For that I may need your help."

"What do you want me to do?"

"What *can* you do?" Che Lu asked.

Duncan frowned. "Not much. Your country has completely cut itself off from the outside world. If UNAOC or the United States made another attempt to penetrate Chinese territory, it could lead to war." Duncan didn't want to add that she didn't exactly trust UNAOC anymore and she was playing her U.S. cards to the max with South America.

"Nevertheless," Che Lu said, "I must go inside. And to go inside I need the help of those with me. And to get their help, I must give them some hope."

Duncan thought for a few moments, then replied. "I'm sorry, but I have to be honest. I'll do whatever I can, but I'm very limited in what actions I can take."

There was a short pause. "Thank you for telling me the truth."

"What are you going to do?" Duncan asked.

"I am old," Che Lu said. "I wish to see what is hidden in the bottom of Qian-Ling before I die. The others here will have to make their own choices."

"Good luck," Duncan said.

"Thank you. I will talk to you again."

The phone went dead and Duncan slumped back in her seat. The headache was worse than ever, the pills seeming to have affected it not in the slightest.

She looked up as the door to her cabin opened. A

crew member handed her a message sheet. Both shuttles were going to launch at the same time, inside of
eight hours.

Was there a connection between the shuttles and the
Earth Unlimited launches? She didn't see how there
could be, but that didn't mean there wasn't. The information that Earth Unlimited had been affiliated with
the biolab at Dulce had certainly been a shock. When
she had been tasked to take a look into Majestic, she
hadn't found that link.

What if there was another ruby sphere in the bottom
of Qian-Ling? She remembered the ruby sphere they
had found in the cavern under the Terra-Lel compound
in Ethiopia. Set there as a hedge by Artad against Aspasia coming back to Earth. Hell of a deterrent, Duncan
thought. Of course, she knew that threatening to destroy the planet to keep Aspasia away was not much
different from the MAD doctrine—mutual assured destruction—that the United States and Soviet Union had
maintained for decades during the Cold War. Except
the Airlia had maintained their cold war for millennia.

The power of that ruby sphere, dropped into the gap-
ing chasm in the bottom of that massive cavern, explod-
ing deep inside the Earth's magma would have caused a
ripple effect throughout the planet along the rift lines
between tectonic plates. It was a doomsday scenario as
devastating as nuclear winter.

She also remembered the black stone, like a dark
finger inside the cavern in the Rift Valley, with the Chinese words written on it. There was a connection between Africa and China. And no matter how faint the
dots, she was willing to draw any line in the hope it
might help Che Lu.

She called a contact of hers at the NSA, National
Security Agency, and told him to keep a tight look not

only over South America, where Turcotte was heading, but also over Qian-Ling, and to copy her on any intelligence reports, no matter how trivial. Then she called Fort Bragg.

Another knock on her door. "Your flight is ready, Ms. Duncan," a sailor informed her.

Turcotte looked across the interior of the bouncer. The two USAMRIID men had their heads bowed together, speaking in low tones.

"Experts," Yakov said with a tone of disgust.

"We need them," Turcotte said.

"People like them are the ones who make situations that people like them have to get us out of," Yakov said.

Turcotte tapped Yakov, and the two of them walked around the small depression where the pilot of the bouncer sat to the two USAMRIID men. The interior of the bouncer was crowded with plastic boxes, and looking through the skin of the craft, Turcotte could see the larger boxes attached by slings to the side of the craft.

"What do you think?" Turcotte asked. "You sure it was a bug?"

Kenyon nodded. "There's only so much we can tell from the video, but we always start by ruling out what it isn't before we try to figure out what it is. Work from the known to the unknown.

"The vomiting. The bleeding from everywhere. Bleeding around the needle happens in some cases of severe viral infection. What's essential is we find out the transmission vector. For example, AIDS requires body fluid—blood or semen—contact.

"Most deadly viruses are not easily transmitted. The odds are great that it isn't transmitted through the air, because most viruses don't last long when exposed to ultraviolet light. That's why they usually go through a body fluid."

"I might be a little slow here," Turcotte said, "but what exactly is a virus? I'm just a soldier—you guys are the experts, and we need to have an idea what we're dealing with here."

Kenyon looked at Turcotte for a second. "There are different types of invasive organisms. The two major forms are bacteria and viruses. Tuberculosis is a bacterial infection. AIDS is a virus.

"Most people think of these things as little bugs that are out to kill humans, but really they're just creatures trying to live. In some cases we just happen to be the host through which they live and reproduce." Kenyon paused. "Well, actually, bacteria are alive. Viruses are and they aren't."

Turcotte looked at Yakov and noted the Russian was also paying close attention.

"Bacteria," Kenyon continued, "are living cells. They cause problems in humans because our body mounts a response to their infection and in many cases the response is so strong it destroys good cells along with the bacteria.

"Sometimes it's the bacteria cells themselves that cause the problem. Cholera is a good example of that. The toxins from the bacteria attack cells in the intestine, causing severe diarrhea that dehydrates the body to the point where many of those infected die. So it's the by-product of the effect and not the bacteria itself that kills in that case.

"A virus is different. A virus is genetic material—DNA or RNA—inside a protein shell. They sort of just hang around and exist. Then they come in contact with a host. The problem—for the host, that is—is that to reproduce, a virus needs a living cell. In the process of reproducing, a virus kills the host cell.

"You can treat most bacterial infections," Kenyon said, "although there are more and more strains appearing that have mutated and are resistant to traditional drug treatments such as penicillin. But there are very few antiviral drugs. The best defense against viruses is vaccination. And you have to have a vaccination *before* you get infected for it to do any good. So, most of the time, finding out that someone has a viral infection doesn't do you much good, because in many cases there are no cures."

"So Harrison and anyone else in Vilhena that got this bug are screwed."

"In layman's terms, yes," Kenyon said.

"How long does it take?" Turcotte asked.

Kenyon shook his head. "I don't know. From the video and what Harrison said, it sounds like this thing acted incredibly fast. That's the paradox of viruses that has saved mankind from being wiped out. The quicker a virus kills its host, the less chance it has to be transmitted. If a virus takes someone down in a couple of days—which it sounds like our friend here did—it only has a small window to be passed on. If it takes years, like AIDS, then it has more of a chance to be spread. Thus, the more effective a killer it is, the less chance that a virus will propagate.

"To really answer the question," Kenyon continued, "we need to find out exactly where Ruiz picked this thing up."

Turcotte glanced out the bouncer. He could see the shoreline of South America approaching. "We'll know pretty soon." Something else occurred to him. "The Black Death—"

"Yes?" Kenyon said.

"You said it was caused by fleas on rats?"

"It still is," Kenyon said.

"But the disease itself, where did it come from?"

Kenyon shrugged. "There are millions and millions of microscopic organisms. They are evolving, changing, just as we are, except they do it thousands of times faster than us because their life spans are so much quicker."

"But there are labs," Turcotte said, "such as what the UN is looking for in Iraq, where people are trying to make bugs such as the Black Death—biological weapons."

"Yes." Kenyon frowned, not sure where Turcotte was taking this.

"Could the Black Death have been man-made?"

Kenyon laughed. "You're talking the Dark Ages. When they still bled you to get the bad spirits out. When they believed you could change lead into gold. There's no way the Black Death could have been man-made."

"You're forgetting something," Turcotte said.

"What?"

"The Airlia were here over eight thousand years before the Black Death. Don't you think they would have had the technology to come up with it?"

13

Duncan stepped out of the plane, feeling the warm California breeze in her face. She felt light-headed for a moment. She wasn't even sure what time it was, as she'd crossed so many time zones in the last couple of days.

She looked around. The Pacific Ocean crashed onto the rocky shore to the west. Vandenberg was halfway between Los Angeles and Monterey, home of the Air Force's missile test base. It was also home to the alternate launch site of the space shuttle.

The launch pad for that craft was the dominating feature between Duncan and the ocean. Standing over 184 feet tall, the shuttle *Endeavor* was mated to its solid-rocket boosters and external fuel tank, sitting next to its tower.

Even as Duncan caught her first glimpse of the shuttle, a loudspeaker crackled and a voice rolled across the tarmac.

"T-minus six hours zero zero minutes. The count has resumed. Next planned hold is at T-minus three hours. Tower crew perform ET and TPS ice/frost and debris evaluation. ET is ready for LOX and LH2 loading. Verify orbiter ready for LOX and LH2 loading."

"Something, isn't it?"

Duncan turned. Six men and one woman were waiting to the rear of the C-7 she'd flown in on from the

Stennis. There was a patch on their left shoulder—a half-moon on one side and a star on the other, with a dagger in between the two.

The man who had spoken walked forward, hand extended. He was a tall, black man, well built, head completely shaved. He wore camouflage fatigues with the "budweiser" crest of the Navy SEALs sewn on the chest above the name tag. Duncan returned the handshake, feeling the strong grip.

"I'm Lieutenant Osebold, *Endeavor* Mission Team Commander."

"Lisa Duncan, Presidential Science Adviser."

Osebold smiled. "Here to spy on us." He turned. "Here's the rest of our team."

As Osebold introduced, they stepped forward.

"Lieutenant J. G. Conover is my executive officer."

Conover was a skinny, red-haired man. He was sporting a bandage on his right hand. Seeing Duncan's glance, he held it up. "Slight training accident."

"Chief Petty Officer Ericson is our weapons specialist."

Ericson was a small man, compactly built.

Osebold moved to the next in line. "Lieutenant Lopez is our medical officer."

Lopez was a dark-skinned Hispanic, a smile on his face as he shook hands with Duncan.

"Lieutenant," Duncan greeted him.

"Lieutenant Terrel is our engineering specialist," Osebold continued.

Terrel had a big hook nose, a balding head, and tight lips. He nodded at Duncan, not moving forward.

"Terrel's always thinking," Osebold said. "He's actually not too happy about the job your friend Captain Turcotte did on the talons and the mothership, because he's been working with the NASA team on how to fix them.

"Chief Maxwell is our communications specialist."

Maxwell was a short, stocky man, with a bright red face.

"The last member of our team is Ms. Kopina. She's from NASA. She's the mission specialist and our ground coordinator. She won't be going up with us."

Kopina was a solid-looking woman in her mid-thirties. She had brown hair, cut short. Her face was unadorned with any makeup and marked with worry lines.

"Ms. Kopina is our jack-of-all-trades," Osebold said. "She's the one who makes sure we can do our job in space."

At the mention of space, Duncan looked once more at *Endeavor*.

"Ever see a shuttle launch in person?" Osebold asked.

Duncan shook her head.

"It's pretty impressive," Osebold said. "It goes up in less than six hours. We're doing a polar insertion."

"A what?"

Kopina answered that. "We have a different launch window into orbit from here than they do at the Cape. Vandenberg's launch limits are 201 and 158 degrees. The orbital trajectory will be within 14 degrees of due north.

"Most people think the shuttle goes straight up, but that isn't even close." She pointed from the ocean inland. "The Earth rotates on its axis at about 950 miles an hour from west to east. We take advantage of that also when we launch."

Duncan assumed Osebold and Kopina were telling her these facts to impress her that they knew their stuff. She knew quite a bit about the shuttle, but she had learned long ago to pretend to be ignorant in order to get people to disclose more than they should.

The loudspeaker crackled once more. *"Initiate LOX transfer line chilldown. Verify SRB nozzle flex bearing and SRB nozzle temperature requirements. Activate LCC monitoring software."*

"What now?" Duncan asked.

Osebold extended his hand toward the van they had driven up in. "We do last-minute prep and fitting."

"Fitting?" Duncan asked as she followed.

"Our TASC-suits."

"Task-suits?" Duncan repeated.

"T–A–S–C–suit," Osebold spelled it out. "Stands for Tactical Articulated Space Combat suit."

"The bitch," Terrel muttered as they climbed into the van.

"The what?" Duncan was surprised.

Osebold laughed. "We call the TASC-suit 'the bitch' among ourselves. No offense, Ms. Kopina."

"No offense taken," Kopina said. "It is a bitch." She didn't smile. If anything, the lines on her face got deeper.

Duncan buckled her seat belt. "Can I ask something?"

"That's what you're here for," Osebold said.

"What exactly are you going to the mothership for?"

"To secure it," Osebold said.

"Secure it?" Duncan repeated. "For what?"

Osebold threw up his hands. "Hey, I just follow orders. We're to rendezvous with the mothership and try to get a secure atmosphere inside."

"That's a big project," Duncan said. "Can you carry up enough material to do the job?"

"They've got some lightweight, highly expansive material," Kopina said. "I think they can do it."

"And then what?" Duncan asked.

Osebold shrugged. "That's up to UNAOC. I assume we might be able to bring the mothership back down. Maybe back to Area 51."

Duncan was startled. She hadn't even thought of that. "And the talon?"

"The crew of the *Columbia* has to ascertain its status, then a decision can be made," Osebold said.

"Isn't this all a little rushed?" Duncan asked.

She picked up some nervous rustling among the crew, but Osebold's answer was confident. "We can do it."

"Flank and far security report in all clear," Faulkener whispered, one finger pressing the earpiece from the small FM radio into his ear.

Toland nodded, watching through his binoculars at the small clearing on the other side of the border. He and Faulkener were lying in a shallow trench they'd dug the previous evening. Toland had dismissed most of the patrol, keeping only two other men besides Faulkener. All people he had worked with before and trusted, as far as you could trust anyone who was a mercenary. Which, Toland had to admit to himself, wasn't very far.

There was another reason besides the better split on the money for going light. Several of the men were ill, and he didn't want to be burdened with them. Toland wanted to travel light to get his job over with as fast as possible. They'd put two of the men on the far side of the clearing and one on each flank to make sure nobody else moved in during the night.

There was a distant noise, getting closer. Toland recognized it—a car engine. Ten minutes after he first heard the sound a Land Rover pulled into the clearing.

The vehicle was covered in mud and looked as if it had had a long trip.

"Long way from the nearest town," Faulkener whispered. "They been on the road awhile."

"Yeah." Toland had half expected a helicopter. Travel by vehicle was very difficult in this part of South America. But maybe The Mission still had to be wary of the Americans' drug trafficking surveillance in this part of the world. The Americans tracked everything in the air in the top half of South America.

The Land Rover came to a halt and two men armed with AK-47 assault rifles jumped out. A man in a dark gray jumpsuit exited more slowly from the front passenger seat.

"Damn Nazi," Faulkener hissed.

The man was over six feet tall, with straight blond hair. Even at this distance, Toland could tell he had blue eyes. The man would have been considered the perfect physical specimen in the Third Reich.

The man began unloading several green cases from the back while looking about the clearing. The two guards moved ten feet from the vehicle and waited, weapons at the ready.

"Professionals," Faulkener muttered. "Why don't *they* take this fellow in?"

"We know the terrain," Toland replied, but it was a good question. Any adequate soldier with a map could navigate in terrain they hadn't been in before. There were a lot of pieces that didn't fit together here.

The man in the gray suit was done. The two guards climbed back in the Land Rover and drove away, back the way they had come. Toland waited until he could no longer hear the engine. He glanced at Faulkener.

"All clear," Faulkener reported after checking on the FM radio with the security men.

Toland stood up. "What's in the cases?" he called out.

The man was startled by the sudden apparition. He stood. "Equipment." He spoke with an accent, which Toland tried to place. European.

"Step away from it," Toland ordered. When the man complied, he gave more orders. "Kneel down, forehead in the dirt."

"Is this really necessary?" the man asked.

Now that he was closer, Toland could see that the man's skin was pale, indicating he had not spent much time in the outdoors.

Toland gestured with the muzzle of his Sterling, and the man reluctantly got on his knees and bent over. Toland walked forward and looked at the three cases. They had hard plastic cases and locks on the opening snaps. He turned back to the man. "What's your name?"

"Baldrick."

Keeping out of Toland's line of fire, Faulkener quickly frisked Baldrick. No weapons.

"You can stand up, Baldrick," Toland said. "Open the cases."

"No," Baldrick said.

Toland closed the distance between the two men in a breath, jamming the muzzle of the Sterling into the skin under Baldrick's chin. "I didn't hear that. Say it again."

"I can't," Baldrick said in calm voice. "I'm under orders too. You aren't authorized to see what's in the cases."

"Bad answer," Toland said.

"I can open one," Baldrick said. "I have to for us to get where we're going."

Toland glanced at Faulkener, who met the look and shrugged. Toland removed the weapon. "Open what you can."

Baldrick flipped open the lid and pulled out a laptop computer with several cables coming out the back. Next he took out a small folded-up satellite dish with tripod legs.

"SATCOM?" Toland asked. It looked more sophisticated than the rig Faulkener carried in his rucksack.

"Not quite," Baldrick said, unfolding the fans that made up the dish.

Toland stepped forward, bringing up the barrel of his submachine gun.

"Don't do that!" Baldrick glared at the soldier. "Do that again, I call this off and you can forget your bonus. Plus I tell The Mission you blew this. You wouldn't want that. They are most ruthless. I and my equipment are more important here than you or any of your men. Is that clear?"

Toland stepped back and gritted his teeth. He waited as Baldrick hooked up the computer to the satellite dish.

"What I have here," Baldrick said, "is a terrain map of this area loaded in the computer. When I hit the enter key here, we get a kick burst up to a satellite, which activates the homing device in the object we're looking for, which bounces back up and gives us a location." With that Baldrick hit the enter key.

Two seconds later there was a glowing dot on the electronic map. "That's where I need you to take me," Baldrick said.

Toland looked at the screen. The dot was located in the foothills just over the border in Brazil. Very rough terrain. Toland pulled out his map case and looked at it, comparing it to the screen.

"How long to get there?" Baldrick asked, turning off the computer and beginning to repack it.

"About forty kilometers," Toland said. "My men can make it in a day. Maybe less."

"Good." Baldrick snapped shut the case. "I'll need help carrying this."

"Bring in the security," Toland ordered Faulkener. He turned back to Baldrick. "Mind telling me what we're looking for?"

"Yes, I do mind," Baldrick said, shouldering his own small pack.

Toland smiled, but Baldrick didn't see it. Faulkener did see the smile, and it sent a chill through him. He'd seen Toland smile like that before, and it meant trouble.

"That's it," the pilot called out.

Turcotte looked down through the clear bottom of the bouncer. "Goddamn," he whispered. Vilhena looked deserted, not a single person visible.

"Where do you want me to set down?" the pilot asked.

Turcotte turned to Kenyon and Norward.

"There—that empty field on the east side of the town," Kenyon said.

"Are you sure it's safe?" Turcotte asked.

Kenyon shrugged. "We don't know what the transmission vector is, so I can't answer that. But it should be safe; plus we'll gear up before venturing out."

The bouncer silently floated down until it was less than a foot above the ground. Kenyon and Norward opened a couple of the cases they had inside and pulled out blue, full-body suits.

"One size fits all," Kenyon said, handing one to Turcotte. He also handed him a hood and a large, heavy backpack.

Turcotte stepped into the suit. He gave Yakov a hand and they zipped each other up. The hood had a full-face, clear plastic mask. With a little help from Norward, they got completely garbed, settling the heavy backpacks on their shoulders and hooking up the hoses from it to the suit properly.

Turcotte felt the slight rush of bottled air as Norward turned a switch on the pack. A small boom mike was built into the hood.

"How much air do we have?" he asked.

"Three hours," Norward's voice sounded tinny coming through the receiver.

The pilot of the bouncer had just a hood on, breathing from a tank strapped next to his seat. He hit a release and the cargo nets on the outside of the craft dropped loose, tumbling the large cases the USAMRIID men had brought to the ground. The bouncer still had not touched the ground, hovering two feet above the earth.

Turcotte climbed the ladder to the top hatch. He opened it, then, with great difficulty, clambered outside. He slid down the sloping side of the bouncer until he was at the lip. He then hopped off onto the ground. Kenyon came next, followed by Norward, then Yakov, who had shut the hatch behind him. The bouncer immediately went back up into the air, to hover a hundred feet above their heads.

"Norward," Kenyon's voice came over the radio. "You and Yakov set up the habitat. I'll find us a specimen."

Turcotte listened to the quiet thump of the rebreather tank on his back. He'd never worn a suit like this before and hoped it was working properly. He could easily remember the sight of the man dying on the video.

He followed Kenyon as the other slowly walked

toward the town. Behind them, Yakov and Norward were opening a large case.

A dusty trail led through the trees at the west end of the clearing. Kenyon led the way. Turcotte was already hot inside the thick suit, feeling a small stream of sweat making its way down his back.

They passed a small hut. Kenyon swung the door open and leaned in. "Nothing."

They continued down the path. A cinder-block building appeared on the left side of the road. The rest of the town of Vilhena lay beyond it, going downslope to the muddy river. It wasn't very large, less than a mile and a half long by a half mile cut into the jungle. Turcotte estimated about five thousand people could live there.

Kenyon walked to the opening of the building, which was covered with a blanket, and pulled it aside.

"We've got bodies," he said.

Turcotte followed him inside. There were six bodies. All had bled out badly. Turcotte glanced at Kenyon, but he couldn't see the other man's face behind the glazed plastic of the suit mask.

"I've never seen symptoms exactly like this." Kenyon was kneeling next to the body of a woman. "They're like Ebola, but the rash is something different." With a gloved hand he touched flesh. "Notice these pustules on the black welts? Does sort of remind me of the plague.

"The thing that bothers me is the timing," Kenyon continued. His fingers were probing the body. "Ebola takes two weeks. Here it sounds like a couple of days, maybe three." He reached into a waist pack and pulled out a sample kit. He pressed the end of a tube into the body's flesh, then capped it and put it back in the case. He also got a sample of the body's blood.

The process was repeated several times, Kenyon moving from body to body.

"We'll know shortly what it isn't," Kenyon said as he headed toward the door.

Back at the field, Yakov and Norward had been hard at work. The first large case they had opened had contained a medical habitat. Norward knew it had not been designed for this use. It was an inflatable tent designed for MASH units to be able to operate in a chemically contaminated environment. It had two flexible Kevlar walls—an inner and outer—with the space between filled with compressed air from tanks they had brought with them, allowing it to be set up very quickly. On the inside it was relatively spacious, with just he and Yakov in there along with their gear.

The air coming in and out was ventilated through special air filters. It wasn't the most perfect Biolevel 4 facility, but it was the best thing Kenyon had found available in the government inventory when he'd conducted the jaunt.

The entryway was cramped, and with great difficulty Yakov and Norward had disinfected the outside of their suits and the other plastic cases they stacked in the entryway. Then they unsuited, placing the garments into sealed plastic bags and shoving the empty cases back outside.

Norward was setting up the equipment when Turcotte and Kenyon arrived at the entry. The two disinfected and unsuited, passing through the air lock. Kenyon carefully carried the samples, sealed inside his waist pack.

To handle a Level 4 bio-agent required either a full suit or a glove box. On top of the table, Norward set up the latter. It was a device four feet wide, by three tall, by three wide. It had its own one-way mini air lock so they could put samples in—once in, the sample had to stay there until they took the box back to the Level 4 lab and could sterilize the inside.

There were numerous compartments so they could keep samples separate and not contaminate each other. There was also a microscope built into the box, so they could examine the samples.

"What are you doing?" Turcotte asked. He was wiping sweat off his forehead with a towel. Yakov was sitting on the floor of the habitat, taking a drink of water from a canteen.

Kenyon was placing the waist pack inside the air lock for the glove box. "What we have to find is a brick—a block of virus particles. A brick contains billions of virus particles, gathered together, waiting to move on to the next host."

Turcotte glanced at Yakov. The Russian shrugged.

Finished with the mechanical task of getting the box ready, Kenyon went to work. Stepping up to the side of the box, Kenyon stuck his hands through two openings, flexing his fingers into the heavy-duty gloves inside. Deftly, he opened the pack, removing the tubes holding the various samples. He sorted those out, placing the tubes in racks.

"I'm going to test it for Ebola, Marburg, and Ebola3," Kenyon said. He took samples and mixed them with solutions in preset tubes that had an agent that would react to the specific virus. The tubes were blue.

"They'll turn red if the virus was recognized," Norward explained as Kenyon worked.

While they waited for a possible reaction, Kenyon put another sample from the brick onto a slide and put the slide into the other end of the scope and pressed his eye up against it.

Kenyon's voice startled Turcotte. "I don't think it's

Ebola3." Kenyon pointed at the microscope and gestured to Norward. "Take a look."

Norward bent over and peered. All he could see was a mass of particles—there was no chance of seeing an individual virus to get a visual ID.

"How can you tell that's not Ebola3?"

"I know Ebola3 and I've seen bricks from Ebola3," Kenyon said. "That doesn't look like an Ebola3 brick."

"One of the other two Ebolas?" Norward asked.

Kenyon looked down into the box at the four test tubes with the various Ebola reactants. They were still blue. "No."

"Marburg?" Norward asked, hoping that at least they would know what they were up against. Even though there was no cure or vaccine for each of the viruses he had just mentioned, knowing the enemy would help clarify the situation.

Kenyon was looking in the box. "No." All test tubes were still blue and the requisite time had passed. "It's not a known. Could be a mutation of a known."

Despite the air-conditioning pumping outside, Norward felt a trickle of sweat run down his back.

"Any idea what it is?" Yakov asked.

"It's definitely a virus," Kenyon said. "But it's moving way too fast. It's got to be passed on quicker than blood contact to hit this many people so quickly. And it looks like it's one hundred percent fatal."

"We didn't check the town," Turcotte said. "Maybe someone's alive."

"Maybe." Kenyon didn't sound very optimistic.

"Could it be airborne?" Norward whispered, the very thought enough to make him wish he were very far away from here.

Kenyon stared at the isolation box. "I never thought we'd see an airborne virus that killed this quickly and could stay alive in the open. It doesn't compute in the natural scale of things," Kenyon said. "But . . ." He shook his head. "But it's got to be vectoring some way quicker than body fluid."

"The Black Death was transmitted by fleas," Yakov said. "Could this virus be carried by some sort of animal or fly or something like that?"

Kenyon was still looking through the microscope. "Possibly. But then, it probably doesn't kill its host. We need more information. And quickly."

Peter Shartran carefully dipped the tea bag in a mug of hot water. He placed it on a spoon, then wrapped the string around, squeezing the last drops out, then discarded the bag into the waste can next to his desk. He cradled both hands around the mug and leaned back in his large swivel chair, staring at the oversized computer screen in front of him. He had six programs accessed, and his eyes flickered from one to another.

The NSA was established in 1952 by President Truman as a replacement for the Armed Forces Security Agency. It was charged with two major responsibilities: safeguarding the communications of the armed forces and monitoring the communications of other countries to gather intelligence. The term "communications" had changed from the original mandate in 1952. Back then the primary concern was radio. Now, with the age of satellites and computers, it involved all electronic media.

Shartran had been "given" a special tasking by his supervisor—to watch two separate locations, one in South America and one in China. So far it had been uninteresting, but mainly because he had spent the last several hours shifting through the communications and signals generated by Chinese forces and trying to get an order of battle on forces deployed near Qian-Ling, a routine task for an intelligence analyst. There had been nothing from the South America locale.

Shartran's ears and eyes were a battery of sophisticated and tremendously expensive equipment. A KH-12 satellite had been moved over to a fixed orbit over Qian-Ling in China. Covering South America was much easier, as he had simply tapped into the Department of Defense antidrug network that blanketed that region of the world.

Shartran took a sip of his tea, preparing to get back to work on the order of battle, when a flashing symbol on one of the displays caught his attention. Several minutes before, something most unusual had happened: someone had bounced a signal off a GPS satellite and then received a back signal through the satellite.

The signal was strange because the satellite uplink went to the GPS satellite instead of one of the commercial satellites that handled SATCOM traffic.

GPS, which stood for ground positioning system, was a series of satellites in fixed orbits that continuously emitted location information that could be downloaded by GPRs—ground positioning receivers. The transmission had been sent up in such a frequency and modulation that it piggybacked on top of the normal GPS transmission on the way back down both times.

Shartran looked at the data and took another sip of tea as he considered the brief burst. Why would someone do that? The first and most obvious reason was to hide both brief transmissions. Shartran knew that even a one-second burst using modern encoding devices was enough to transmit a whole message, but maybe this wasn't a message. The key question was why use the GPS satellite?

"Because they want to know where something is,"

Shartran said out loud. But then, why didn't the people on the other end simply tell the first transmitters their location? The answer came to him as quickly as he thought the question: because there was no one at the second site. It was all clicking now, and the more Shartran thought about it, the more his respect grew for whoever had thought of this. Using the GPS signal allowed the first transmitter to get a fix on the response, which was blindly broadcast up. And there was more. Maybe, just maybe, Shartran thought, the second signal was very weak and needed the GPS signal to add to its power.

"Most interesting," he muttered as he summarized the information on his computer and e-mailed it into the Pentagon intelligence summary section. As the report flashed along the electronic highway, it fell in among hundreds of other summaries coming out of the vast octopus of intelligence agencies the United States fielded. And there it spooled, waiting to be correlated and even perhaps read. But Shartran also made a copy and sent it to the address his supervisor had told him to.

14

"This is our main training area," Osebold told Duncan.

The dominating feature of the large hangar was a three-story-high water tank, almost a hundred meters in diameter. The exterior of the tank was painted a flat gray. Several ramps went up the side of the tank. There were also tracks suspended from the ceiling over the top of the tank, several having various devices hanging down from them.

There were several men gathered around the top edge of the tank, looking down at something inside. They wore shorts and black T-shirts with the trident, eagle, flintlock pistol, and anchor symbol of the Navy SEALs on the front. Each of the men looked as if he spent his entire day split between the gym and the beach—bronzed, well-muscled warriors. Captain Osebold led Duncan over to the side of the tank where his crew was.

"Aren't you cutting it tight for launch?" Duncan asked.

As if on cue, the speaker blared once more. *"Perform IMU preflight calibration."*

"We'll make it," Osebold said.

"How did the SEALs get tagged for this?" Duncan asked.

"Because we're used to operating in a nonbreathing

environment. Plus we have some degree of familiarity with a sort of zero-g operational area."

Duncan knew about the SEALs. The acronym stood for sea, air, land—which pretty much had covered the three environments the naval commandos had been asked to work in up to now. Duncan wondered where they would add the "space" to their name.

SEALs were the most physically fit of all the special operations forces, taking great pride in their conditioning. They were adept at operating underwater with a variety of equipment, and it did make sense for them to be picked for a combat space force.

The SEALs had grown out of the Navy frogmen in World War II, called UDTs—underwater demolition teams—at the same time Turcotte's Special Forces had grown out of the OSS, Office of Strategic Services. The SEALs had always been less of a sneaky-Pete type organization, more oriented toward combat. Along with Special Forces, the SEALs had been the most decorated force in Vietnam. The thing Turcotte had impressed Duncan with was that the SEALs had never in their entire history left behind one of their own—be he dead or wounded. No Navy SEAL had ever been taken prisoner.

But Duncan had to wonder why the military had been brought in on this operation. The military had run Area 51 and Dulce. Duncan returned her attention to this new unit. A rack was behind the team, holding five roughly human-shaped suits.

Osebold saw Duncan's glance. "Those are our TASC-suits. We use them instead of NASA's space suits."

Duncan looked more closely at the suits. They were long, almost seven feet from the top of the helmet to the legs. The exterior seemed to be made of a hard black material with articulated joints. The helmet had no visor, just a camera and several lights and sensors on top and in the front.

The arms ended in a flat black plate instead of a glove. The same with the legs—no feet, just the plate. Before Duncan had the chance to ask, Captain Osebold was pulling her to the side.

"What is that?" Duncan demanded.

A large gray tank, like a coffin, was raised off the floor. The lid was open. It reminded Duncan very much of what they had rescued Johnny Simmons from in Majestic's secret biolab in Dulce.

"That's how we get fitted for the TASC-suit," Osebold said. "A person gets in, we pump it full, and it basically makes a body cast. Much like a dentist makes a mold of your teeth—except we need the entire body."

Duncan stared at it. "Can I ask why the military is involved in this?"

Osebold smiled, revealing even teeth. "Ma'am, I just do what I'm told to. Space Command put together my team a couple of years ago and we've been preparing for a combat mission in space ever since."

"Do you anticipate combat?" Duncan was confused.

"No, ma'am. Just a recovery mission. But—"Osebold shrugged. "You never know."

"Welcome to the bitch." Lieutenant Terrel walked up, interrupting her train of thought. He pointed at the suits. "Getting in one of those isn't much better than the mold tank."

"Why does—" Duncan began, but Ms. Kopina, the mission specialist, slapped her palm on the tank.

"The TASC-suit is an exoskeleton." She jerked a thumb over her shoulder at the rack. "See how much thicker each one is than the human that goes inside? Once inside, a person has about four inches all around. That includes protective armor, power system, environmental system, and external suit nervous system. On top of that, a computer system gets carried on your back, but we'll get to that in a little bit."

Kopina walked over to the rack and stood next to one of them. "This suit has taken fifteen years of development. We put as much work into this at Space Command as the Air Force put into the Stealth bomber. This suit represents four billion dollars of research and experimentation."

"I'm surprised I haven't heard of this program."

"It was highly classified," Osebold said, as if that explained everything quite satisfactorily.

It was dark inside the Cube conference room, only a single light in the corner giving any relief. Larry Kincaid had his feet up on the conference table, leaning far back in a seat, a cigarette dangling from his lips. He was staring at his computer screen.

"No smoking," Major Quinn said with no emphasis on the words. He sat down across from Kincaid, several file folders under his arm.

Kincaid took another puff. "What ya got?"

"The bodies from the vats at Scorpion Base have been flown in. They're not the same as what we got here with the two STAAR bodies."

"What's different?"

"These don't have any of the Airlia genes. Just plain human clones."

"So they were growing their own people down there?" Kincaid wasn't surprised by much anymore.

"Looks like it."

"And what exactly are these STAAR people?"

"Autopsy's done on the ones we had here. Or as done as the UNAOC people can do."

"And?"

"And those two STAAR people aren't people, but they aren't aliens either. Some kind of DNA combination. Mostly human"—Quinn thumbed through the papers—"eighty-six percent human. Other than eyes, there's some discrepancy in the skin pigment, the hair. That's the obvious stuff. The not-so-obvious stuff is that the brain is a little different."

"Different how?" Kincaid asked.

"The frontal lobe is a little bigger, and they have more connections between the two hemispheres."

"Does that make them smarter?" Kincaid wanted to know.

"Maybe. Maybe not." Quinn smiled. "Hell, *we're* doing the autopsy on them, remember, not the other way around."

"Yeah, well, Turcotte and those USAMRIID guys are doing autopsies on some human bodies down in South America."

"Another strange thing."

"Yes?"

"Their genitalia are underformed. The UNAOC people think they must reproduce mechanically. Perhaps using the cloning vats."

"They can't have sex?" Kincaid asked.

"Doesn't look like it was important to them." Quinn pointed at the cigarette. "Got a spare?"

Kincaid pulled a pack out of his shirt pocket and extended it. There was only one cigarette in it.

"Damn." Kincaid shook his head. "The stuff keeps getting deeper and deeper."

"What about South America?" Quinn asked as he fired up.

"They've forwarded what they've found to USAMRIID. Hope to get some sort of readout shortly on what the bug is. Imagery shows it's spreading. Two more villages wiped out. Closing in on two thousand dead. Anything on Temiltepec?"

"The classified records say that the guardian was recovered at Temiltepec," Quinn said. He ignored the look that statement garnered him from Kincaid. "But no matter how well someone tries to cover up, there's always a loose end."

"And what thread did you find to pull on?" Kincaid asked.

"I pulled the classified flight record for Groom Lake," Quinn said.

"And?"

"And on those dates that the classified record shows that someone from Majestic went to Temiltepec, the flight log from the Groom Lake tower indicates an Air Force executive transport plane with a flight plan for La Paz."

"Bolivia."

"Long way from Mexico," Quinn said.

"Indeed."

"In fact, it's pretty close to the ruins at Tiahuanaco."

"So the guardian might have been there?"

"It's possible."

Kincaid thought about it. "What about The Mission?"

Quinn pulled out a file folder with a red TOP SECRET stamp at the top and bottom. "I found this in the files. The CIA rep to Majestic-12 asked the same question a couple of years ago. There's not much here, but what is written is pretty remarkable.

"The CIA had reports of a place called The Mission in South America." Quinn smiled. "When they chased Che Guevara, they thought that was where he was heading."

"You're pulling my leg," Kincaid said. "Che Guevara?"

"I'm not kidding. This Mission place sounds like it's been around awhile. The CIA tried backtracking it. The most current report says it might have been in Bolivia—where Che was killed—but that it moved sometime in the seventies. Current location unknown, but they think it's still in South America somewhere."

"Come on—" Kincaid began, but Quinn cut him off.

"No, wait a second. This is interesting. This report says that before he went to Cuba, Che first spent a couple of years traveling all over South America on foot and by bicycle. He then made his living by writing articles about ruins in South America."

"Could he have come across the guardian or The Mission?" Kincaid asked.

"I don't know," Quinn replied, "but according to the CIA he was heading toward a place called The Mission when he was caught by the Bolivian Army, backed up by U.S. Special Forces troops, another little fact that's not well known."

Quinn turned the page. "The CIA wanted to find this Mission, as they thought it might be a Communist front organization. Checking Che's writings, they found he paid special attention to an ancient site called Tiahuanaco in Bolivia." He scanned down the page.

"The dots are connecting," Kincaid commented, "but I can't figure out why."

"Before Che, in the late forties, the OSS, the forerunner of the CIA, had interest in a place called The Mission because it was reported to be a gathering place for members of the defeated Third Reich. It's well known that there was an escape pipeline to South America for Nazis during and after the war. The OSS/CIA heard rumors that the scientists who weren't snatched up by our Operation Paperclip or the Russians went to The Mission," Quinn added.

"Despite that, they weren't able to find the exact location of The Mission. They got word from some contacts that it was originally from Spain, and that it had come over the Atlantic sometime in the fifteenth century. But beyond that, it seems like the CIA stopped the investigation."

"Wait a second," Kincaid said. "Columbus didn't discover America until 1492."

"I'm just telling you what the CIA uncovered. Perhaps those date problems are why the CIA didn't follow through on the investigation."

"Or perhaps there was another reason they dropped the investigation." Kincaid looked around the Cube. "Like they've stopped digging at Dulce."

Quinn shut the folder. "I don't know." He opened another folder. "But my computer whiz kid has managed to pull something out of one of the hard drives Turcotte got out of Scorpion Base and it references The Mission."

"What is it?" Kincaid asked.

Quinn smiled. "You think the Che Guevara stuff is weird, wait until you read this." He slid a computer printout over to Kincaid, who picked it up and read:

```
THE MISSION & The Inquisition
(research reconstruction and field re-
port 10/21/92-Coridan-)
  Overview:
  The Papal Inquisition was instituted
in 1231 for the apprehension and trial
of heretics. The Mission, now estab-
lished, as previous entries note, in
central Italy, seized upon this oppor-
```

tunity to expand its power, aligning itself with the church. It was to continue in this role both in the Old and New Worlds for the next four centuries until the hysteria that fueled the Inquisition waned. The Inquisition was only one of several actions The Mission undertook during this time period, but one that bears our interest.

While the Inquisition focused on heretics, The Mission's task in this quest was more specific. It was to weed out those individuals who posed a threat in terms of theoretical advancement.

That they were effective in this effort can be seen by the lack of scientific advancement by mankind for the next several centuries.

The Mission seemed to want to ride a line between encouraging economic development, to increase mankind's numbers, and holding back scientific development, to decrease mankind's potential.

Examples:

In 1600 Giordano Bruno was burned at the stake for postulating a heliocentric system. I found direct evidence of Mission involvement in both designating Bruno for the Inquisition and forcing through his conviction and execution.

More interesting is The Mission's involvement in the case of Galileo. The 1616 Edict on Copernicanism can be laid to The Mission's desire to keep mankind from looking to the stars, even at the most base level. As a result, in 1624,

after publication of his   Dialogue on
the Tides," Galileo was brought to Rome
to be tried for heresy. Again, involvement of The Mission can be found through
the office of the Fiscal Proctor, one of
the officers of the Inquisition. In this
case, the Proctor went by the name
Domeka, which I have traced to The Mission and other actions (see App. 1 for
cross-references).

That the Inquisition was not completely successful-Galileo was only
sentenced to house arrest for the rest
of his life-indicates not the waning
power of The Mission, but rather the influence of TOWW.

"What's TOWW?" Kincaid had finished reading.

"I have no idea," Quinn said. "I'm having my computer guy check."

Kincaid handed the printout back. "Geez, if they put
Galileo away—" He didn't finish the sentence, just
shaking his head.

"I'm forwarding this to Dr. Duncan," Quinn said.
"She can figure out what to do with it." He looked up at
the red digits on the clock that glowed at one of the
rooms. "Under four hours until they launch at the Cape
and Vandenberg."

Quinn held the cigarette up. "Better get a carton."

"I have lived many years by saying no to stupid
ideas," Lo Fa said.

"I have lived many years also," Che Lu said. "But
there is more to life than just breathing."

"Ah, don't start that with me." Lo Fa tapped the side

of his head with a crooked finger. "I have also had many people try to play with my mind over the years."

Che Lu laughed. "Your mind is like a rock. Who would want to play with it?"

Lo Fa's dark eyes were looking about the guerrilla camp. The women were gathered to one side, talking quietly among themselves, while the children played around them. The men, those who weren't on guard, were resting. Finally his eyes returned to Che Lu.

"I will go with you. But only me. I will order the others to move west, to get away from the army."

"How will we get in the tomb?" Che Lu asked.

"I will get us in. The same way I was able to get you away from there when the army was shooting at the Russians and Americans. You get us out once you find what you are looking for."

"It's a filovirus." Kenyon had finally isolated the bug.

"A filovirus?" Turcotte asked.

"A 'thread virus,' " Kenyon said. "Most viruses are round. A filo is long. Looks like a jumbled string. Ebola's a filo, as is Marburg."

"So this is a cousin to Ebola?" Yakov asked.

"We don't know," Kenyon said. "This thing is an emerging virus."

"Emerging from where?" Turcotte asked.

"We don't know," Kenyon said.

"What *do* you know?" Yakov demanded.

"Where did it come from?" Turcotte asked, glancing at Yakov. "Is it man-made?"

"Man-made?" Kenyon frowned. "Why would anyone let something like this loose? Many viruses are simply nature's defense against mankind's incursions into places we never were before."

"What do you mean?" Turcotte asked.

"We're tearing up the rain forest," Kenyon said, "and so far, most of the nastiest bugs we've seen—the variants of Ebola and Marburg—have come out of the rain forest in Africa. It was only a matter of time before something came out of the Amazon. Humans have upset the ecological balance, and these viruses are fighting back against humans to re-right the balance."

"Are you saying this virus was always there in the forest and we came in and activated it?" Turcotte asked. Yakov was shaking his head.

"This virus," Kenyon said, "is what we call an emerging one. There are three ways viruses emerge: they jump from one species—which usually they are relatively benign in—to another, which they aren't benign in; or the virus is a new evolution from another type of virus, a mutation, basically; or it could have always existed and move from a smaller population to a larger population. In the last case, this thing could have been killing humans out in the jungle for thousands of years, but now it's moved out into the general population."

"Is that possible?" Turcotte asked. "Wouldn't someone have noticed?"

"Not necessarily," Kenyon said. "We're now beginning to believe that the AIDS virus might have been around for quite a while. Cases as far back as forty years ago are now being uncovered. They just didn't know what it was back there and called it something else. And it stayed in a very small population."

"Isn't there a fourth way a virus develops?" Yakov growled. "A man goes into a lab and tinkers with something, and out comes a virus that kills?"

Kenyon stared at the Russian. "The sophistication to produce a biological agent of this order is beyond our capabilities."

"The key word is *our*," Yakov said. "We haven't built a ship capable of interstellar travel either."

"Which do you think this thing is?" Turcotte pressed Kenyon. "How did it evolve?"

"I don't know exactly," Kenyon said. "To find that out I need patient zero."

"Patient zero?"

"Patient zero is the disease's human starting point. If we can backtrack and find patient zero, then backtrack patient zero's steps, we can find what and where the disease jumped from to get to humans and we would be that much further on our way to understanding not only the disease itself, but how it started.

"A virus has to have a 'reservoir'—a living organism that it resides in that it *doesn't* kill—or at least kill as quickly as the filoviruses kill humans. Otherwise the parasite would destroy its own source of survival. If we can find the reservoir, we might find out how that organism held off the effects of the virus, and that might point in the direction of a vaccine or cure. It has to be the village that Harrison talked about."

Turcotte stared at Kenyon in disbelief. "Are you nuts? We don't have any time to be coming up with vaccinations!"

Kenyon returned the look in kind. "We've got to find where it came from or else this thing will burn and it will only stop burning until it kills everything and there are no more hosts for it to consume."

"The satellite," Yakov said.

"What satellite?" Kenyon demanded.

Turcotte explained about the satellite that came down west of their location.

"You think this came from a satellite?" Kenyon asked. "What is this Kourou place?"

"It's the launch site for Ariane, the European Space

Consortium," Yakov said. "It's located on the coast of French Guiana."

"Why is the European Space Port located in South America?" Kenyon asked.

"Several reasons," Yakov said. "First, it's got a low population density. Second, it's located near the equator, which is advantageous for a space launch. Third, it's right on the ocean, so rockets can go up over water instead of land. And fourth, there's little likelihood of hurricane or earthquake in that specific area.

"Even though it's run by the European Space Consortium," Yakov continued, "anyone with enough money can buy a rocket and a launch window from them. Many U.S. firms launch their commercial satellites from Kourou."

"Do you have proof that this virus came off a satellite?" Kenyon demanded.

"We need to find exactly where Harrison and his crew picked up this thing from. That will help prove or disprove what Yakov says," Turcotte said. "He said in the video that he went upriver, but there's a lot of rivers here."

"What do you suggest?" Norward asked.

Turcotte tapped the scientist on the chest. "You and I go to the boat, try to see if there's a map or anything on board that shows where they found the dead village."

Guide Parker stood on top of a dune, looking down at the encampment of the chosen. Only one hundred and forty had made the commitment to leave behind all they knew and follow him to the desert.

This was the place. They had left the last hard surface road at Alice Springs, the center of Australia, and followed an old mining track into the Gibson Desert. Even that had disappeared hours before, but the Guide

Parker had kept his people moving through the desert, the sun beating down on the roofs of the four-wheel-drive vehicles that made up the makeshift convoy.

When he arrived at the right spot, he had just known. He'd ordered them to stop and set up camp. Then he had walked out of the camp and up this dune.

Parker looked around. He saw no sign of life other than the tents his people had pitched. He dropped to his knees, feeling the sand shift beneath them. He looked up to the sky.

"We are here," he whispered to the clear night sky. "We are here. Come take us away."

He didn't notice the drops of blood coming out of his nose, falling to the sand and being absorbed immediately.

Duncan read the report from Major Quinn once more. The Mission was real and STAAR had been investigating it. That was important, but did little to help the situation right now. It did back up Yakov's story about the existence of The Mission and that The Mission had obviously interfered with mankind in the past. She called Quinn and told him to get his computer experts working on finding the current location of The Mission and whether there was any connection between The Mission and the Black Death.

Duncan punched in another number on her SATPhone. The other end was picked up on the third ring.

"USAMRIID," the voice pulled the letters into one word.

"Colonel Carmen, please," Duncan said.

"Who is calling?"

Duncan paused—this was Carmen's direct number. "I'd like to talk to Colonel Carmen."

"I'm afraid that isn't possible."

"Why not?"

"Colonel Carmen had an accident."

Duncan's hand gripped the SATPhone tighter. "Is she all right?"

"I'm afraid the accident occurred on the Level Four containment facility. The entire base has been quarantined. Colonel Carmen is dead. There's a Colonel Zenas here from the Pentagon, and he's taken over. Would you like to speak to him?"

Duncan pushed the off button. She stood in the shadow of the space shuttle *Endeavour* for several minutes, waiting until she could stop her hand from shaking.

15

Che Lu thought it quite ridiculous, two old people crawling around in the dark. She and Lo Fa were a kilometer from the base of Qian-Ling, edging ever closer. They were moving so slowly it had taken them an hour to go the past hundred meters, but Lo Fa was in no rush. He had told Che Lu before leaving the guerrilla camp that they would proceed very cautiously. He reminded her for the hundredth time of another reason he had lived to be an old man—his ability to move carefully when it was called for.

The rest of the camp had packed up their meager belongings and begun their trek west to the Kunlun Mountains. It was reported that large numbers of refugees were flooding into those hills, occasionally coming out to strike at the army. It had tugged at Che Lu's heart to see the women and children pick up their satchels and fade away into the night. It seemed as if that was the story of China—the people always walking to escape one government while hoping for another.

"Hush!" Lo Fa hissed, even though Che Lu knew she had not made a noise. There was a quarter moon that threw down a feeble light. Even on the darkest night, it would be impossible to miss the looming bulk of the mountain tomb of Qian-Ling.

Che Lu heard what it was that had halted her partner. A plane's engine, very faint but getting louder. She peered into the night sky, searching.

Lo Fa grabbed her arm and pointed. "There."

Chė Lu looked, but she couldn't see what he was pointing at. The plane had to have been blacked out, as there were no lights. The sound grew louder, then she spotted it, a black cross in the dark night.

It came in low over the mountain, then circled. As it did so, screams rang out in the night, emanating from the Chinese soldiers bivouacked all over the mountain.

"What is happening?" Che Lu asked.

"I don't know, but we wait," Lo Fa said.

On the second time over, white parachutes blossomed in the plane's trail. Lo Fa stood. "Now!"

He scrambled across the creek, Che Lu following. He pushed aside a heavy overgrowth of vegetation and then they were in a narrow cut in the side of the mountain, less than three feet wide and six feet deep, almost completely overgrown across the top. Che Lu felt smooth stone under her feet and she remembered scrambling down these same stairs after splitting from Turcotte and Nabinger as they escaped from the tomb the previous week.

The stairs went up the side of the tomb, invisible unless one stumbled right into the narrow cut. Che Lu wondered why it had been made. She assumed it was for the warriors who guarded the emperor's tomb so many centuries ago to be able to move across the mountain from one side to the other without being seen.

Whatever the reason, the steps took them up the mountain to within twenty meters of the hole that Turcotte had blown at the end of the exit to the Airlia storeroom.

By the time they got there, Che Lu could hear men

moving in the darkness, commands shouted in foreign tongues, some of which she recognized.

"What is going on?" she asked Lo Fa, who was peeking over the edge of the trench toward the opening.

"I think someone else wants to get into the tomb." Lo Fa slithered over the edge of the trench, then reached back. "Let us hurry!"

Che Lu took his hand, and he lifted her out. Together they hustled through the dark. Che Lu could see bodies lying about—the soldiers who had been guarding the entrance.

Lo Fa reached the small opening that had been blasted. "Come on, old woman!"

Che Lu put her foot into the hole, and Lo Fa hissed. "Don't move."

"What?"

Lo Fa was turning, his hands raised. "Look at your chest," he said.

Che Lu looked down and saw three bright red dots of light on her khaki shirt. "What is it?"

"Laser sights."

Che Lu put her hands up also as men loomed out of the night and surrounded them.

Turcotte looked down at the body. The walk had taken twenty minutes. He had made sure to control his breathing the entire time, trying to keep the suit's mask from fogging up. His clothes under the suit were soaked with sweat. The dirt lanes between the buildings had been empty. Turcotte tried to imagine the streets of New York looking like this once the Black Death spread.

Norward was next to him, walking very slowly. They'd left Kenyon trying to get hold of his headquarters at Fort Meade—to no apparent avail. Turcotte knew Kenyon's scientific methods weren't going to work. One look at the empty streets told Turcotte this was out of control. The one thing that Kenyon had said that Turcotte did think was valid was that they had to find out how the Black Death had originated.

The river appeared. Several docks stuck out into the brown, murky water. Turcotte recognized the boat from the video.

"That one." He pointed with a blue arm at a flat-bottomed boat tied up at one of the docks. They made their way out on the shaky wooden pier and onto the boat.

There were two bodies. One was covered with a poncho. The other was slumped, half sitting with its back against the front of the bridge shield.

Harrison had not waited for the Black Death to take him down. Very carefully, Turcotte knelt down. He nudged the pistol in the man's hand and pushed it away, along the deck. There was something around his neck. Turcotte pulled apart the shirt, ripping it off the open black welts. A thin metal chain. Whatever was on it had slid into Harrison's left armpit. Turcotte pushed the arm out.

The chain passed through a ring. Harrison must have taken it off recently, as his body began to swell with the infection and his finger wouldn't take the ring. Turcotte lifted the ring up and looked at it. The face was almost half an inch diameter, slightly bulging. Turcotte was looking at it for several seconds before he realized what the design was—an eye, pupil inside of iris inside of eye. It was the same design as the one that had left the mark on the tree near Duncan's house in Colorado. Turcotte looked around. There was the smallest of indentations in the forward wood of the bridge. Turcotte checked the ring against it. It fit exactly.

He ripped the ring off the chain and stuck it in his waist pack. He went onto the bridge. There was a leather-bound binder. Turcotte opened it. A map was inside, covered with acetate. Blue marking traced a route from Gurupa near the mouth of the Amazon, upriver thousands of miles.

It passed by Vilhena and continued to the foothills near the border with Bolivia, where it ended. Farther to the west there was a small circle of yellow highlight off the south tip of a lake in Bolivia. Turcotte read the label: Tiahuanaco.

He tucked the binder under his arm. "Let's go," he ordered Norward. "Back to the habitat."

"What is that?" Duncan was staring at a large black helmet that had no mask or eyepieces. She remembered the photos Turcotte had brought back from Scorpion Base. She was trying to concentrate, to make sense of everything, but events hard outpaced her ability to keep track.

"That's our helmet," Osebold said.

"How do you see?"

"It's something that's come out of the Air Force's Pilot 2010 Program." Kopina had walked up and heard the question.

"So what's this 2010 program thing?"

Osebold answered. "The Air Force knows that their equipment, specifically their jet fighters, are outstripping the men who fly them. Most modern jets are capable of maneuvers that the pilot's body can't take. What good does it do to have a jet capable of making a twenty-g turn if the pilot can only handle half that before passing out?"

Duncan thought of the pilots of the bouncers and how that alien craft was far beyond anything the Air

Force could develop. How come Area 51 had not had access to this technology was the unspoken question that crossed her mind. Or had it had access to it?

"Also," Osebold continued, "another big problem is the time lapse between the brain receiving information, processing it, and then executing a response through the nervous system."

"You're talking reaction time," Duncan said.

"Correct. Like the time it takes you to see someone jump out in front of your car to the time your foot is on the brake. In a jet going at several thousand miles an hour, even a tenth of second lapse can lead to a pilot missing a target by dozens of miles.

"Pilot 2010," he said, "is a program where the Air Force worked on both problems. The TASC-suit utilizes everything they've managed to develop, including the SARA link."

"SARA link?"

"The SARA link is a direct link into the brain. It—"

"Wait a second!" Duncan said. "How does it do that?"

Kopina leaned over the helmet and pointed. "See here?" She was pointing to the interior. There was a black band. She pointed down. There was one around the back part of the head portion. "You can't see it, but there are very small holes in that black band. Very small," she repeated.

"The SARA probes come through those holes. They are extremely thin wires that go directly into the brain and—"

"Hold it." Duncan held up her hand. "Directly into the brain?"

"It's perfectly safe," Osebold said. "Scientists have been using thermocouples—which are very similar to the SARA links—for years to study the brain. We're just taking them to a higher level of use. The wire goes into a specific part of the brain. It's a two-way feed."

"Feed of what?"

"Electrical current. That's how the brain works. The SARA link can send coherent current in and can also read activity in the brain. It's an extremely sophisticated device, built at almost microscopic levels."

"You're putting electric current into the brain?" Duncan thought of the EDM—electrical dissolution of memory—research that they knew for sure had been done at Dulce on the second-to-last level—which had been done to Kelly Reynolds's friend Johnny Simmons and led to his "suicide."

"We're talking about less power than you would get from a double-A battery. It's safe, I assure you," Osebold said. "We've all been through it."

"I've never heard of this," Duncan said.

"Compartmentalization," Osebold said. "No one can know everything that's going on, especially when it's covered under the Black Budget." She reached out and felt the helmet. The black metal reminded her of the skin of the mothership. "Tell me more."

Kopina nodded. "Okay, what we do is two things. We fit the suit to the body using the impression tank, then we fit the SARA link array to the brain." She held up a small black box. "This is SARA, which stands for sensory amplifier response activator. The box goes on the back of the suit. SARA is a very special computer. It adds sensory input to the brain and receives immediate commands back from it which it relays to the suit even as the body is still responding through its own nervous system."

Duncan stared at the black box. "You're joking."

Kopina shook her head. "No, I'm not."

"Have you used it?"

"In the tank," Osebold said, referring to the large water tank in the hangar. "It's been experimental."

"But it's not experimental now?" Duncan asked.

"We're operational," Osebold said.

Duncan looked at the members of the team. "Have any of you ever been into space?"

"I have," Kopina said. "Aboard the shuttle."

"Has this team ever conducted any sort of mission with these TASC-suits in space?" Duncan asked.

"No," Osebold said, "but we're ready."

"T-minus three hours, thirty minutes," Kopina said. "They have to go suit up."

"Someone's alive." Norward's voice sounded weak in Turcotte's earpiece.

Turcotte had to turn his whole body to look at the other man. Norward had his arm raised, pointing at a small building to their right. A figure was standing in the doorway. The robes had once been white, but now they were badly stained with blood and other material that Turcotte had no desire to know. The woman wearing them was old, her white face lined and weathered.

As he got closer Turcotte could see the trace of black lines on her skin, indicating she had the Black Death. Her pale blue eyes watched them approach in their protective suits.

"I am Sister Angelina." The old woman's English was heavily accented. She looked up and down at their suits. "I see you are a bit better prepared for this than we are. Who are you people? We have not been able to communicate with anyone since this began."

"We're from the CDC," Norward said. "America. What's the situation?"

"Over half my staff is down," Sister Angelina said.

"High fever, headaches, bloody diarrhea, vomiting. We've tried to do all we can, but nothing works."

Sister Angelina led them into the building. Turcotte looked around. Through a curtain made of a sheet, he could see a ward. There were bodies in the beds and two nuns moved among the people, ministering to them. He felt totally immersed in a different world. The nuns didn't have the slightest form of protection, not even surgical masks.

"I was in Zaire in ninety-five," Sister Angelina said. "This looks very much like Ebola."

"It's not Ebola," Norward said. "At least not one of the known strains."

"But it is a virus," the nun replied. "Or else you would not be wearing those suits."

"Yes," Norward confirmed. "It is a virus."

"Can you help us?" Angelina asked.

"We have to track down the source," Norward said. "I'll have them send you some equipment. Gowns, masks. That will help."

"If it isn't already too late," Sister Angelina said.

To that, Norward had no answer. Turcotte knew that she knew she was dead.

"We would like to look at some of your patients," Norward said.

Sister Angelina pointed to the ward. "Follow me."

They moved through the archway, careful not to scrape their suits on either side. There were fourteen people in the beds.

"My native support left when they first feared this was a virus," Sister Angelina explained as they moved. "All that is left are my Sisters. And these are the only ones left in town alive." She pointed at the bodies.

"How many people used to live in Vilhena?" Turcotte asked.

"That is hard to say. Maybe five thousand. Some have fled into the jungle or downriver, although I heard that the next town in that direction has set up a blockade on the river and is killing anyone who tries to cross it."

Turcotte knew that also meant the native support workers might have run away with the disease in their system. This was the horrifying danger of trying to contain an epidemic. Nobody wanted to hang around in the area where the sickness takes root, but by running they spread it to new areas.

They walked down the aisle. Turcotte was glad that he had the suit. The smell must be horrendous. The overworked nuns were trying their best, but the soiled sheets from vomiting and diarrhea could be replaced only so often.

They'd seen Ruiz's body, but at that point the virus had been at full amplification, taking over the host completely. Here they could see what it did to flesh prior to death.

"The rashes," Norward said briefly.

Turcotte had noted that too. Streaks of pustulant black cut across the skin of most of the victims. He leaned over one bed. Blood was seeping out from the patient's eyes, nose, and ears. The eyes were looking at him, wide open, rimmed in black and red, fear and pain evident.

Turcotte glanced about. There were no IVs or any other signs of modern medical procedures in sight. Just the nuns in their habits, using what they had to comfort the people, wiping sweat and blood from ravished flesh. Giving aspirin for the sickness and pain. In his time in the Special Forces, Turcotte had served on MTTs—mobile training teams—and MEDCAPs—medical civilian assistance programs—in several third world countries.

"We have to go," Turcotte said, tapping Norward on the shoulder.

"Will you help?" Sister Angelina asked.

"We'll get you some help," Norward promised.

Turcotte turned for the door, then paused. "Sister—"

"Yes?"

"Have you ever heard of The Mission?"

The nun stared at him for several seconds, then she nodded ever so slightly. "Yes."

"Where is it?"

She lifted an arm under her stained robe and pointed to the east. "I have heard that The Mission has made a pact with the Devil where the sun rises out of the ocean."

"Where exactly—" But Turcotte was cut off as she asked her own question.

"When will the others arrive?"

"The others?"

"Help."

"They should be here in the morning," Norward answered, feeling Turcotte's disapproving gaze upon him even though it was hidden by the plastic mask.

She put out a hand and touched Turcotte on the arm. "There are no others, are there?"

"It takes time to mobilize people," Norward said.

"You're with the American army, aren't you?"

"I . . ." Norward halted.

Sister Angelina was looking at Turcotte, her face calm.

"Yes," Turcotte answered.

"There will be no others coming to help, will there? We're on our own, aren't we?"

"Yes."

"Thank you for being honest." She looked down the row of beds, the sound of people vomiting and moaning in pain filling the air. "I need one more answer. Did your people cause this?"

Turcotte blinked. "No. I think it came from The Mission."

"I would not have believed that answer if you had not told me you were with the army."

Norward was leaning over one of the bodies, staring at a young man through his thick plastic shield. The man suddenly reached up and grabbed his suit on the shoulders, screaming, blood pouring out of his mouth. Norward pulled back, the man rising off the bed.

Norward threw his arms up to knock the man off and the man suddenly released. Norward staggered backward, minus the weight, and fell on his back, knocking over a table in the process.

Turcotte reached down and gave Norward a hand, pulling him to his feet. "You all right?" he asked as he helped him get up.

Norward didn't answer. He was looking down at his suit. He reached up and pulled off his helmet.

"What are you doing?" Turcotte was shocked by the other man's action.

Norward pointed to the side of his suit. A foot-long tear ran from his hip along to the middle of his back. The edge of the table that had caused the cut was covered with blood-soaked sheets.

"I can feel the open wound." He peeled off the space suit, and Turcotte could see the blood seeping through the jumpsuit he wore underneath.

"Doesn't matter what the vector is," Norward said. "Air or blood. I've got it."

Sister Angelina pointed toward the door. "You'd better go back to your people."

Norward shook his head. "I'm going to stay here where I can be of some use. Since I can't go back into the habitat without destroying its integrity, I'm going to remain here and lend a hand and try to learn what I can."

"What should I tell Kenyon?" Turcotte asked.

"We just got a look at the symptoms," Norward said. "I need to get an idea of the timeline of this thing. Interview some of the patients that are coherent." He looked around the hospital. Sister Angelina had moved off to one of the beds. "Look at this. It's the way it is all over the third world, where they spend more money in a day on bullets than on medicine in a year. And I'll tell you something else. I don't think our modern medical facilities in the United States are going to make much difference when the Black Death hits them."

"If we can quarantine this here, then—" Turcotte began.

"It's already out," Norward said. "You heard her. People ran into the jungle downriver."

Turcotte thought of the Earth Unlimited rockets waiting to be launched at Kourou. He had a very good idea what the payload in those nosecones was going to be. "Nobody's going to be safe from this if we don't stop it now."

"Why are they going armed?" Duncan asked.

The SEALs had left for final mission prep before loading the shuttle. Kopina had led Duncan back into the large hangar, to an area in the rear. A table held copies of the weapons the SEALs would have with them.

"They're military," Kopina said, as if that explained everything.

Duncan was troubled by the advanced technology that was being used in the TASC-suits. She knew one of the biggest concerns of UNAOC was the discovery of

Airlia weaponry—she wanted to know what Space Command issued in conjunction with the suits.

"What kind of weapons are they using?" Duncan asked.

Kopina turned to the table.

"They didn't have many options when it comes to stand-off weapons in space. The powers that be have always been more concerned with things like missile defense, Star Wars–type stuff, than actual combat in space. Space Command keeps an eye on all weapons-development programs and tries to see which ones we might adapt and use."

Kopina ticked off on her fingers. "We checked everything, and contrary to science fiction a lot of stuff just isn't practical. Chemical lasers are out. They require too much mass in terms of a laser reactant unit. Free-electron lasers offer more promise, but the current level of technology doesn't give us a powerful enough beam to do more than blind someone if you hit them directly in the eyes. So that's out.

"Another exotic weapon that's on TV shows but isn't even close to being up to specs is the particle beam. Nice idea, but no one's got it down yet to a workable size, or a beam coherent enough to be functional in combat."

She turned and waved her hand over the table. "So what we ended up with is here."

Duncan looked at the items laid out as Kopina picked up what appeared to be a jackhammer with an open tube where the chisel would be. About five feet long, with a thick cylindrical shape that tapered to the end, where the tube was about an inch in diameter. At the other end, there were two pistol grips, one about six inches from the flat base, the other eighteen inches in with a trigger in front of it. The nonfiring end ended in a flat plate. The entire thing was painted a flat black. There was some sort of sighting mechanism mounted on the top.

"This is the"—Kopina paused, thinking how to describe it—"consider this the M-16 of space." She held it out to Duncan. "Its official designation is the MK-98."

Duncan took the weapon and almost dropped it. "How heavy is it?"

"Empty weight is thirty-eight pounds," Kopina said. "Each magazine adds about ten pounds."

Duncan hefted it, hands on the pistol grips. She knew Turcotte would find this most interesting, but it just seemed like a heavy piece of machinery to her.

"It will be easier to handle in space," Kopina said. "No weight there."

Duncan put it down on the table with a thud. "What does it shoot?"

Kopina picked up a two-foot-long cylinder that was about the same diameter as the MK-98. She touched a button on the side and a two-foot-long section on the top sprung open. Leaning the end of the barrel against the tabletop, Kopina pressed the cylinder into the well. She swung shut the cover and it latched into place.

She picked up the gun and aimed it at a six-by-six beam set inside of a concave concrete range against the wall of the hangar. The muscles in her arms bulged as she handled the weapon.

"Laser aiming sight," Kopina explained, flipping a switch. A red dot appeared on the six-by-six. "You also have to turn on the gun's main power." She flipped another switch on the side. A loud whine filled the air. "Now we're ready to fire." A small light turned green near the switch.

Kopina pulled the trigger. There was no explosion, but rather a loud ping as the gun fired. Splinters flew in the target and then chips flew off the concrete in the rear. Kopina put the gun down and led Duncan to the beam. There was an inch-wide hole in the front that went straight through to the back. There was a three-inch divot out of the concrete retaining wall. Duncan couldn't see what had caused the damage.

Kopina looked around, then picked something up and held it out to Duncan. It was a shiny piece of metal, an inch wide, six inches long, with both ends pointed. "This is the round. Depleted uranium, very hard."

"What gives it velocity?" Duncan asked as they walked back to the table holding the gun. She knew that depleted uranium rounds used in the Gulf War were being blamed for some of the Gulf War Syndrome.

"Springs."

"Spring?" Duncan repeated.

Kopina smiled as she tapped the MK-98. "Yep, you could consider this the most powerful spear gun in the world. The spears are a mite small, but I wouldn't want to get hit by one. The technical term, of course, is not a spring gun, but a 'kinetic-kill' weapon."

She pulled out the cylindrical cartridge. "There's ten rounds just like this one, being held under high tension. When you pull the trigger, the spring is released and the round is fired. The barrel is electromagnetically balanced so that the round goes right down the center, never touching the walls and thus not losing any velocity and staying exactly on course. That's why you have to turn the gun on—to charge the barrel."

"How fast does it fire?" Duncan asked.

"As fast as you can pull the trigger," Kopina said, "which is not as fast as *you* can pull the trigger. It's as fast as the ninety-eight will allow you to pull. The trigger locks up until the barrel is set. The cylinder also rotates, aligning a new round. You can fire once every one point seven seconds. It will be attached to the firing arm of the TASC-suit." She slid aside the back plate of the gun and showed Duncan. "See these adapters? They go right onto the end of the TASC-suit arm."

Kopina slid the place back. She moved down the table to another weapon that looked very similar to the MK-98. "This packs a bigger punch. Works on the same principles as the ninety-eight—spring-fired—but the round is different." She picked up a black pod, about six inches long by two in diameter. "This is the round. It's not solid. Rather, it's filled with high explosive. I'd test it for you, but it would piss off the NASA people if I blew the wall of the hangar out. This is the MK-99, and they're taking a few of these with them."

"I still don't understand why the military is in on this," Duncan said. She found it strange that the TASC-suit and its helmet were so advanced yet these weapons so primitive in comparison. She remembered Yakov telling how The Mission had controlled human development, increasing one thing while taking away in another.

Kopina turned her back on the weapons. "That's a question I don't have an answer to."

"Who are you?" Che Lu asked.

The figure in the black robes finished directing the mercenaries to deploy around the entrance to the tunnel above their heads. Che Lu and Lo Fa had been forced inside the tomb at gunpoint, carefully using the ropes to get down the slope to the large storage area inside the mountain tomb.

The light had come on as they entered, just as it had the previous week when they'd come from the other direction, through the tunnels of the tomb.

They were inside a large open space. Metal beams rose from the nearest wall, curving overhead to follow the dome ceiling around to come down the far side, which was hard to see because of the obstructions in the way. There were numerous black rectangles spaced across the floor ranging from a few feet in size to one over a hundred meters long by sixty high. There were other shapes scattered about here and there also. The far wall was over a mile and a half away.

To the far right a bright green light glowed, brighter even than the one overhead. Che Lu knew that inside of the room that green light came from was a guardian computer, hidden behind a wall.

At the base of the sloping tunnel they had come down, the mercenaries were building a barricade pointing machine guns toward the outside. Che Lu wondered how long it would be before the People's Liberation Army returned to the area in force and what would happen then.

"My name is Elek," the figure replied, pulling a hood down, revealing pale skin and sunglasses.

"What do you want here?" Che Lu demanded.

"Perhaps the same thing you want," Elek said.

"The lower level," Che Lu said. "Can you get past the ghost guard?"

"The ghost guard?" Elek bared his smooth white teeth in a quick smile. "I can get past that with the proper information and equipment." He lifted a long thin hand and pointed. "You recovered Professor Nabinger's notebook, did you not?"

Che Lu knew there was no use lying. "Yes."

"And what did he discover?"

"He believed Artad and other Airlia are in the lowest level."

"What else?"

"There was something about the power of the sun." Elek nodded. "Very good." He yelled some more

commands at the mercenaries. "Come with me," he said
to Che Lu and Lo Fa.

They followed, guards with weapons ready surrounding them. There were a half-dozen control panels of the
type Che Lu now associated with the Airlia, hexagon-
shaped patterns filling the surface with Airlia high rune
symbols inside of each hexagon.

Elek walked right up to a console in the front of the
room, facing a wall where the trace outline of a door
was visible. Che Lu knew the guardian was behind that
door.

"You are with Artad?" Che Lu asked. She remembered what Nabinger had said after making contact with
the guardian behind the wall.

Elek said nothing.

"STAAR?" Che Lu tried.

"Very good," Elek commended her. "STAAR is one
of many names we have had over the years." He put his
right hand on the console. A red glow suffused the black
top, outlining more high rune symbols. A new group of
hexagons, fitted tightly together, appeared. Elek's hand
flew over the pattern, touching.

There was a loud humming noise. A crack appeared
along the edges of the door in the far wall as it began to
slide upward. Che Lu noted that the mercenaries
brought their weapons up. Lo Fa had not said a word
since they had encountered the mercenaries and their
strange leader.

Elek disappeared into the next room. Che Lu and Lo
Fa followed. A six-foot-high pyramid, the surface glowing with a golden haze, rested in the center of the room.
Elek stopped and looked at it. Che Lu picked up in him
the same reverence she felt when in the presence of her
ancestors' tombs; a deep reverence.

"What are you going to do?" Che Lu asked.

"We need the power—the ruby sphere."

"The ruby sphere was destroyed," Che Lu said.

"One of the ruby spheres was destroyed," Elek said.

"The second one is down there?" Che Lu pointed to the floor.

"It had better be," Elek said.

Elek walked forward and placed both hands, palms out, on the glowing gold surface. Within a second, he was completely covered by the glow.

16

The patrol was making good time. They were moving along the east bank of a river. The patrol crested a tall, grassy ridge and Toland halted briefly to peer about. He could see a long way in every direction, and there was nothing. No sign of civilization. They could be the only people on the face of the planet, based on the information his senses were giving him.

Toland glanced at Baldrick. "Got a reading?"

Baldrick pulled his pack off.

Toland gestured for Faulkener and the two remaining merks to form a close perimeter.

Baldrick was opening the plastic case when one of the men leapt to his feet, cursing. A thin strand dangled from his right arm.

Toland whipped his machete out of its sheath and dashed toward the man. With one sweep of the blade he cut the snake in two just under the head, which was still attached by its teeth to the man's arm.

"Hold still!" Toland ordered. "You're just pushing the venom through you."

Toland carefully reached and spread the teeth, pulling the head off. He knew the make—a krait. He pushed the man to the ground. "Take it easy."

Toland knelt down to the man, whose screams had descended to gasps of pain-filled breath. "Easy, man, easy." He shifted around to the side of the man, one hand on his shoulder. With the other he brought up the Sterling, out of the man's sight, and holding the muzzle less than an inch from his head, fired a round into his brain.

Baldrick didn't react.

"Do you have a fix?" Toland demanded.

Baldrick pointed. "Five kilometers that way."

"Let's move." Toland got to his feet.

As they left behind the body, Faulkener moved over next to Toland. "Well, more for each of us now."

"I know," Toland repeated. He felt warm, and his head was throbbing. He looked down at his hand. There were faint traces of black under the skin. He remembered the bodies being carried by the patrol they had ambushed.

"You all right, sir?" Faulkener asked.

"No."

"I got you!" Waker yelled out, startling the men and women in the other cubicles in the NSA surveillance room. "I got you!" he repeated, his fingers tapping keys quickly.

On his computer screen the silhouette of the South American continent appeared, then grew larger, the edges disappearing, the computer focusing in on the west-central part. It narrowed down to a spot just over the border from Bolivia in Brazil, a hundred kilometers west of the town of Vilhena.

Waker quickly summarized the information and sent out a priority intelligence report to Duncan via secure Interlink.

"T-minus three hours. The count has resumed. Perform T-3 hours snapshot on flight critical and payload items."

The same voice carried over the launch pads on either end of the United States. Lisa Duncan heard them as she peered once more over the papers that had been faxed to her by Major Quinn.

The partial history of The Mission was interesting, but what she really needed was a location and he had not yet uncovered that. She thumbed quickly through all the information that had been forwarded. She paused as she saw the e-mail from the NSA.

She frowned. Someone had piggybacked a GPS—ground positioning satellite—signal in the area near the border between Bolivia and Brazil. Even as she was looking at it, the printer attached to her computer chimed and another sheet slowly came out.

Same thing. Slightly different location. This one pinpointed a spot. It was in the very west of Brazil. Duncan took a pencil and slowly wrote on a pad of paper:

Tiahuanaco.

The Mission.

Coming from Spain in the fifteenth century.

The Airlia.

STAAR.

Guides.

Yakov and Section IV being destroyed.

Guardian.

Dulce.

Easter Island.

Che Lu and Qian-Ling and a second ruby sphere.

Duncan paused. If there was a second ruby sphere then—

"The next planned hold is at T-minus two hours. Go for flight crew final prep and briefing."

Duncan's eyes flashed toward the window. The space shuttle was ready. If there was another ruby sphere, then the mothership could still be used for interstellar flight. If it could be repaired—but hadn't Kopina said they were going up to get a breathable atmosphere inside?

Duncan picked up her SATPhone and dialed the number for Turcotte in South America.

The mechrobots continued to do the guardian's bidding. The hole in the floor of the chamber had reached the thermal vent. A power system to tap that was being built two miles down.

Under the black shield guarding Easter island, all was progressing quite well.

Elek stepped away from the guardian. His dark sunglasses turned in the direction of Che Lu and Lo Fa, but before he could say anything, the tough-looking mercenary leader spoke.

"We got trouble," Croteau said. "My man in the top says he can hear tanks and other heavy equipment. The Chinese army is back, and they're pissed seeing all their buddies dead."

"Your men have mined the entrance?" Elek asked.

"Yes, but that doesn't stop them from dropping satchel charges in here or even gassing us like you did them."

Elek walked past Croteau to stand in front of Che Lu.

"Where is it?"

Che Lu stepped back, feeling the malevolence coming off of him. "Where is what?"

"The key."

"I do not have a key."

"Search them," Elek ordered Croteau.

Croteau did the job quickly.

"They don't have any key," Croteau said. "We're wasting time here. We need to get out, if we still can."

Elek shook his head. "No, we will make the time we need." He headed back into the control room. As they entered, an explosion rumbled through the cavern.

Croteau was listening to the small FM radio on his combat vest. "The PLA is attacking!"

Another explosion came amid the sound of automatic weapons firing. Elek stood at the main control panel. He ran his hands over the hexagons. A loud rumbling noise overrode the sounds of battle. Croteau dashed to the door and looked into the cavern.

"You're shutting the inner door!" he exclaimed.

"We need time," Elek said.

"But I left ten men up there!" Croteau's right hand came up, the submachine gun pointing at Elek.

"I am the only way you will get out of here alive," Elek said. "And sealing the tunnel was the only way we are going to stay in here alive. There were no other options."

"Goddammit!" Croteau exploded. "You don't just leave men to die like that."

"You do it all the time," Elek said. "It's called war."

Turcotte ripped off the suit, passing directly into the isolation lock, then into the habitat. Yakov had imagery and intelligence printouts spread out on the floor in front of him. Kenyon was looking through his microscope.

"Where's Norward?" Kenyon asked.

"At the hospital in town." Turcotte told them of the tear in the suit. The USAMRIID man did not seem surprised or particularly upset. Of course, Turcotte knew both Kenyon and Norward had had more time to

think about such a fate, just as a soldier was more prepared to go into battle.

"We're all going to get this thing if we can't figure out
its vector and come up with an antidote or vaccine,"
Kenyon said.

"Anything from your headquarters?" Turcotte asked.

"I can't get through to Fort Detrick," Kenyon said.
"It will take time for the vector experiments to work."

"We don't have time," Turcotte said. He looked at
Yakov. "What do you have?"

Yakov drew a circle. "The satellite came down somewhere to the west of here. I think—" He paused as the
SATPhone rang.

Turcotte picked it up. "Turcotte."

"Mike, it's Lisa. We've got something."

Turcotte listened as she told him about the strange
transmission picked up to their west. He got the grid
location from her.

"There's something else," Duncan said.

"What's that?"

"Colonel Carmen, my friend who authorized the
USAMRIID mission, is dead." Duncan went on to tell
Turcotte of the phone conversation.

"So someone's covering up on the Stateside end" was
Turcotte's summation of that information.

"Looks like."

"Can you get me any help?"

"I can try," Duncan said. "What do you need?"

Turcotte rattled off a quick list of support.

"I've already got some of that moving. I talked to
Colonel Mickell at Bragg already."

"Good. What about the shuttles?" he asked her.
"Have you figured out what is going on?"

"I think someone wants to get the mothership, because there's a second ruby sphere hidden somewhere, maybe in the lowest level of Qian-Ling."

Turcotte considered the situation. "That's putting the cart before the horse," he said. "Whoever wants the mothership has to survive the Black Death first."

"The Airlia on Mars don't have to worry about that," Duncan said.

"True," Turcotte acknowledged. "But what about whoever is helping them? These Guides?"

"The guardian didn't care much about the people it used on Majestic-12. Humans are just tools for it."

Turcotte thought about that. "Yeah, but if the second ruby sphere hasn't been found yet, the guardian still needs those tools. Maybe they're securing the mothership for a different reason."

"I don't . . ." There was a pause from Duncan's end. "Oh my God. Major Quinn told me something and I didn't think it was important, but maybe that's why there's a rush to get to the mothership."

"What?" Turcotte asked.

"Quinn got some information off the hard drives about The Mission, but it's old stuff, although it does back up Yakov's claim about The Mission being around a long time. I'll forward you a copy. I've told him to try to find something more recent.

"The only other solid thing they've gotten out of STAAR's hard drives you recovered from Scorpion Base was that they were doing a keyword search with the word *ark*. Maybe the rush to get to the mothership is to use it as an ark. The gravity drives still work, so it could land on Earth and get back up into orbit without having the ruby sphere."

"Like Noah's Ark," Turcotte said.

"So the chosen ones can survive the Black Death and do the Airlia's bidding."

Turcotte looked across the habitat at Yakov, who was following his end of the conversation. "Like they've done before in the past. Culling out the human race to make it controllable. And if the Black Death spreads and kills everyone at NASA, then there's no one there to launch the space shuttles to secure the mothership. I think that has to come first."

"We can't let that happen, Mike."

"Get me that support," Turcotte said.

Lexina looked at the crater, trying to imagine a mountain here. She had seen images of this place before the destruction. It had dwarfed Mount Kilimanjaro in size and bulk.

She was near the center of Ngorongoro Crater, a most intriguing spot in north Tanzania. Ngorongoro was the second-largest crater on the surface of the planet. Over twelve miles wide, it encompassed over three hundred square miles, including Soda Lake in the center. The crater was over twenty-two hundred meters above sea level, the top of a huge, ancient volcano that had been worn down, obviously much further than its cousin to the east, Mount Kilimanjaro.

The crater was a spectacular place, considered by those who had made the arduous journey there to be almost an unspoiled Garden of Eden. Even if one reached the rim, which was not easy by itself, the steep, almost vertical rim of the crater made travel into the crater very difficult. There was only one overgrown road that switchbacked its way down to the interior floor. The land was mostly open grassland, although near the rim there was thick forest. Soda Lake was a broad expanse of water, but it was not deep, less than four feet in most places. Because of its isolation and the relative lack of human intrusion, the crater teemed with wildlife.

She reached into her pack and pulled out a small gray device about six inches long by three wide and one deep. The top surface was covered with hexagons. She knew she was close enough now, but the big question was whether there was anything left here.

Lexina pressed a pattern on the device and the hexagons were lit from behind with a green light. She then tapped out a code and the front edge of the device glowed orange.

Slowly she turned in a circle, holding the device at arm's length. She completed one complete revolution. Then she tapped in a new code. The front shifted from orange to red. She again began turning, holding the device out. It had been so long and the obvious destruction so great, she expected nothing.

Thus when there was a beep from the device and a bright scarlet line appeared in the center of the red, she didn't stop, but completed another circle. When the device repeated its report as she faced in the same direction—toward the center of the crater—she stopped. She began walking forward in a perfectly straight line, ignoring the bushes that grabbed at her cloak.

Soda Lake came into view, and the device still pointed her forward. As she approached, she pulled her backpack off, holding it with one hand. With the other, she removed her black robe. Underneath she wore a tight, gray bodysuit. She stuffed the robe in her backpack as she walked.

She didn't pause, striding right into the lake, feeling the cool water splash around her ankles. She had studied this area before going on her trek and knew the lake covered a large amount of area, but it was very shallow, never more than four feet deep.

The device kept her on an unerring straight line. The shore was soon far behind and the water just above her waist, slowing her slightly, but she kept moving. A flock of birds resting on the water took off in startled flight at her approach. Off to her left front, beady eyeballs in large gray heads watched her warily. She knew the water buffalo were to be feared, as they were unpredictable in their behavior, but her course wavered not in the least. She passed within twenty feet of the water buffalo.

The beeping on the device was growing quicker, the pauses less. Despite that, she was startled when her right foot touched nothing and she fell, the water going over her head. She kicked, coming back up to the surface and backed up, regaining her foothold on the bottom.

Carefully she felt in the murky brown water with her foot. There was a smooth cut in the bottom. She traced its circular pattern to the left until she had outlined a round hole in the bottom of the lake twenty feet wide. The entire way, the device in her hand pointed to the center. She turned the device off and put it in her soaked backpack, making sure the top was sealed.

Lexina took a deep breath and then dove headfirst into the hole. Her legs kicked as went straight down. She could feel the pressure building on her ears as the seconds went by and still she descended. She let air out of her lungs in a trickle of bubbles, going ever deeper.

Then her outstretched arms hit something smooth and flat. Her fingers scrambled in the murky water, searching. They closed on a semicircular metal object sticking up from the flat surface. She gripped it with her left hand and continued to feel around with her right.

Her lungs were low on air; she'd been under now for over a minute. Her fingers hit a thin, raised ridge of metal, less than half a millimeter high. She traced it, running into a junction where three ridges went off at exact angles. Exploring further, she realized she had a series of hexagonals.

Her lungs struggling, her mind beginning to blacken with lack of oxygen, she felt out the entire series. There was one in the center with six surrounding. Quickly she hit the code she had memorized long ago.

The rod in her left hand swung up, the surface underneath it rising, pushing her upward. She scrambled to avoid being caught between the hatch and the side of the tube. A bubble of air blew past her, too quick for her to even consider trying to get any.

She pulled herself around the hatch that had opened. She scrambled around, feeling the walls, searching for the controls to close it. She realized she had to find it in the next couple of seconds or shoot for the surface, and even as she thought that, her fingers touched a similar pattern of hexagons on the wall. She hit the code. She could feel water sweep by her, forced by the hatch closing.

Now she was trapped. The last of the air in her lungs dribbled out of her mouth. Her mind flickered, going blank, when she was slammed against the metal wall by a rush of water. Then all went dark.

17

Turcotte looked at the map as Yakov and Kenyon peered over his shoulder. "NSA picked up some SATCOM transmissions out of this. Earlier today someone piggybacked a GPS—ground positioning satellite—signal."

"And?" Kenyon asked.

"And someone has to have very good gear to do that, *and,*" Turcotte continued looking at the map, "the NSA analyst thinks that the whole thing was designed for whoever broadcast the first signal to find something on the return piggyback."

"Find what?" Kenyon asked.

"The satellite," Yakov said.

Turcotte nodded toward Kenyon. "That would be your zero point."

"No," Yakov disagreed. "That would be the start of your vector. The zero point is The Mission."

Duncan looked out the blast windows. The shuttle *Endeavor* and its launch pad dominated the view between his location and the Pacific Ocean beyond.

"NASA's never done a dual launch." Kopina had quietly appeared at her side.

"Can they handle it?" Duncan asked.

Kopina nodded. "We prepared contingency plans for this exact occurrence."

" 'We'?"

"Space Command." Kopina pointed at the shuttle. "Right now that's the only way we can put people into space. At least in the States. And each shuttle can carry only eight personnel, ten if we disregard some safety requirements. Not exactly a large number. Of course, that's considering only the crew compartment," Kopina amended. "Rockwell has been working on a personnel payload pod to fit in the cargo bay, but it's never been tested.

"Right now, the crew of each has ten people. Most from SEAL Team Six and two from NASA—pilot and copilot."

"With those two shuttles launched, will we have any space capability?" Duncan asked, thinking about Turcotte's theory that the shuttles had to be launched first, before the Black Death spread too far.

"There will be one remaining shuttle—*Atlantis*. It's currently being refitted."

Kopina had a model of the shuttle in her hand. "Just so you know a few basic terms that will help." She tapped the shuttle on top of the large rockets. "This is the orbiter." She touched the two rockets on the outside of the large center tank. "These are the two solid rocket boosters, which are called SRB. This big tank in the center is not a rocket, but rather carries fuel. Most people don't know this, but each SRB is bolted to the launch platform by four bolts.

"At launch, the three space shuttle engines, these three nozzles here at the bottom, are ignited first. They're fed fuel from the external tank so the orbiter can get into space with a full load. It's a special liquid hydrogen fuel with liquid oxygen oxidizer. When feedback indicates all three are working properly—we're talking the last six seconds in the countdown here—the SRBs are ignited." She touched the bottom of the two rockets.

"But we still want to make sure everything's working right. When it's determined that there is sufficient thrust-to-weight ratio, initiators—small explosives—cut the eight hold-down bolts on the SRBs and the whole system is now free to go. That's liftoff.

"Maximum dynamic pressure comes approximately sixty seconds after launch, but it never exceeds three g's. Two minutes up, the SRBs are just about empty and they're jettisoned from the external tank. They still have a little fuel left that keeps them going while a small side rocket pushes them away from the shuttle."

Kopina pointed out to sea. "The SRBs are reusable and deploy a parachute. They come down over a hundred miles out to sea. By that time, the shuttle is moving pretty quickly. For the next six minutes, until eight minutes after launch, the orbiter engines fire. Then, just before reaching orbital velocity, the external tank is jettisoned. It is not reusable."

"Where does it come down?" Duncan asked.

"Point of impact is the extreme South Pacific, but most of it breaks up coming back down. Two of the orbiter engines are then used to finalize thrust into orbit. Which can be anywhere from 115 to 250 miles up. The mothership and talon are at about 175 miles. *Endeavor* should be able to link up with the mothership without any problem. It's not like they could fly by and not see it."

"What's in *Endeavor*'s cargo bay?" Duncan asked.

"Equipment to seal up the mothership and for beginning repairs on the talon."

"The hole in the side of the mothership must be

huge," Duncan said. "How are they going to be able to seal it?"

"They've got high-tech material that can stretch and seal in the vacuum of space," Osebold said. "The big advantage they have is they'll be working off of a good base, the mothership itself. Plus they're working in space. The key is to make the bay able to take an atmosphere.

"*Columbia* is also carrying material to help make the bay livable. That makes just about sixty tons of material," Osebold said. "But *Columbia* is also carrying extra fuel, as we're afraid it's going to have a harder time linking up with the talon than *Endeavor* will have with the mothership. Also, *Columbia,* after it links up, is going to have to tow the talon to the mothership."

"Do you guys think this is going to work?" Duncan asked.

"It's a long shot," Kopina said. "They'll need a couple of breaks to succeed. First make both linkups before the shuttles run out of fuel. Then being able to repair the mothership. Then . . ." She paused. "Well, you get the idea."

The speaker gave the latest orders. *"T-minus one hour and thirty-five minutes. Verify all systems ready for crew module closeout. Perform air-to-ground voice checks."*

"Is that necessary?" Duncan asked.

Kopina smiled. "The speaker? No. Ops has several different channels to the shuttle and the ground crew that they do all the real work on. But it's sort of a NASA tradition to do a speaker countdown. And, you never know, it's a redundancy that just might be important."

"Close crew compartment hatch."

"That's it. They're in," Kopina said.

·   ·   ·

Lexina blinked. The first thing she felt was the air in her lungs. It was stale and there was a foul edge to it, but it felt wonderful. She opened her eyes. She was lying on a black metal floor. She sat up and looked about. The room she was in was twenty feet wide and round. The top was the hatch that she had come in through. Light came from a series of blue, glowing tubes spaced vertically every five feet. To her left, she made out the outline of a door, with a hexagonal panel next to it.

As she stood to go to it, she noticed something. There was the faintest trace of a jagged line going around the entire circumference of the tube. It took her a second, but then she realized what she was looking at—the tube had gone farther, probably much farther, when the top of the mountain had been here. The line was what was left after this place had been blasted. Whoever had come later and added the air lock had put it right on the end.

She thought of the power that had been involved in taking off the top of the mountain. She shook that thought away and went to the panel. There was much to do. She went to the side door and entered a code into the panel.

In Vilhena, Norward tried to conquer his fear as he lit a cigarette. He was a doctor first and foremost, and he had seen much pain and suffering in his time, but nothing like this. And never before had he worked knowing he would be on the other end, a patient, very soon. He was taking a short break, sitting behind the infirmary.

He had used Sister Angelina as an interpreter and questioned the few patients who could still speak. He had a good idea now of the timeline of the disease.

Finishing the cigarette, he went back inside. A figure was shuffling down the hallway, a body in her arms.

"Sister Angelina!" Norward moved forward to help.

"I have been trying to move the dead to A wing," Angelina said. Her white robe was caked with blood and other material that Norward didn't want to identify. She lowered the body to the floor and pulled the dead nun's habit over her face. She knelt and crossed herself, her lips moving in prayer.

Norward moved past her and looked into the main ward. There were bodies on all the beds, some on the floor where death spasms had thrown them. He could smell the odor of death. He forced himself to look. They were all bled out. Blood had exploded out of every orifice of the body, including their eyes and ears. That was the virus looking for a new host, having finished with this one. He forced himself to look more closely. The blisters in the black streaks had broken open on all of them. There was no one left alive other than he and the nun.

Norward turned. Sister Angelina was still kneeling, praying. She didn't even look up as Norward walked past, out the door into the street. A thunderstorm seemed to be forming on the horizon, and a strong gust of wind blew down the empty street, carrying a few leaves and pieces of paper with it.

Vilhena was dead.

Norward headed toward the boat he and Turcotte had visited. He remembered the gun that the man had used. It was still there.

"We have another message," Faulkener said, holding out the message flimsy.

Toland put a poncho over his head and used his red lens flashlight to see the letters. Quickly he decoded it.

```
TO TOLAND
FROM THE MISSION
PAY UPPED TO TWO MILLION A MAN
US DOLLARS
ALREADY IN YOUR ACCOUNT
TIME IS OF ESSENCE
DO NOT HALT FOR ANYTHING
CALL FOR AIR EVACUATION WHEN
BALDRICK CONFIRMS ARTICLE RECOVERED
AIRCRAFT REQUIRES RUNWAY
MINIMUM LENGTH THREE HUNDRED METERS
SIDE TO SIDE CLEARANCE FIFTY METERS
MONITOR FM FREQUENCY 32.30
YOUR CALLSIGN GALLANT
AIRCRAFT CALLSIGN SPARROW
END
```

"Wake up, sleeping beauty," Toland ordered Faulkener. "We're moving *now*."

A dim red glow appeared twenty meters down the main tunnel. Che Lu put her hand on Lo Fa's thin shoulder; she knew he was brave but also superstitious.

The red glow changed shape from a circle, stretching and narrowing, touching the floor. The form of a person began to coalesce, but a strangely shaped person. The legs and arms were too long, the body slightly short. The large head was covered with red hair. The skin was pure white. The ears had long lobes that almost touched the shoulders. The eyes were bright red with scarlet, elongated pupils.

The figure was not solid. Che Lu could see through to the corridor behind it. As it had the last time she saw it, the figure raised its right arm, the six-fingered hand spread wide.

A deep, guttural sound echoed up the tunnel. The language was singsong.

"Do you understand it?" Che Lu asked.

Elek had watched as silently as the rest. "Why should I tell you?"

Che Lu shrugged. "Because we're all here together. Because I am curious?"

"No, old woman," Elek said, "I do not understand the language. It is the language of the Airlia. Only another Airlia could understand what it is saying."

The figure had spoken for almost a minute, before fading.

"What it says is not important," Elek said. "What is important is this. . . ." She paused and walked forward a few steps, then threw a jacket down the tunnel. There was a flash of light and the jacket settled to the floor in two pieces.

"Damn!" Croteau exclaimed from his position at the rear.

"And there is worse beyond the beam," Elek said. "What is important," Elek repeated, "is that all the defenses are still in place. We must have the key!"

Duncan grabbed the phone and pressed the on button before the first ring was finished.

"Duncan."

"Dr. Duncan, my name is Lexina. I am a member of the organization you know as STAAR."

Duncan felt her pulse quicken, and she sat up straight in the seat. "What do you want?"

"I am not your enemy," Lexina said.

Duncan remembered the two STAAR representatives and how they had tried to stop Turcotte from taking off in the mothership. "Why should I believe you?"

"You can believe whatever you wish," Lexina said.

"But your wishes and your beliefs don't concern me. What is essential is your cooperation."

"What do you want?"

"How much of the dig at Dulce has been uncovered?"

"You should know better than me," Duncan said.

"I don't know what you're talking about," Lexina said.

There was a pause, and Duncan let the silence ride. She saw no need to confirm that or give up any information.

"I need something," Lexina finally said.

"Exactly what do you need?"

"Don't play games," Lexina said. "We don't have much time."

"You're the one playing," Duncan said. "Your organization has been playing for a long time. I want to know who exactly you are before this conversation goes any further."

"We're The Ones Who Wait."

"Wait for what?"

"We wait."

"Oh, that clears everything up."

"I assure you, our goals are the same."

"I don't think so," Duncan said.

"I need the key."

Duncan frowned. "What is it the key to?"

"That is why I need it," Lexina said. "You have no idea what you have. If you have it."

"This conversation is going nowhere," Duncan said.

There was a long pause. "You don't have it, do you?"

Duncan wasn't sure how to answer that. "We know that you aren't human."

"You know nothing. I need the key. It would be in your interest to give it to me if you have it. There are enemies everywhere, and they will want the key too. I will call back."

The phone went dead. Duncan thought for a few moments, then she placed another call.

Turcotte opened up a footlocker bolted to the floor of the bouncer. There were four MP-5 submachine guns inside. He tossed one to Yakov, then one to Kenyon, who almost dropped it.

"What am I going to do with this?" Kenyon asked.

Turcotte was leaning between the two pilot seats, showing them where he wanted to go. He ignored Kenyon.

The bouncer began moving to the west.

"The objective is a hundred kilometers away," Turcotte announced. "ETA in six minutes."

"What do you think is out there?" Kenyon asked. He was holding the gun as if it were as toxic as the samples he'd just finished dealing with.

"Somebody's out there in the middle of all this death," Turcotte said. "Using SATCOM and looking for something. I don't have a clue whether that somebody has anything to do with this disease, but it's a bit too much of a coincidence."

"Wait a second," Baldrick said.

Toland went down to one knee, Sterling at the ready. Baldrick flipped open the lid on the case. He pulled out the GPR into which he had programmed the location of whatever it was he was looking for. "That way," Baldrick said. "Four hundred meters."

Toland didn't have to say a word. He stood, the other men deploying around in a wedge. They were in steep terrain, with small clusters of trees every hundred meters or so rising above the thick undergrowth. By Toland's pace count they had moved three hundred meters when he saw something silhouetted on the top of a ridge ahead.

Toland twisted the focus on his goggles. A tree, twisted and shattered by some powerful force, was leaning to the right.

Baldrick checked the GPR one more time. "Wait here for me."

"We should go with you to the top of the ridge," Toland said. "If there's someone—"

"I said wait here," Baldrick said. He picked another case and took it with him.

Toland gestured and the other two men went to earth, facing out, weapons at the ready. Toland watched as Baldrick walked up the ridge and past the broken tree. As soon as the doctor was out of sight, Toland followed.

As he came up to the tree, Toland crouched low. He slowly peeked over a broken bough. The terrain dropped off on the other side, but Toland's attention was focused on the gouge in the grassy slope. Starting from the tree and going downslope, the dirt was torn as if a large tank had ripped through. Baldrick was at a large piece of crumpled metal at the end of the gouge, opening the third case.

Toland heard the screech of metal as Baldrick leaned into the wreckage. A downed aircraft? Toland wondered. Perhaps Baldrick was here for its black box, or maybe classified equipment or something else that had been on board.

Toland turned and worked his way back down the slope considering the possibilities.

"What's happening?" Faulkener asked.

"There's a plane or chopper crashed on the other side of the ridge," Toland said, his mind working.

"Must be pretty damn important to be worth this much," Faulkener said.

Toland looked upslope. Baldrick had appeared, moving quickly toward them.

"Let's get moving," Baldrick said.

"Change in plans," Toland said. "Last message I got from The Mission said to call in for air evacuation as soon as you recovered what you were supposed to."

"Well, I got it," Baldrick said. "So call."

Toland's head snapped up like that of a bird dog on the scent. "Something's coming." He scanned the sky, then, in a flash of lightning, spotted the bouncer passing by to the south, heading for where they had been.

Toland stuck the muzzle of his Sterling in Baldrick's stomach. "Maybe *you* already called someone and we're getting double-crossed here?"

"I don't have a radio!" Baldrick said calmly.

"You have that SATCOM thing you used to get this position," Toland said.

"I left it here," Baldrick pointed out.

"Then who's on the alien craft?" Toland asked.

"I don't know."

"It's setting down to the south of here," Faulkener noted. "Where we were stopped last."

Toland removed the gun from Baldrick's stomach. "Someone picked up our satellite transmission."

"How can they do that?" Faulkener asked.

"I don't know how," Toland said, "but it's the only thing that makes sense." He took a deep breath and cleared his head. "All right. Here's the plan. We call on the SATCOM. If someone's intercepting, that means they get a fix on us here, but we start moving right away. In the message we designate a linkup point." Toland studied his map. "Here. Eight klicks north." He knew the spot. It was an abandoned dirt strip that had been used occasionally by drug smugglers before the American crackdown on air traffic.

"What if they decode the message?" Faulkener asked.

"I don't think anyone can break a one-time pad," Toland said, not even really aware of where he was for the moment as his brain worked. "No, I think we're just getting the signal picked up. Get the rig set up."

Toland blinked as Faulkener threw his ruck down and scrambled to pull out the radio. He focused on Baldrick. "What did you get out of that aircraft?"

Baldrick was adjusting his pack straps. "What are you talking about?"

"What did you just get? What did we come here for?"

"That's not—"

Toland drew his knife and slashed, the blade cutting across Baldrick's right cheek, a thin line of blood following the cut.

"Why did you do that?" Baldrick was calm, staring at the other man.

Toland stepped forward and slammed a knee into Baldrick's chest, pinning him to the ground. He pressed the point into the skin under Baldrick's right eye. "What crashed over there?"

"I can't—"

The point of the knife edged forward until it was a scant millimeter from Baldrick's eye. "I'll take one eye, then the other. Nothing in Skeleton's orders about you keeping your eyes," Toland said. "Just get you and your cargo back. What crashed?"

"It was a satellite," Baldrick said.

"A satellite?" Toland frowned. "What did you get out of it?"

"Film," Baldrick said.

"Film of what?"

"The Amazon rain forest," Baldrick said. "The satellite wasn't supposed to come down so soon."

"That's worth millions?" Toland didn't wait for an answer. "Bullshit."

"This type of photo is worth a lot." Baldrick spoke quickly, eye still focused on the knife so close by. "The camera used special imaging. With thermal and spectral imaging the specialists can determine areas under the rain forest that have a high likelihood of holding diamonds, particularly alluvial flood areas."

"It's set," Faulkener reported.

Toland sheathed his knife and pulled out his one-time pad. He quickly began transcribing. He finished the message and punched it into the SATCOM and burst it out.

"Where did you say for the transportation to meet us?" Baldrick asked.

Toland laughed. "I don't think that's information you need. You just stick with us. We'll get you there."

"Both launches are go so far," Kopina said.

Duncan checked the red digits on the large clock, then returned her attention to the *Endeavor*. She thought of the crew, strapped to their seats, essentially sitting on top of a tower of high-explosive fuel.

"T-minus nine minutes. The count has resumed. GLS auto sequence has been initiated."

Five thousand meters to the south of Toland and his small patrol, Turcotte looked around, weapon at the ready. The bouncer was sitting a short distance away, silently floating.

"What do you think?" Yakov asked, looking about in the dark at the rolling terrain around them.

"They were here," Turcotte said, pointing at where the grass was pressed down. "Maybe three, four men."

"So where'd they go?" Yakov asked.

"They could have gone in any direction," Turcotte said. "We need help. Let's get back on the bouncer."

"T-minus one minute."

The shuttle on the pad directly in front of Duncan, three miles away, was mirrored in the TV screen in the observation room, with a view of *Columbia* on the pad at Cape Kennedy.

"T-minus fifty seconds. Ground power removal."

"If they have an abort now, there is an escape mechanism built in," Kopina said. "You can't see them, but there are seven twelve-hundred-foot-long wires from the top to the ground. Each has a basket big enough to carry three people.

"The wires come down right next to bunkers," Kopina said. "The theory is you get out of the orbiter, into the basket, ride the wire down, jump out of the basket and into the bunker."

"T-minus thirty-one seconds. Go for auto sequence. Start SRB APUs."

Duncan could see gas venting out of the bottom of the shuttle.

"T-minus twenty-one seconds. SRB Gimbal Test. Activate sound suppression water. Perform SRB AFT MDMS lockout. Verify LH2 high-point bleed valve closed. Terminate MPS helium fill."

More gas venting, lines falling off the shuttle from the tower.

"T-minus ten seconds. Go for main engine start! Nine. Eight. Seven. Six."

"Engine three on the shuttle has started," Kopina said as a loud roar rumbled by them.

"Five."

The roar grew louder as the second main engine kicked in.

"Four."

The third main engine on the shuttle now ignited. But still gravity held the shuttle in its grip.

"Three.

"Two.

"One. SRB ignition."

The ground shook as if the hand of God had come down and was waking up all nearby.

"The bolts have been cut," Kopina said. "It's free."

Rising on a plume of fire, *Endeavor* lifted off the launch pad. On the other side of the country, *Columbia* was climbing into the sky at the same rate.

"How long until linkup?" Duncan asked.

"Three hours for Alpha with the mothership. A half hour later for Bravo at the talon."

Duncan watched the tower of fire go higher and higher.

18

"Okay, okay," Waker said as he read the intelligence request. He was pumped. He was hooked in to his electronic network, everything coming in and dancing in front of his eyes in letters and symbols his brain automatically translated.

"Perfect timing," Waker muttered. The KH-12 had picked up the SATCOM transmission as it was being made. Within thirty seconds it had come up on Waker's screen. And now, three minutes later, someone on the ground in South America wanted the location of the transmitter.

This time, though, he was talking direct back to the man in the field, and that gave Waker a rush. It was as close as he was ever going to get.

He typed, each finger slamming down on the key with authority.

```
TO: TURCOTTE
FROM: NSA ALPHA ONE ONE
TRANSMISSION SENT BY SAME SATCOM
LOCATION UTM GRID 29583578
```

Waker hit the send button.

·   ·   ·

"We've got an AWACS on channel two," the pilot of the bouncer informed Turcotte.

Putting a headset on, Turcotte switched to channel two. "This is Bouncer Two. Over."

Circling two hundred miles to the northwest, just outside of the international boundary of Columbia, an Air Force plane was always on station, its mission to catch drug traffickers, part of an electronic wall put in place.

At 45,000 feet, over eight miles, above the Pacific, the Boeing E-3C Sentry AWACS—airborne warning and control system platform—could "paint" a picture of everything within a three-hundred-mile radius using the thirty-foot radome above the center of the fuselage.

Colonel Lorenz was the officer in charge (OIC) of the rear compartment. Most of his crew were veterans of the Gulf War and numerous missions over both the subsequent no-fly zone and this drug zone south of the United States. There was no real threat to the plane itself on this mission, but that didn't mean Lorenz let things get slack as they "rode the southern fence," as the drug mission was known among the AWACS crews.

Lorenz spoke into the boom mike in front of his lips as soon as he received acknowledgment. "Bouncer Two, this is AWACS Eagle. We have new coordinates for you."

The point man stumbled and fell. Faulkener was quickly at his side. The man reached up, grabbing Faulkener's arm.

"Damn!" Faulkener hissed as the man vomited over his arm.

Toland came up and looked at the man. He was a mercenary who had served with Toland for the last two years. "Can you go on?"

The man groaned and rolled on the ground. Faulkener stood, flicking his arm to shake off the black vomit.

Toland rubbed his forehead. He brought up the Sterling. The man raised an arm weakly. Toland fired twice, then his arms slumped to his side, the Sterling hanging by its sling.

"Let's go," Baldrick said.

Toland thought of the two dead drug runners in their poncho stretchers. Two million dollars. Would he make it out of here in time to buy help? "Let's move." As they went forward in the darkness, he noted that for the first time Faulkener had not added up their suddenly higher shares.

"Lock and load," Turcotte yelled. The bouncer came in fast, the pilot using the craft's superb turning capability to keep them just above the treetops.

In a small open area, less than a hundred meters short of the location they'd been given by the AWACS, the pilot touched down. Turcotte was out of the hatch, followed closely by Yakov and Kenyon. The bouncer lifted and hovered ten feet overhead.

Turcotte scanned the area, but he saw nothing. He began moving forward, and Yakov grabbed his arm.

"What's up there?" Yakov was pointing with the muzzle of his MP-5 upslope at a tree that had been sheared off halfway up its trunk. Turcotte ran up the slope and crested it. A pile of twisted metal lay at the end of a trail of torn-up earth.

"The satellite," Yakov said as he knelt next to the wreckage. The scene was lit by a bolt of lightning. Thunder rumbled a few seconds later.

•   •   •

Toland had his small band of survivors moving. He checked out the sky as everything was brilliantly lit. He'd seen this before. Heat lightning, soon to be followed by a torrential rain. Perfect. There was no way they would be found, no matter how close their pursuers were.

"Here!" Kenyon called out.

Turcotte ran over, the others following. A body lay in the grass. Yakov shined a light down and they immediately saw the blood and the bullet holes. But there was also the sign of the disease. Black welts crisscrossed the man's exposed skin.

"We're exposed," Kenyon said.

"Everyone will be exposed sooner or later," Turcotte said. He was tired of hiding in the suits. There was no way they were going to track down the source by hiding.

Turcotte looked out into the dark. The wind was picking up, and he could feel dampness being carried with it. "Weather's changing," he called out. "Back to the bouncer."

19

The pilot checked his map one last time, then carefully folded it so that the portion he needed was faceup. He used a band of elastic to attach it to his kneeboard. He had no electronic devices on board other than the engine, windshield wipers, and the rudimentary instrument panel, so this truly was going to be a seat-of-the-pants navigation job. He did have a small FM radio to be used to contact the people on the ground when he got close. The pilot was used to such missions and felt confident he could find the target runway. He looked like Baldrick's brother—tall, his six-foot-two frame crammed into the cockpit, with straight blond hair and brilliant blue eyes.

He'd been waiting here for two days, the aircraft—a specially designed, top-secret prototype named the Sparrow—under camouflage nets at a deserted airstrip as close as he could get to the target area without actually entering the suspected infected zone.

He flicked the on switch and the engine coughed once, then smoothly started. It was a specially designed rotary engine, quieter than a conventional piston engine and mounted directly behind the cockpit in a large bubble. The propeller shaft extended forward from the engine, over the pilot's head to the high-mounted propeller, supported by a four-foot pylon mounted on the nose. The long shaft allowed a high reduction ratio for the prop, and the very large blades—over eight feet long—turned very slowly. The resulting sound was no louder than a moderate wind blowing through the trees.

The Sparrow was made by a South African company off of designs stolen from Lockheed's Q-Star (Quiet Star) program. The company was a subsidiary of Terra-Lel. The entire aircraft was designed with two factors in mind: reduced noise and radar signature. It wasn't built for speed or endurance, but the target was only sixty miles away. The pilot knew he would be there in less than forty minutes.

The runway was dirt, and the rain had further complicated what was going to be a difficult takeoff with no lights. The pilot released the brakes and the plane began rolling. Peering through the Plexiglas with his night-vision goggles, the pilot ignored the sweep of the wipers and concentrated on staying straight. In two hundred feet he had sufficient speed and pulled back on the yoke, lifting off. As soon as he cleared the trees, he turned due west.

Colonel Lorenz had moved the AWACS until they were now farther south along the coast, opposite Peru. The only aircraft on his screens was moving in this direction, because he had ordered it to.

He keyed his mike. "Spectre One One, this is Eagle. Over."

"This is One One. Over."

Lorenz quickly relayed to the pilot of the Spectre gunship what he wanted. The AC-130 didn't look like a bloodhound, but it was the best Harris could come up with in the inventory. A C-130 transport plane modified to be an airborne gun platform, the Spectre could throw a lot of bullets in a very short period of time. From front to rear, along the left side, the Spectre boasted 7.62mm Gatling guns, 40mm cannon, and a 105mm howitzer, all linked to a sophisticated computerized aiming system on board the craft. The crewmen's job was to shovel away expended brass from around the guns so they could keep firing.

Using its low-light-level TV—LLTV—Lorenz wanted the Spectre to head to the bouncer's location, then begin a circular search pattern, literally looking for the people they were after.

"Roger that," the pilot of the Spectre acknowledged when Lorenz was done with his instructions. "ETA at target sight, fifteen minutes. Out."

"Another kilometer," Toland said. He pulled his canteen out and drank deeply while still walking, trying to replace some of the fluid he was losing and keep his temperature down.

He looked over. Faulkener and the other man weren't doing too well either, but Baldrick seemed all right. Of course, Baldrick hadn't been with them at the ambush.

Lexina listened to the report from Elek in Qian-Ling and then one from Gergor and Coridan, still making their way south. Neither was good. Gergor's description of what happened when he turned on the ship link did not bode well for current events. And Elek being trapped inside the tomb without access to the lower level was frustrating. The fact that the guardian in Qian-Ling could give no information on the location of the key had not surprised her, but she had had a faint hope it might. That hope was now gone.

She was seated in a tall black chair, a few inches too

big for her. One small screen glowed in front of her, the rest of the devices in the room dark and powerless.

She knew little of this base from the records other than that the Airlia had established one at this location during the height of their domain on Earth. Its purpose was unclear, and who had attacked it, and why, were also unknown, although Lexina had to assume it had happened during the long struggle between Aspasia and Artad, and their minions: the Guides and The Ones Who Wait. There was so much that had been lost over the years, so much information.

There was little power left in the base's energy source, and she had carried few supplies in with her. Until Gergor and Coridan arrived with more, she would have to make do. Her sat-link still worked—after she had hooked it into the facility's monitoring array. That allowed her to talk to them, but there was little she could do other than monitor. The conversation with Duncan had not gone well.

But one thing she had learned in her years with STAAR was that there was always a way to turn what looked like a negative into a positive. She punched into her sat-link.

The other end was answered promptly.

"Duncan."

"Dr. Duncan, this is Lexina. Have you thought more about my request that you give us the key? If you have it, that is."

"Oh, we have it," Duncan said. "But I see no reason why we should give it to you."

"My people are in Qian-Ling."

"Is that where the key goes?"

"It is possible," Lexina said.

"But you don't know for sure?" Duncan pressed.

"My people in Qian-Ling have Professor Che Lu in their custody."

"Are you threatening to harm her?" There was a touch of anger in Duncan's voice.

"Perhaps I should," Lexina said. "After all, you killed two of my agents at Area 51. But I would prefer to act in a more civilized manner if we can. Qian-Ling has been sealed off from the outside world. The Chinese army has it completely surrounded. Unless you give me the key, Che Lu and those with her will never get out of the tomb."

"What does the key have to do with Qian-Ling?"

The question gave Lexina pause. Exactly what did Duncan have? Or were they ignorant?

"That is why you must give me the key," Lexina said. "I know how it is to be used."

"So do we," Duncan said. "And maybe you're lying to me. Maybe it doesn't go to Qian-Ling."

Lexina realized this was going nowhere, a poker game where both sides were refusing to show their cards.

"I understand your shuttles have launched to link up with the mothership and the remaining talon."

"The whole world knows that," Duncan said.

"But I know something that could critically affect their mission," Lexina said.

"What?"

"You don't get something for nothing."

"I'm not giving you the key," Duncan said. "We not only don't know who you are, we don't know what you are. Until then, there are no deals."

"You are making a mistake," Lexina said.

"Perhaps, but we didn't think STAAR had our best interests at heart before, and now that we know you aren't even human, we think it even less."

"I'm human," Lexina said.

"That's not what the autopsies on your two people revealed."

"We are here to protect you," Lexina said.

"And it was an easier job when we were ignorant," Duncan said. "But we're not ignorant, and frankly, protect us from what? Yourselves? Sort of like the Mafia? We'll protect you from us? If it's to protect us from Aspasia, we took care of that problem on our own."

"So you think," Lexina said.

"We will take care of the Airlia survivors on Mars on our own also."

"So you think," Lexina repeated.

There was a pause. Then Duncan spoke. "What do you know of the Guides?"

"They are your enemy."

"The Mission?" Duncan asked.

"They seek to destroy you," Lexina said.

"Using the Black Death?"

"They have done that in the past."

"But we have always survived."

"You do not even know who you are, yet you think you can do all this? You are children! Ignorant children playing in a very grown-up universe."

"If you are willing to work with us," Duncan said, "perhaps something can be arranged. But I do not respond well to threats."

"On your head be it." Lexina cut the connection. She sat back in the chair designed for the Airlia, her feet dangling just above the floor.

"Is there any other way out of here?" Croteau kept his voice low, even though it appeared Elek was totally engrossed in the golden pyramid.

Che Lu shook her head. "The main passageway was

blown up by the army. Our friend there closed off the tunnel."

Lo Fa had been silent the entire time they had been inside the tomb. Che Lu had attributed it to his displeasure over being captured by these mercenaries on what she knew he considered a foolish mission. But he broke his long silence.

"How did those others get in here last week?"

"What others?" Che Lu asked.

"The Russians," Lo Fa said. "I know they did not go in the front door of the tomb, because I cleared that for you. And they did not go in the large tunnel, because that was how you got out. So—how did they get in?"

"A side tunnel," Che Lu said. She remembered Colonel Kostanov, the Russian officer who had been in here before she arrived last time. He had pointed to the side of the large chamber. "Over there. But he said it was sealed from the outside."

"Yes, but I have some explosives," Croteau said.

"The army will be waiting outside," Lo Fa said.

"I'd rather take my chances out there than in here," Croteau said. "This Elek fellow doesn't have what he wanted, and I got a feeling he'll sit in here forever. Every hour we wait, the more troops are going to be outside. Now is our best shot. Plus it'll be light soon. We wait another day, we'll never get away."

"I agree," Lo Fa said.

"I must stay," Che Lu said.

"Suit yourself," Croteau said.

Raindrops pelted Toland. He had quit using his night-vision goggles, because nothing could help a person see in this. He was back to the basics he'd learned as a young lieutenant in the Canadian Army: compass direction and pace count. He looked down, then knelt and felt with his hand. Dirt, no grass. He squinted into the dark. It appeared that the runway ran perpendicular to their path.

"We're here!" he yelled, reaching out and grabbing the back of Faulkener's backpack. The signal was passed and the men gathered in close.

"How will we know when the aircraft lands?" Baldrick asked.

Toland was shivering now—a down spike in his fever—as water rolled down his body. "If I knew what type of aircraft, that would help. We might have to wait until this thunderstorm passes and the pilot gets an opening. When it lands," he pointed out, "we'll see it. Don't worry. Let's just hope it gets here."

He hadn't told Baldrick about the FM frequency. Toland had his survival radio in an ammo pocket on his vest. So far nothing. His stomach twitched, and he leaned over as he vomited into the mud.

The pilot of the Sparrow was circling on the edge of the thunderstorm, just above stall speed, creeping west with this part of the storm. There was another thunderstorm behind him, and he estimated he'd have about a five-minute window to hit the landing strip, make the pickup, and get back in the air.

Two kilometers to the west, Turcotte and the others in the bouncer waited. Turcotte tapped Kenyon on the arm.

"Could this thing be some sort of space bug that Earth Unlimited gathered?"

"There's nothing alive up there," Kenyon said. "But I've been thinking about it ever since you told me about the satellite, and I think I know what they did. Zero g."

"What?"

"Zero g," Kenyon repeated. "Things work differently under zero gravity. Biology, physics—at the molecular level the rules change." He was tapping his forehead. "I read a paper about manipulation of the RNA under zero gravity.

"There's a thing called transduction. A virus infects a bacterial cell that has a toxin . . ." Kenyon shook his head. "Forget about all that, it's not important right now. But this is starting to make some sense. The blisters on the black rashes. I think that's the way the virus moves—the blister explodes, the virus goes into the air. And this is different than, say, Ebola, because it lasts in the air. It holds together under ultraviolet light longer. And zero g would be the only way to manipulate the virus to get that effect."

"Then the satellite wasn't sent up there to spread the virus," Turcotte said.

Kenyon shook his head. "No. It was a zero-g lab."

Turcotte looked over at Yakov.

The Russian had been silent for a long time. He continued his silence, not responding to the look.

"You shot it down, didn't you?" Turcotte finally asked.

Yakov raised a bushy eyebrow. "Excuse me?"

"Sary Shagan," Turcotte said. "The Earth Unlimited satellite was over that site when its orbit began to suddenly deteriorate."

"Ah." Yakov waved a hand. "Yes. We fired a laser at it."

"Why?" Turcotte demanded. "You started all this!"

"We started all this?" Yakov was incredulous. "You give me too much credit. This started ten thousand years ago! It has been a war that has lasted that long, and we humans have been pawns. Well, we fought back. This disease—do you think they were going to put it in a

bottle at The Mission? What do you think those four
scheduled Earth Unlimited launches from Kourou are
for?"

"Can they spread this via a satellite?" Turcotte asked
Kenyon.

"This"—Kenyon indicated the immediate area—
"was spread via a satellite coming down, but it's not very
effective. A single point to start from."

"Tell that to Vilhena." Yakov snorted. "The payloads
in those four rockets are different. A Section Four man
lost his life finding that out. They hold multiple atmospheric return crafts that can spray the virus. Between
the four payloads there are sixteen craft. Enough on
their flight paths to blanket the world. You would have
preferred we waited until they perfected their plan? We
acted, and Section Four was destroyed in retaliation."

"Are you sure of that?"

"I am sure of nothing," Yakov said, "except that we
have to stop this Black Death."

In the Spectre gunship the storm didn't matter in the
slightest. The four powerful turboprop engines cut
through the wind and rain and the men in the inside
were on task, particularly the targeting officer, watching
his TV set. The thermal imaging also wasn't affected by
the weather. He could see as clearly as if it were broad
daylight.

They were flying low, doing shallow S-turns. They'd
started at the bouncer and were ranging out in a clover-
leaf pattern, always coming back and then back out at a
slightly different angle.

In the back of the AWACS a young technician stared
at her screen. She played with her computer for a little
while, then she reached up to the rack above it and

pulled down a three-ring binder. She flipped through, searching. Finding what she was looking for, she tapped the man next to her. "Hey, Robbins, align with me."

Robbins switched to the same radar frequency. "What do you have, Jefferson?"

"Just watch."

"What am I looking for?" Robbins asked after a minute.

"There! See it?"

"A shadow," Robbins said. "There's a thunderstorm outside, in case you didn't notice."

Jefferson ignored him. "Look what happens when I let the computer project a cross section based on the shadow."

"What the hell is that?" Robbins asked.

Jefferson handed him the binder. "You haven't been doing your homework. Colonel Lorenz wouldn't be pleased."

Robbins read. "The Lockheed Q-Star. It says here that it's an experimental aircraft, and not in production. Hell, it says this thing was tested back in the early seventies."

"That doesn't mean someone couldn't copy it and make their own," Jefferson said. "And they didn't have the radar technology and computer systems we have on this plane back in the seventies. It would be invisible back then. But it isn't now."

Robbins handed her back the binder. "Your find, you do the honors with the colonel."

The Sparrow pilot knew he was very close now. He pressed the send button on his stick. "Horseman, this is Sparrow. Over."

·   ·   ·   ·

Toland sat up straight, ignoring the pain in his stomach and head. He fumbled, then pulled out the radio.
"Sparrow, this is Horseman. Over." He squinted up into
the rain. It was getting lighter. The worst was passing.

"Horseman, this is Sparrow. I'll be down in three
minutes. Be ready to load fast. Over."

"Roger that. Out." Toland stood with difficulty. "Aircraft's inbound. Let's get ready."

"Got him!" Colonel Lorenz called out. "Got them
both!" He had the small airplane on screen for sure
now, and they had pinpointed the FM ground source.

"Direct in the Spectre and the bouncer," he ordered.

Inside the Sparrow, the pilot held the stick between
his knees as he pulled the bolt back on his pistol. He
had room for only one man, and that man was Baldrick.

The pilot of the Spectre gunship leveled off. "What
do you see?" he asked his targeting officer.

"I've got them on the ground. Four people." The
man played with his camera controls. "I have the plane
too. Off to our left. About a half a mile away."

"Eagle, this is One One. What are your orders?
Over."

Colonel Lorenz didn't really understand what was
going on. He relayed that question to Captain Turcotte
on board the bouncer.

Turcotte's reply was curt.

"Take the plane out."

The pilot of the Spectre blinked. "Say again. Over."

"Shoot down the aircraft. Over."

As far as the pilot knew, no Spectre had ever even

engaged another aircraft, never mind shot one down. "Keegan," he asked his targeting officer over the intercom, "did you hear that?"

"Yeah," Keegan said. "Far out. We're a fighter now. The jet jocks will crap when we tell them this. Give me level flight, azimuth, two one seven degrees."

The pilot of the Sparrow saw the edge of the runway through his NVGs. He nudged the stick forward, descending. He had about a second and a half to figure out what was happening as a solid line of tracers appeared just in front of him before the plane—and him with it— was torn to shreds by a combination of 7.62mm and 40mm rounds.

"What the hell is that?" Faulkener called out as they watched the tracers streaking over head, parallel to the ground.

"Sparrow, this is Horseman," Toland called into the radio. "Sparrow, this is horseman!" There was only static.

They all turned to look as a bouncer flashed out of the rainy dark and silently flew by.

"There they are!" Turcotte cried out. "Put us down!" They landed, a hundred meters from the four men.

The radio dropped from Toland's fingers into the mud. His head drooped on his shoulders for a long second, then came back up, and he looked about. There was just the slightest hint of dawn in the east, and the clouds appeared to be clearing.

The third man from Toland's patrol was lying in the mud, black vomit coming out of his mouth, blood seeping out of his eyes, nose, and ears.

20

"*Endeavor* has visual on the mothership," Kopina said, tapping the TV screen that showed the long black cigar shape above the curve of the Earth. "That's a forward view from the shuttle cabin."

She and Duncan were in a small room off the training hangar. Two TVs perched on the edge of the table, one tuned to *Endeavor,* the other to *Columbia.*

As the shuttle approached the mothership, the damage caused by the nuclear explosion became evident. There was a long gash, over six hundred meters long down the side. At its widest—where the cargo bay had been—the cut appeared to be about fifty meters wide.

"That thing actually held up a lot better than I thought," Duncan said.

Kopina nodded. "We think the skin of the ship was ripped open in the explosion, but the main structure—the load- and stress-bearing beams, remained intact. It's obvious that in order to be able to sustain the stress of interstellar travel, the structure of a spaceship has to be incredibly strong."

"How soon will they make linkup?" Duncan asked.

"They're closing relatively quickly," Kopina said. "They're going to be in range and try to grab a hold with the robotic arm in about thirty minutes. Let's hope they get it."

"If they miss, can't they try again?" Duncan asked.

Kopina gave her a sidelong glance before answering. "*Endeavor* has enough fuel for only one try. If they miss, that's it. And," she added, "if they use up too much fuel trying to link up with the mothership, they won't have enough to get back down. The shuttle wasn't designed to do much moving once it got into a stable orbit."

"What about *Columbia*?" Duncan asked.

"It'll be in the vicinity of the talon about thirty minutes after that."

"Do you have us fixed?" Turcotte asked, holding the handset for the FM radio close to his lips. "Over."

"Roger that," the Spectre replied. "We've got the bouncer clear. We'll track each individual as you come off. You have four people, about one hundred meters due south of your position. We can finish them for you. Over."

"Negative," Turcotte replied. "We need them alive. There is something you can do, though." Turcotte quickly finished giving instructions, then signaled for Kenyon and Yakov to follow him.

Turcotte hopped off and slid through the ground fog and the half light of a sun just clearing the horizon, weapon at the ready. Turcotte sidled to the right, getting off the mud of the runway and into the waist-high grass. He got down on his belly and began slithering forward, his clothing immediately soaked by the wet grass, the others following.

When he had made about fifty meters, he halted. "Stand up," he yelled. "Throw down your weapons and put your hands on top of your heads."

"Screw you!" A burst of semiautomatic fire ripped a few feet over Turcotte's head.

·   ·   ·

Toland looked at Faulkener. Faulkener returned the look with a glare, his eyes wild. "I'm not going to die like some animal." The NCO fired another burst from his AK-47.

"We've got a chance," Toland said. "They want to talk!" He looked at the third man. He was unconscious now, blood seeping out of every pore, covered in black vomit.

A noise caught Quinn's attention. Baldrick was turning a knob on one of the cases. "What are you doing?"

"Orders," Baldrick said.

"Everyone just freeze," Toland hissed. "I'm in charge here, and I'll make the decisions."

Baldrick didn't stop. Toland rolled twice to get close, then slapped Baldrick's hands away from the case. "I said stop."

"The Mission—" Baldrick began.

"I don't give a damn about your Mission," Toland said.

"I ain't going to die like that," Faulkener said. He began to stand. Toland grabbed him and pulled him down.

"What do you think you're doing?"

Toland didn't have time to dwell on Faulkener, though, because Baldrick began fiddling with the case. Toland finally understood that he was working on a small keypad—activating a destruct device. Toland drew his knife, grabbed Baldrick's right hand, and slammed the knife point through the center of the palm, pinning it to the ground.

He spun about as he heard a shot. Faulkener's body was crumpled on the muddy ground, blood pouring from the self-inflicted shot to the head. "Oh, goddamn," Toland muttered.

"Hands up!" the same voice called out.

"Who are you?" Toland called out.

"U.S. Army."

"Why do you want us? We have nothing against you."

"We want to talk!"

"Talk?" Toland returned. "You shot our plane down."

"We'll shoot *you* if you don't put your hands up."

A line of tracers came down from the sky and tore into the earth less than ten meters from Toland's position.

"Next burst is on top of your position," the voice called out.

Toland reached over. The third man was dead. Bled out. Everyone was dead, except he and Baldrick.

"You can't surrender that case," Baldrick said through a grimace of pain.

"Oh, yeah," Toland said. "So we blow it up and then we don't have anything to deal with these people."

"You can't deal this!" Baldrick said, his one good hand reaching for the case.

"The Mission's got you brainwashed," Toland said. "Nothing is worth that much." He raised his voice. "You want the imagery—we'll give it to you, if you'll give us free escort out of here."

Turcotte looked at Kenyon, who had come up during the exchange. "Imagery? What's he talking about?"

"I don't know what they might have," Kenyon said. "But we need to see it, whatever it is."

"All right," Turcotte called out.

"You can't!" Baldrick said. "It's not what you think."

Toland reached over and with one move withdrew the knife from Baldrick's hand. "Next time, I won't be so nice," he said. Baldrick tucked his bleeding hand into his armpit. "Move and I'll kill you," Toland continued.

"Stand up where I can see you!" Turcotte called out. He was relieved when a man stood, a Sterling submachine gun in his hands.

"Put the weapon down," Turcotte called out.

"You've got the big gun in the sky," the man said. "All we've got is our personal arms. You want to talk, we talk like we are now."

Turcotte glanced at Kenyon, who shrugged.

"Your call," Yakov said.

"I'll meet you halfway," Turcotte stood up. He let the MP-5 hang by its sling and noticed that the other man did the same with his Sterling. Turcotte walked forward—the other man doing the same—until they were five feet apart.

"I'm Toland."

"Turcotte."

Toland looked Turcotte up and down. "I don't see a uniform."

"I don't see one either," Turcotte replied. The other man looked ill, with the beginning of a black rash running down one side of his neck—which didn't surprise Turcotte. Everyone out here seemed to be sick. *Was sick,* Turcotte amended in his mind.

"You want the imagery?" Toland asked.

Turcotte didn't have a clue what he wanted other than answers. "Yes."

"What assurance can you give me that you'll let me go?" Toland asked.

"What assurance *could* I give?" Turcotte asked in turn.

Toland smiled despite his pain. "Good answer, Yank."

Turcotte had had enough with sparring. He also was surprised at Toland. Where did the man think he was going to go now?

"You know you're sick?" Turcotte asked.

"Oh, yeah."

"Do you know how sick?"

"I've seen them die," Toland said. "I know."

"The satellite you were just at," Turcotte said. "We think it had something to do with the disease."

This time Toland did show surprise. "I was told it simply took some pictures."

"Who told you?"

Toland looked over his shoulder. "You say this has something to do with the disease?"

Turcotte nodded.

Toland turned. "Come with me."

Turcotte hesitated. "I need to bring someone."

"Who?"

"A scientist who specializes in viruses."

"All right."

Turcotte gestured, and Kenyon rose and joined them. Together they walked back to Toland's group. Turcotte looked at the dead men lying there.

"This is Baldrick." Toland pointed at the man holding a bloody hand. "He's the one who knows what's going on." Toland kicked Baldrick. "Open the cases."

"I can't," Baldrick said without much conviction.

Toland's hand strayed to the knife on his web gear.

Baldrick kneeled and turned the combination knobs. He flipped the lid open. Inside sat a large metal box, battered and heat-streaked.

Kenyon looked at the box. He reached to his belt and pulled off a multipurpose tool and used the Phillips head to work on the screws holding the top on. Baldrick sat back down, nursing his wounded hand.

Kenyon flipped the top off. Inside lay sophisticated machinery.

"What is it?" Turcotte asked.

"Could it be a camera?" Toland asked.

"No." Kenyon lifted the machine out and turned it over. He was looking it over very carefully, then pointed. "This canister." It was as large as a gallon milk jug. "I'd say it's the biolab."

"Of?" Turcotte asked.

"The Black Death."

"The Black Death?" Toland repeated.

"The virus that's killing us."

Toland's eyes opened wide, and he turned to Baldrick. "You mean this thing we got. He made it?"

"He either made it or he knows who made it," Kenyon said.

"You—" Toland was speechless. His knife was out, and he was just about at Baldrick's throat when Turcotte intercepted him.

"Easy. We need answers from him. We need him alive."

"I'm not talking," Baldrick said. He glared back at Toland. "You can use your knife all you want, but I'm not going to say anything more."

"Let's take it back," Turcotte ordered.

"What about safe passage?" Toland asked.

"You're free to walk wherever you want to," Turcotte said. He turned and headed for the bouncer.

"Can I come with you?"

"This," Kenyon said, using a ruler to point, "is some sort of chamber in which the virus was manipulated in zero g. I can't tell you much more without taking it apart." He moved the ruler. "The virus was then shunted down this tube, to this holder. It must have been held there until the booster came down. Then it leaked."

Turcotte looked at the machinery. "Then they need this supply?"

"Looks like it," Kenyon said.

"No," Yakov said. "They need this supply to fill all four payloads, but they have quite a bit of Black Death stockpiled from the previous two launches."

Turcotte looked up at Baldrick. He had held true to his word and said nothing since they'd boarded the bouncer and flown back to the habitat at Vilhena.

"He doesn't seem too worried about catching the Black Death," Yakov noted.

"Do you have a vaccine for this?" Kenyon asked. Everyone in the habitat turned and stared at Baldrick.

Baldrick simply looked away.

"We know he works for The Mission," Toland offered.

"Where is The Mission?" Yakov asked.

Baldrick's face was expressionless.

"He's got to be vaccinated," Kenyon said. "He wouldn't have handled this," he tapped the device from the satellite, "like he did if he wasn't vaccinated."

"A vaccine won't do us much good," Turcotte noted.

"But it will save a lot of lives," Kenyon said. "The Black Death hasn't finished burning yet. It hasn't even really started."

Turcotte walked over to Baldrick. "You need to talk to us."

"I have an idea," Yakov said. He walked over to the isolation box and pulled out a small plastic kit from a drawer on the side.

"What's that?" Turcotte asked.

"You can't—" Kenyon began, but Yakov silenced him with a glare. He opened the case and withdrew a hypodermic syringe. Then he drew out a small bottle of murky liquid, checking the label. He inserted the needle into the bottle and drew back on the plunger, filling about an inch of the clear plastic tube with the liquid. He took out another bottle and did the same.

Yakov walked over to Baldrick. "We've all got the Black Death. I think you're vaccinated for it." Yakov shook the needle. "But this—this is Marburg. It might not kill you. Fifty-fifty on that. But it'll make you very sick even if it doesn't." Yakov looked at the others in the tent. "From what I know about it, Marburg seems to especially like the eyes and the testicles. Gets in there and really does—how do you say in English—a number?

"I also put Ebola in here," Yakov continued. "So if the Marburg doesn't kill you, the Ebola will." He looked at Kenyon. "Have you ever seen what effect on a human the two combined has?"

Kenyon could only shake his head.

"I do think it will be quite terrible," Yakov said.

Baldrick was staring at the needle. He finally spoke. "You can't do that to me."

Yakov laughed harshly. "I can do it without a second thought. You're an animal that deserves to die if you were in on the making of this thing." He pressed the tip of the needle against Baldrick's neck.

A nerve on the side of Baldrick's face twitched. His eyes were turned, watching the needle.

"Just a prick," Yakov whispered, "and you're infected."

The needle began pressing down on the skin.

"Take it away," Baldrick hissed.

Turcotte leaned forward into the other man's face. "You work for The Mission?"

"I work for them, but I'm not one of them," Baldrick said. "There are only a couple."

"Them?" Turcotte asked.

"Guides?" Yakov interjected.

"Yes," Baldrick said.

"Is there a vaccine?" Kenyon asked.

"No."

Yakov frowned. "But you've been exposed!" He pulled the needle back slightly. "Is there a cure?"

Baldrick looked away.

"Answer the man, you son of a bitch!" Toland yelled.

Baldrick looked around the habitat. Half the people there already had the beginnings of black welts on parts of their bodies that could be seen.

"Is there a cure?" Yakov demanded one more time.

Baldrick looked the Russian in the eyes. "Yes. There's a cure."

Yakov nodded. "And once you are exposed to the Black Death, and then cured, you'll be immune. Dangerous living, my friend. If you don't get back to The Mission on time, you're dead like us."

"Where is The Mission?" Turcotte asked.

"I cannot tell you that," Baldrick said.

Yakov put the needle back at the man's neck. "Where is The Mission?"

Baldrick smiled. He jumped forward, the needle tearing at his neck. He grabbed the MP-5 Kenyon had leaned against a case. As he brought it to bear, Turcotte shot him once in the upper right arm, knocking him back. He still struggled to bring the gun up.

"Stop!" Turcotte yelled.

But Baldrick ignored the order. The muzzle swung through horizontal. Turcotte's finger twitched on the trigger, but he hesitated to fire again, knowing they needed Baldrick alive.

Toland reached for the gun and Baldrick fired, hitting the mercenary in the chest and killing him. The muzzle kept going up, and Turcotte realized what he was going to do. Turcotte jumped forward, but Baldrick pulled the trigger once more a half a second before Turcotte could grab the gun.

The round went up through the mouth and blew off the top of Baldrick's head.

21

It was an intricate and very difficult task that the *Endeavor* was trying to accomplish. First, the mothership was slowly tumbling. Second, both it and the shuttle were moving relative to Earth. Third, the shuttle had to approach on the side of the gash and try to grab hold of the side with its fifty-foot manipulator arm at such slow relative speeds to ensure that the arm held and wasn't ripped off.

The crew of the *Endeavor* and those at NASA knew all these difficulties. But the history of America's space program had been full of long shots, and once those involved were briefed on the stakes, there had been no question that the mission would be accepted.

But, as expected, as the *Endeavor* maneuvered close to the mothership, the first pass didn't succeed. This had been anticipated.

A second pass was attempted. And failed, the end of the fifty-foot arm missing the rip in the mothership's side by a hundred meters—a relatively tiny distance given the scale of the maneuvers, but a tremendously large one given the length of the arm.

The point of no return had been reached. A third pass was attempted, the crew—and those running the mission on the ground—now knew that *Endeavor* did not have enough fuel to return to Earth.

The third one worked. Barely. The arm grabbed hold of the edge of the blasted-out black metal and the claw on the end locked down. The shuttle swung around on the end of the arm, bumping against the side of the massive alien ship, bouncing off, then coming to rest.

Within minutes, the boarding team, led by Lieutenant Osebold, was preparing to space-walk in their TASC-suits to enter the mothership.

"We made the decision during planning to have both shuttles take as many passes as needed to link up, regardless of their fuel situation," Kopina said. "We're prepping some Titan rockets with fuel payloads. They won't be ready for a couple of days, but we will get the payloads up and we will get *Endeavor* down."

"So they're stuck?" Duncan asked.

Duncan nodded. "It's mainly a psychological problem. They have enough air, water, and food to last three weeks."

"They could also fly the mothership back down," Duncan noted.

Kopina looked at her. "That's a possibility, but not one that has been approved yet."

"What does approval matter if they have control of the ship?" Duncan asked.

Kopina shifted her attention to the other screen. "*Columbia* has visual on the talon," she announced. "Let's hope they have better luck on linkup. *Columbia* is carrying more fuel than *Endeavor* because not only do they have to catch the talon, they then have to maneuver it to the mothership. So there was a sacrifice in payload so she could take more fuel into orbit.

"I'm putting *Columbia*'s cockpit intercom on speaker," Kopina said as she flipped a switch.

A woman's voice filled the room. *"Range three hundred meters, closing at relative four mps."*

"That's Colonel Egan, the pilot of *Columbia*," Kopina said.

Duncan could see the talon on the screen in front of her. Unlike the mothership, it wasn't tumbling, at least as far as she could tell. "How come the talon seems to be stable?" she asked.

"We noticed that a day or two ago," Kopina said. "Best guess is that there was some internal shifting inside that counteracted the initial rotation."

"How can that be?" Duncan asked.

"Any one of a lot of things," Kopina said. "An internal bulkhead giving way. Shifting of liquid inside of tanks. A system can degrade over time."

"But it happened in such a way to exactly counteract the original rotation?" Turcotte asked.

"Not exactly," Kopina said. "There's still some yaw and pitch. Hey, let's be thankful for small favors. If it was still tumbling like it was initially, it would practically be impossible for *Columbia* to get close."

"Two hundred meters," Egan said. *"Closing at three mps. Adjusting and slowing."*

The talon, although nowhere near as large as the mothership, still dwarfed the shuttle. The lean, black ship was over two hundred meters long and thirty meters in diameter at its thickest point. It was slightly bent to one side, giving the appearance of a very large black claw.

"One hundred meters. One meter per second. Rotating cargo bay to face target."

"They're putting the arm closest to the talon," Kopina explained. The camera view shifted. They were now looking up out of the cargo bay of the *Columbia*. The talon was a lean dark shape filling the space above the shuttle. The thin form of the manipulator arm could be seen, slowly extending.

"What the hell!" Colonel Egan's voice conveyed her surprise. *"Something's happening!"*

Turcotte and the others in the room could see it also—there was a small golden glow on the tip of the talon.

"Get them out of there," Duncan ordered.

"Boarding team deploy! Deploy!" Colonel Egan was yelling into the intercom. *"We're too close. I'm going to have to keep closing."*

"We're going out," a voice replied.

"That's Lieutenant Markham, Bravo Team Leader," Kopina said.

A TASC-suited figure appeared, cutting across the camera. An MK-98 was in the figure's gloved hands. A tether line was attached to the figure and a bulky maneuvering pack was on its back.

"There's Markham," Kopina said.

Markham was about twenty feet outside the shuttle's cargo bay now, between it and the talon, which was less than fifty meters away. There was a bright gold burst from the tip of the talon.

"Oh, God," Duncan muttered.

A thin golden line of light flashed. It went to Markham's left, then adjusted, cutting right across the SEAL commander.

The scream that echoed out of the speakers lasted less than a second. Markham was in two pieces, neatly sliced, the top half still attached by the tether, the bottom half tumbling away. Frozen blood floated about both parts.

"I'm up!" a voice yelled. A second space-suited figure appeared, this one with no tether.

"Jesus!" Kopina exclaimed. "He must have just jumped out of the cargo bay."

The man held an MK-98 in his hands and he was bringing it to bear when the ship fired again. Duncan admitted the bravery of the SEALs while recognizing the futility of their action.

"Emergency firing!" Colonel Egan's voice was terse. *"We're getting the hell out of here."*

Another, larger golden beam lanced out. The camera recorded that for the briefest of moments, then the screen went black.

"We can blow this door," Croteau said.

"And bring the army down on top of us," Lo Fa noted.

Croteau shrugged. "At least we'll have a fighting chance. It's still dark out there. In the confusion, many of us can get away."

There was a murmur of assent among the mercenaries gathered in the corridor. They were two hundred meters away from the main chamber, where Elek was still working at the console. They did not have much time before she realized they were gone.

Che Lu remained silent, having already made her decision to stay. Croteau looked around, getting assent.

"Blow it," he ordered.

As the mercenaries' demolitions men rigged the charges, everyone else moved back down the corridor.

Che Lu pulled Lo Fa to the side. "I wish you well."

Lo Fa shifted his feet. "You should come with me. This place is not good."

"I have to stay."

Lo Fa grimaced and looked away.

"You only promised to get me in, and you did," Che Lu said. "You must take care of yourself."

"I didn't get you in like I planned," Lo Fa said. "Getting you captured was not part of it."

"I will be all right."

Croteau raised his voice so the cluster of people could hear him. "We blow the blocked entrance, we're going to have to move fast. I recommend everyone move west. According to our man here"—he pointed at Lo Fa—"there are guerrilla bands in that direction you can hook up with. They might be able to pass you through out of China."

The demo men came down the corridor unreeling their detonating cord. Croteau pulled back the charging handle on his weapon and made sure there was a round in the chamber.

"Ready?" He looked about. "Fire in the hole!" He pulled the ignitor.

There was the sharp crack of explosives, amplified by the tight confines of the tunnel.

"Let's go!" Croteau dashed up the corridor, the rest of the mercenaries following.

Lo Fa took Che Lu's hand and shook it. He bowed, then he was gone up the tunnel.

Che Lu turned away.

"What have you done?" Elek was hurrying across the large open space.

"They desired to leave," Che Lu said. "And they did."

"They breached the perimeter!" Elek was looking down the corridor.

"When there was the opening up top," Che Lu noted, "the army was in no rush to enter. I don't think they will try now either."

"Then who is that?" Elek asked as they heard footsteps coming from the corridor. Che Lu cocked her head and listened. A smile came to her face as a familiar figure appeared.

"You could not leave me, old man." She gave Lo Fa a hug.

"Ah, don't flatter yourself, old woman."

Che Lu stepped back. "What is wrong?"

Lo Fa tapped his ear. "Listen."

"I hear nothing," Che Lu said.

"Correct," Lo Fa said. "By now there should be firing between the mercenaries and the army. There is none. I went out. As the mercenaries ran, I looked about. The army is gone. There is no one out there."

There was silence for a few seconds as all three thought about that strange occurrence.

"Why do you think they have done this?" Che Lu asked, although she had a suspicion that was so devastating she dared not voice it.

Lo Fa had no such reservation. "They are going to try to destroy the tomb," he said. "The troops have been pulled back to prevent them from being caught in the destruction."

"They seek to destroy us," Elek said. Che Lu could not tell if it was a question or a statement, but Lo Fa nodded.

Elek turned and headed for the control room. After a few moments, Che Lu and Lo Fa followed.

"*Columbia* has been destroyed." Kopina threw imagery on the conference-room table. "We've had the closest satellite take some shots. All it picked up was the talon and some wreckage."

"There were ten people on board?" Duncan confirmed.

Kopina nodded. "Yes."

"Any chance someone might still be alive."

Kopina sat down. "No."

There was silence in the conference room for several moments.

"Could there still be Airlia alive on board that talon?" Duncan asked.

Kopina shrugged. "I have no idea. The hull seems to be intact. The blast might have damaged its drive system but nothing else."

"Did you have any—" Duncan began, but Kopina cut her off.

"Do you think we would have sent those people there like that if we had had the slightest clue? It looked dead, we assumed it was dead."

"Maybe—" Duncan began.

"What?" Kopina asked.

"Maybe there weren't any Airlia still alive on the talon. Maybe it was controlled remotely?"

"It doesn't matter," Kopina said. "*Columbia* is gone either way."

"What about the mothership?" Duncan asked.

"Osebold is preparing to board," Kopina said. "There is no sign any of the Airlia that were in the cargo bay survived the blast."

"How far apart are the mothership and the talon?" Duncan asked.

"About eight hundred kilometers."

"So no chance the talon could attack the mothership?"

"I would think," Kopina said, "that if they had been capable of doing it, the Airlia would have maneuvered to the mothership already."

"Unless they were playing possum to draw us in," Duncan said.

"Look," Kopina snapped, "I'm just the mission specialist here. I didn't make the plan."

"No." Lisa Duncan's voice was harsh. "But I wonder who did."

Croteau halted, raising his fist. His band froze behind him at the signal. He estimated they'd made two klicks from the tomb and no contact yet. The other merk groups had scattered in slightly different directions, all heading generally west. And no shots from anywhere.

Croteau knelt as another mercenary came up next to him. "Something's wrong," Croteau whispered. "There were PLA crawling all over this place. And they got to be pissed about their buddies getting gassed."

"Maybe they're scared and have backed off," the other merk suggested.

"Yeah, and the Legion loved me," Croteau said. He rose and signaled for the patrol to continue.

Inside of *Endeavor*'s cargo bay, Lieutenant Osebold had his TASC-suit on. Inside of his helmet, the left side of his face was twitching. He could feel a tear slide down his left cheek—at least he thought it was a tear. In reality it was a drop of blood.

The massive bulk of the mothership filled the space above their heads. The shuttle was less than twenty feet away, held in place by the remote arm.

"We go as planned," he announced in the radio.

The first pair of SEALs—Ericson and Terrel—jetted out of the cargo bay, heading toward the open gash on the side of the mothership. Right behind them went the second pair—Lopez and Conover.

Osebold still waited, inside the cargo bay. He could see the other members of his team, dark black silhouettes, against the blackness of the mothership.

His head was pounding, spikes of pain lancing across

his brain. More tears of blood were flowing now, out of both eyes. He raised his MK-98 and fired.

The six-inch steel darts ripped through his team, tearing through the exoskeleton. The screams echoed inside of Osebold's helmet.

"What's going on?" Duncan yelled.

"A Guide," Kopina hissed. She pulled a small device out of her pocket.

"What are you doing?" Duncan demanded.

Kopina flipped open the lid of the device. She pressed down on a large red button.

The small charge was right against the shuttle's fuel tank. There wasn't much fuel left in it, but more than enough to multiply the initiating explosion.

Inside the cargo bay, Osebold was consumed by the momentary fireball, along with the entire shuttle. His last thought, fleeting and free, was of gratitude that death had found him.

"Who are you?" Duncan demanded.

Kopina closed the cover on the device. The screen that had showed the feed from *Endeavor* was now blank.

"They wanted the mothership," Kopina said.

"Who?"

"The Guides. They were going to bring it back to Earth, load their chosen people on board, and go back up to space while the Black Death took care of the free people of Earth."

"If you knew that, why did you let the shuttle launch?" Duncan asked.

"We only suspected," Kopina said. "There is no way to tell if someone is a Guide until they act."

"I ask you again," Duncan repeated. "Who are you?"

Kopina raised her left hand. A large silver ring was on her ring finger. "I am a Watcher."

"And what is that?"

"As long as the Airlia have been here, there have been Watchers," Kopina said. She was backing up, moving toward the door.

"Stop!" Duncan yelled.

"I have to go."

"The Mission! Where is it?"

Kopina shook her head. "We don't know. We sent one of our people to look for it. You know him as Harrison. He failed."

With that the other woman dashed out the door. Duncan ran after her, but she was gone.

22

Inside Qian-Ling, Che Lu and Lo Fa watched as Elek was one with the guardian, surrounded by the golden glow.

"I do not like this," Lo Fa said. He spit. "Talking with that thing like that."

The golden field snapped off and Elek stepped back. He walked past the two Chinese without a glance, into the main control room, and up to the console.

"What have you learned?" Che Lu asked as she followed.

"I have no time for you," Elek snapped. His hands moved over the panel.

A loud rumbling noise came through the door leading to the storage cavern. Che Lu and Lo Fa went into the large room. In the center of the floor, the black metal covering was sliding back on one of the largest of the containers. Inside was a drum, about fifty meters long, by ten in diameter. It was mounted on both ends by a cradle of black metal that attached at the center of each end. The drum itself was a dull gray.

As they watched, the drum began to rotate, faster and faster. Streaks of color—red, orange, violet, purple—began shooting through the gray.

"What is that?" Lo Fa asked.

"I have no idea."

"It is of the devil," Lo Fa said, and he spit in that direction.

"Hear that?" Croteau held up his fist, halting the patrol once more. The faint light of dawn was touching the eastern sky, and the men were nervous.

Another mercenary cocked his head. "Yah."

They both turned and looked back the way they had come. Qian-Ling was highlighted in the flush of the first rays of the sun.

"What's that?" the mercenary whispered.

The air around Qian-Ling was shimmering.

"I don't—" Croteau paused as he heard another noise. The roar of a jet engine. He barely had time to look up as a CSS-5 cruise missile flashed by overhead at a height of less than forty feet. The contrail of the missile headed straight for Qian-Ling.

"Oh, God," Croteau whispered.

The missile hit the shimmering wall and detonated.

Croteau saw the flash, which instantly destroyed his retinas, a millisecond before the blast wave incinerated him and everything within ten kilometers.

"China just nuked Qian-Ling." Duncan was holding up several satellite photos. Turcotte was seated cross-legged on the floor of the bouncer, the laptop hooked to the SATPhone on his lap. He could see her and the photos on the twelve-inch screen.

As Turcotte looked at the photos in the computer screen, she kept speaking. "From following the time sequence, it appears that a shield was activated just prior to the detonation." She reached and pulled one of the photos out and put it on top. "See this wavy effect? That's what the Easter Island shield looked like before it went opaque."

Turcotte checked the next couple of shots. "It apparently doesn't completely stop a nuclear blast."

In the imagery, Qian-Ling had been stripped bare of vegetation, trees blown away, the ground scorched.

"It didn't completely stop this blast," Duncan agreed, "but it did seem to stop the missile." She used the tip of her pencil to show a point to the west of the mountain tomb. "Point of detonation was right here, about a kilometer and a half from the tomb. Right where the shield wall is. I think it was targeted for the tomb itself."

"The Chinese probably used a cruise missile," Turcotte said. "The shield wall detonated it when the missile touched the shield because the wall picked up the EM emissions."

Duncan nodded. "Yes, but I think the wall still dissipated the blast somewhat. The experts are going over the information, but initial impressions are that damage was not as extensive as the Chinese would have liked. The tomb appears intact."

"And sealed off now like Easter Island," Turcotte noted. "What about Che Lu? Was she inside?"

"We don't know. Imagery caught several groups of people outside the tomb just prior to the blast."

"If they were outside, they're dead," Turcotte said.

"Radius of blast is ten kilometers. I'm hoping Che Lu stayed inside."

"But if she's not in the tomb activating the shield," Turcotte wondered, "then who is?"

"STAAR."

Turcotte slumped down in a chair. "I've been thinking. STAAR knew there were Airlia still alive on the talon or that it was being remote-controlled—whichever—that's the card Lexina was holding."

"Most likely."

"So they could be in communication with the talon?"

Duncan shook her head. "I don't know about that."

"So we're back to not having a clue as to where STAAR is, who they are, what their goals are, and most important, what they are up to," Turcotte summarized. He rubbed his hand across his forehead. "Plus we now have these Watchers. I don't understand why they need to put their people on board the mothership if they have a cure."

"Maybe they can't get the cure to all their people," Duncan said.

"More likely they want to keep them vulnerable to the Black Death," Turcotte said. He shook his head, trying to clear it of the confusing information. "We've got to find The Mission. It's our only chance."

"Kopina didn't know where it was. And . . ." Duncan paused, looking off to her right. "I've got a message from Major Quinn at Area 51. Hold on."

The entire mountain had shaken with the blast, but there was no visible sign of damage inside the tomb. Lo Fa had gone down the tunnel the mercenaries had left from and reported back that it was again sealed with dirt and rock.

Che Lu had gone with him up the left corridor, where there had been a small shaft to the outside world. That shaft was also closed off now. Che Lu had stood for several moments on the right side of the corridor, where the shaft went down into the heart of Qian-Ling, trying to imagine what lay down there on the forbidden lowest level.

They had finally returned to the control room where Elek was.

"All those men had to have died in the blast," Che Lu said.

Elek simply stared at the old Chinese woman, his dark glasses hiding his eyes.

"You are responsible for their deaths," Che Lu added.

"I did not detonate the nuclear weapon," Elek said. "The Chinese government did. That is who is responsible."

"You brought those men here," Che Lu said. "I don't believe you really had a plan to get them out."

"Perhaps not," Elek granted. "But that was their destiny, what they were. They fulfilled it."

"What destiny?" Che Lu challenged.

"They were mercenaries. Soldiers for hire. Death is the natural conclusion to such an existence. It is what they are for." Elek pointed a long pale finger at Che Lu and Lo Fa. "You think too much of yourselves."

Lo Fa muttered something, and Che Lu placed a hand on his shoulder. "Who thinks too much of themselves?" Che Lu asked.

Elek smiled, revealing a perfect set of teeth. "Most people. They think they are important and they aren't."

"An interesting perspective," Che Lu said. "What now?"

"We wait."

"For what?"

"Until someone brings us the key."

"What makes you think someone has it and what makes you think they'll bring it here? And even if they do, how are they going to get it in to us?" Che Lu challenged.

"We wait" was all Elek would say.

The inner hatch opened with a splash of water. Coridan and Gergor dropped several packages in before entering themselves and shutting the hatch behind them.

"The Chinese dropped a nuclear weapon on Qian-Ling" was Lexina's way of greeting them.

"Elek?" Coridan asked.

"Inside. He was able to get the shield up before the attack."

"The key?" Gergor asked.

"The guardian in Qian-Ling has no record of it returning to China. It confirms that Cing Ho did take it with him in 656 B.C. to the Middle East."

Gergor shook his head, water flying off. "Fantastic. So we don't have a clue."

"Be careful how you speak," Lexina warned.

Gergor arched an eyebrow. "I spent years in the ice and snow watching that place. My patience was sorely tested. But I did my job. It was your job--and the job of those before you—to maintain the records. You did not do your job well. That is our problem now. So be careful of how you speak to me."

"The records were lost long before my time," Lexina said. "We have tried to reconstitute them."

Gergor shrugged. "I don't care whose fault it is. We need the key. Now."

"The human shuttles were destroyed," Lexina said.

"*Both* of them?" Gergor was surprised.

"The talon's automatic defense system—which we knew was active—destroyed the one that went to it. Someone among the other shuttle's crew was a Guide. But as soon as he acted, the shuttle imploded."

"The Watchers?" Gergor asked.

"It could be," Lexina allowed.

"So they cannot use it to pick up their Guides and their followers," Coridan said. "What will The Mission do now?"

Lexina had been considering that same question. "I don't know."

As he waited for Duncan to get back with him, Turcotte pored over a map of South America, Yakov looking over his shoulder.

"Could The Mission be at Tiahuanaco?" Turcotte asked.

Yakov shook his large, shaggy head. "No. I was there."

"Well, Harrison had Tiahuanaco highlighted."

"That is because he knew of The Mission's involvement with the death of that Empire," Yakov said. "The records I found indicate the Black Death finished off the Aymara."

Turcotte ran a hand through his short hair. "Sister Angelina said The Mission was to the east, but that seems like the wrong direction."

"Perhaps—" Yakov began, but Duncan was back on the screen.

"I'm forwarding you some text that Quinn's people got out of the Scorpion Base hard drive."

"Does it pinpoint The Mission?" Turcotte asked.

Duncan shook her head. "I don't think STAAR knew where The Mission was either, but they were on its trail. You have to read it."

The screen cleared and then the rest of the document appeared.

```
THE MISSION & South America
(research reconstitution and field
report 6/16/97-Coridan-)
  Overview:
  In a previous report I described how
The Mission appears to have been instru-
```

mental in the complete annihilation of the Aymara civilization, whose capital was in Tiahuanaco. This is connected to contact between the Aymara and the people of Easter Island (cross-reference an entry made on 5/24/96).

The Mission departed South America for a long period of time; some records of its actions and locations are in other entries.

It appears, though, that The Mission returned to South America sometime during World War II. After the war, it was a magnet for expatriate Nazis, particularly scientists who had worked in the camps.

Due to the presence of these Nazis and their strong influence in their new land, The Mission has a built-in level of secrecy and security, a tactic it has used throughout the ages. Initially, I believe The Mission was located in Paraguay. However, I am certain it moved from that country sometime in the 1970s.

So far, I have only been able to cull some rumors out of those who might know something.

One word that keeps coming up is the Devil, but The Mission has often been associated with demons or devils due to the nature of its work.

Recommend we send an operative to search for the site of The Mission with the highest priority.

"Sister Angelina mentioned the Devil," Turcotte said, having finished reading the document.

"Ah." Yakov was disgusted. "Our base for Section Four was called the Demon's Station. This does not get us any closer to finding where The Mission is. Even STAAR had not found it."

"Or the Watchers," Duncan said through the computer link.

"Damn it!" Turcotte slammed a fist into his side. "South America is a big place. If these people had been looking for years, there's no way we're going to . . ." He paused. "Kourou."

"What about it?" Yakov asked.

"When is the launch of the next four satellites scheduled?"

"Tomorrow morning."

"Then The Mission will have to put their Black Death payloads into the rockets soon, right?"

Yakov nodded.

"But we got the payload from the last launch," Turcotte said.

"They were either refining the virus with this launch," Kenyon said, "or making more. Most likely the latter, as they were confident enough to schedule the four launches for tomorrow. You said there were two previous launches. They most likely have Black Death virus from those that they can use."

"So they don't have to have this load?" Turcotte asked.

"I doubt it," Kenyon said. "One thing, though—even as tough as this virus is—I'd say they'd have to keep it viable, which means keeping it refrigerated and not loading the payload dispersers until the last minute."

"I doubt they're holding it at Kourou unless all of Europe is in on this," Turcotte said. "The previous launches—where did they come down?" Turcotte asked.

Duncan answered that: "Off the coast of French Guiana in the Atlantic."

"I saw something," Turcotte muttered. He grabbed the map off the floor of the bouncer. He ran his finger along the coast, up from Brazil to French Guiana where Kourou was located.

"It's there," he whispered. "It's been there right in front of us all this time."

"What?" Duncan's voice out of the speaker echoed Yakov's.

"The Mission." Turcotte stabbed his finger on a spot on the map. "Right off the coast from Kourou. The old French prison. Devil's Island."

23

"If you are wrong, we will have wasted critical time," Yakov said. The Amazon rain forest was flashing by beneath the bouncer as they headed northeast toward the coast.

"You got a better suggestion for the location of The Mission?" Turcotte asked. He held up his hand. A faint trace of black was under the skin. He felt terrible, a pounding headache on top of a fever. He held on to Baldrick's last statement about a cure. It was their only chance.

"If you are wrong, at least we will be close enough to Kourou," Yakov said. "I will ensure those rockets never launch in the morning."

"Better to burn out than fade away," Turcotte said. He knew what Yakov had in mind—a Special Operations warrior conducting a suicide mission was a most formidable foe. He had no doubt the two of them would be able to make a good charge at disabling those rockets no matter what security there was at the field. The problem, though, was that the Black Death would still continue burning through South America and eventually move outward from there.

"What does that mean?"

"It's a song," Turcotte said. "Means it's better to go out with a bang than a whimper."

"A bang, yes," Yakov said. "That is what it would be."

"According to the information Dr. Duncan was able to find," Turcotte said, "Devil's Island has been abandoned since the Second World War. She's having the NSA get some overhead shots and she's tracking down the plans for the prison there.

"From the little we know of it, this Mission uses people and things that are already established. Devil's Island seems custom made for it. Add in the fact that Kourou is right next to it on the mainland and the first two satellites were recovered to the east of the island in the Atlantic and it all fits. Plus the name Devil's Island, which corresponds to what Sister Angelina said." Turcotte nodded. "This is it. I can feel it."

"I hope you are correct, my friend." Yakov pointed to the left. "Because if you are wrong, that is our next stop."

Brilliantly lit by spotlights, four Ariana rockets sat on the four launch pads at Kourou about eight miles to the north of where they were flying.

"NSA Seven, this is Eagle Leader. Over." Lieutenant Colonel Mickell released the transmit button on the radio and waited. He was in the cargo bay of an MC-130 Combat Talon—a specially modified version of the venerable four-prop Hercules transport plane that had been in the Air Force's inventory for decades.

The Talon was special in that it could fly very low, hugging the terrain, thus evading getting picked up on radar. This was a relatively easy flight so far, given that the flight path had been over water since reaching the Atlantic off the coast of South Carolina.

The radio crackled as Duncan answered. "This is NSA Seven. Over."

"This is Eagle Leader. I'm calling for final mission authorization. Authenticate, please. Over." Mickell released the send button.

The radio hissed. "I authenticate NSA Directive 6-97. I say again, I authenticate NSA Directive 6-97. Over."

Mickell nodded. He at least had a pretense of legitimacy. "Roger, NSA Seven. I copy NSA Directive 6-97. Over."

"NSA Seven. Out."

Mickell keyed the mike again. "Tiger Leader, this is Eagle Leader. Did you copy NSA Seven? Over."

From two hundred fifty kilometers to the south the reply came back. "Roger that. I'll get it cranking. Over."

"Good luck. Out."

Lisa Duncan put the SATPhone down. She was on board a bouncer, flying back to Area 51. She had far overstepped her bounds giving authorization for military action in a foreign country. NSA Directive 6-97 gave her some power, but not that much.

"We're six minutes out from Area 51, ma'am," the pilot announced.

"Thank you," Duncan said. She called ahead and had Major Quinn patch into the SATCOM frequency for the Delta Force operation.

Turcotte sat on the opposite side of the tree trunk from Yakov. Kenyon was slightly behind him. They were near the top of a knoll. Below them were the old walls of the abandoned French prison. Beyond the prison, the Atlantic Ocean crashed into the rocky shoreline with thunderous breakers.

The bouncer had dropped them off on Devil's Island, on the opposite side of a ridge behind the supposedly long-abandoned prison. The island was rough and heavily vegetated. The prison was on the western side, a walled compound about two acres in size. Turcotte, Kenyon, and Yakov had quickly hiked over the ridge to their present location.

"The Mission must be in the old prison," Yakov said.

Turcotte pointed to the right. "Two boats are tied to the pier." The pier was about a mile from the prison.

"One is a patrol boat." Yakov noted the dark silhouette, dimly lit by a couple of lights on the pier. "Russian made. We have made some good money selling items like that to the highest bidder in the past several years. *Pauk* class. It could have been used to pick up the satellites in the water. The other boat is smaller." He turned his attention back to the prison. "There's a helicopter inside the walls," he noted.

Turcotte pulled a set of night-vision goggles out of his pack and put them on. "Guards. Four on the dock. Others along the top of the wall and inside the compound. About fifteen."

"I think you have—how do you say—hit the jackpot," Yakov said.

Turcotte slipped the pack off his back and pulled out a SATCOM radio. He unfolded the tripod legs of the little dish and angled it up to the sky, then hooked in a scrambler and put on a small headset. He did a trial shot and got a successful bounce back from the communications satellite, indicating he was on the right direction and azimuth.

He hooked a small portable printer into the radio along with the laptop computer. It was a long way from his time in the infantry when he'd gone to the field with just a bulky FM radio for communications.

"I've got a link to both Duncan and Area 51," Turcotte confirmed to Yakov.

The printer came alive and a sheet of paper scrolled out. "Current real-time thermal of the island from a KH-12 spy satellite," Turcotte said. He tapped two small red dots. "That's us."

"Amazing" was Yakov's take on that.

"And we're not alone." Turcotte slid his finger along the paper. "This dark blue square is the other wall of the prison. This building inside has people in it." There were about a dozen red dots on the paper. "And the guards at the dock and people on both boats."

Turcotte frowned. "The chopper is red. The engine is still hot."

"You think they have already delivered the payload to Kourou?" Kenyon asked.

"I don't know," Turcotte said. "You said they needed to keep it refrigerated. Let's hope they haven't taken it out yet. I'd say if the boats are still here, the Black Death is still here."

"So what do we do now?" Yakov asked.

"We wait for just a little while, then we go visiting."

"I will stop those rockets from taking off at Kourou no matter what," Yakov vowed once more.

"Let's start here," Turcotte advised.

Lisa Duncan was walking a fine line. She had told no one other than Turcotte about Kopina's action in destroying the shuttle *Endeavor.* She wanted to stay clear of the official reaction to that event and the destruction of *Columbia* by the talon. With one fell swoop, two-thirds of America's space fleet was gone; only the shuttle *Atlantis,* currently being refitted, was left.

She'd arrived in Area 51 and was now in the Cube, coordinating all the forces she had set in movement. Major Quinn was helping her, his military experience invaluable, his links to intelligence networks critical.

The progressives were using the events to further their own cause, as were the isolationists. China firing a nuclear weapon within its own borders had the world's governments fixated on that event and how it affected their own little backyards.

Now that she had a slightly better view of the playing field, Duncan had to wonder how much of that was due to the influence of the Guides, The Ones Who Wait, and the Watchers.

Meanwhile, from Quinn's intelligence, Duncan knew the Black Death was spreading in the Amazon rain forest and the four rockets were set to launch at Kourou in less than six hours.

"They have to have a Level Four biolab somewhere in there," Kenyon said.

"We'll find it," Turcotte promised. He cocked his head as the SATPhone gave a very low buzz.

"Turcotte," he spoke in a low voice.

"Mike, this is Colonel Mickell. We're en route."

"Yes, sir."

Mickell gave him the satellite radio frequency they would be working on and the call signs that would be used.

Turcotte switched from the phone to the more secure radio. "Eagle Leader, this is Wolf Leader. Over."

The reply from Mickell was immediate. "This is Eagle Leader. Go ahead. Over."

"Roger, we've got the prison under surveillance. One thing—we've got to recover a cure for the virus inside the prison, so tell your people to be careful who they shoot and what they blow up. Over."

There was a moment of silence on the other end. "Roger. Over."

Turcotte knew the Delta Force men with Mickell had

no idea that they were here outside the normal chain of command. And if they knew, they wouldn't really care—as Colonel Mickell hadn't cared—given the urgency of the mission.

The trend in Special Operations over the past two decades had been for fewer and fewer people to be informed and involved in actual operations. The after-action report on the debacle at Desert One had shown up glaring faults in the number of people who were actively involved in the decision-making process, from the President on down. The military had pushed for less outside involvement and more autonomy for the leader on the ground. It also allowed those on the inside to use Delta Force for this mission without having to inform everybody and their brother about what was going on and having the chance of a Guide becoming involved. After what had happened to *Endeavor* there was most definitely a need for keeping this in close.

"They'll keep the cure with them," Kenyon said. "If they move the payloads with the Black Death, they'll move the cure."

"Why?" Turcotte asked.

"If you were going to handle snakes, wouldn't you keep your antivenom kit close at hand?" Kenyon asked.

Sergeant First Class Gillis signaled to the pilot. "Crank her up, Corsen."

The pilot started his helicopter. The aircraft was an OH-58, the military version of the Bell Jet Ranger. The twin-bladed helicopter could hold only the pilot and the three men of Tiger element. They were flying out of the airfield at St. George's in Grenada, where, as members of the Seventh Special Forces Group, they were always on standby for counterdrug operations. Gillis was glad to be doing something other than chasing drug runners for once, even though the plan looked half-assed at best.

The four men were dressed similarly, all in black, including black balaclavas that left only their eyes exposed. Night-vision goggles hung around their necks, and each man wore a headset for communication among the team and with the other elements. They wore combat vests with the various tools of their trade hanging on them.

The single turbine engine started to whine as Corsen began his start-up procedures. Gillis glanced at his watch just before getting in and taking the left front seat, next to the pilot. Since the OH-58 was the slowest aircraft involved in the operation, it would leave first, even though it was two hundred fifty kilometers closer to the target than the Eagle element currently in the air. Just a few hours earlier they had received a real mission tasking and the Delta Team had worked out a rough plan with them over the radio. The plan depended on split-second timing from the various elements involved.

As soon as Corsen had sufficient engine speed, the blades started turning and the aircraft began rocking. Gillis looked over his shoulder at the two men seated in the back. Shartran and Jones both gave him a thumbs-up. Their guns were between their knees, muzzles pointing down.

Gillis pulled out the acetated map with their flight route on it. Written in grease pencil along the route were the time hacks for the various checkpoints on the way in. A stopwatch was taped to the map. Gillis checked his watch. Corsen lifted the aircraft to a three-foot hover. When his second hand swept past the twelve and the watch indicated 5:41, Gillis indicated "go" and clicked the stopwatch. Corsen pushed forward on the cyclic and they were on their way.

. . .

Four powerful turboprop engines drilled the night sky, pulling the Combat Talon troopship. Inside the cramped cargo bay, Mickell sat as comfortably as his parachute and equipment would allow on the web seats rigged along the side of the aircraft. He wore a headset connected by a long cord to a SATCOM radio nestled in among the electronics gear in the front half of the bay. The other members of his team were spread out in the rear half.

They had an hour and forty-two minutes to their infiltration point. Since they were coming in over the ocean, the Combat Talon was going to rely on something besides its terrain-following ability for this flight. The electronic-warfare people in the front were sending out a transponder signal indicating that the Talon was a civilian airliner en route to Rio de Janeiro. The aircraft would fit this profile except for the brief one-minute slowdown over the infiltration point for the drop.

Mickell's ears perked up when he heard the radio come alive.

"Eagle, this is Hawk. I have lifted and am en route." Mickell checked his watch: 8:44. The HH-53 Pave Low helicopter had lifted from the USS *Raleigh* off the coast of Panama on time. All the pieces were moving.

Turcotte waited at the base of the tree with Yakov and Kenyon.

"We are wasting time." Yakov was sweating, his hand rubbing back and forth along the muzzle of the MP-5.

"We're only going to get one shot at this." Turcotte understood the Russian's anxiety. With every passing minute people died and the Black Death spread farther. On a more personal note, the more time passed, the more the virus infiltrated their own bodies. "We have to do it right."

Turcotte stared at the old prison below. His adrenaline was starting to flow. He forced himself to calm down. They still had a while to go before things started happening. Another hour and twenty-five minutes.

At Area 51 Lisa Duncan looked at the latest imagery forwarded from the NSA of South America. There were now eight villages that were cold, all downriver from Vilhena. The next six were hot, indicating the disease was raging in those towns. The one farthest from the site where the satellite had gone down was on the Amazon. She knew that meant the disease would be down the river to the coast in the next twenty-four hours, if it wasn't already. For all they knew, carriers, fleeing the disaster, had reached some of the major cities on the coast.

Focused on China and the shuttles, the media had not yet caught on to what was really happening, although some scattered reports were beginning to trickle in. She knew by the time the media was aware of the story, it would be far too late for anyone to do anything to stop the Black Death. The most chilling aspect of it all was that there appeared to be no survivors in the affected areas.

She turned to Major Quinn. "I'm going to Devil's Island on one of the bouncers. You're in charge here. If we don't succeed in getting the cure, do your best to get someone to try to quarantine South America."

Quinn stared at her in disbelief, but Duncan didn't have time to discuss impossibilities as she hurried for the elevator.

·   ·   ·

Gillis looked at the fuel gauge. They were down to less than a third of a tank. He checked the map as the helicopter whizzed over a small lighthouse. "Checkpoint fifteen, on route and on time."

Corsen nodded but didn't speak.

Gillis checked the map again. "Turn right. Stop turn." He peered ahead through his goggles. "The route goes slightly to the left."

Corsen made the slight adjustment and the aircraft steadied on the new course. Gillis checked the time again. Another forty-five minutes to target.

Mickell looked up in dismay as he verified the abort code word. The other members of his force were still in their positions. His ops officer was looking at him strangely, wondering what the long conversation was about. Mickell gestured for him to come over. The man waddled over awkwardly and threw himself on the adjacent seat. He yelled in Mickell's ear to be heard over the roar of the engines. "What's up?"

"I just got an abort over the SATCOM from the office of the Chairman of the Joint Chiefs of Staff."

The ops officer rolled his eyes. "Damn! It's a little too late for that. Tiger element is already past the point of no return. They don't have enough fuel to make it back to Grenada."

Mickell had talked personally with Lisa Duncan several times over the past two days, and he knew what was at stake. The fact that Mike Turcotte trusted her was more than enough for him, but someone in the Pentagon must have gotten wind about what was going on and wanted to pull the plug. He keyed the mike.

"NSA Seven, this is Eagle Leader. Over."

He heard Duncan's voice. "This is NSA Seven. Over."

"We've received the order to abort from the Pentagon."

There was a short pause. "Colonel Mickell, I've told you what the threat is. I would be lying to you if I told you I had authorization from higher for this mission. But I also believe that we would not get authorization until it was too late—if at all—given the fact that there have been compromises in security throughout our government.

"We just lost two space shuttles, one of them because of treachery within our own ranks. We don't have the time to play games. Latest imagery shows the Black Death has reached the Amazon and is going downriver.

"I'm on my way to your location on board a bouncer and should be there shortly after you attack. I will take complete responsibility for everything that happens."

Mickell looked down the cargo bay of the Combat Talon. His men were ready. Two helicopters were en route, one without enough fuel to get back. He had Mike Turcotte on the ground. Then there was the matter of his duty to his chain of command and his career.

"NSA Seven, this is Eagle Leader. I am having radio problems. You are the only station I can receive. Over."

"I understand," Duncan said. "Good luck. See you shortly. NSA Seven out."

"Let's go." Turcotte took off the SATCOM headset. He had the plug for the FM radio on his vest in his left ear, a boom mike in front of his lips.

Together, Yakov, Kenyon, and he made their way downhill, staying under the cover of the jungle until they were as close to the wall as they could get. There was about ten feet of low scrub between the edge of the jungle and the ten-foot-high brick wall.

Turcotte was looking at the guard who was walking

along the top of the wall, when there was a loud humming noise and his goggles blanked out. He ripped them off his face and saw the cause: lights had been turned on inside the compound and the glow had overloaded the light enhancement inside the goggles. The guard was clearly silhouetted now. Lights were also on at the docks.

"Time's running out." Yakov brought the MP-5 up and sighted on the guard.

"Wait." Turcotte gently laid his hand on the Russian's arm. "Just wait another couple of minutes."

A caution light appeared on the console of the OH-58. Gillis stared at it in concern. "What's that?"

Corsen kept his attention fixed ahead. "Fuel warning light."

"I thought you said we'd have enough fuel to make it to the target. Are we going to make it or not?"

"We should."

"Should!" That answer didn't please the sergeant.

"Relax. All that light means is that we're low, not that we're out. We should have about twenty minutes left. We'll make it. And if we don't," Corsen added mischievously, "I'll just autorotate."

"Just great," Gillis muttered to himself. "Checkpoint twenty-four. That's the last one before we hit our final reference point." He looked at the stopwatch. "Right on time."

The ramp opened and air swirled in with a roar. Colonel Mickell pushed himself up tight behind the jumper in front of him. One minute out from drop. Mickell kept his eyes fixed on the glowing red light above the ramp. He took a few deep breaths. The light turned green and the ten men shuffled off the ramp in formation.

Mickell felt the plane's slipstream grab him and buffet him about. He spread his arms and legs and arced his back in an effort to get stable. He had barely achieved that state when he pulled his rip cord. His chute blossomed above him and he oscillated under the canopy.

Quickly getting his bearings, Mickell spotted the other members of Eagle spread out below him. He dumped air and caught up with them.

The target island appeared on the low-light-television screen on the helicopter console. Corsen raised their altitude for the final approach.

"The prison is lit up big-time," Corsen said.

Sergeant Gillis's headset crackled as he heard Turcotte for the first time over the short-range FM radio. "Tiger, this is Wolf. I can hear you coming. Situation at target as briefed. LZ inside the south wall has one chopper on the pad and room for you to the east. Over."

Corsen swung the chopper around in a left-hand bank and they approached the island from the south.

The muted buzz of the inbound helicopter reverberated through the air. Turcotte pulled a double-edged commando knife from the sheath on his combat vest. Holding the blade, he stood and threw in one smooth motion. He sprinted for the wall while the knife was still in the air.

The point hit the guard in the neck. The guard's hands went to his throat, dropping his weapon. He staggered, went to his knees, then used one hand to try to steady himself as the other grabbed the handle of the knife protruding from his throat.

Turcotte reached the wall and jumped, grabbing the

guard's left leg and pulling him down on top of him. Turcotte was surprised when the body was lifted off of him as if pulled by a string. Yakov had the guard in his large hands. With a quick twist, he finished what Turcotte had started. He tossed the body into the bushes.

Turcotte stood and, with great effort, boosted Yakov up on the wall, then reached up and grabbed the Russian's hand. Yakov reached down and pulled Turcotte up with one quick heave. He did the same with Kenyon.

They lay on top of the thick prison wall, getting their bearings. The main building was only twenty-five feet away. It had an administration center and two long wings of cells.

Turcotte spotted a guard on this side of the building, inside the wall. The man held a submachine gun in his hands.

Turcotte slithered over the wall, followed by Yakov and Kenyon. There was the sound of helicopter blades coming from the south, drawing the guard's attention.

The inbound helicopter not only drew attention away from the wall, but it covered up the slight noise Eagle Force made as it landed on the roof of the main building and kept anyone from looking up and possibly seeing the black parachutes against the lit sky. One by one, the parachutists touched down, their chutes collapsing.

Mickell was the trail man in the airborne formation. He could see the canopies from the other jumpers draped all over the top of the roof. He braked and felt his knees buckle slightly as he made a perfect landing in the center of the roof. Two of the first jumpers were already at work, prepping a charge on a locked door that barred their way down.

Mickell looked up as the OH-58 swooped in from the

south, its bright searchlight blinding the guards on the ground as it settled in toward the landing pad. The man in charge of the demolitions gave Mickell the thumbs-up. Mickell signaled for him to wait.

The skids of the bird settled on the concrete landing pad. Two guards were moving forward toward the aircraft from the front, trying to identify it. Corsen suddenly twisted his throttle to flap the blades. The two guards bent their heads even farther and covered their eyes at the sudden onslaught of wind.

As they did so Jones and Shartran leaned out of the open back doors, one on either side, and gunned down the guards, using their silenced MP-5s.

"Tiger, two down LZ," Gillis reported over the radio as he got out. Jones and Shartran started sprinting for the front door, their weapons at the ready. Corsen rolled off the throttle and waited, weapon at the ready . . .

Mickell signaled. There was a flash and hiss as the charge ate through the lock. The door swung open and the ten men slipped in, Mickell in the lead. They halted at the foot of the stairs and the team split. Four men headed toward one wing, while the other six began work on the other.

They fanned out on the second floor, moving in a practiced routine. They began clearing, cell by cell. The first indication that anything unusual was happening in the building finally occurred—the muffled roar of a machine gun echoed up from the east wing.

Turcotte slid through a ground-floor entrance that was open and stepped through to the right while Yakov stepped to the left, Kenyon staying safely behind them.

"Turcotte, east wing," he whispered into the mike as he and Yakov turned for the hallway.

A figure stepped out in front of them and Yakov cut the man down in a hail of bullets. The roar of a machine gun to their left startled both men.

Gillis let up on the trigger of the squad automatic weapon, SAW, with a satisfying click. "Tiger, one down first-floor foyer, main building."

He swung the muzzle slightly to the left as another door opened and a half-dressed guard stepped out waving a pistol. As he pressed the trigger, Gillis could see the outlines of other men behind the first. He decided to make a clean sweep of things. Keeping the trigger depressed, he swept the doorway and then stitched a pattern on the walls.

The 5.56mm, steel-jacketed rounds tore through the brick wall and made a carnage in the guardroom. Gillis fired until he expended all hundred rounds in the drum magazine. When the bolt slid forward and halted for lack of ammo, he expertly pulled another drum out of the bag on his hip and reloaded.

"Tiger, a bunch down, first-floor foyer, main building."

Gillis swung his barrel to the left as two figures stepped out of the hallway from the east.

"Friendly, Wolf element!" Turcotte yelled. He looked around the main foyer. Two large double doors were off to the left. "There!" He remembered the plans Duncan had managed to get hold of—those doors led to stairs going down to the old solitary confinement area.

Turcotte led Yakov, Kenyon, Gillis, and the other men to the doors. Gillis slapped a charge on the thick wooden doors. They all dove for cover, then the doors blew wide open. Gillis led the way in with a burst of fire from the SAW.

"We need them alive!" Turcotte yelled, seeing the wide row of stairs leading down. He pushed past Gillis and took the stairs two at a time. They ended at a steel door with dire warnings printed in several languages. Turcotte recognized the international symbol for bio-hazard.

More men came down the stairs, weapons at the ready, Colonel Mickell in the lead.

"Mike!" Mickell called out, seeing Turcotte. "We've got both wings secure. My men are checking the exterior, but I think we've got it all."

"Can you get us in there, sir?" Turcotte pointed at the doors.

Mickell responded by yelling orders. A demolitions man ran up with a heavy backpack. He put it on the floor, pulling a cylindrical black object out. Working rapidly, he placed it on a tripod, one end eighteen inches away from the steel.

Turcotte knew it was a shaped charge, designed to focus a blast of heat and force at exactly the distance it was from the door.

"Fire in the hole!" the demo man called out, causing everyone to scatter for cover. Turcotte grabbed Kenyon and dove behind a desk that had been a security check-point. There was a loud bang, causing his ears to ring. Poking his head above the desk, Turcotte saw a four-foot-wide hole had been torched through the steel.

"Wait for it to cool," the demo man advised as Turcotte approached the hole.

Turcotte threw a chair across the bottom of the hole, the wood arms hissing as they met the red-hot metal. He grabbed a flash-bang grenade off his combat vest, pulled the pin, and tossed it through the hole. As soon as it exploded, he followed it through, diving headfirst, his belly sliding over the chair.

Turcotte rolled left once, then to his feet, weapon at the ready. He froze as he saw the white-coated bodies crumpled all over the floor amid the sophisticated equipment. He slowly stood.

The Mission had completely gutted the level and put in a Biolevel 4 lab. Turcotte considered the situation. Had the virus already taken over here? Had there been an accident? But the guards had seemed fine.

"What happened to them?" Mickell demanded, carefully stepping through the hole in the door.

Turcotte knelt next to a body and looked closely. He had seen this before. Deep under the Great Rift Valley. "They were killed by the people they worked for. The Mission is covering its tracks."

"Exfil is only a couple of minutes out," Mickell said.

"That's not important right now," Turcotte said as he stepped forward into the room. There were six men in the white coats. All dead, their faces contorted in agony. All were middle-aged. Hemstadt—the Dulce Nazi—wasn't here.

There was a lot of complicated equipment in the room along with several high-speed computers. Yakov had a difficult time getting through the hole, singeing his shoulder on the cooling metal but not seeming to notice it. Kenyon followed him.

"Are we too late?" Yakov asked.

"I don't know," Turcotte responded.

"The payloads." Yakov ran over to a large door on the left side of the room. A crane was bolted to the ceiling. He threw the door open. A tunnel beckoned, a set of narrow-gauge rail tracks bolted to the floor. A lone lightbulb every thirty feet dimly lit the way.

Yakov pounded his fist against the rock wall. "They got the payloads out!"

Turcotte oriented himself. The tunnel led to the west. Toward the ocean.

"The patrol boat!"

"The cure!" Turcotte grabbed Kenyon's shoulder. "Is it in here?"

Kenyon unlatched a large freezer door and swung it open. Turcotte looked over his shoulder. There were rows and rows of rubber-lined slots designed to hold test tubes. They were all empty.

Kenyon read the labels below the empty racks. "The first batches of Black Death are gone, along with the cure."

Yakov was staring down the dark tunnel. "There is no time. We must go after them." He headed down the tunnel, shoulders hunched to keep his head from hitting the ceiling.

Turcotte turned to Colonel Mickell. "We need to get to the pier."

Turcotte pushed a man trying to get into the lab out of the way as he bullied his way through the breach in the doors, Colonel Mickell behind him, Kenyon following. They took the stairs up two at a time. Sergeant Gillis was standing guard in the main foyer.

"What's going on?" Gillis demanded as Turcotte sprinted past him.

"Follow me," Turcotte yelled over his shoulder.

Entering the courtyard, Turcotte saw the OH-58. He ran to the passenger side. "Get us in the air!"

Corsen was staring at him. "Who the hell—" He paused as Gillis, Kenyon, and Colonel Mickell crowded into the backseat of the chopper.

"Get us down to the docks as quickly as possible." Turcotte forced himself to speak more slowly.

"Now!" Colonel Mickell added from the backseat.

Corsen turned the generator and fuel switch on, then rolled the throttle. The engine began to whine.

Turcotte felt time ticking away. The blades began to slowly turn overhead. "You have a chopper coming in for exfil?" he asked Mickell.

The colonel nodded. "HH-53 Pave Low." He checked his watch. "Only a minute out."

Turcotte grabbed a headset and put it on. "What's the call sign?"

"Hawk," Mickell said.

Turcotte keyed the radio. "Hawk, this is Wolf. Over."

The pilot of the Pave Low flared the chopper to slow it as he got his new orders from Turcotte. He banked hard right and followed Devil's Island's western coastline.

"I've got one vessel—patrol boat size—moving west, two hundred meters from shore," the pilot informed Turcotte, seeing the ship clearly on his low-light television. He turned slightly, adjusting the camera mounted under the nose of the craft. "Second, smaller one is preparing to get under way."

"Stop the patrol boat!" Turcotte ordered.

The pilot frowned. "Yes, sir." All he had were door-mounted 7.62mm Gatling guns.

He rolled throttle, increased pitch, and headed in for a run, telling his left door gunner to be ready.

The gunner pulled the trigger as they passed the ship, two hundred meters off its port side. The electric drive ran the belt of ammunition through the gun, the barrels rotating, spewing out hundreds of rounds per second. The bullets ripped into the superstructure of the patrol boat, killing and maiming.

The ship retaliated a second later as a surface-to-air

missile leapt out of a tube and headed for the Pave Low's hot exhaust.

"Evasive manuevers!" the pilot screamed as he banked hard left, directly into the oncoming missile, reducing both his target profile and his heat signature.

The missile flashed by to the right, narrowly missing.

Two more missiles were launched.

The pilot saw them coming and knew he had run out of options. They both homed in on the exhaust coming out of the engine.

The Pave Low exploded in a ball of fire.

Turcotte saw the explosion as the OH-58 finally lifted off the concrete pad and cleared the prison walls.

"Goddamn," Colonel Mickell exclaimed.

Yakov heard something ahead. Voices. Speaking in German. His hands tightened down on his submachine gun. The tunnel was narrow, less than six feet wide and the curved ceiling just under six feet high, causing Yakov to walk with knees bent. It went down at a steady angle toward the ocean.

He caught a glimpse of light reflecting off metal about fifty meters ahead and increased his speed.

"What do you want me to do?" Corsen's voice was worried; he had just seen the *Pauk*-class patrol boat take out the HH-53.

A red light went on and a warning tone sounded.

"What's that?" Turcotte asked.

"Fuel warning light," Corsen said. "We have only a minute or two of fuel left."

It took Turcotte less than ten seconds to tell Corsen his plan.

·   ·   ·

A voice echoed back up the tunnel, inquiring in German who was there.

Yakov had the butt of the MP-5 nestled tightly in his shoulder. He could see two men now, with something metal in front of them on the rails. He pulled the trigger once, then twice. Both men flopped backward.

Yakov continued down the tunnel, then paused briefly when he recognized the metal object that was reflecting light—a wheelchair with a bald old man sitting in it.

Corsen headed straight into the first SAM launch, evading the first missile at the last second using his flares. The distance between the chopper and the Pauk patrol boat closed rapidly even as the helicopter gained altitude.

"They're going to launch again!" Colonel Mickell warned.

Corsen reached up and flipped a switch. The sudden silence was startling as the engine emergency shutoff activated.

With a burst of light, another missile launched. And a third. Both flew by the OH-58, unable to find an infrared source because the engine had stopped putting out hot exhaust.

The blades whooshed by overhead as the chopper autorotated, the blades being turned by the air passing through them, in turn providing some lift, enough to keep them from gaining terminal speed.

Corsen was struggling with his controls, manhandling the hydraulics now that he didn't have power from the engine to assist, pushing forward, trying to direct the fall.

He made it as they slammed into the rear deck of the Pauk, the blades cutting into the superstructure with a glitter of metal-on-metal sparks. The landing struts crumpled, and the helicopter ended up precariously perched on the deck, tilted hard to the right.

"General Hemstadt," Yakov whispered, keeping the muzzle of his MP-5 centered on the old man as he slipped past the wheelchair and turned to face his enemy.

"Who are you?" Hemstadt asked in German.

"Where is the cure?"

Hemstadt's face was surprisingly young-looking for a man in his late eighties. His hands were gripping the arms of his chair, his lower body covered in a blanket.

"You are Russian," Hemstadt said. "I recognize the accent. A Russian pig. I killed many of your kind in the war."

"You killed many prisoners," Yakov said. "Where is the cure?"

"Not here."

Corsen was dead, the control panel smashed against his chest. Turcotte had narrowly escaped the same fate. He kicked out the front Plexiglas and rolled onto the deck. He got to his knees and noted green tracers flashing by perilously close. He rolled left.

The sound of a SAW firing roared in his ears and red tracers tracked back down the green ones. Sergeant Gillis was standing on top of the wreckage of the chopper, firing rolling bursts with the automatic weapon, the recoil slamming into his shoulder.

Gillis swept right, then left. In a matter of seconds, he got off five twenty-round bursts before a bullet caught him in the head and knocked him backward on top of Colonel Mickell and Kenyon, who had been trapped below him in the wreckage of the chopper.

By that time, Turcotte had maneuvered up the left side of the ship's superstructure. He killed the man who had shot Gillis with one round through the head, knocking him off the wing of the bridge.

Turcotte blew out the bridge windows with a burst, then threw a flash-bang grenade through the opening. He dashed up the metal ladder onto the bridge. There were two men doubled over, hands pressed against their heads, suffering the aftereffects of the grenade.

"Freeze!" Turcotte yelled, knowing they probably couldn't hear him.

One of the men reached for a pistol on his belt, and Turcotte shot him. The second man saw that and paused in his grab for a weapon. Then the man reached for a lever on the instrument panel.

"No!" Turcotte yelled.

The man's hand closed around the lever. Turcotte fired, hitting him in the shoulder, knocking him back against the wheel. The man's right arm flopped, useless. He reached with his left hand for the lever. Turcotte fired again, hitting him in the chest. The man grinned, then pulled the lever. Turcotte put a round right between the man's eyes.

He ran forward to the console. A digital timer welded into the metal frame was counting down second by second from one hundred. As Turcotte watched, it went from 98 to 97.

Yakov placed the muzzle of the MP-5 on Hemstadt's chest. "Where is the cure?"

"Gone."

"The Mission," Yakov said. "Where are they?"

Hemstadt smiled. " 'They'—as you call them—are long gone. You will never find them."

"Who are they?"

Hemstadt simply shook his head. "Far beyond you. You don't have a clue about what is really going on. What has been going on throughout history. Nothing is as you were taught."

"They helped you in the camps during the Great War."

Hemstadt snorted. "Helped? They invented the camps. *We* helped *them*. You have no idea—"

Yakov jabbed the steel barrel into the old man's frail chest. "Why don't you tell me, old man."

Hemstadt laughed, the sound echoing off the stone walls. "You think you have accomplished something here? You haven't stopped us. The launches have already been aborted and this plan abandoned. They're taking the cure out to sea to sink it."

Turcotte left the bridge and raced aft. Kenyon and Mickell were pushing pieces of the helicopter out of the way. There were several large plastic cases tied down on the deck.

"You've got a minute," Turcotte yelled.

"What?" Kenyon was at the cases.

"This ship's going to blow in a minute."

Kenyon flipped open the latches on the first one. A large stainless-steel cylinder rested on the cut-out foam, about three feet wide by six in length.

"One of the satellite dispersers," Kenyon said. He turned to the next case. It also held one of the satellite payloads.

"Thirty seconds." Turcotte knew that the concussion from an explosion carried well in water. Even if they got off in time, the blast would kill them as they tried to swim away.

Kenyon skipped the next two cases, which were the same size.

The fifth, smaller box was different. Kenyon opened the lid and the top of rows of glass test tubes appeared, each one inserted in the foam padding.

"Black Death?" Turcotte asked.

Kenyon pulled one out and read the German label. "Yes."

He opened the next box. Pulled out a tube. "More Black Death."

Turcotte looked up. A bouncer was hovering overhead. A voice spoke in his earpiece—Duncan had arrived. He swung the boom mike for the FM radio in front of his lips to tell her what he needed.

Two more boxes of Black Death.

"Twenty seconds!" Turcotte yelled.

There was only one box left.

"Grab the cargo net!" Turcotte ordered as the bouncer came in low, hovering just above their heads. Kenyon and Colonel Mickell jumped.

Turcotte grabbed the last box with one hand and with the other grabbed hold of the cargo attached to the bottom of the bouncer.

His arm was wrenched in its socket as the bouncer accelerated straight up, the case almost torn from his grip.

Below him there was a thunderous explosion and pieces of the boat flew by.

"I'll tell you something to show you how ignorant you are," Hemstadt said. "Nineteen oh eight. Tunguska. The great explosion. You should know what caused that, but you don't, do you? Your own government hid that from you. And you are Section Four, aren't you? You are a naive child."

Yakov saw that the old man's right hand had slipped under the blanket. He ripped the blanket off the German's lap. The hand flopped down, a small needle clenched between two fingers. When Yakov looked up, Hemstadt's face was slack with death.

The bouncer came down very slowly over the courtyard of the prison on Devil's Island. Turcotte's feet touched the ground and he collapsed, cradling the case.

The bouncer slid over to the side and touched down. The top hatch opened and Lisa Duncan slid down the outside and ran over.

"Are you all right?"

Turcotte didn't have the strength to reply. He forced his other hand to let go of the handle of the plastic case. Kenyon unsnapped the latches and opened the lid. Rows of glass tubes were nestled in the foam lining. He pulled a tube out and held it up.

24

Inside of Qian-Ling, Elek had been in contact with the guardian for the past hour. He stepped back, the golden glow retreating from his head. "I have sent a message," he said.

"To who?" Che Lu asked.

"To my superior. She will get us the key."

Four hundred meters down, the crew of the *Springfield* also waited. The foo fighters had not moved. Admiral Poldan, commanding the USS *Washington* on the surface, fifty kilometers from Easter Island, spent most of his time imploring his chain of command for permission to attack the island with nuclear weapons. So far, he had not received permission.

Deep inside Rano Kau on Easter Island, the guardian received input from The Mission. The Black Death mission had been aborted because the attempt to seize the mothership had failed.

The news was noted, but it was only a stone thrown in the stream of action the guardian had planned.

The power from the thermal vent had the guardian running at 100 percent. In a corner of the cavern, the microrobots had been working. In a curious assembly line, the production of each successive generation had grown smaller. A circle of half-inch-long microrobots were at work on a new model. When they were done, a quarter-inch-long robot skittered across the floor on six tiny legs. Then it joined the production line.

The Guide Parker pulled the cellular phone connection off his laptop. Wind blew sand into the keyboard, but he didn't care. He stood up. The Chosen were gathered around him. The time had come and passed. The Prophecy was unfulfilled. He felt a spike of pain in his left temple.

"The time is not now!" His voice was taken by the wind and whipped away. "But it will be soon. We must go back and prepare once more!"

Turcotte made a fist with his right hand and pumped his arm. There was already swelling where the needle had gone in. Next to him, Lisa Duncan did the same.

"Will Kenyon be able to stop it?" she asked.

Turcotte nodded. "He thinks so. He's sending samples of the cure to every disease-control agency on the planet, as well as the World Health Organization. The governments may have their heads buried in the sand, but he's confident that if the Black Death shows up, the agencies and WHO will deal with it. He's pretty sure he can contain it in the Amazon and help those already infected."

"Several thousand are already dead," Duncan noted.

Turcotte grimaced, whether from the soreness in his arm or the subject, Duncan couldn't tell. "It's like when people in the States read about a flood in India or a landslide in Mexico killing a bunch of people. Very few people really care if it's not happening in their hometown."

"This came very close to happening in everyone's

town," Duncan said. "At least we stopped The Mission."

"The Black Death has been stopped," Turcotte amended. "The Mission is another matter."

"Yes, it is," Yakov said. The Russian had been unusually quiet the past hour, since Kenyon had taken off in the bouncer with the case of vials containing the cure for the Black Death. Yakov had dragged Hemstadt's body out of the tunnel and thrown the old man into the sea, letting the sharks have him. "We are going to have to find out about The Mission on our own."

"We'd better find it and take care of it," Turcotte said, "because we just won a skirmish in a long line of battles here. I've got a feeling the war really hasn't started yet."